"This isn't a retelling, this is Alice in Wonderland 2.0."

—BLACKSCI-FI.COM

"*A Blade So Black* is a novel that roars mightily in the face of all those Wonderland tales that have come before. L.L. McKinney is on her way to someplace special with this debut; get onboard now."

—*LOCUS* magazine

★ "An explosive, kickass debut . . . The *Alice in Wonderland* retelling the world has always needed."

—*BOOKLIST,* starred review

"Relentless action, spiraling stakes, and a fierce heroine . . . A heartbreaking cliffhanger will leave fans clamoring for a sequel."

—*PUBLISHERS WEEKLY*

"A thrilling, timely novel that ensures readers will be curiouser for a sequel."

—*KIRKUS REVIEWS*

"With a modern flair, a rich backstory, and just enough emotional heft, this particular looking glass will have readers eagerly falling through it."

—*THE BULLETIN*

"Teens will root for Alice as a strong, multidimensional black girl usually unseen in YA fiction . . . A must-purchase."

—*SCHOOL LIBRARY JOURNAL*

"*A Blade So Black* is a modernized version of a well-known story that retains enough of the original to be lauded by both fans of the classic and readers wholly new to Wonderland."

—SHELF AWARENESS

A BLADE SO BLACK

A
BLADE
SO
BLACK

L.L. McKINNEY

NEW YORK

SQUARE
FISH

An imprint of Macmillan Publishing Group, LLC
120 Broadway, New York, NY 10271
fiercereads.com

Our books may be purchased in bulk for promotional, educational, or business use.
Please contact your local bookseller or the Macmillan Corporate and Premium
Sales Department at (800) 221-7945 ext. 5442 or by email at
MacmillanSpecialMarkets@macmillan.com.

Library of Congress Cataloging-in-Publication Data is available.

ISBN 978-1-250-21166-8 (paperback)   ISBN 978-1-250-15389-0 (ebook)

{Imprint}
MAKE YOUR MARK

Originally published in the United States by Imprint
First Square Fish edition, 2019
Book designed by Heather Palisi
Imprint logo designed by Amanda Spielman
Square Fish logo designed by Filomena Tuosto

1   3   5   7   9   10   8   6   4   2

AR: 4.9 / LEXILE: HL660L

If you don't want a streak of bad luck,
then you best not mistreat this here book.
That means stealing's a no,
and illegal downloads
equal curtains for all likely crooks.

For my Granny,
who put a pen in my hand
and told me I had the power
to shape the world

*"Begin at the beginning . . . and go on
till you come to the end: then stop."*

—LEWIS CARROLL

A BLADE SO BLACK

Prologue
CURIOUSER

Alice couldn't cry. She couldn't scream. All she could do was run.

Her boots slapped the vinyl floor. Light flickered in the red leather. Someone shouted her name. Maybe her mother. Maybe a nurse. A hurricane of rushing blood and her thrashing heart wailed in her ears.

Out. She had to get out.

A feeling like a hammer beating at the inside of her skull made everything fuzzy. She didn't see the white man in the middle of the hall until she was on top of him, but she couldn't stop. It was like hitting a wall. Then they both hit the ground. The smell of bleach and disinfectant coated her throat.

She fought to untangle herself from him.

"Dammit, kid, hold on a second!"

"Alice!" Mom's voice chased her past the lobby and through the sliding doors.

Get. Out.

Bright red letters danced in the puddles peppering the concrete.

EMERGENCY

Grady towered over her, casting a shadow across the night.

Warm water misted her skin and hung in the air, a rain that wasn't really committed to falling.

She raced into the street. A car swerved to avoid her, horn blaring and headlights flashing.

"You crazy?" the driver hollered at her back.

Alice had no idea where she was headed. She just ran. Past parking garages and a couple shops. Squat, beige buildings lined the street. The GSU campus. She kept going.

He was okay.

And going.

All day, he was fine. Why did he do this?

And going.

Why did he leave me?

Her lungs kicked at her rib cage, strangled by the hollow feeling clawing at her chest. Her legs pumped until the burn in her stomach rolled to her feet. When they refused to carry her any farther, she dropped to the ground. Water soaked her gloves. Dirt stained the white fabric. Uneven asphalt dug into her knees, scraping them as she crawled the last few feet to sink against a wall.

Tears and snot ran down her face. "Daddy." But he was gone. Dead.

"Poor child," someone nearby whispered, the words dragging across their tongue in a growl. "So alone. So afraid."

Panting around hiccups, Alice shook her head, her face in her hands. "Go away."

"Oh, I can't just leave you. Not when your fear is so . . . inviting."

Alice lifted her head to search the emptiness around her. She sat in the mouth of an alley, god knows where. Her tears made it hard to see. Snot and the stink of something sour made it hard to breathe.

"I can take it away." The darkness shifted with movement deeper in the alley, coming toward her. "Let me help you."

A dog stepped out of the black. Huge paws ended with long, wicked claws that clacked against the ground. Inky skin, no fur, rippled as it moved. Illuminated eyes blinked at her; one pair, then two, and three. Lips curled in a flash of fangs the size of her fingers.

The trembling in Alice's gut shuddered through the rest of her.

She screamed.

It lunged. Teeth snapped shut just inches shy of her face. Drool that smelled like rotten meat splashed across her chest and cheek. She scrambled backward, trying to call for help, the words choked in a wail. The roughness of the brick at her back caught her clothes and scraped her skin. She was trapped.

Instead of attacking again, the creature collapsed and flailed, ripping at the ground. "Traitor!" it shrieked.

"Yeah, yeah."

The air quivered, steeped in shadows that seemed to recoil

as a white boy stepped into view. He gripped the end of something sticking out of the monster's back.

A sword, Alice realized. The thunder of her heartbeat against her skull sharpened.

What little light that managed to thread the gloom hovered along the length of the blade, as if afraid or unable to touch it.

"You will suffer! You will all suffer!" Pinned to the ground, the beast thrashed. Yellow blood slid against the blade, coating the onyx metal, dripping onto the pavement beneath it.

"What's that? I couldn't hear you over the sound of . . ." The boy pulled the sword free and drove it in again with a *slurch*.

Alice jerked. So did the monster. Then it fell still. The glow in its eyes slowly faded.

Stepping over the body, the boy wiped his sword clean then slipped it into a sheath over his shoulder. As the hilt clicked into place, light poured in from the street, saturating the alley.

Confused, Alice blinked against the stinging bright, trying to focus on what and who was in front of her. Wearing dark jeans, boots, and purple T-shirt with the words *We're All Mad Here* scrawled across the front, he looked like a regular dude. With a weapon strapped to his back.

She didn't realize she was staring until the beast's body jolted with a loud pop, startling her. Its leathery skin bubbled and folded, shrinking in. A smell like old milk and mold filled the air. She gagged, her stomach roiling.

Oh my god. There was really a dead monster. She was going to be sick.

Unfolding his lithe frame from a crouch, the boy turned to go, though he paused as if noticing her for the first time. Blinking, he shifted to the left, then to the right as Alice watched. "You see me?" He had an accent. Sounded English.

It took a second for Alice to realize he was speaking to her. She nodded, her eyes darting between him and the dissolving creature. "Curiouser." He tilted his head to the side and came toward her.

Alice jerked back, fear cold in her limbs.

"Whoa." He lifted both hands and went still. "I just wanna make sure you're okay." He took another, slower step. When Alice didn't move—she wasn't sure she could—he took a couple more, then knelt in front of her. Light from the street slid across his moss green hair and spilled into gray eyes looking her over from beneath a furrowed brow. "Anything hurt?" he asked.

Alice stared. She couldn't manage words. Her thoughts tumbled over themselves as her mind tried to make sense of . . . she wasn't even sure. Talking dog-monsters, some dude with a sword, he killed—what the hell just happened? She couldn't breathe. When she tried, sour air stuck in her throat. Her stomach quivered.

"Hey. It's okay." His quiet voice managed to fill the alley. The gray in his eyes shifted, colors catching and dancing like a kaleidoscope in the dark.

Chest heaving, Alice shook her head. Blond strands from her wig clung to her face. Her thighs stung where she'd crawled across the ground. The pounding in her head worsened, made it hard to think. She had to get up. She had to go.

Dad was waiting to take her to the con. Only he wasn't. He was gone.

"Can you walk?"

"Wh-who—" She couldn't get the rest of the words out. They weren't even words anymore, just small sounds on the edge of more sobs. *No.* She gripped her mouth with both hands, her fingers digging into her cheeks. *Stop it. Stop. It.* The ache in her jaw spread to her throat and slithered behind her eyes as she fought back tears, bottling them up to throw them away. She wouldn't break down like this. Not out here. Not in front of . . . whoever this was. Hiccupping around slow breaths, she fixed the boy with a stare and pushed the question free. "Who are you?"

"Oh good. I thought you might pass out on me." He pressed a hand to his chest. "I'm Addison Hatta." He offered her the other. Bands of silver gleamed on each of his fingers. "Can I help you?"

She watched those fingers for a long moment. When he wiggled them, her eyes shot to his face, then the hilt of the sword peeking over his shoulder.

A freaking sword.

This is too much.

She took his hand.

Addison stood, drawing her up as well. Her legs shook but held, though she braced her free hand against the wall. Dirty water and lord knows what else stained her gloves and her sailor fuku. Her costume was ruined. She'd worked so hard on it.

But that didn't matter anymore.

Swallowing thickly, she forced words over the sand in her throat. "Thank you."

"You're welcommme." He drew out the last syllable, trailing off with a lift of his eyebrows.

"A-Alice."

"You're welcome, Alice." A smile stretched his face, and the color of his irises shifted again, brighter now.

"Your eyes!" She pointed, nearly poking him in one. "They changed!"

"Yeah." He rubbed at the back of his head. "That happens when I come to this side . . . of town."

"This side—where are you from?"

"Not anywhere near here."

The burbling body nearby gave a loud *crack*. It was nearly gone, the ground stained black beneath it.

She aimed her finger at that mess. "What was that thing? Where did *it* come from?" The questions leaped free on their own, her brain latching on to something, anything to try and make sense of what she was seeing. Shifting to the side a few steps, she eyed Addison and his sword once more.

"The same place as me?"

"And where the hell is that?"

"You wouldn't believe me if I told you." Addison chewed at his lower lip, watching the body before looking to Alice. He eyed her up and down, then nodded to himself. "But I think I will."

One
HERE WE GO

Alice ran her fingers over the ivory handles of the daggers on the desk in front of her. Cold light filled the blades, their surfaces more like silvered glass than steel. You'd think after three months of knowing Addison Hatta, she wouldn't be surprised whenever he pulled random weapons out.

"Pretty." She plucked one up and raised her eyebrows. "Light. What are they?"

"Figment Blades." Addison dug around in the drawers where he sat on the other side of the desk. The old metal rattled and creaked.

"For real?" She trailed her fingers over the flat of one of the glittering blades, the only things capable of killing Nightmares. She'd never held one before or seen one, really.

"They'll help focus your Muchness."

"Munch-what now?"

"Muchness." He slammed a drawer then jumped with a curse, shaking out his hand. "*Your* Muchness, to be precise." The fingers he'd shoved into his mouth muffled the words. "The part of you that believes in yourself, even when the rest of you doesn't."

Alice blinked a few times then set the dagger down. "Right. They look a lil small for killing monsters." She'd only ever seen one Nightmare, when Addison rescued her the night her dad died. While it wasn't huge, it was big enough to be scary as all hell.

"That's not what matters." He slammed another drawer. "The weapon is only part of the equation. A small part."

The desk took up most of the cramped space he called his office—more like a slightly large broom closet—along with the small love seat Alice sat perched on. There were a couple lamps, but the place was mostly bare. No file cabinets, no computer, just a little shelf in the corner with a funky teapot on it.

"Says the dude who carries around a big fuck-off sword." She'd glimpsed the black blade a couple times since that night. When he wasn't fighting monsters, Addison kept it in a metal locker that filled a corner of this "office."

"Aha!" Addison straightened and set a leather belt beside the daggers. The sheaths strapped to it clapped together. "You'll have to be specific; I have many swords." There was a room in the back of this very building full of weapons, but they were blunted for training.

Alice twisted her lips to the side and leveled a look at him. "You know the one I'm talking about."

"Do I?"

"Addison."

"*So many.*"

"*Addison.*"

"Well, firstly: It's not a Figment Blade, and secondly: I'm not human, meaning I don't have Muchness, so I need a little something extra." According to Addison, he could destroy a Nightmare's physical body, but it would just re-form after a while. Since Nightmares were a manifestation of humanity's fears, humans were the only ones who could put them down permanently. That's why people like him trained people like her.

"And last: you play too much." She narrowed her eyes at him, but there was no real heat behind it. "Talkin' 'bout some 'you'll have to be specific.' Specific deeze."

Addison grinned, his dimples popping into view, as he came around from behind the desk and tilted against the front of it. In the harsh fluorescent lighting his hair was dark green, his eyes a subtle though somewhat rainbowy gray. Piercings lined his left ear, shining silver as he cocked his head to the side. Metal glinted over the rest of him, too: the studs in his shirt at the shoulders, the chain around his hips, the zippers and buckles on his boots. A punk rock Prince Charming. Damn, he was fine. Lucky for him.

She turned her attention to the weapons, picking one up, the ivory warm in her palm. "This what you wanted to show me? I mean they're cool and all, but you made it sound like you had some big surprise set up."

"Those are now yours, luv."

Alice nearly dropped the dagger. "For real?"

He nodded, his smile widening. "You're ready."

She jerked straight in her chair. "So soon?"

"I wouldn't call three months soon, but yeah. I knew there was something special about you." He angled forward, closing off a bit of the space between them.

Heat filled Alice's face. She turned her attention to the weapons, hoping he couldn't see her blush. Not that she actually turned red or anything—she don't blush for real, for real. "Special how?"

"Well, you were able to see me, for one thing."

She smiled. "Hard to miss a dude stabbing a monster to death three feet in front of you."

"That's not the p—I'm trying to be serious and give you a compliment. May I get through my serious compliment?"

Alice lifted her hands, fighting laughter. "Excuse the hell outta me for having eyeballs."

"That somehow see me even when I mean not to be." Addison narrowed his eyes before folding his arms over his chest. "Nope. Never mind, moment's ruined. I now deem you unspecial. Give the daggers back."

"Wait—" The laughter burst free.

"Nope! Damage is done. Come on, hand them over."

"No, no," Alice said, still laughing as she waved off his reaching hands. "No, I'm sorry. I didn't mean to hurt your feelings."

"And they're so fragile." He grabbed for one of the daggers.

"Waaaiiiiiiit." She pressed her hand over his, still snickering. "Go on, serious compliment away."

He watched her, his eyes crinkling at the corners as he fought his own smile. "Where was I?"

"I was special." She wiggled her eyebrows.

He finally chuckled. "Right, then." Lifting her hand and

the dagger she still clutched, he curled her fingers around it and his fingers around hers. "I knew you were special. That's why I told you about the Veil, the monsters that cross it, and my duty to stop them. Well, my duty to train someone to stop them. I have trained three others before you, and none of them learned so quickly. It was a pleasant surprise."

Hell, if Addison was surprised, she was floored. He gave her a sword to start, and it was like she'd been carrying the thing her whole life. Maybe not her whole life—she did smash a table once. And a few chairs. On accident. But when she got her hands on a pair of daggers, that was a whole different story. It was like in the movies where someone says something about becoming one with the weapon, blah blah, it's an extension of your body, blah. No joke, it really felt like that, like her body somehow knew what to do. She still had to practice, though. A lot.

"I had motivation." More like a need to beat the shit out of something. Ever since her dad died, whenever Alice was alone she was just so . . . angry. She swallowed it. Bottled it up. Her mom needed her. Her grandma needed her. She got through the funeral. She got through the first days back at school. She cried. She hugged it out. But she wanted to punch things.

So when Addison presented her with the chance to be like him, to kill monsters that crept across what he called the Veil, a border between the real world and the world he came from, a realm of dreams called Wonderland, well . . . she called him crazy. Then she apologized; that was rude.

But she'd seen the monster. She'd smelled the damn thing. She'd felt its breath hot on her face, and after going back to that alley near the hospital the next week and seeing that stain on the concrete, after talking with him out in the open and noticing how no one else seemed to notice him, she decided to take him up on his offer.

"Alice?" Addison's voice sliced through her thoughts.

"Hmm? What?" She blinked up at him, her cheeks warm again. "Sorry."

"Right in the middle of my serious complimenting." He huffed, but she could tell he didn't mean it. "Where'd you go this time?"

"I was thinking about that night." And meeting him, but "that night" was safer. "And how everything changed."

"Mmm. Well, it's about to change again. Strap those on." He gestured to the daggers, then pushed away from the desk.

Alice fought with the belt for a few seconds before managing to get it fastened around her waist. Her hands shook, a combination of nerves and excitement. For three months she'd been coming here, learning how to fight with a handful of blunt weapons. When she figured those out, Addison said he would give her real ones and take her across the Veil. Now, it was happening. Like, for *real*, for real. These were real daggers hanging from her hips.

She pressed her fingertips to the hilts again, just to make sure. *Dude. This is really going down.* She took a slow breath. *Keep it together, Kingston.*

"You ready?" Addison stood at the door, holding it open for her.

Alice swallowed and nodded. "Y-yeah, yeah." She followed him out into the hall.

"Need to let Maddi know we're going through." He led the way out to the main part of the building that had served as her training grounds.

The Looking Glass pub was every bit the midtown Atlanta dive it pretended to be, from the mirrored wall of liquor behind the bar to the pool tables, high-top tables, and chairs grouped on the worn wood floor. Strategically mounted TVs meant you could see a number of shows or games from any spot on the floor. Her first time here she didn't believe this was some secret gateway to another world; it just looked like a bar.

"Looks can be deceiving, which is the point," Addison had said.

A patchwork of memorabilia from ages past covered the pub's walls. Hats, pocket watches, monocles, beat-up old canes and parasols, photographs of flappers in Paris and World War II vets in London, an autographed picture of someone named the Big Bopper. A cacophony of sight.

A cat-shaped clock hung on the wall behind the bar—the creepy kind where the huge eyes swish back and forth while the tail wags to mark the passing seconds. Black stripes covered its dark purple body. A grin spread beneath its wiry whiskers.

Tick-tick-tick-tick.

Underneath the clock, Maddi mopped the countertop in slow, lazy circles with a dingy rag. A mousy girl with a round, brown face, she was the pub's bartender, although Alice believed she took more naps than she mixed drinks. On cue, Maddi yawned, covering her mouth with the rag.

Alice grimaced. *Gross.*

Like Addison, Maddi was from Wonderland. The two of

them were stationed here to keep an eye on one of four openings in the Veil, called Gateways. As a front, they opened the Looking Glass, a functioning bar with drinks and food and regulars, which just happened to have a portal to another realm in the back. Addison owned it. He and Maddi looked young, late teens, early twenties, but they were both super old. Like, immortal old. Still fine, though. They looked like regular people until you got a *good* look at them, especially their eyes.

"Madeline." Addison knocked against the bar as he stepped up to it. "I'm taking Alice through."

Maddi blinked her big blue eyes slowly. With each fall of her lids, the color of her irises shifted, first green, then brown. "Whistle while you work?"

"Yup. She's ready."

A thrill slid through Alice at those words. She'd worked so hard. So many long hours, sleepless nights, and sore-as-hell days. This was it, though. She made it. She just had to keep telling herself that. And to breathe.

Addison ducked around behind the bar, glass clinking as he searched for something. He emerged with three small vials of purple liquid, most likely Maddi's handiwork. The girl was a bomb-ass Poet, but not in the Still I Rise way.

In Wonderland, Poets were like witches or wizards, mixing potions and wielding the magical essence of the realm in spells called Verses.

Alice never saw Maddi do more than mix mild potions to help Alice heal faster after training. Still, the stronger the Poet, the more potent the Verse, and the weirder they talked as a result. Alice figured Maddi was powerful as hell, the way she barely made sense half the time.

"Hold the fort—we'll be back in a tick," Hatta said.

Maddi saluted with the rag. There weren't humanlike races in Wonderland, at least not the way it was in the real world, but people had different skin tones and features. Maddi, with her warm, copper complexion and high, round cheekbones looked almost Latina to Alice. Addison was white. Like, super white, saying stuff like "in a tick." They both spoke English, Spanish, French, Japanese, Russian, and pretty much every other language on the planet. That's what happens when your homeland is the collective unconscious of the entire world.

Hatta offered Alice his arm. "Let's go, luv."

While the front of the building housed the pub, the back was a labyrinth of hallways and random-ass rooms. Bathrooms. Bedrooms. A kitchen. Hatta and Maddi lived here after all. There was even a room that looked like a hotel somewhere downtown, had windows and everything. It was fake—the building was magic, but still, it was wild.

Alice wondered which of these rooms held the Gateway. She'd never seen it, and now she had that feeling like getting ready to open Christmas presents: giddy, bubbly, and kinda worried that you wouldn't like what you got. It was as if her stomach didn't know if it wanted to do the butterfly thing or tie itself in knots. It left her feeling gassy and decidedly unhero-like.

Keep. It. Together. Kingston.

Addison stopped in front of a ratty-looking door. Inside, he flipped on the light.

Alice blinked, staring at the buckets in the corner and the shelves lined with stacks of toilet paper, towels, and cleaning supplies. The sharp scent of bleach hit her nose. "A broom closet?" Was he playin' with her?

"The last place you'd look for an interdimensional doorway, right?" Addison bowed and waved her in. "After you, milady."

Shaking her head, Alice stepped into the narrow space.

Addison followed, shutting the door behind them. Then he took a moment to strap a sword Alice hadn't noticed he'd been carrying—he was always pulling things out of the air—onto his back. It wasn't the big Fuck Off black one, but it looked dangerous enough. "Okay, the next bit is a tad . . . intense. It's probably best if you hold on to me."

Alice blinked. "Hold on to you."

"The first time through can be a bit rough."

"Um." She cleared her throat before swallowing thickly. "All right. How should I—" She stepped forward, lifting an arm to wrap around his shoulders mindful of the sheath. "Like this?"

He nodded, watching her with those slightly shimmering eyes. "Whatever you're comfortable with, so long as you've got a good grip."

"Right." Alice stepped in a little closer, trying to concentrate on anything but how he smelled faintly of spiced rum, cologne, and something sweet she couldn't place.

His arm slipped under hers, hooking around her back. The other reached out to flip the switch, plunging them into darkness.

"Last chance to back down," he murmured, his lips near

her ear. "You've accomplished a lot. No one will think less of you."

She couldn't say she hadn't thought about walking away—he was talking about fighting monsters—but she wanted this. Needed it. She shook her head, then nodded quickly. "No, no, I'm ready."

"Here we go," he warned. His voice rippled through her.

The ground dropped, and a sudden sense of falling yanked her stomach against her diaphragm. She screamed, the sound lost to a howl of wind and thunder. Her heart thrashed in her chest. Her hair slapped at her cheeks and ears. She latched on to Addison.

I'm gonna die, I'm gonna die!

Light burst across her vision. She shut her eyes against the sting and buried her face in Addison's chest. His arms tightened around her. His hand cupped the back of her head. The shrieking rush grew louder, drowning out the pounding in her ears.

She whimpered. *Pleasepleasepleasepleaseplease* . . .

When solid ground pushed up beneath her feet, her knees buckled. She would've dropped if not for the arms holding her up.

Everything in her stomach curdled, her last meal climbing toward the back of her throat. Shoving away from Addison, she stumbled across the floor toward what looked like a rosebush and threw up everything in her gut.

"Oh god," she groaned between retches.

A hand pressed between her shoulders. Addison knelt beside her, his brow furrowed. "Told you it would be rough."

"Rough? No, Mondays are rough. The first few days of your

period are rough. That?" She jerked her thumb over her shoulder. "Was three kinds of hell." She groaned again, spitting to clear her mouth of that coppery taste. "Uck."

"Here." Addison offered one of the vials. "You can rinse your mouth out."

She snatched the vial. "You coulda warned me I'd puke all over the place."

"Didn't expect you would." He shrugged. "Wouldn't have helped, anyway."

She tipped the rim against her lips. The liquid was cool and minty with a hint of . . . banana? After swishing thoroughly, she spit it out at the roots of the rosebush as well, and was wiping her mouth when she realized those weren't roses.

It was definitely a bush, though the coloring was off, more blue than green, but the bursts of red she thought were flowers were actually little orbs of what she could describe only as fluffy light. The tufts glistened softly, shivering as they hovered close together. Alice stared, filled with a sudden want to see what they felt like, but also an understanding that touching random shit is how people lose fingers.

"That is a Flit." Addison stood and offered her a hand. "They grow here in the Glow."

"The—" Alice took his hand, glanced up, and froze.

They stood on one side of a marble terrace, the surface opalescent. Pillars cut from the same material encircled the structure, giving it the look of an ancient, open temple. At the center, the very air had split but was falling closed with a sucking sputter. The world filled in the open space, leaving the structure whole. It shone, reflecting the light from the forest surrounding it. From the trees' silver bark to their sparkling leaves, everything glistened as if spun from glass.

"Glow," Addison finished. He guided Alice along the terrace. The clap of their shoes resonated outward. The pillars hummed faintly in response, like massive tuning forks. The sound rose into the air and then fizzled out as they moved down a set of steps to the ground below.

Addison shifted around in front of her, and she looked to him, her eyes widening. Her breath caught, just as it had the night they met. Everything about him had changed and yet . . . not. He was brighter, his skin moon-kissed, his hair more pale than moss green now. It stood up a bit instead of pressing against his head. And his eyes, now more silver than gray, glowed gold at their center.

His smile was exactly the same, though, stretching his face in that way that always left her feeling warm. He swept his hand out in a wide gesture. "Welcome to Wonderland."

Two
BEYOND THE VEIL

She held on to Addison, her eyes wide, her mouth open. He'd tried to describe Wonderland a few times, but always wound up saying it was like talking about a memory that was half-forgotten: a dream faded at the edges of your mind but somehow whole in your heart. None of it made sense until now.

He led her farther along, an amused twist to his lips. She didn't walk so much as shuffle. Their steps stirred the mist creeping along the ground. It crawled over the white grass and hung just beneath the silver branches in a few places.

"Beautiful." She looked to him, then to the forest again. Actually, she looked everywhere she could—this place was incredible.

"This is Wimble-Di'Glow Woods, though most just call it the Glow." Squeezing her hand, he turned them around to face the pillared platform. "That's the Gateway. It's closed at the moment, and now you must defend it from Nightmares seeking to enter your world. With my help, of course."

"Oh, right." A shiver slid like an icy finger down the curve of her spine, banishing the joy that had been bubbling up. The mention of the monsters sunk like a stone in her gut. "Are we here to stop one?" She hated the slight tremble in her voice.

He nodded. "Small one. Not far. I said you were ready, and I meant it."

Oh shit.

This was really happening. She was really here. They were going to do this.

This is what you wanted.

She cleared her throat and squared her shoulders.

This. Is. What. You. Wanted.

"Everything all right?" Addison watched her from nearby, a single eyebrow arched.

"Fine. I'm fine." A deep breath helped calm the flurry of anxiety skittering through her. A little.

"We can go back if you don't think—"

"I said I'm fine." Though the fearful flutter in her chest was distracting.

His other brow shot up to join the first one. "Very well."

She didn't mean to put that much bass in her voice, but she had to hold on to this. But what if she didn't come back? No. No, she had to do this. But her body wouldn't listen to her. She just stood there, frozen.

"Do you remember why it's best to slay a Nightmare before

it crosses into your world?" Addison asked, those multicolored eyes still on her.

Alice nodded. Of course she knew. They'd gone over it a hundred times. Humans were the source of a Nightmare's strength, and the closer the beasties got to people, the more powerful they became.

Humans were the source of everything, really. Wonderland was the literal world of dreams. Now-I-lay-me-down-to-sleep dreams. Good dreams made this world healthy. Bad dreams messed it up. Get enough bad in one place and *poof*! Nightmare. Maybe not poof. And nightmares . . . affected people.

Folk might not see the monsters themselves, but they sure saw the end result. On the news, reports about someone snapping and killing their whole family, or shooting up their job for no reason? Yeah, people were still messed up, dudes not able to take no for an answer, KKK mofos, the "lone wolf" bullshit, all that mess . . . but sometimes? Nightmare. And she was here to face one.

Oh god.

"Can you tell me?" Addison's voice cut through her thoughts.

Alice swallowed thickly, her fingers twisting around each other. Something bitter coated the back of her throat. "Um, s-so they don't get bigger."

"Good." He tilted his head to one side then slowly to the other as he spoke. "And what is it that actually kills a Nightmare?"

She pressed her shaky hand to one of the pommels at her side.

"That's just part of the equation." His fingers folded over hers, his touch light but warm. "Remember?"

Part of—? A combination of her growing fear and Addison being so close filled her mind, but his words from earlier rang clear in her ears. "M-Muchness."

"Right. What's in here." He gently tapped the tip of one ringed finger against her forehead, then her chest. "And in here. You are the one thing capable of ending a Nightmare's terror for good, and now you stand between them and their goal. If there is anything to fear here, it's you."

As Addison's words poured over her frenzied thoughts like water over coals, the thumping between her ears began to fade. "Me?"

"You." His hands fell to her shoulders, squeezing gently. "But only if you believe you can do this. I think you're ready; do you?"

Alice continued to breathe deep, in through her nose, out through her mouth. In and out, in and out. Seconds ticked by. She even counted a few in her head. Gradually, the pressure behind her eyes lessened. The wild dancing of her heart evened out. The buzzing in her limbs subsided.

"I can do this," she whispered. "I can do this." Louder this time.

Addison smiled, his eyes crinkling at the corners. "I know. Let's go." He turned to lead the way farther into the bright haze of the Glow.

With another deep breath she followed him, now able to fully concentrate on taking in the . . . well, the wonder of it all. Every so often, tiny, hazy arms and legs materialized in the branches, accompanied by bell-like laughter. She jumped a couple times, even took a swing at something bright blue that dipped in front of her face.

Addison laughed.

"Hey, it was a reflex."

"Few things here will harm you." He paused, angling his head back. "Intentionally, that is."

"So comforting." Some of the tension melted from her muscles. She half listened to Addison's tips as they went along.

"Remember to keep your core tight when you move, especially when you jump or dodge."

Maintain your grip. Eyes on your opponent. All stuff she'd heard before.

"And, I haven't mentioned this before, but you'll need to adjust for your newfound speed and strength. It'll be—"

"Wait, my what?" She blinked at him.

"When a trainee crosses the Veil for the first time, the same essence that feeds this place empowers them, enhancing their natural abilities and bestowing a few new ones." Addison continued on, leaving Alice staring after him. "That's when, and how, you become a Dreamwalker."

"Wait, wait wait wait, wait." She hurried to catch up with him. "You never said anything about superpowers." She was hearing this right, right? That's what he was talking about, *right*?

"It only happens *if* you cross the Veil, so there was no need to mention it before, in case you decided not to."

"Uh, I kinda think *superpowers* are something you bring up when training to fight monsters."

"I didn't want to influence your decision in any way. Crossing was your choice to make."

She looked to her hands as they moved along. "I don't feel any different."

"You will. Trust me."

She curled and uncurled her fingers, grinning a little. *Cool.* Dad would flip if he knew she was pretty much a superhero now. Only, he would never know.

Her vision blurred, and that hollow place in her chest deepened. *No.* She sniffed and wiped her eyes. *Not here. Not now.* She couldn't come apart here.

She smoothed her hands over her hair, fingers catching the coils a couple times. That trip had blown her hair all over the place, so she worked it into the large ponytail holder she always kept on her wrist. She stole a glance at Addison, who looked to be caught up in searching their surroundings for something. If he noticed her brief break, he didn't say anything.

"So, what else haven't you told me about this place?" She waved a hand. "Not wanting to 'influence me' or whatever."

"I can't very well tell you everything. Wonderland is as wide as your world and as immense as the human imagination." He shoved his hands into his pockets.

"Uh-huh. So this is you sayin' you don't know everything." A corner of her lips lifted.

"What I'm *saying* is your training covered a lot, but 'there are more things in heaven and earth, Horatio, than are dreamt of in your philosophy.'"

Alice snorted. "You know poetry don't work on me, right?"

Addison grinned. "I'm simply saying there's a lot here. A lot of history. A lot of . . . complications." His tone dipped around that last word. "And I'm here to be your partner and tour guide all rolled into one. And that wasn't poetry."

"You know what I mean." She wanted to ask what he meant by complications, but they'd reached the end of the Glow. At least, she assumed they did, because everything was suddenly less bright.

A meadow opened before them; a sea of tall grass—or what looked like grass—waved back and forth in the night. The color shifted in a gradient of pink and yellow. Purple clouds drifted overhead, rimmed in silver, and bloated from soaking up moonlight. *Blue* moonlight. The moon was freaking blue.

"Wow," Alice whispered, stepping forward. The grass brushed against her thighs. She could feel the tickle through her jeans. She was so focused on the sky, the moon, that when a luminescent blue blob bounced out of the grass, she yelped and stumbled back.

Addison laughed.

Alice puffed her cheeks, trying to ignore the burn in them. She slugged him in the shoulder, which only made him laugh harder. "It's not funny."

"No." He snickered, trying to breathe. "It's hilarious. And these little guys are harmless. Frubbles. They just want to play."

She rubbed her arm as a few more Froo-bles, Frubbles, whatever, rolled around at her feet, shining different colors. "Play?"

"Yeah. They're like puppies. Round, glowing puppies. Just

run, you'll see." He smiled, those dimples appearing again. "Go on," he urged when she hesitated. "Fast as you can."

She looked to the Frubbles, then to the meadow. It was about a hundred yards or so to the next tree line, which wasn't as bright as the Glow. With a quick breath, she took off, crossed ten yards in a burst of speed that shook her core, and promptly tripped over her own feet. "Whoa!"

She hit the dirt with a *whuff* as all the air was pushed out of her lungs. "Uggghhhh." Cold from the ground seeped through her jeans and her shirt. She shivered and struggled to her knees, then hugged herself to ward off the nighttime chill. The rich smell of damp earth mingled with the sharp scent of moss and fresh water from somewhere nearby.

Addison knelt beside her. "You all right?"

"Yeah." Though her torso ached a bit, but the pain was already starting to fade. "I didn't—I was so fast, I couldn't keep up with my damn self. How does that even work?"

"Heh, told you you'd feel it." He offered her a hand up. "Try again."

Alice took a second to gather herself, flexing her arms, shifting her legs. The Frubbles rolled about in the grass, trilling softly like birds. She grinned. They were so cute!

Okay. She glanced across the meadow again. *Super speed.* Well, not super, just faster. *I can handle this.* With a deep breath, she pushed into a run. Slower at first, getting a feel for her Wonder-legs? Now that was corny.

She stumbled a bit, but didn't fall. She turned at the tree line and kept going. Faster now. Faster. Faster! Luminescent blobs bounced out of the thigh-high grass, racing beside her, surfing the meadow like dolphins. The Frubbles trilled cheer-fully, dipping in and out of her path, arcing through the air like shiny beach balls.

She pushed into a full run, her head buzzing as her chest heaved. Her legs and arms pumped. Wind swept over her face and through her hair. She whooped and kept going until she pushed off into a jump. Her momentum carried her forward, propelled her up.

"Whoa!" Her arms and legs flailed, throwing off her center of gravity. She managed to get her feet under her before hitting the ground and tumbling to a stop.

On her back again, she stared at the starless sky and the moon overhead. Her muscles sung, jerking here and there. Her nerves were alight. She laughed and whooped again, panting.

The Frubbles rolled back and forth beside her, cooing like doves. She patted a pink one gently, her hand black against its shine, gliding across the smooth surface. Sitting up, she glanced around for signs of Addison when an odd sort of pressure slid along her limbs, like dozens of tapping fingers. Goose bumps prickled her flesh. The Frubbles gave high-pitched trills before darting away into the grass.

"Um . . . okay."

"Alice?"

"Over here." She brushed herself off, glancing around. She was at the edge of the forest across from the Glow. It was much darker. Shadows filled the trees. Tangled branches and vines choked the canopy, keeping the moonlight at bay.

Alice tensed when she thought she saw something move out of the corner of her eye and scanned the undergrowth.

"Alice?" Addison called again.

She lifted a hand out of the grass and waved, not wanting to shout again. Something was out there. Her senses strained to take in everything they could.

The forest remained still, quiet enough for her to hear the wind sweep through with a low, heavy *whuush*. *Whuush*.

Not wind. Breathing.

Movement to her left.

Oh shit. She pushed to her feet, scrambling back from the forest just as a roar shattered the quiet like an air horn. Her ears rang. Her bones rattled.

"Alice!" Addison was racing toward her when the Nightmare burst from the brush, looking like a hippo with more limbs than a squid.

The beast charged. She twisted out of the way, barely avoiding a swipe of claws. She screamed, fear jolting through her as she tried to get her legs to work.

"Alice!" Addison stood a short ways off, gold eyes wide and dancing between her and the Nightmare. "You can do this!" He gripped the hilt of the sword at his back but hadn't pulled it free yet.

"It's too big!" She backed away from the Nightmare as it lumbered around, looking between her and Addison as if trying to decide which of them to eat first. She shook her head, feeling the sting of tears. "It's too much!"

"But you are much more!" He sidestepped, putting distance between them, drawing the monster's attention. It sniffed the air and growled, turning to focus completely on him. "You can beat it. You trained for this. You're faster, stronger than you know."

Alice whimpered, shaking her head. She drew back a few more steps, her whole body cold and shaking.

The beast charged Addison. Alice's heart practically uppercut her it jumped so hard, but Addison spun out of the way, unsheathing a sword and slicing across the beast's side in the same move. The monster roared. Yellow blood spattered the tall grass.

Addison slid into a ready stance, his weapon lifted, the silvery blade shining against the night.

"We can go back," Addison called without taking his eyes off the beast. He dodged again, rolling under a swipe of claws. "I can stop it, and we can wait for it to re-form. Try again later."

No no no. Alice lifted her trembling hands to the sides of her face. How could she suck so bad at something she trained so hard to do? But she couldn't. It was too much.

Breathe, Baby Moon. Dad's voice filled her head. It did that a lot lately, memories of him laughing with her, talking to her, chastising her. The tears spilled free and she shook her head. "I can't," she whispered.

Breathe.

"I *can't.*"

Breathe . . .

"I'll try."

Ain't no try. You know that. What you gone do?

Alice's hands fell to the daggers at her hips. She palmed the pommels before gripping them tight and yanking them free. Azure moonlight filled the crystalline surfaces of the blades.

Across the meadow, Addison fended off a swipe of claws,

the shriek of grating metal filling the air. He leaped back and shot a glance Alice's way. Their eyes met.

What you gone do?

Her fingers tightened their hold on the daggers. Something swept through her, pushed outward from the center of her chest to the top of her head and the soles of her feet. "This. I'mma do this."

The Nightmare whipped around to face her. It loosed a roar and pounded the ground with its feet.

Alice adjusted her weight, then pushed off into a run. The smell of grass and dirt snapped crisp against her senses. Her steps thudded against the ground, mirroring the pounding of her heart, a storm in her chest. She darted across the meadow, coming around the monster's flank. It stood out against the black, her vision sharpening. Before the Nightmare could turn to take her head-on, she jumped.

"Aim for the core!" Addison's voice reached her above the scream of wind in her ears.

The Figment Blades burned against the night. Their fire stampeded up her arms, filling her, fueling her, igniting something inside her that would never dim again.

As she came down on the beast, she tightened her grip and threw her weight into the thrust. The monster roared.

So did she.

They collided.

Three

DREAMWALKER

One year later...

Alice dropped into a slide as a barbed tail lashed through the air overhead. The Nightmare, a massive thing with a rhino's body and spindly, almost-human arms sticking up from its back, tumbled past. She twisted out of the slide and caught her balance in a crouch before exploding forward to drive her dagger at the monster's side. The blade glanced off with a *crack* like striking stone. Armored hide. She spun outside another swing of the tail and leaped, aiming to land atop the creature. It swatted her aside like a gnat instead of her tall-ass self.

The impact robbed her of breath and the ability to scream when a white-hot throb lanced up her arm. She hit the ground in a roll, then twisted out of it, her knees on fire. Blood ran warm and slick where claws had torn into her forearm.

"Dammit." She swapped her weapon to her other hand,

shifting to shield her wound. "Hatta!" Her eyes flickered between the monster and the treetops. Where *was* he?

The Nightmare howled and came at her again.

Every inkling of self-preservation shouted to jump, dive, get out of the way. At the last instant she jerked to the side. The beast crashed into a tree, tearing it up from the roots. Wood groaned and snapped. Leaves shivered and fell like rain. Blue moonlight spilled into the clearing.

Alice ducked a spindly, talon-tipped arm. She jabbed the dagger into the rippling flesh of the monster's underbelly and yanked. Something wet, thick, and rank spilled over her hand. She gritted her teeth and pushed.

Come . . . on . . .

The knife sank farther into the creature and, with a snap and hiss, pierced its core.

Yes! A thrill blazed through Alice. She smiled. *That's right, you sonuva—*

The Nightmare loosed a keening cry and lashed out, slicing into the trees and scoring the earth. Alice shuffled aside, dagger ready as her target staggered, limbs twisting, body buckling. The creature collapsed inward like crumbling stone. Its wounds popped and fizzed, spewing yellow goop across the dirt and onto her shoes.

"*Augh.*" She danced backward and wobbled as she shook each foot. Too late—the pus had already soaked into the material. "Really? Really." Another pair of kicks ruined. Along with her good mood. "Perfect." She couldn't afford a new pair of shoes right now! Or jeans. And asking her mother was not happening. Who knew being a superhero meant going broke.

Pop. The body started to dissolve. She pinched her nose against the stink, which no doubt clung to her, thick and gross.

As she wiped the dagger on her already-ruined jeans, a second shadow dropped from the branches of a nearby tree. She whirled, body sliding into a defensive stance, weapons up.

"Easy, luv." Silhouetted in shadow, Hatta's face was hidden, but Alice knew he was smiling. Bastard was always smiling. "It's just me."

Alice straightened and glowered at him. "It's just me," she mimicked, scrunching her nose and pitching her voice higher. Releasing a heavy breath, she sheathed the blades and tilted against the toppled tree to assess her injuries.

Her legs throbbed but held. Scuffed knees peeked through holes in her pants, stinging with each subtle movement. A torn sleeve revealed nearly invisible slices in her dark brown skin. They burned and bled a fluorescent green mixed with deep red as her body expelled toxins from the Nightmare's claws. One of the *actual* perks of being a Dreamwalker, along with getting to stab things, not some bull like "the honor of serving her fellow man." Was her fellow man gone pay for a new pair of Converse? Or keep her mom from wringing her neck if she got this crap on the carpet?

Didn't think so.

"Nothing serious, I hope." Hatta gestured to her arm as he approached. The rings on his fingers glittered. "May I?"

She snorted and thrust the injury toward him. "Where the hell were you?"

"Close." His long fingers curled around her wrist, their press gentle as he inspected the wound, his head bowed slightly. In the Wonderland light his moss green hair paled, the wavy strands clinging to his forehead and face. His white skin shone like polished porcelain.

"Close," she repeated, hoping the darkness concealed her flushed state. He'd know, though. Hatta had this way of *knowing* when he was getting under her skin. Usually, she was annoyed, but sometimes? Sometimes heat filled her face, her palms prickled, and her stomach tried to wedge itself between her lungs. Like now as he traced the edge of one of the cuts with a gray-painted fingernail.

"I was ready to jump in if needed." He glanced up. His eyes practically glowed. Over time she'd noticed the gray wasn't just one color but a mix of different flecks and dabs, like stained glass at sunset. Weird but gorgeous, and god, she was weak. And sappy. And staring. And he was smiling again.

"Uh-huh." Alice withdrew her hand, certain he'd feel her rising temperature or heartbeat in her wrist. "So helpful, considering you said we were after a Chihuahua, then ran into a pit bull."

"That . . . was unexpected. I'm sorry." He shoved his hands into his jeans pockets, slouching a bit. "But you're strong, adaptable. I could tell you had things handled."

Okay, so that lifted her mood somewhat. She smirked. "Thanks." He hadn't even brought his sword, so he must've really thought she had this.

"And my plan worked." He glanced at the Nightmare carcass.

What was left writhed and squirmed as the land absorbed the remains, leaving a shadowy scorch mark.

"It was a stupid plan." Alice yanked a dagger free from her belt. Seriously, having her sit out in the open like bait? Here's a human, come and get it! *Ass.*

"It still worked."

"Meh-meh-meh." Covering her nose again she drove the blade into the tainted ground with a "Cosmic moon power!" The dirt gave easily, and the blade lit up like a Roman candle. White sparks skittered across the ground, leaving jagged marks like lightning in the earth. They pulsed a few times, brighter and brighter, before fading entirely and taking the taint with them, leaving no trace of the fallen Nightmare.

"Why do you say that?" Hatta tilted his head to the side, eyeing her. "The moon has nothing to do with it."

"True." She yanked the dagger free and resheathed it. "But it feels cool." Purging Nightmares so they wouldn't rise again didn't require moonlight or magic words, just a Figment Blade and Muchness—the Wonderland equivalent of believing in yourself or something like that, it didn't make a lot of sense whenever Hatta tried to explain it—but the words didn't hurt, so Hatta could suck on that with his logic.

He chuckled, eyes on the newly purged ground. "If you say so."

"Yup." Alice started toward the Gateway, happy to put as much distance between herself and that lingering stank as possible. Hatta moved at her side, seeming to glide over the brush while she plowed through, smacking leaves and vines out of her way. Cool, crisp air gradually banished most of the foul smell, though a faint whiff did follow them. No doubt her shoes and clothes. *Ugh.*

"Are you sure you're all right?" Hatta watched her from the corners of his eyes. "You're favoring your left leg."

"Eh. Hit my knee pretty hard when I landed. I'm cool, though."

"Mmm." He didn't sound convinced. He drew a hand from his pocket, fingers wrapped around the handle of an ornate mirror, the kind the Queen of England would own, and much too big to be carried around in someone's pants but, y'know, Wonderland. An intricate curl in the mirror's metallic back formed the raised profile of a woman's face. Alice had seen the mirror a number of times and asked about it. It belonged to a friend, Hatta explained, and that was all she got.

"I'll have Maddi prepare something for the pain."

Alice rolled her eyes. "I said I'm fine."

"I know." He knocked three times against the reflective surface of the mirror. "Open my eyes."

The glass rippled before swirling into itself. Color poured through the chaos, like drops of paint in water. Alice had a similar mirror, though much smaller and less fancy. Hatta gave it to her after she killed her first Nightmare. Was in it for the long haul, then.

The mirrors acted like magic phones, but you could only use FaceTime. She preferred actual phones and kept her mirror buried in her locker. It used to stay in her room, until Hatta "called" her one evening and Mom was certain Alice was smuggling boys into her room. She took the door off the hinges and kept it. For a month. *Who does that?*

Finally, the swirl of colored light and silver evened out to reveal Maddi's yawning face. "Twinkle who?"

"Madeline, wake up!" Hatta said cheerfully.

"But it's star time," Maddi huffed.

"I know, but Alice got a little banged up and needs something to set her right."

"Nuh-uh," Alice called as she stepped around a large pink stone. "And no, I don't."

Hatta ignored her. "Do you think you could whip something up by the time we get back?"

Maddi blinked again, her eyes now orange. She nodded, and a veil of stringy black curls fell around her face. "Full moons mean empty glasses." She gave a thumbs-up.

"Great. See you in a tick."

Maddi waved before her image faded and the mirror was a mirror again.

"Do you not know what 'I'm fine' means?" Alice cut him some side-eye.

"Yes," Hatta drawled, and shoved the mirror back into his pocket. "And you probably are. But if your knee bothers you in the morning, you'll have something."

Yeah, he was right. And it would likely help her arm, too, which still throbbed slightly. She'd had worse, but this didn't tickle.

Finally, they broke through the forest's edge into the meadow. Another cloudy night hung over them, pale green clouds puffy and shining with blue moonlight. Breaks in the billows revealed the splintered, starless sky. A faint golden glow peeked through the cracks. The Midnight Breaking had come and gone, but that didn't mean anything. Time passed much more erratically here than in the real world. Sometimes, an hour back home could equal a day here. Or a week. One of the reasons Hatta suggested she never spend more time here than absolutely necessary. Across the meadow, Wimble-Di'Glow Woods stood as a beacon in the night.

"Curiouser." Hatta glanced around as they approached the Glow.

"What?"

"Nothing. But maybe everything."

Oh boy, here we go. Wonderlandians may speak every language, but sometimes they don't make a lick of sense.

"That was the ninth incident this month," Hatta said.

"Tenth," she corrected. "There was the twofer this past Saturday."

"Right," said Hatta. "How're you doing?" His voice softened and sent butterflies skittering through her insides.

"Better." She swallowed. Said twofer hit a little close to home.

Normally, Dreamwalkers were immune to the influences of Nightmares, but if it was a fear close to your heart, it could get to you anyway.

A week before the fight, police shot a Black girl, seventeen, same age as Alice. Her name was Brionne Mathews. It happened in the parking lot after a football game at a school across town. Nothing the news said made sense, something about a fight between gangs and some people had guns. The girl had on one gang's colors, but so did a lot of people. They were the same colors as one of the teams playing that night.

Over the next few days, things were kinda chaotic. Protests and arrests. Course some mofos came in trying to start trouble. So many people were hurt, angry, and so afraid. It was enough to create *two* Nightmares. Alice had felt that fear, a physical thing that ate away at her from the inside. It left her hollow, shaking, and useless. If Hatta hadn't been there . . .

"Alice?" Hatta's voice pulled at her. He stood at the edge of the Glow, eyes on her, concern illuminated in their light. "Are you all right, luv?"

"Fine," she breathed, and nodded. "Just tired." She was seriously feeling every bone and muscle in her body right now. A hot shower and her bed were singing her song.

"Ahh. Let's get you home, then." He curled his fingers, beckoning.

She grasped his hand, the rest of her body stiff with chills, and followed him into the Glow. Its haunting shine wrapped around her. In all of Wonderland, this was her favorite place.

She swatted at bouncing Flits and Sparks as they dipped in and out of her vision like fiery cotton balls, and she took care not to step on the blossoms scattered across the ground like Christmas lights. Flowers never wasted an opportunity to whine about being trampled.

They walked in silence until, eventually, soft earth gave way to the hard stone of the Gateway platform beneath their feet. Hatta released her hand. Her skin prickled at the loss, and she tucked her hand under her arm.

At the center of the terrace, he stretched out his arm. For a few seconds, nothing happened, then the air in front of him split down the middle and curled outward like a well-used scroll. Pale light spilled out around him, the Gateway drawing open to about the size of a large door.

Turning to her, he angled forward and extended a hand. "Your chariot awaits, milady."

Feeling a familiar warmth crawl up the back of her neck, she grasped his hand and stepped through the Gateway and into his arms. They wrapped around her, muscle concealed by lengthy sleeves.

As light enveloped the two of them, he settled his chin atop her head. Her arms wound around his waist, and she got a faint whiff of Nightmare stink. It amazed her how the smell didn't seem to bother him. Every time she ended up covered in the stuff, he took her into his arms like it was nothing. Her cheeks warmed at the thought as the Gateway folded in behind her, the air sewing itself shut. The light faded, leaving them floating in darkness.

She closed her eyes and held her breath.

Man, she hated this part.

◊ ◊ ◊

When the scream of wind died away, and the floor solidified beneath her feet, she stood shaking and trying hard to keep her stomach in check. She hadn't eaten before going through the Veil; what was even in there to come up?

"You okay?" Hatta murmured near her ear.

She nodded rapidly, fighting to regain control of her

breathing enough to manage words. "'M fine," she half gasped, half burped, then groaned. *Sexy, Kingston. Real sexy.*

"After all this time, still not used to it." He chuckled and let go, taking with him her means of stability.

One hand shot out to brace against the wall. "My stomach does not appreciate being spun through the universe like old socks in a washer." She flapped her other hand at him. "Open the door."

Light and sound burst into the space as he stepped out. Stable, Alice moved to follow, but something caught her foot. With an undignified squawk, she fell against the doorjamb. A mop lay across the floor, snagged on the toe of her shoe. Grumbling, she kicked it into the closet and slammed the door.

Blessed with increased speed and agility, incredible strength and dexterity, abilities no normal human being possessed . . . and she trips over a mop.

"Complications?" Hatta had stopped at the end of the hallway, where it angled to the left and out of sight. The sound of laughter, music, and clacking billiard balls poured in from behind him.

Shaking her head, Alice waved him on. "I'm fine. Gonna clean up." She steadied herself against the wall, the faux wood cool beneath her fingers.

"I'll wait for you out front." He disappeared around the corner. A chorus of cheers greeted him.

Alice shuffled after him but veered left into the ladies' room. She locked the door and turned the water on full blast. Cupping her hands beneath the spout, she splashed her face again and again. The sudden shock of cold helped tamp the nausea churning in her gut. She snatched paper towels from the dispenser to wipe her face and jerked when their roughness scraped a tender area near her temple.

Staring at her reflection, she pushed her hair back to reveal scratches on the side of her face. They were barely bleeding. Smoothing her fingers against her brown cheeks, she wrangled her ebony locks and tied them off. If she didn't count the stains on her jeans and shoes, she looked presentable. She couldn't do anything about the smell, though. It wasn't so bad anymore, but her nose still scrunched whenever she caught a whiff. Yeah, this outfit was definitely done. She'd spent a grip on these shoes, too. After a few finishing touches, she made her way out front.

Hatta stood behind the bar, talking to Maddi. Above them the cat clock ticked and wagged away. 10:34 p.m.

Crap. It wasn't *too* late, but Mom would still probably have a cow.

"Hey, I need to head out. Pretty sure my mom's already gonna bust my ass. Better not make it worse."

"Right." Hatta sat a small vial of purple liquid on the counter. "Maddi worked her Poetic magic."

"It was," Maddi muttered, her head tilted against her hand on the bar, "nothing not worth everything."

"Thanks." Alice pocketed the vial as Hatta produced her backpack and purse from behind the bar. She traded him her belt and daggers, then hurriedly pulled out her phone. Technology didn't work in Wonderland, so she usually left it at the bar or with her best friend, Courtney, who would cover for her. Court had tennis practice today, so Alice was on her own. Six missed calls and twice as many texts. *Yikes* . . .

She didn't read any of them, but caught a glimpse of a threat to put her ass in traction if she didn't pick up her phone. "I'll see you guys later," she said as she struggled into her pack with one hand, the other speeding over her phone to let Court know she was back but probably wouldn't be at school tomorrow since her mom was going to eat her alive.

"Be safe." The door swung shut behind her, cutting off Hatta as Alice stepped out onto the street. Downtown Atlanta sparkled in the distance.

She took off toward the nearest MARTA station, praying the Red Line hadn't run yet. Hopefully, by the time she made it home, Mom would be asleep. Alice *really* didn't wanna have to explain why she was burning a brand-new pair of shoes.

◊ ◊ ◊

As Alice raced up the sidewalk toward her house, she grimaced when she noticed a glow from the living room windows.

Shit.

And the front door wasn't even locked.

Oh shit.

Ruined shoes in hand, Alice slipped inside and headed straight for the stairs. She took them two at a time as quietly as she could. In her room she dropped her shoes and bag at the foot of her bed and peeled off her clothes. Those and her Converse went into a shopping bag, and she tied it up to throw away tomorrow. She'd scrubbed the last of the Nightmare gunk from her arms and pulled on her pajamas when, "Alice?" Mom's voice floated up from the kitchen.

Hnnnnnnnnnnnnnshit. "Yeah?" Alice stuck her head out of the door.

The soft thump of her mother's footsteps preluded her appearance down in the den. She stood in yoga pants and a T-shirt, her hair a bushy halo around her head, somehow perfect. Alice never managed to get her hair to look that good.

Mom folded her arms over her chest. The curious look on her face flattened under a stormy stare. "Where the hell you been?"

Every muscle in Alice's body stood at attention. "I fell asleep at Courtney's." The lies leaped free with ease now. A year of practice helped. "She put in some sappy love movie, and I was out."

Hopefully, Court would be okay with a retroactive cover-up. What're best friends for, right?

"And you didn't—Get down here."

Resigned, Alice exited the safety of her room and slumped back down the stairs.

Mom met her at the bottom. "You didn't hear your phone? I called at least twelve times." The dim light from the nearby lamps painted her rich brown skin in gold flame, intensifying the irritation rolling off her.

"It was on vibrate." Another lie. And Mom had only called six times, but she wasn't bringing that up.

"Mmmmmmmmhm." Mom pinched her lips and arched

an eyebrow. "I don't appreciate these games, Alison." She shuffled toward the kitchen.

Alice flopped against the stairs. She buried her face in her arms, a sudden heaviness pouring through her. "I'm not playing games."

"—late enough this week. And don't blame the phone; it ain't ignoring my calls."

"I'm not ignoring you."

"—got too much to do around here and can't do it by myself. Specially since I'm leaving town next week. I'll be gone for four days. This house, work, your grandma, I can't do it alone."

Alice stiffened. *Alone? Alone?!*

For months after her dad passed suddenly, heart failure the doctors said, Alice did everything. She spent hours before and after school, when she wasn't training with Hatta, cleaning the house from top to bottom. Every day. She cooked, she did the yard work, she fielded calls from family and friends, lying to them about how she and Mom were doing okay. They weren't. Then, when Mom recovered, Alice kept the work up. She'd felt that if she eased even the smallest burdens—like mating socks or making sure the dishes were always done—it would lessen the chances of her mother sinking into herself again. If *anyone* had been alone, it was her! She wanted to scream the words, tasted them and the anger charring the back of her throat, coating her tongue with ash.

Instead she swallowed it all, like acid, and croaked, "You're not alone."

A hand squeezed Alice's knee. Reluctantly, she lifted her head, and blinked in surprise.

Mom held a culinary offering aloft, the heady spice of shrimp scampi mingling with the sweet tang of olive oil and tomatoes over angel-hair pasta. Her favorite.

Alice's wide eyes lifted to her mother, who settled a warm plateful of food into Alice's somewhat shaky hands. Then her mom leaned in to kiss her forehead and smooth her hands over her hair.

"You're all I got left. I can be worried."

Alice's throat swelled. Heat filled her face, stinging her eyes lightly.

"Especially after what happened to that baby." Mom came around to sit on Alice's stair and slipped an arm around her shoulders. She was talking about Brionne. Had to be. That's all anyone was talking about anymore. Well, anyone around here.

Mom kissed Alice's temple and smoothed fingers against her baby hairs. "The story was on again tonight, and I just . . ." Mom pursed her lips, her eyes shining with tears. "With you not answering your phone, I didn't know what to think."

Alice rested her head against Mom's shoulder, careful to balance the plate on her knees. "Anything new?"

"Same old, same old." Mom shook her head and rubbed Alice's arm. "That baby's gone, and nobody got answers. It wasn't even a full story, just some words on the bottom of the screen saying the investigation is still ongoing in the death of a young woman and some other mess. Won't even say her name."

Alice straightened when Mom stood up. "Promise me you'll be careful. I know you already are, just"—she lifted her hand from Alice's knee, made a fist, then forced her fingers loose to pat her knee again, squeezing—"even when you're careful, even when you play by the rules, it might not be enough. Gotta go the extra mile out here."

"You're scared I'll end up like Brionne?" Alice asked quietly, her shoulders hunched.

"Maybe. Or maybe it'll be those little girls down the street. That boy you used to catch the bus with." Mom sighed, shaking her head. "A lot of us are scared, but I don't wanna scare you, baby. I just want—"

"Me to be careful."

"For you to be okay." Mom leaned in for another kiss, this one on Alice's cheek. "Eat. Then go to bed." Mom headed for the kitchen again. "I don't wanna hear no mess about you too tired to go to school tomorrow."

"Good night." Alice shuffled up to her room.

Stretched across her bed, she couldn't bring herself to eat more than a few bites. She pushed the rest around on her plate. Normally, she was starving after a trip through the Veil, or anytime really—a girl burns some serious calories fighting monsters and motion sickness—but her appetite was MIA, even for her fave. Something wet and cold brushed her feet. Peering over her shoulder, she spied a familiar face of dark fur and blue eyes. "Hey, Lou."

Lewis, her Siamese cat, purred and pressed into the attention as she rubbed his ears.

"Been keeping my bed warm?" She kept scratching. "Where's Carol?"

Lewis paused in licking his paw to pin her with a look.

"Right, Mom's room."

The stub-tailed tortie preferred Mom's California king, fit for feline royalty.

Alice sighed, her gaze drawn to a picture of her father on her desk across the room. It had been a year and some months. That's one Father's Day. Almost two birthdays. Almost two Christmases, Thanksgivings, everything else. Two anniversaries for her mom.

But it wasn't all bad. There was a whole year of Hatta. A whole year of Wonderland. A whole year of being a secret hero. Beating the shit out of monsters was what kept her from losing it. Doing something, saving people. Now, everything was okay. At least, she thought it was okay. She needed it to stay okay.

Setting aside her now-cold plate of pasta, she crawled under her blanket, turned off her lamp, and curled up in the dark. Mom's words from earlier played through her head.

Even when you're careful, even when you play by the rules, it might not be enough. Gotta go the extra mile out here.

Having special powers might count as going the extra mile. But was she faster than a bullet? Was she strong enough to survive one? She could fight monsters, but she couldn't fight this. She was out there protecting everyone from some bad shit from another world, but bad shit still happened in this one. What if it *did* happen to her? What would the news say? No one would know she was a superhero. Would it matter? Or would she be another story with people waiting to hear both sides but only listening to one before forgetting her completely? She'd protected this world, but would anyone protect her?

Mom wasn't alone, but if anything happened to Alice, she would be. And like Brionne's family, Mom would be left with all questions, no answers, and no one else.

No. Alice curled tighter under the blanket and squeezed her eyes shut. No, she couldn't let that happen. *Wouldn't* let that happen. She couldn't control Nightmares, and she couldn't control bullets, but she could control this. She could quit. She could stop putting herself out there like this. She could just walk away, and the sooner the better. Tomorrow. She'd do it tomorrow.

Her mind made up, she relaxed a little. This was for the best. For her family. There was no arguing with that. Still, she sighed and tried to ignore the twist in her chest.

She was going to miss him.

Four

UNDATE

"Oh my gawd, you're bananas." Courtney shoveled a helping of peas into her mouth, the plastic spoon coming away stained neon pink like her lipstick. "You're seriously going to bail on the best job ever? Taking tests by day, fighting monsters by night. You're pretty much a Black Buffy."

"Thanks? Or just Buffy. Whatever." Alice lowered her voice, glancing around the cafeteria as she toyed with the top on her soda. Maybe talking about her plans to retire before actually retiring wasn't such a good idea. "She died. Repeatedly. Remember?"

"Well, if anything happens, you have Maddi."

"And?" Yeah, Maddi was pretty powerful. Still not revive-the-dead powerful, though.

"*And* you literally save the world at least two times a week."

"Not the world—"

"Aaddahdahdah!" Court gestured for silence with her pink spoon. "If you didn't help Hatta slay these things, we'd all be in serious shit."

"I'm the one who does the slaying in this relationship, so he helps me."

Court slid her a side-glance. "So you admit it's a relationship?"

"*Partner*ship," Alice emphasized.

"Whatever-ship. Addison Hatta is six kinds of hot, two of which are illegal in some states. Where did I go wrong with you?" Court narrowed her eyes and pursed her lips. Thus began her almost daily recounting of the many reasons Alice should try and talk to Hatta. Court had made it her mission to improve Alice's love life. Or torment her endlessly. Same thing.

"There's nothing *wrong* with the way things are." Alice stole a baby carrot from Court's plate. "Plus he's old. Like, centuries old."

"Is he, though? Because I remember when y'all talked about how time is funky in Wonderland."

"Shhhh!" Alice hissed, glancing around. "I fail to see your point."

"The *point* is, you geeked out hard about how everyone there ages super slow, like that pretty boy you like with the ears. LEGOS?"

"Chile, it's Lego*las*."

Court waved off the correction. "Anyway, I know Hatta's actually nineteen. Oh, I paid attention to *that* part of the conversation, so don't look so surprised. And you'll be eighteen in six months, so stop making excuses."

Alice fought not to scowl at her friend. "Don't be using *Lord of the Rings* against me. You don't even like those movies. Either way, me and Hatta just friends."

"Blasphemy." Court jabbed the business end of her spoon in Alice's direction. With her frost blond pixie cut and full face of makeup, she looked more model than menace. "If this were ancient times, wars would be waged for that gorgeous piece of man meat."

"Man meat." Alice ticked an eyebrow over the rim of her Pepsi bottle. She brought it from home, where Mom usually kept a stash, just like Granny used to. Hard to find anything but Coke around here, and Mom's side of the family were Pepsi people, a closely guarded secret. "You just said the phrase *man meat*."

"Yes, I did. I own that. And you are forbidden to be 'just friends' with someone so dangerously delicious."

Alice shook her head and rolled her eyes. "Imaginary relationships aside, I've already thought about what not being a Dreamwalker anymore might mean. Not seeing him. But it's not personal. I mean, it is, but not like that. It's family." She sighed and sank down in her chair a little. "Last night Mom got really upset when I got home. I was in Wonderland and missed her calls. She saw another story about Brionne, I guess, and started talking about how I'm all she has left and she's scared something will happen to me, even when I'm being careful and following the rules. She's not wrong. You know how it is. There's no right way to be but dead in these situations."

Court frowned, fidgeting with her spoon. "That's heavy."

"Mmm. She's been like that since Saturday. Most of the neighborhood has, if I'm being honest."

"'Cause of the girl killed at the game?"

"Brionne," Alice insisted.

"Brionne, sorry."

"And yeah. I mean, I like kicking ass and taking names, but I been thinkin' 'bout what'll happen to Mom if something happens to me, too. Her and a bunch of ladies at church were all 'it could've been my baby,' and they're right." Alice shook her head, and stared up, at nothing really. "Folk ready to shoot me for being who I am. I mean, I could die walking down the street in the wrong color T-shirt. Why add monster hunting to that?"

"'Cause you're a badass." Court took another bite from her plate.

Alice stole another baby carrot. She'd already finished two slices of pizza and a turkey sandwich. "I'm serious."

"Me too!" Court licked her spoon, then dug around with it in the bottom of an obviously empty yogurt cup. She concentrated on scraping together about a pinkie nail's worth of strawberry banana. "I can't pretend to know what this is like for you. I'm sorry for Brionne. For her family. That this happened. Again. But I don't know what to say other than I'm here. As a shoulder to cry on or scream into about anything. Shit with your mom. Racism. Fucking white people."

Alice snickered, though her gaze shot around the cafeteria again. "Really?"

"Oh yeah." Court tossed the cup and the spoon onto her tray. "Have you met any? They're a mess. They only believe, like, in three seasonings."

Now she laughed.

"And one of them is pumpkin spice." Court lifted a mani-cured finger.

Alice doubled over, her face pressed to the table as she howled.

"Tell me I'm wrong!"

"No, stop! I can't!"

By the time Alice could breathe again, a few people were staring and Court sat with her chin on her folded hands and a smug look on her face.

Alice stifled another snicker. "I dunno, you and Chess are pretty cool."

"And you're amazing." Court squeezed Alice's fingers.

"I hear my name?" A chair scraped the ground to her left, and Chess dropped into it. "And that I'm pretty cool?"

"As far as white people go," Court added before eyeing him across the table. "How many spices can you name?"

"Um, what?" He sank against the back of the chair, long legs sprawled under the table, oddly colored eyes flickering back and forth between Alice and Court curiously. Chess had turned their duo into a trio sophomore year, but the violet tint in his gaze took Alice by surprise at least twice a week.

"Court was just going on about how ridiculous white people are for pumpkin spice." Alice shook her head.

Chess snorted. "Hard truths."

"Always." Court shoved her tray aside and dug into her designer backpack.

"Forget targeting the economy or our infrastructure. If any-one managed to kill the pumpkins, America would fall in a week.

Panic in the streets." Chess gestured questioningly at Alice's half-empty soda bottle.

She handed it over. "I hear no lies. Hell, *I* like pumpkin. Except pie. Sweet potato all the way."

Chess took a few swigs, then handed the bottle back with thanks.

"I'm a salted caramel mocha girl, myself." Court fished out a compact mirror. After generously reapplying a layer of psychedelic lipstick, she blew a kiss at her reflection. "Hopefully, that means I'd survive the fall of the western world."

Court always looked flawless: shoes, clothes, and especially makeup. Alice couldn't help being jealous sometimes. She'd yet to find a foundation that didn't turn her gray or orange. There were so many choices for light complexions—all with sassy names like Honey-Tan, Beige Bomb, or Pearl—but usually only a handful for her skin tone: all named some variation of Dark. Dark Chocolate, Dark Onyx, just Dark.

'Cause I need reminding.

A hand landed on her shoulder, squeezing. "Alice."

She shook herself free of her thoughts, turning to face a frowning Chess. "Say what, now?"

"I was . . ." He trailed off, pitching a glance at Court—who watched the two of them from behind her mirror, pretending to inspect her brows—then back. "I asked if you wanted to see the new *Black Panther* tonight. Supposed to be better than the last one."

Alice froze. Her throat closed up and something heavy in her chest pulled her heart toward her stomach. She was fiendin' to see that movie, but she'd promised her dad she'd see it with him first and—he wasn't here to go with her. Not anymore. Not to see this or any other movie, ever again.

Unable to speak for a whole new reason, Alice stumbled over a few *ums*.

Chess's hand slid down her arm, his frown deepening. "You okay?"

"She can't," Court offered, clipping her compact shut. "Birthday business."

He straightened in his chair, eyes on Court. "Your birthday's *tomorrow*."

"I know, but we have this tradition where we spend the day before shopping, then she sleeps over at my place. Plus we have to make sure everything is ready." Court went on about the venue (which was just a fancy way of saying her house), the food, the DJ, even the custom invitations she sent out weeks ago. This year's theme was Haunted Masquerade Ball. Court loved Halloween and always threw parties Alice would describe as scream-queen chic.

Chess arched an eyebrow, effectively distracted. "You can't just say 'costume party,' can you?"

"Chester," Court gasped, clearly affronted. Chess flinched slightly at the use of his gov'ment name. "This isn't some party. It's an *event*."

Thankful for the save, Alice took that moment to swipe at her eyes and swallow the fist jammed in her throat. Relief and guilt battled for dominance inside her. She hadn't meant to lock up like that.

Court was still talking, going over her full plan for Operation B-Day: the big One Eight. She'd moved on to playlists and coordinating outfit changes. Some brides didn't even put this much thought into their weddings.

Chess nodded slowly, his eyes somewhat glazed. He made the occasional sound of interest or affirmation, but he'd obviously checked out.

Alice smirked. "We could plan for Sunday," she managed, cutting off Court's rambling.

Chess blinked out of his stupor. "Sunday?"

"Sunday night, after we've all recovered from Carnival de Courtney."

Court scoffed. "*If* you recover."

A smile stretched Chess's face. "Sunday it is."

"It's a date," Alice said, then her eyes widened and she swatted the air as if she could catch the escaped words. "But not a *date* date. Just a day when planned things happen."

"An *un*date, then." Chess nodded. "I can dig it." He shifted his attention to Court. "Back to birthday business, then?"

"Actually, we should hit the little girls' room before the bell or we'll get crowded out." Court put her stuff away and swung her bag onto her shoulder.

Alice rose, tray in hand. "Catch you after school?" she asked Chess.

"Sounds like a plan," Chess said as the three of them maneuvered their way to the end of the cafeteria, dumped what remained of their meals, and added their trays to the growing pile.

They split at the hall into the main building, Chess promising to text as he headed for the science wing.

"Sooooo." Courtney dragged the word out as the two of them made for the bathroom. "A date."

"An undate," Alice corrected. "Thanks for the save back there."

"Of course. This won't help your Hatta situation."

"There's no situation to be helped or hurt." Alice sneaked a glance at her phone, less than eager to have this conversation. Again.

A message from Hatta stood out on the screen.

Checking in. Did you—

The screen went black. A white pinwheel twirled at the center.

Great.

"I hope you're not making a habit of ignoring me," Court grumbled.

"What?" Alice glanced up right into her friend's irritated face.

Smack in the middle of five gorgeous girls, Courtney Marroné grew up struggling to be seen and heard among her sisters. She tended to take it personal when people spaced out on her, even if by accident.

"Sorry, was trying to answer a text from Hatta, but my phone died."

Court's frown morphed into an annoying and knowing-but-oh-so-wrong smirk.

The bell rang and kids flooded the hall, saving Alice from explaining for the hundredth time how it wasn't like that.

"Come on, or we'll get stuck at the back of the line." Court pulled her into the flow of bodies. She had a point. Teachers didn't view girls' room gridlock as a valid excuse for being tardy.

Alice tucked the phone in her pocket. She wouldn't be able to charge it again until after school. That meant she would have to use the mirror Hatta gave her to find out what he needed.

Perfect . . .

Five

LOOSE ENDS

After the final bell, Alice pushed through the throng of student bodies to reach her locker. She took a moment to swap out books, pitching glances over her shoulders. Everyone seemed occupied enough.

Reaching past a few books, she knocked three times against the small mirror hanging at the back and whispered, "Open my eyes."

Like Hatta's mirror, the surface rippled and swirled before Hatta's face appeared. He smiled. "Afternoon, luv."

"Got your message, but my phone died."

"Message?" He cocked his head to the side while his gaze roamed the room as if searching for a lost thought.

"Yes. The text you sent." She huffed a sigh and rolled her eyes. "I couldn't get the details."

"Details. Devils. Always hiding. I think I may have uncovered the reason why we've had so many visits from our friends lately."

Friends, code for *Nightmares* whenever Alice was in public and they couldn't speak freely. She threw a couple glances over her shoulder, then looked back to the mirror. "And?"

He glanced over his shoulder as well. "Excuse me a moment." Then he . . . ducked. The angle drifted, leaving her staring at the ceiling. He must have set the mirror down.

Rude. Alice peered up and down the hall. No one noticed her talking to the back of her locker yet. She shifted closer to the locker. "Hatta," she hissed. "Yo, Hatta. Hat. Ta!"

The top of his head popped back into view, but only so far as his nose. "Who said that?" Something shattered in the background.

"*Me.* You—you okay? What was that?"

He looked around again. "What was what?"

She huffed through her nose. "Look, I'll see you in a few. You lucky I planned on coming in anyway."

His attention returned to her, brows lifting. "Oh really?" The mirror righted itself, revealing the rest of him. His smile returned full force. "What for?"

She chewed at the inside of her cheek. "To talk. 'Bout stuff."

The corners of his mouth crooked slightly, lending a sly twist to his grin. "Stuff."

"Mmmm-yup." She lowered her gaze briefly. "I gotta go. Ride's waiting on me."

"Ahh. Then I'll see you soon, luv." He bowed his head

and his image faded, swirling out of sight before the mirror solidified into a plain mirror once again. Alice's reflection stared out at her. She bit back a groan and slammed her locker shut, twirled the lock, and followed the waning flow of students through the doors.

Chess waited at the bottom of the stairs, his wide grin stretching into place when he spotted her. "Hey. Where's the birthday girl?"

"Probably powdering her nose." She tilted against him with a dramatic sigh of exhaustion. He draped an arm over her shoulders and settled against the huge stone banister with his own sigh. Warmth spread from where he held to her lightly. Part of her shouted to pull away. Another part noticed how good he smelled, like fresh rain and mint, and suggested she press closer. She ignored them both and just watched him, watching her. She cleared her throat and glanced out over the grounds as other students filed past.

"Soooooo got a costume picked out for Courtney's party?"

Chess grinned. "You mean the ball?" He put on a posh accent.

Alice waved a hand. "The *event*."

He chuckled. It vibrated through her, and she felt a faint shiver slide up her back. "I'll probably just slap a glow-in-the-dark sticker on a T-shirt and go as Tony Stark or something."

"Slacker." Alice rested her head on his shoulder. "You should've let me know; I woulda made you a costume."

Surprise lifted his brows. "You make costumes?"

She shrugged, fidgeting with the hem of her Triforce T-shirt. "Not really. I mean, I haven't for a minute. I'm only making one for Court's party, but I used to cosplay a bit." That was an under-statement. She would put hours upon hours into her cosplays, making sure to get every little detail just right. *If you're gonna do a thing, you do it right*, Dad used to say, *even if that thing is costumes*. He got her into it. Into all her geekery stuff.

"Really?"

She nodded. "That was before we met."

"Why'd you stop?"

That sinking feeling from earlier in the lunchroom came back. Alice swallowed the tart taste coating her tongue. "It was something I did with my dad. I stopped after he passed."

"I'm sorry." Chess squeezed her shoulders.

"It's cool." She breathed through the tightening of her insides.

"What're you going as? To Courtney's ball."

Heat filled Alice's face. She glanced away. "This character from a show I used to watch."

"Which was?" he pressed, shaking her a little.

She cut him a look. "Princess Serenity. From *Sailor Moon*."

Chess stared at her for a few seconds before shaking his head. "You are seriously the coolest girl I know."

That wasn't the reaction she expected. Usually, people poked fun at her for things like watching lots of anime, listen-ing to rock music, cosplaying. They called her names like Oreo and Wannabe-White Girl, all kinds of bull. She didn't expect Chess to say stuff like that, but still.

The smile broke over her face before she could stop it. "Thanks."

"You two look cozy." Court clicked her way down the stairs to join them.

"He is quite comfy." Alice patted Chess's arm, then slipped out from under it.

He rolled his shoulders. "I try."

The three of them headed for the parking lot, Alice tugging her dead phone free along the way. "I need to use your charger."

"No prob, Bob." Court fished her keys from her bag. The purple Camaro at the end of the lot honked a response. It took a moment for everyone to climb in—Chess insisted on opening the doors for them and they'd given up trying to stop him.

Alice plugged in her phone, fastened her seat belt, and braced herself. "Aaaaand I need a ride to the pub."

Court froze, finger on the ignition button. "You were just there last night. And it's Pre B-Day."

She lifted her hands. "I know! I know. It'll be quick."

Chess's head slid between them, eyes on Alice. "You working today?"

"Just gonna work out something with my schedule." Sometimes she nearly forgot the cover story she fed Chess about working at the Looking Glass part-time. Unofficially, being underage and all. He thought it was cool, rebellious and such, and didn't ask questions, which was peachy.

"This really can't wait?" The look Court gave her could've singed her brows off.

"I got a call. It didn't sound serious." It didn't sound anything, really. "But I wanna make sure. So there won't be any B-Day interruptions."

Court continued to stare. "Won't take long."

"I swear."

"In and out."

"Quick, like a bunny."

Court drummed her nails against the wheel before nodding. "Fine." She threw the Camaro in gear and peeled out of the parking lot, flinging Chess and Alice against the side of the car as she turned onto the street.

"This is how I die," Chess groaned from the back seat.

◊ ◊ ◊

Court pulled up in front of the pub, and Alice climbed out of the car. She bent to peer at the two of them through the window. "Won't be long."

Chess nodded. Court tapped the clock on the dash. Alice rolled her eyes and turned to head inside. As usual for this early in the day, the pool table was the only occupied area inside the Looking Glass. A handful of people sipped beers between shots. One white guy was busy feeling up his scantily clad emo Katniss-looking girlfriend while she did her best to choke him with her tongue.

A Black woman in biker gear and a hijab stood at the bar, hands on a tray stacked with a few open bottles of beer and glasses of water. Maddi milled about behind the counter, topping off a drink and setting it among the others. The woman handed Maddi a bill, waved off the change, then took the tray and headed toward the pool tables at the back.

Alice slid onto a barstool. "Where's Hatta?"

Maddi shrugged. "Not where he isn't."

Alice blinked. "'Course not." *Why do I try?*

"The raven flies?" Maddi asked.

"W-what?"

Maddi gently tapped Alice's injured arm. "South is finer than north."

"Oooooooh." Alice ran her fingers lightly over the concealed bandages. The slices beneath itched with the telltale tickle of accelerated healing. "Doing lots better, thanks. That voodoo that you do is legit."

At the end of the bar an old Black man harrumphed, then tipped his drink down his gullet. He clacked the glass against the counter and swiped his hand across his mouth before scratching his wispy white hair. It stood up in two tufts on either side of his otherwise bald head, earning him the nickname Sprigs. He was a regular. He tapped the counter next to his empty shot glass. Maddi sighed and tossed the rag over her shoulder.

"Duty sings her siren song, a peril ignored." She hummed as she grabbed a bottle of amber liquid from the mirrored shelves, refilled Sprigs's glass, and plinked it onto the bar. "Thar she blows," she called, then covered yet another yawn. "Sleep time, be mine." She folded her arms over the counter and laid her head against them. After a few seconds, she actually started snoring.

Alice stared for a second. "Ooooookay." She climbed down off the stool. "I'm just gonna go see if he's in his office."

Leaving Maddi dozing and Sprigs drinking, she slipped into the back hall. She paused when she found the office door closed, *weird*, then knocked.

"Come in," Hatta called.

Alice stepped through to find him staring into his fancy mirror, his face pinched with concern. She'd never seen him frown so hard.

"Everything okay?"

His head snapped up, and he stood and waved her in, all smiles. "Isn't this a pleasant surprise."

She blinked. "I told you I—never mind." She moved to plop onto the little couch. "What's up?"

Humming a drawn-out breath, he retook his seat, folded his hands together, and fixed his faintly glowing gaze on her. "Last night, after you went home, I crossed the Veil again to do a little investigating, try to see what's causing our friends to come out and play so often. Normally, Nightmares rise out of the Nox, but the one you killed last night looks to have come from the east."

The Nox was the dark part of Wonderland, where the bad dreams collected and occasionally spit out Nightmares. Hatta told her, according to Wonderland's wonky history—trying to keep time straight between here and there was truly headache inducing, and pretty much impossible—maybe a few Nightmares a year would rise. That was a couple thousand years ago, give or take a century. Then the human population started growing. People started living longer and having more people. More people meant more dreams. More dreams meant a thriving Wonderland, but also more Nightmares. Now, instead of the here-and-there nasties, Alice killed around one or two a week. *Used* to kill one or two a week. The past couple weeks it had been more like three or four.

"The east?" She frowned. "What's east?"

Hatta hesitated. "Ahoon."

A shudder hitched her shoulders, and her back went rod straight. A steady throb radiated from her left arm, and it took every ounce of self-control to keep from rubbing it. *You're fine. It's fine.*

Ahoon was a quaint little village in Wonderland and the site of her hardest fight ever.

Fueled by the fear that ate at people, her people, Black people, when shit like what happened to Brionne went down, the Nightmare Alice fought in Ahoon was some nasty business. Evil the size of a Mack truck, all teeth and claws, stronger and deadlier than anything she'd faced before. Alice nearly lost an arm to it. Hell, she nearly lost her damn head, and almost threw in the towel back then. It was the first time she'd felt a Nightmare's influence so keenly, and it took more than a month before she worked up the courage to go back to Wonderland. Hatta had been patient, telling her she could take all the time she needed, that he was there for her. She eventually pulled herself together, like you have to in these streets, but if he had a mission for her involving one of those things, he could keep it.

"Ahoon," she whispered. "Is it another . . ."

"No, no."

Oh, thank god. Instant relief left her sinking back against the couch.

Hatta bounced his chair into a steady rock. "I couldn't go too far, so I'm not certain if that's where this last nightmare came from. But if there was anything outside of the Nox strong enough to produce a Nightmare, I'd say the site of an unpurged one that powerful might do the trick."

Alice chewed at her lower lip as a feeling like cold oil coated her stomach. This was her fault. Hatta didn't say it, but he didn't have to. It was her job to purge the kill site. Sure, she'd been a beaten-up hot mess, but she should've been more thorough. Or gone back to double-check. He'd even suggested it, but she was too shaken to listen, so he let it go. Now, it would come back to bite them in the ass.

"I'll go through, make sure," she said.

Hatta blinked at her like she'd just started singing from her forehead. "What?"

"I'll check the village, see what I find." Her knees started bouncing as she spoke. "If there's anything left of that Nightmare to rise again, it's my fault."

Hatta's expression fell and Alice looked away. She *hated* when he looked at her like that, all pity and softness, like she might break. Happened every time they talked about Ahoon, and now every time they talked about Saturday and Brionne. "Alison, I didn't mean—"

"I know, but that doesn't make it less true. This is my mess; I'll clean it up." Besides, she couldn't just leave it for whoever he trained next to deal with. Plus the training itself would take at least three months, and leaving a Nightmare unpurged for so long was bound to mess things up even more. No, no, she had to set this right, especially since she planned on quitting. Right after this.

He was watching her. She could feel his eyes on her

even as she kept hers on the ground. Silence filled the empty space around them, pushing against her almost like it blamed her, too.

"All right," he said finally. "You can go. But it's too far in for me to come with you."

"Is that ever gonna change?" Alice shifted forward, happy for the subject change.

Hatta averted his gaze this time. "Not as far as I know."

"That's bullshit. You *know* this, right?"

He lifted his shoulders in a shrug. "It can't be helped."

"You *helped* end the war."

"Doesn't make up for having helped start it."

"But it should at least get you something! Wonderland is your home; they're really gonna kick you out forever?"

His lips pursed, Hatta puffed his cheeks and scratched an eyebrow, fixated on his mirror. "That's what exiled means. Besides, there are stipulations. To perform my duties, I'm allowed to cross the Veil, to train Dreamwalkers. I just can't go too far from the Gateway."

Alice shook her head. "It's not fair. You made a mistake. You realized it. You even helped fix it."

"Nothing will fix—"

"Then, you tried! You tried, and if you hadn't, they'd've lost. You're a good person, Addison. It's been decades—the White Queen has to see that. I mean, I see it."

"I have my head. That's more than most traitors get." He finally looked at her. Something wavered in his eyes, his expression softening. His lips lifted just the faintest bit. "Thank you, Alice."

She blinked. "For what?"

His smile widened a little. "Seeing it."

"Yeah, well, you're my partner. I got your back." *At least until I tell you I'm done. Which will be when we get back.* That conversation was going to suck.

He nodded, seeming to consider her words a moment. "All right, then, partner."

She flinched but hid it in a smile. "Mmhm."

"I'll see if I can't get you some help."

Alice jumped to her feet. "My friends are waiting for me. I need to let them know I'll be a while."

Hatta nodded as he knocked against his mirror. "Open my eyes—of course, luv."

As Alice slipped out of the office a woman's voice spilled out of the mirror. The closed door made it impossible to hear what she said, or Hatta's response. Alice hurried for the front of the bar, passing Maddi still asleep on the counter. Sprigs had joined her, his face buried in his arms.

Outside, Court had turned off the car and sat scrolling through her phone. Chess had pushed the passenger seat forward and kicked his ankles up to cross them on the open window. Court looked up as Alice approached.

"About time." She swatted at Chess's legs. "Sit up."

He grumbled something, and his feet disappeared into the car.

Alice swallowed a groan as she bent to fold her arms where Chess's feet had been propped. This was not going to be good. "Change of plans."

Court snapped around so fast her neck popped. "What?"

"I have to stay. For a couple hours." As each word passed her lips it was like dropping a stone into her stomach.

Courtney stared at her, fingers tight around the wheel, her knuckles white.

"I know I said it'd be quick, but something came up and they really need me." Alice stressed those last few words, hoping Court understood their meaning.

If she did, there was no sign of it on her face, or anything. Her expression smoothed out completely.

Shit.

"It's Pre B-Day." Court's voice was silky as hell. She was *pissed*.

"I know."

"This has been our thing since we were *five*."

"I—I know."

"This is gonna be the biggest, most important day of my life; you're supposed to share it with me, you're my *best friend*."

"I know, I know, and of course I'll share it with you. I'll even be there for Pre B-Day things, just not all of them."

The leather on the wheel whined as Courtney wrung it between her hands.

"Look, it's just a lil after four. You still have to take Chess home."

"Please don't bring me into this," he called from the back seat.

Alice shot him a look, then turned back to Courtney. "While you do that and maybe grab some dinner or something, I'll pick up a couple hours, have Maddi give me a ride to your place, be there by seven. Plenty of time for lots of Pre B-Day stuff."

She flashed what she hoped was a winning smile. *Love me*, it would say. *Forgive me.*

Court drew in a hard breath through her nose, then pushed it out through her lips. "Seven sharp, Kingston."

Relief swept through Alice, but it was short-lived at the use of her last name. *She's so pissed.*

"Seven sharp." Alice gave a thumbs-up, then opened the door to grab her things. She unhooked her phone from the charger. Thirty percent, that should be plenty. Chess climbed into the front seat and flashed her an apologetic grin. "See you at the party tomorrow. If, y'know, I make it home alive." He fastened his seat belt.

"Shut up, Dumpsky," Court snapped. "You're buying my Pre B-Day dinner."

"I am?"

"Yup, since my previous date canceled on me."

Alice winced and stepped back from the car as Court started her up and roared off. "That could've gone better." Alice called her mom, explaining that she was gonna hang with Court and Chess for a while, doing some last-minute birthday stuff for tomorrow. Mom said she was going to see Grandma Kingston after work, so Alice needed to figure out dinner for herself tonight.

"No prob," Alice said. "Give Nana K. my sugar."

"Sure thing. Be careful, Baby Moon."

Words caught in Alice's throat at the nickname. Mom tended to use it without realizing, especially when she was missing him.

"I will. Love you."

Mom reciprocated and Alice hung up, then fought to breathe evenly, to banish the sting behind her eyes before pushing into the pub.

Hatta was at the bar, mixing a few drinks. Maddi was still knocked out nearby. He glanced up as Alice approached. "All good?"

"I guess." She handed him her pack. He handed her an empty belt. She arched an eyebrow. "Um, I like being hands-on as much as the next girl, but isn't this a bit much?"

He chuckled and produced two brand-new Figment Blades. "I noticed your other pair was starting to dull."

Alice's lips curled into a smile "Lethal weapons, a girl's best friend." She took one of the daggers by its ivory handle, admiring the curved, foot-long blade. She ran her thumb against the surface of the hilt. A frown creased her brow. "You don't just keep these things lying around, waiting for me to break 'em, do you?" Alice tended to go through weapons a little faster than most Dreamwalkers, according to Hatta. She wasn't sure if that was because she fought more Nightmares, or because her Muchness was lacking. The blades were only as strong as the person wielding them. There was no way to sharpen them, so once they started to dull it usually meant getting another pair.

"I'm all for preparation, luv, but Dust tends to run in short supply."

Dust was an element as natural to Wonderland as fire or water, but far more uncommon. It was produced during the Midnight Breaking, when the sky cracked open and silver particles fell from the heavens like glitter. She'd seen it a few times. Figment Blades were forged from that stuff.

"I'm not entirely certain what we're dealing with, so I'm not sure what to tell you to expect." Hatta finished the drinks he'd been working on, then set them at the end of the bar and snapped his fingers. One of the dudes from the group near the pool tables, white guy, claimed them with a nod that Hatta returned. "So just keep an eye out for anything strange."

"Strange." Alice strapped the belt in place and slipped her new daggers into the sheaths. "You know *everything* about Wonderland is strange, right?"

Hatta smiled. "And everyone."

"So define *strange*."

"You'll know it should you see it. Trust me."

"So helpful."

"I try." He came around the bar and offered her his arm. "Ready?"

She nodded and took hold of his elbow, letting him guide her to the back.

One last mission, to tie up any loose ends. That way, whoever Hatta found to take her place could start off with a clean slate.

Take my place . . .

As they moved down the hall, the idea that someone else would be standing here with Hatta, walking with him, working with him, twisted itself around in her head furiously. She couldn't be *replaced* replaced; it would just be another Dreamwalker. Who Hatta would have to spend all his time with, training them, teaching them. Would she get to spend any time with him? Of course she would; they were friends. She was being dramatic.

At the broom closet, Hatta held the door open for her. Inside, he joined her in the center of the room and curled one arm protectively around her shoulders to pull her in. "Despite everything, I wish I could go with you," he murmured into her hair.

She shut her eyes and pressed her face to his chest. "I know."

"Ready?"

She took a handful of deep breaths to shake off the jitters clamoring through her. "Yeah. Yeah, I'm good."

"Here we go." Darkness flooded the room when he flipped off the light, save for the sliver of brightness at the base of the door. Soon it vanished. The slight feeling of motion slithered up her legs, like standing in a boat gliding over water. She shut her eyes and tried to focus on anything but what was coming.

Hatta's chest rose and fell against hers, slow and steady. His breath tickled the top of her head. A pang of regret centered in her chest. This was one of the last times he'd hold her like this. That they'd be this close. The steady thumping of his heart eased her anxiety, and his spicy-sweet scent like bourbon-flavored cotton candy took the edge off anticipatory nerves. She was going to miss this.

"Hold tight," he whispered.

Then the floor opened and swallowed them whole.

Six

CONTRARIWISE

The sugary scent of Wonderland's fresh air worked won-ders on motion sickness. Alice drank deep gulps, bent for-ward, hands on her knees.

"Oh god," she groaned around a hiccup, glad her diaphragm had ceased trying to worm its way through her guts. She was *not* going to miss this.

"Easy now." Hatta rubbed slow circles between her shoul-ders, then brushed her face with the back of his hand. "Don't want you blacking out."

Without thinking, she tilted into that touch, his hand cool and soft. His fingers cupped her cheek, and her eyes rose to meet his. They crinkled at the edges as he grinned, and the warmth moving through her intensified with new meaning.

"I don't faint." She tilted against a nearby pillar. The cold of the marble bit through the fabric of her shirt, easing the rising heat in her body and face. The smell of wildflowers and spice tickled her senses. Over Hatta's shoulder the Gateway glowed faintly, the air curled back like the corners of worn pages.

"Blacking out and fainting are two different things." Hatta sat a hand atop her head. "Are you okay?"

She swallowed and nodded. "I'm good." She let her gaze wander away from him, over the terrace. It was a skeleton of a structure, crumbling in places, flawless in others, time slowly eating away at it. Daylight dulled the marble's shine and made the decay stand out even more. "Should've grabbed one of Maddi's potions."

"I'll have her prepare one for your return." He rubbed her arm in passing on his way to the stairs.

Beyond the platform, Wimble-Di'Glow Woods spread out around them. The grass shimmered between red and blue like a chameleon. Silver trees shivered in the wind, filling the air with the tinkling of chimes as their crystal-like leaves rustled.

"In the meantime, I suggest you find a Follyshroom to set you straight," Hatta said.

She made a face at the thought of eating one of the tart mushrooms. Of all the edible things in Wonderland, and the odd side effects that went with them, it was a cruel joke to match the ability to settle an upset stomach with something that tasted like sautéed donkey butt.

"You wouldn't happen to have one on you?" She smoothed a hand over the front of her shirt and checked her weapons.

"Nope. But we can find them near water. Lots of it."

"Lots of water," she repeated, her hands on her hips. He

couldn't mean the river. It was at least a day's journey north and super far out of her way.

"Mmhm." He inspected a tie-dyed colored fruit the shape of a banana. "Gratuitous amounts. Which means?"

Well, it didn't rain in Wonderland. At least, not unless something was really, *really* wrong. There was only one place he could be talking about. She groaned. "The Bubbles."

He lifted his shoulders, an apologetic smile on his face. "The Bubbles."

She *hated* the Bubbles: a field where mushrooms the size of houses flourished thanks to the beach ball–sized spheres of water given off by weird holes in the ground. The spheres floated through the air, but never went far. They popped at the slightest disturbance, dousing anything in the area, including girls with a fresh press.

"I just got my hair done." Alice tugged the dark strands from the ponytail and proceeded to retie them, pinning them and looping the band in a defensive bun.

"You always 'just got your hair done.'"

"You got no idea what it takes to get this straight." She wiped excess grease from her hair onto her jeans. "Blow-dryers, flat irons, hot combs, hours of sitting still while someone holds what's essentially a branding iron centimeters from your naked skin."

He kept smiling. "Sounds terrifying."

She shrugged. "Beauty is pain, as the saying goes."

"So it seems." He glanced in one direction, then the other. "I can go with you as far as the Bubbles. From there you can cut across the Glays plains. Ahoon won't be much farther than that. Should take an hour at the most."

Alice nodded and pushed away from the pillar. The world didn't spin too hard, but her stomach still burbled angrily.

As she descended the platform, a faint whoosh behind her signaled the Gateway closing. She paused to watch the open air sew itself shut with a soft sucking sound, then the terrace was empty.

Hatta offered his arm. She took it and they started on their way. They walked in silence for a while, just . . . together. Alice could practically hear Courtney's teasing.

Thinking about her friend sent a bitterness twisting through Alice's insides. Court looked soooooo angry. She had every right to be; it was Pre B-Day and Alice pretty much bailed on her. Not for the whole day, but still. She'd never missed any part of Pre B-Day before now.

"Your mind seems aboil."

Alice blinked and glanced up to find Hatta gazing down at her as they walked, those brilliant eyes taking her in. "Uh . . . what?"

"Deep in thought. And not a pleasant one I take it—you look like someone just curdled your whompus."

Alice stopped. She stared at Hatta. He blinked at her. Then she busted out laughing, and this was a good laugh, had her bent over and everything. When she managed to catch her breath and straighten, they continued. "I promise my . . . whompus is just fine." More than a year of stuff like this, and it still managed to completely catch her off guard.

"Good." His smile widened, and he patted her hand, his

skin warm in contrast to the cool touch of his rings. "A curdled whompus is a fairly unfortunate situation."

"I'll take your word for it." She wiped a couple tears from her eyes, then looked up to gauge the time. Hard to do without a sun, but the sky had already sewn itself shut and washed afternoon green instead of morning pink. The Mending, the sky recovering from the Breaking, marked "noon" in Wonderland. It was a beautiful twelve-hour cycle where the heavens would shatter, then heal.

As they went along, Hatta talked about how this area used to be famous for its produce; all sorts of funky fruits and vegetables would grow here, most of them delicious.

"There would be festivals during the harvest, grand parties the royal family would attend." He smiled, going on about the decorations, the music, the food.

It was good to see him like this, so bright and lively. He didn't talk about the past. She understood that, not wanting to go back. Afraid of having to return. It was the same reason she didn't like talking about how things were before losing her dad. It seemed like so long ago. Another world. Another life.

"So this area was pretty busy?" Alice asked.

"Very, comparatively. War tends to leave things less . . . vibrant."

"Where did everyone go?"

He rolled his shoulders in that I'm-pretending-this-doesn't-bother-me way of his. "Away from the Gateways. More humans, more Nightmares trying to get through, more problems for the locals. The Queens decided relocation was best for lots of villages and towns."

That explained why she never ran into any other Wonderlandians. She wasn't sure if that was a good or bad thing. "The Queens decide a lot." She tried not to sound salty. And failed.

"That's what Queens do."

"Do they still have festivals?" Alice asked. "They" being the Red and White Queens. Well, the White Queen, mostly. The Red Queen vanished long before Alice became a Dreamwalker, leaving the White Queen to rule alone—but not before she and her sister banished Hatta and a few others for their crimes during the war. Alice had never met either Queen, but she'd have words with them about this exile thing if she ever got the chance.

"No." His smile fell slightly as he shook his head. "At least, not the one this area was known for. I'm sure there are others, but I'm not exactly up-to-date on royal social events. It's not like I can attend them." He probably meant it to be funny, but it only irritated Alice.

The war was so long ago, and he'd done so much good since. "That doesn't outweigh the bad," Hatta would say. Which, okay, yeah, he had a point. A pretty valid one. That didn't mean she had to like it. And the war was pretty horrible—like most wars—from what she'd pieced together talking to him and Maddi. Hell, it split Wonderland in half. Not like physically, but one kingdom ruled by one Queen became two. A family and a people fell apart.

"I still don't think it's fair," Alice pressed.

Hatta groaned faintly, shoving a hand through his green hair. "I thought we were past this."

"You might be, but I'm angry enough for the both of us."

"It can't be help—"

"I know, I know, but I can still complain. I mean, the *Black Queen* started this mess. It's not your fault."

"But I made a choice." Hatta kept his eyes on the path. His shoulders tensed, his jaw set. "I thought it was the right one. Just like her." After her youngest daughter died, the Queen of Harts tried to harness the power of the Nox to bring her back.

Maybe it wasn't the smart thing, but when you lose someone like that? They're just gone? There's this hole inside you you'd give anything to fill. You don't think, you don't plan, you just pour shit into it, anything that will fit. Sometimes, it's bad shit.

Alice understood that much. "Yeah, but you didn't stick with the choice. She did."

The Nox corrupted the Queen of Harts, turning her into the Black Queen. Consumed by rage and pain, she used her new, dark powers to raise an army of Nightmares unnaturally, making them even more deadly.

"And her people, her family, paid the price. I was part of that," Hatta said. "Even if I didn't see it through, I'm still responsible." The Queen's remaining daughters tried to talk her down, but it was too late. The influence of the Nox was too strong. If they were going to keep the rising darkness from consuming both Wonderland and the real world, they had to fight their mother. This led to the war, one the Red and White Queens almost lost.

"But your switching sides changed the game." Before Hatta defected, the Black Queen and her most loyal and lethal warrior, the Black Knight, nearly destroyed everything. Then Hatta gave the Red and White Queens the secret he discovered to the Black Queen's weakness, something to do with her heart. She and her knight were defeated, Wonderland came under the rule of the Red and White Queens, and there'd been peace ever since. Mostly. "And as a reward they exiled you. Yeah, it was better than execution, but you're clearly happier here than on earth."

"What makes you say that?"

"You get all bright and colorful when you're here. No, for real." She flapped a hand in a vague gesture at him when he arched an eyebrow. "You hair is brighter, your eyes glow, even your skin shines kinda. You perk right up like a daisy."

That made him laugh, his shoulders rolling back as his posture eased into his usual slouch. "I'm more of an orchid."

"You can make jokes, but I'm serious. They may not have cut off your head, but cutting you off from the place that literally feeds your life force is just as bad." Sure, Hatta could survive in the real world, but people from Wonderland could never go too far from the Gateways or they'd fade.

"Oh, I don't know, the human world has its charms. Cotton candy, for instance."

Alice snorted. "Yeah, and it's got plenty of problems."

"It's got you."

She nearly tripped over her own feet at that. The butterflies in her stomach took a nosedive at the jostle, and her insides felt like they might upend themselves. She slapped a hand over her mouth with a groan, the back of her throat burning but tingling at the same time. "Oh no."

The world tilted to the side, but a hand on her arm helped steady her. "Nearly there, luv."

By the time the shining spheres of water came into sight, floating in the sky just over the approaching hill, she was ready to dive headfirst into an ocean if it meant settling her stomach.

"This is where we part ways, milady." Hatta moved his hand down to hers and held it. He traced his thumb along the backs of her fingers, his face slightly strained.

"What's wrong?" Alice asked, concern a needle between her shoulders.

He shook his head. "Nothing. Just a little farther in than I've been in a while."

That needle became a knife. She'd been so caught up in her nausea she hadn't noticed the obvious pain Hatta had to be in this far from the Gateway. The Verse that exiled him only allowed him so far into Wonderland, to facilitate his duties as a Gatekeeper, training his Dreamwalker and the like. He'd explained that it was like wearing one of those invisible fence collars that shock the weaver when it passes over the boundary, only instead of being around his neck it was around his heart.

"Oh my god," Alice squeaked. She wasn't even embarrassed; all she felt was guilt. "I'm so sorry."

Hatta shook his head. "This is only ever my fault. I need to get back."

"Y-yeah, of course." She nodded. And nodded. And nodded—god, why was she such a goober. "You'll be all right, though?"

"I'm not worried about me." He lifted her hand, hesitated a beat, then pressed his other one on top of it. "Take care, luv. I'll be waiting."

Alice's heart stuttered in her chest as she stuttered over her words. "Y-you're the one who needs to take care. Go, go." She pulled her hand free and turned him around, pushing him back the way they came. "Hurry up before you pass out on me."

Hatta chuckled as he went, lifting a hand to wave over his shoulder. "I don't faint."

"If you do, I'm kicking your butt. Go!" She waved him on and watched him for several seconds before turning to continue on her way. She couldn't help stealing a couple glances after him, to make sure he didn't fall over or something. By the time she reached the hilltop he was a blot barely discernible against the chameleon-colored grass. She lifted her arm above her head to wave, hoping he saw her, then started downhill toward the Bubbles.

It didn't take long to collect a piece of Follyshroom, but all hopes of remaining dry had been popped early on. Literally. Alice grumbled as she tromped along, glad to put the soggy landscape behind her. Her shoes squelched, and her bangs were already coiling against her forehead like springs. When they dried, they'd fan out like frizzy plumage. Thankfully, the knot at the back of her head kept the damage minimal. And at least the Follies had eased her nausea.

As she ventured farther along the Glays plains, the sky paled to palettes of gray and white. Ahoon wasn't far now. A change filtered through the atmosphere, through the land itself. The faint scent of smoke and coals left the air bitter. Grass didn't grow as tall, and there was less of it. Patches of cracked earth peeked through, as if the ground was balding. The trees thinned out, their bare branches like spindly arms reaching for the sky, or scattered and broken.

Coming upon a road, she stopped. Clusters of aged cobblestone marked the route like islands in a river of dirt. She followed them, keeping to the path until it eventually split. According to a weathered sign posted in the fork, the turnoff led toward what remained of the small village of Ahoon. The other way led to some place she couldn't pronounce. The ache in her arm returned full force. The break had been bad. She'd told her mother she'd fallen down the stairs at Court's house.

Massaging the muscle through her sleeve, she hesitated, the fingers of her free hand tapping the hilt of one blade. She took a steadying breath before starting forward. Every now and again a shadow danced along the edge of her vision. She did her best to ignore them; they were just Shadow-Wisps—Wisps affected by the Nightmare before it was killed. They weren't strong enough to result in a full-formed Nightmare rising; she needed to keep looking for other signs.

The closer she drew to the village, the kill site, the more the land seemed to be affected but not tainted—there was a difference. There were signs that life was slowly coming back to the area, a few fledgling plants here, a faint critter call there, but nothing near as vibrant as the rest of Wonderland. Even the wind had fallen still, silent. The immensity of nothing went on in every direction.

Everything's fine. You're fine. Calmed though still alert, she put one foot in front of the other. Eventually, the crumbling remains of half-formed houses and shops came into view, jutting up from the ground like bones. Stone blackened from fire, wood splintered and rotting seemed to suck the daylight from the air, leaving a shadowy haze over the entire village. She slowed, her eyes dancing over the ruins. Anything could be hiding here in the shadows, waiting to pounce. Her hands on the pommels of her daggers, she stepped over what remained of a wall.

Ahoon was small, but the emptiness made it seem so much larger. It reminded her of something out of the Middle Ages, old and fantastical even in decay. The main square lay ahead. Every half-fallen wall, decrepit doorway, and shrouded corner wound her a little tighter than before. Like in the woods, there were signs that nature was beginning the daunting task of reclaiming this area. Maybe the people would eventually return as well, then harvest those fruits and vegetables Hatta talked about.

Movement caught in her peripheral vision, and she stiffened, daggers partially drawn. That wasn't a Shadow-Wisp. It was bigger, quicker. She remained still for a moment before picking her way across the square, pace brisk, eyes fixed ahead. Several more steps and it happened again, to her right. She turned and saw nothing but broken stone and rusty dirt. But she knew better. Her skin prickled. The hairs on her arms stood on end.

She wasn't alone.

Alice's heart beat faster. Her muscles tensed. The faint buzzing of alarm bristled at the base of her skull. Stopping in the center of the square, she crouched, reaching to trace the fingers of one hand against the ground, scrutinizing nonexistent tracks.

Calm.

Wait.

Something emerged from a building at her four o'clock, several paces back. It slunk forward, movements measured and deliberate. The sound of steps against cobblestone held a significant difference from the sound of those same steps on dirt, and when they reached the patch of stone on which she now knelt, she struck.

Her calf caught legs and swept them loose, sending her stalker sailing for the ground with a startled cry. She drew both Figment Blades and leaped onto him, one knee in his gut, the blades pressed against both sides of his neck like scissors waiting to lop off his head.

"Stoy!" he shouted, hands lifted and fingers splayed to show he was unarmed. He stared at her with wide, surprised eyes belonging to a face she recognized.

"Dee?" She narrowed her eyes.

He nodded slowly, mindful of the blades poised on either side of his neck. "Da."

Every muscle in her body turned to water, and by force of will alone she didn't sink down on top of him. "I coulda *killed* you."

"I am very aware." He swallowed, tension thickening his Russian accent. He didn't relax until she withdrew her weapons.

"What the fel you doin'?" Sheathing her blades, she rose and offered him a hand up.

"Trying to surprise you." He brushed his hands over his front, then ran them through his blond hair. "Just a joke."

She snorted and folded her arms over her chest, her

bandaged wound aching dully. "You gone get yo ass kicked behind these jokes one day." Her attention shifted as she eyed the rest of the ruins for Dee's other half. "Where's Dem?"

Laughter rang out, rich and thick like syrup. Alice followed it to a nearby house as Dee's twin brother swung into view, holding on to the doorjamb.

"Idiot," Dee muttered, still brushing dirt from his clothes.

"That was priceless." Dem snickered as he jogged over to join them.

"Har har. Jerk." Her glare bounced between two identical sets of ice blue eyes.

Dimitri and Demarcus Tweedlanov—Dee and Dem for short—were mirror images of each other: tall, teenage versions of Spike from *Buffy*. Dreamwalkers as well, and only a couple years older than her, they comprised a well-oiled killing machine that sometimes pulled dumbass pranks. She worked with them whenever there was a job to do farther in than Hatta could come, like the fight at Ahoon. They were there, and probably the only reason her ass didn't end up filleted. They had to be the backup Hatta mentioned.

Alice jerked her chin at the twins. "The Duchess would lay y'all out if she knew you were dicking around."

Anastasia Petrova, aka the Duchess, was to the Tweedles what Hatta was to Alice, only less patient and far more strict. Alice had never met the woman, but she heard plenty about her from the twins and from Hatta. After the war, the Duchess was exiled as well, but kept her formal title at court as a sort of code name. She watched over the Northern Gateway somewhere in Saint Petersburg.

"Contrariwise to popular belief, she doesn't mind if we loosen up from time to time." Dem grinned, his hands clasped behind his head.

"That's not even a word." Dee shoved his brother. "But yeah, we're here to back you up."

"No orders to be on our best behavior, though."

"It was implied," Dee countered. The two of them were dressed in their customary black and gray, with leather, spikes, the works. Semigoth, or whatever it was, worked for them. Alice was careful not to appreciate the look for longer than a few seconds.

She shifted her weight to hide her fidgeting. "You know what you're backing me up for?"

Dem turned his attention to her, then out over the village. "See if any trace of the Nightmare remains. If it wasn't purged completely."

"If I messed up." Alice snorted.

The Tweedles fixed their gazes on her, heads swiveling in tandem. So hot, and yet, so *Children of the Corn* creepy sometimes.

"That is not what was said," Dee emphasized, no doubt trying to make her feel better. The twins were good for that, getting her to laugh when she felt like crap.

Alice shrugged, hands dropping to rest against her weapons as she scanned the village again. "It is what it is." The twins had been there, had helped her fight, but it was her weapon that struck the final blow to the monster's core. That meant her weapon had to perform the purge, and she had to be the one to do it. Figment Blades were funny like that, drawing off the strength of their wielder. Muchness and whatnot. Guess she wasn't that strong. "Either way, it won't hurt to make sure. Last thing I wanna do is be in my feelings for no reason."

"There she goes with her feelings again," Dem murmured before barely managing to dodge a kick aimed for his balls.

"How 'bout you feel my foot up yo ass," she threatened as he shuffled away, laughing as he went. She couldn't help grinning herself. "Keep it up, Dem. Ain't nobody playing with you."

Dee slid to her side, scratching at the faint shadow of hair on his chin. "You know that only encourages him, yes?"

She waved a hand as Dem slipped into the nearest half-worn building. "Like I could discourage him. You guys check any of the buildings?"

"A few in the north end." Dee shrugged. "Nothing so far. We have not been here long."

Alice turned her attention heavenward. "Sky's going blue." It would be dark in a few hours.

"We should keep searching, then, da? At least for a little while."

"Da." She nodded, and the three of them split off, moving to hunt through separate areas of the ruins.

Figment Blade in hand, Alice scuffed through a few patches of dirt, uncovering little more than hunks of stone and wood. With the twins nearby, she was less antsy and able to concentrate on the job. Even so, she didn't find any trace of Nightmare taint. "This place is full of a whole lotta nothing." She brushed a bit of dust from her hands.

She was searching her third building when Dee called out, "Zdyes'! Over here."

Alice rushed to the square, joining Dem as he raced from another direction. The two of them floundered briefly before a sharp whistle drew their attention. Dee stood near the eastern edge of the town, waving them over.

Inside one of the more intact buildings, the air hung heavy, musty.

"Look." Dee pointed at the far corner.

Dem made a face like he'd caught a whiff of something rank. "What the hell?"

The same question played through Alice's mind as she eyed what looked like black water spilling out of the ground. Instead of soaking the dirt and spreading, the liquid bubbled in on itself. It hissed and popped, glopping but never landing anywhere.

"I *did* screw up the purge," Alice murmured, the words bitter on her tongue. How could she have been so sloppy?

"I don't think so." Dee knelt to get a closer look, still a respectable distance from the spill. "It looks like corruption, but not."

"Whaddya mean?" She kept her eyes on the phenomenon. Something about this wasn't right, but she couldn't put her finger on what. Aside from it being . . . gross.

"This does not behave like taint," Dee said. "It doesn't affect the ground, or spread. It's . . . isolated."

"You guys notice it's in the corner farthest from the light?"

Both boys looked up, blond heads turning to take in the room. Three of four walls remained intact. The position of the two broken windows made it impossible for sunlight to reach the corner. The roof was still in one piece as well.

"Coincidence?" Dem stepped closer to his brother, his hand on the hilt of the dagger at his hip, similar to Alice's.

"Baba taught us not to believe in coincidences." Dee produced a small glass container along with a tiny pair of tongs.

Alice's gaze bounced between the twins. "What you doing?"

"Sample." Dee uncorked the vial and, with steady hands, extended it toward the liquid via the utensil.

"You sure that's a good idea?" She had no idea why she whispered or held her breath as the liquid trickled into the vial.

"We take this to the Duchess, we maybe figure out what it is." Dem kept his eyes on his brother, shoulders tense, jaw locked.

"She told you to bring it back?" Both brows rose. Anything the Duchess told them to do, they often did the opposite, meaning she probably told them not to touch anything. And here they were bottling it like a fifth-grade science experiment.

Dee corked the vial and gestured for his brother to join him. "Idee syuda."

Dem edged closer, only to jump when Dee latched on to the edge of his twin's shirt with one hand, the other slicing a small section of cloth free with a switchblade.

"Ah!" Dem pulled away, clutching at the hole in his shirt like a wound. "Mudak, why'd you do that?"

"I needed something to clean with." Dee wiped the vial with the cloth, then tossed it aside.

"Use your own damn clothes." Dem glared at his brother, muttering while he fingered his torn shirt, and Dee slipped the vial into one of the pouches along his waist.

"The Batman belt finally came in handy." Alice smirked, earning a glare from Dee and a snicker from Dem. "Way to go, Bruce. What now?" She eyed the gurgling fountain.

"Now?" Dee glanced around. "You try to purge, I guess."

Alice eased one of her daggers free. She dug one shoe into the ground, not wanting to approach whatever the hell that stuff was just yet. It gave her a serious case of what Nana Kingston called the heebie-jeebies. "Okay," she said more to herself than anyone else. A few careful steps brought her to the edge of the shadow. It continued to pour outward, running over itself and into nothing. She didn't know whether to stab it directly, or the ground beneath it.

Kneeling in the dirt, she tightened her grip on the dagger and looked to the twins. Dee nodded, eyes on her. Dem stared at the . . . whatever it was. With a deep breath, she lifted the dagger and drove it into the floating yuck.

Crack! With a flare of light, the Figment Blade went flying. Alice shouted as pain danced up her arm. The twins called out to her, moving forward, weapons sliding free.

"I'm all right!" She cradled her throbbing hand against her chest. "I'm all right."

"Do you need our help?" one of them asked, probably Dee.

She shook her head, shaking her fingers out. The pain faded, leaving them tingling. "No, I got this." She drew her second dagger.

Hatta's words from her training played across her mind.

The Figment Blade is an extension of your will, your courage, your confidence. It is very much you. Your Muchness. If you believe you can slay monsters, you will.

"I believe I can slay monsters," she mouthed. She hadn't had to talk herself up like this since . . . well, since the last time she set foot in this village. *I believe I can slay monsters.* "Cosmic moon power."

Light bled along her lifted blade, or maybe it was a trick of the shifting shadows. It only lasted for a brief second before she drove the dagger into the yuck as hard as she could. There was another flare, but this time the bubbling liquid vanished, hissing as it evaporated into gray mist. The Figment Blade sank into the ground beneath it, spewed the usual sparks and lightning, then went quiet.

Alice stared for a few seconds, panting faintly. She yanked her blade free and dropped back to sit on the ground, her muscles aching from how tense they'd been. The throbbing in her hand had faded completely.

"Ey." Dem held her other blade out for her, wiggling it.

"Thanks." She took it, slid them both into their sheaths, then took the offered hands.

The twins pulled her up, both clapping Alice on her shoulder or back, nodding. Alice smiled, giving a thumbs-up. A quick glance at where the liquid had hovered revealed nothing but the empty, bare ground. Whatever it was, it was gone, but she kicked at the dirt a bit just in case.

"You think that's it?" she asked.

"Maybe. We should look, just in case." Dem started for the door.

"It may not be the usual taint, but thankfully it purges like one." Dee followed his brother.

"Thankfully." Alice stole one last glance at the shadowy corner. She couldn't shake this cold, slimy feeling trying to crawl its way through her. "You're just freaked at being back here. Grow up, Kingston," she said to herself. Wrinkling her nose, she hurried after the twins to search the rest of the village.

◊ ◊ ◊

By the time the three of them finished searching, finding nothing else, the dimming light had further bruised the sky. If they didn't leave right the hell now, she wouldn't reach the Glow before dusk: prime Nightmare time.

"You want company?" Dem stood with his brother at the entrance to Ahoon.

Alice glanced back from where she'd already started toward the main road. "No, I'm good. Thanks, guys." Gratitude warmed her. Annoying as they could be, the twins had her back and she had theirs. At least, she used to.

Remembering her plans to quit, she was hit with a sudden sinking feeling at the thought of never seeing them again, never kicking butt with them again. She was gonna miss them and, unlike Maddi and Hatta, she couldn't pop over to Russia for a visit whenever she felt like it.

"Hey, Dee." She stepped back over the crumbling wall to join them. "You got a pen and paper in the Bat-belt?"

Dem snickered while Dee glowered, but he produced a small pad and tiny pen.

Alice took them, smiling. "Here, this is my number." She handed over a freshly scribbled-on scrap of paper. "Country code and all. I'm . . . I'm retiring. From Dreamwalking," she explained at their dual looks of confusion.

Confusion flashed to double incredulity.

"What?" they both barked.

"You're quitting?"

"Why?"

"Is everything okay?"

"Did we do anything?"

"May talk too much, about her feelings."

"Is just jokes!"

"Guys! Guys." She lifted her hands to calm the storm. And she was starting to get whiplash. "It's complicated. Family and stuff, nothing you or your jokes did." She smiled, hoping to reassure them. They just fidgeted, looking like someone had kicked their puppy. It was sweet. "I promise, it's not you. I'd go into details, but it'll be dark soon. So call me. I wanna keep in touch."

"We understand," Dee murmured as he pocketed his pen and pad.

"We promise to call. All the time." Dem nodded.

"Maybe not all the time." Dee elbowed his twin. "But we will miss you."

"Very much."

"Ahh, guys." She waved them over. "Bring it in." She hugged both of them, wheezing faintly when Dem squeezed a bit too tight. Like being hugged by a brick wall, that boy. After a few more minutes of hugs and lamenting, she actually did have to go. She had a lengthy walk back, by herself.

"Take care, Alice." Dem waved, as did his brother, and the two headed north.

She headed west. As she went, she thought over what they'd found back at the village. Maybe she had failed to purge the Nightmare, but this made up for it, right? She cleaned up her mess. On the flip side, if whatever that gunk was didn't have anything to do with her screwup, this was an entirely new mess, one the twins had never seen, and they'd been at this longer than her. And she couldn't shake the feeling that it was all centered around some major bad juju. Could she really leave Hatta to deal with it all on his own? Or the twins? Sure, they had each other, but some things required a team, not just a partner.

Then there was what happened with her blade. Had she imagined it? She tugged it free, holding it out as she walked. It looked fine now, no special glow or anything. Maybe if she concentrated. She focused on the weapon, pushing every ounce of will into it. Right when the area behind her left eye started to throb, a faint light poured over the weapon. Her heart leaped in her chest for a split second before she realized it was the moon. Then her heart dropped to the soles of her feet. It was the moon.

She was still a good twenty minutes from the Gateway, and the dark had caught up with her.

Seven
A MESSAGE

Night in Wonderland was similar to home in many ways. The moon burned the sky with its cold light. The woods came alive, teeming with nocturnal creatures—only the ones here were a bit deadlier. She had to hurry. Surely Hatta would be near the Gateway, waiting for her, worried out of his mind. Rule #1 of being a Dreamwalker, you didn't go wandering Wonderland alone after nightfall.

Alice picked her way through the thick brush. No dazzling flowers or trees illuminated her path, but she moved with the sure-footedness of a jungle cat. The Gateway wasn't far ahead, maybe another fifteen minutes? She couldn't see the telltale brightness of the Glow just yet. *Almost there, girl. One foot in front of the—*

Something snapped in front of her. She froze. Silence descended like a plague. She scanned the brush, following sounds she thought she heard. Her fingers curled tight around the hilt of her dagger.

Another snap. A crunch of leaves, at her seven. Whatever was out there was fast, and circling her. The twins? If they were playing another prank, she was going to hand them their asses. But they wouldn't follow her clear to her Gateway for no reason, or risk pissing off the Duchess by dicking around *this* much.

No, this was something else.

Alice held steady. Listening. Waiting.

It came at her from the right.

The ring of metal against metal filled her ears as an inky blade clashed with her silver one. Her attacker pressed the advance, driving her back with the momentum from a lunge. She stumbled, unable to plant her feet.

Shit!

When their blades came free, she twisted to avoid another strike and tumbled to the ground. The sound of her heart blasted in her ears.

Get up! She swept around to a crouch, her blade lifted and ready.

"You're fast, I'll give you that." Amusement coated her unseen opponent's tone, his voice smooth despite the mask he wore. Or was it a helmet? Black, it held a faint shine, along with the rest of the material covering him. Some sort of high-impact body armor. "But sloppy, tsk tsk tsk."

Ignoring the remark, she stood, brandishing her dagger, her muscles tense as her chest heaved.

He seemed at ease, one hand at his waist while the other

lifted his sword to rest against his shoulder. Her eyes locked on the blade: long, black, single-edged, and sleek, appearing to hang in the atmosphere as if snagged on the air itself. It didn't reflect the moonlight so much as suck it in and snuff it out.

"You like?" He lifted the sword. "It was a gift."

"Who are you?" Alice demanded through clenched teeth. "What do you want?"

"She speaks." His smile was audible as he tilted his head. "And I wanted your attention."

"Shouting 'hey, you' would've worked."

"Boring." He shrugged. "And a little silly."

Alice snatched her other dagger free, whipping them both into a defensive stance, ignoring the throb moving through her arm.

"Easy, kitten," he chuckled. "We'll get to the fun. But first, a bit of business. I need you to give a message to your handler."

He's not *my handler.* She bit back the retort.

"Tell him I want the Eye," he continued. "He has it, and I'm coming to get it."

Eye? She blinked rapidly, frowning. "Not that I give a damn, but who do I say sent this message? Some rando SWAT ninja?"

"The Black Knight."

She barked a laugh. "Seriously? The Black Knight? That's what you're going with?"

He shrugged again. "The Dark Knight was taken."

"The Black Knight is dead."

"I'm afraid reports of my demise were greatly exaggerated."

"Sure, Jan. Either way, I ain't no errand girl. So you can shove that and any other message up your ass."

"If you won't tell him, I'll have to come up with a more . . . creative way to get my point across." He lowered his sword, sweeping the ground with the tip.

Where the weapon touched the dirt, darkness spread outward, bubbling up out of the earth like in Ahoon. But this muck flowed on, coating the grass like oil.

Alice recoiled, her daggers lifted as if to fend off the taint. It spread, devouring everything in its path. Plants wilted and grass withered.

"Last chance, kitten." He purred the nickname.

Shoving down the panic that kicked at her heart, she lifted her gaze from the grime and glared. "Screw you."

He pressed his hand to his chest and gasped. "So aggressive! Have it your way." He took a step forward and vanished.

Movement on her left.

She dodged in time to parry his blow. The force of the impact dug into her joints. She twisted to drive her second dagger at his hip. He pulled away.

His next blow was easily blocked and left him open, but she hesitated. She'd never fought an actual person before. If she struck, she could kill him.

WHAM.

Something connected with the side of her head. Pain erupted in her skull and hammered through the rest of her body. The world winked out and she stumbled.

"Keep your head in the game, kitten." His voice rattled between her ears.

Fingers curled around her wrist and squeezed so hard her bones ground together. The slices beneath her bandage screamed.

So did she, her fingers jerking open. Her dagger dropped. She swung with the other. He spun with the swipe, whirled her around, and slammed her into a tree. Her vision doubled with the pain. She sank to her knees, but he kept hold of her wrist. He pressed his sword to her palm and pulled. Cold and hard, the pressure gave way to searing agony.

Her voice cracked.

He let go.

She dropped her other dagger and gripped her throbbing wrist, blinking away the haze. Her stomach roiled at the sight of flesh split from her middle finger to the heel of her palm. Blood filled the gash, running over her hand in rivers.

"Looks like that hurts." The flat of the Black Knight's sword tapped the side of her cheek. She twisted away to protect her wounded hand. The other slid through the dirt in search of her weapons. Tears filled her eyes. Her teeth tore a hole in her lower lip.

"Now, about that message." His boot connected with her shoulder and pinned it to the tree. She fought for freedom as he tapped the tip of his sword to her injured palm.

The pain faded, replaced by a low burn that traveled up her arm. Her entire body quaked as the wound sewed itself shut. Blood blackened against her skin, seeping into it, staining it.

"W-what . . . what did you do?" Her heart thrashed in her chest. She scrubbed at her palm in vain.

"What I had to. It's not permanent, I promise." He sounded far more chipper than a psychopath should. "Deliver the message. You can do that for me, can't you?"

It wasn't coming off. It was inside her. It wasn't coming off!

She shrank in on herself, muscles tensed to aching, head pounding. *No no no.*

He knelt at her side. "Calm down, you'll give yourself an aneurysm." One of his hands closed over the mark, and he brushed her cheek with the other.

"No!" She lashed out with a kick as he disappeared, her foot connecting with nothing.

"If you keep fighting me, I'm going to have to do this the hard way, kitten," he called, from everywhere.

Alice jerked away from the tree as the echoes of his voice crescendoed. She scrambled to her feet, to chase him down, make him undo this, but she couldn't keep her legs under her. "What did you *do!*"

The Black Knight appeared a short distance away. "My job, unfortunately." He held his sword toward her. Her eyes fastened on the blade, a slice of black in the light of the moon.

"The sword, the sword, a blade so black," he said. The words danced on the wind, echoing faintly.

Each one drove into Alice like nails.

He tapped the tip of the sword against the ground. The same blackness that had spilled free before, probably what tainted her hand, crawled outward. Decay followed, chewing up the dirt and grass, surrounding him.

Alice wanted to run. Everything in her screamed to get away, but she couldn't move. She could only stare, trembling, hot tears scorching her face. "N-no."

"The Vorpal Blade went snicker-snack." He flicked his wrist. The sword swallowed the moonlight, defiling the very air around it.

Alice's head buzzed. Her skin flushed, her muscles threatening to burst out of it. This was wrong. "Stop." Something inside her shouted: *This. Is. Wrong.*

"He left her dead, and with her head." Lifting his sword, he plunged it into the dirt. The blade sunk in clear to the hilt, same as hers did with the purge, only this was different. The ground shuddered before the area encasing the sword rose, hilling itself beneath the hilt.

"Stop!" she screamed.

He couldn't hear her. She could barely hear herself over the shrieking wind. It whipped up a hurricane of dust and leaves, snatched at her clothes and hair, battered her body and senses. She pressed her hands against her ears.

"He went galumphing back." The knight's words somehow rang clear. He pulled his weapon free, but the ground continued to bulge, higher and higher. Branches snapped and leaves shivered as the growing hill broke through the canopy, a huge mass of blackened dirt and stone.

The mound rippled, the various textures smoothing out or melding together to become a single amorphous blob. It shifted and shuddered, solidifying as it took on a familiar inky quality. The wind vanished. The world stilled. A low rumble Alice recognized as a growl filled the air.

The Nightmare spun in a slow circle until the crimson orbs of its pupil-less eyes fixed on Alice. With the body of a bear and the head of a turtle, the damned thing stood twice as tall as her. Its beak parted to reveal dozens of long, thin teeth the size of her fingers. It snarled, a forked tongue darting at the air.

"This is *his* fault." The knight sheathed his sword at his back. "All of it!" he shouted, his voice suddenly thick with emotion. "Now we'll all suffer her darkness."

He was talking nonsense, but Alice didn't give a good gotdayum. Her attention was on the Nightmare, now fully formed.

"I'm sorry it's gotta be this way, kitten, but you can do this." His voice echoed as he faded from sight. "Fight."

Fear slithered cold and wet through her limbs, but something in her moved, lifted her weapon. With the knight gone, whatever spell had held her fast was broken.

Roaring, the beast attacked.

Alice jerked back to avoid a swipe of talons before it reared and swung again. She dropped and rolled, springing to her feet and away to put distance between them.

It lumbered around to face her, then pushed onto two legs.

She lunged to the side to avoid another swing of massive paws. Her dagger scored along its arm, earning a pained howl. A massive scorpion tail with a wicked barb at the tip lashed from over its shoulder. Alice skittered back to avoid being skewered. Dirt erupted where the tail tagged the earth, but she wasn't fast enough to dodge when it came at her again.

She caught it broadside and flew end over end, her bones rattling as she hit the ground in a heap of bruised flesh and rolled to a stop. The smell of dirt and grass filled her nose along with the bronzed scent of blood. Every inch of her throbbed. Her lungs spasmed.

Something punctured her left calf. She shrieked and lashed out. Her knife caught leathery flesh. The Nightmare howled and jerked its tail, the barb ripping free. Fire shot through her leg, her nerves ablaze. She scrambled back and managed to haul herself to her feet.

The Nightmare paced back and forth nearby. Mist curled from its flared nostrils. Another pair of red eyes on either side of its head flickered into view. Both sets blinked vertical lids. Its beak hung open, rivers of drool and venom pouring to the ground. A gash along its tail where she cut it bled green, as did the stab wound in its arm.

It charged.

Alice whirled and threw herself into a dead run. Molten cold shot up her leg and punched her in the stomach with each step, bending her into a hobble. Terror kept her upright, kept her moving. *Hatta.*

The Nightmare gained on her, pounding the ground with large paws. The tremors hit her like a shock wave, and her legs nearly gave.

Hatta. The name sank like a stone in the uproar of her mind. She latched on to it, an anchor.

Hatta! Louder this time, but not enough. Leaves and branches slapped at her as she ran blind through the forest. Twigs stung her face and tugged at her hair. She lifted her hands to guard her head as her legs pumped and her heart hammered. A sudden drop into a ditch took her feet out from under her. She cried out when she hit the ground and tumbled down the incline. She flew off a short overhang and landed in a trench on her side. Agony spiked through her torso. Something hard dug into her hip. Her injured leg felt like little more than wrenched nerves and torn flesh engulfed in hot hurt, but she forced it and her other one under herself. They barely held her weight.

The Nightmare bellowed as it slammed into the trench behind her. Branches snapped. Rocks tumbled. Alice's heart jackknifed between her lungs. The monster flailed, trying to regain its feet.

Her lips pursed, locked between her teeth. Blood coated her tongue, copper sweet. Her scream welled up from her gut, scorched her throat, and nearly knocked her teeth loose as it tore free. "Hatta!" His name echoed through gunk and mud, her mind frantic with fear. He couldn't hear her. She was too far away from the Gateway.

She tried to run, but her now-useless leg gave completely. She fell against a boulder lodged in the dirt, barely pushing away in time to avoid being impaled as talons raked along the stone. Sparks flew.

Scrambling, she rolled in under the Nightmare's arm and hurled herself at its body. Inky fur stuck wet to her skin as she drove the knife into its belly. The beast howled but couldn't get at her, not with its movements restricted by the high, close trench walls.

What looked like tar and smelled like rotting flesh spilled over her hands and forearms as she gritted her teeth, pushing, trying to reach the core with her blade. The Nightmare twisted and turned, finally able to get a swing in. The blow caught her across the face. Stars exploded against the backs of her eyes. Her teeth rattled. She staggered away, her weapon still lodged in the beast. It slapped at the hilt with massive paws.

Alice's vision speckled. She dropped to the ground, her ears ringing. Blinking did little to clear the haze over her eyes. Somehow, she saw the knife, saw how it caused the beast pain.

Hauling herself upright, nearly losing her head to another swipe in the process, Alice gripped a root jutting out from a wall of dirt overhead with both hands and flung her good leg out. Her heel caught the dagger's hilt like a hammer on a nail and drove it farther into the beast.

It loosed a wail, tearing at its flesh with one arm, the other trapped by the trench. The knife was too deep and couldn't be pulled out. The monster bucked and thrashed, putrid pus pouring to the mud beneath it.

Alice dropped, catching herself against a trench wall, exposed stone scraping her back. She crawled through the muck as the beast flopped and rolled. It shrieked and hissed like a tire losing air.

Something struck the back of her head, and everything went white. Pain carved out a hitch between her ears. Her hands groped against the cold dirt. She tried to push, but it was like her arms weren't a part of her body anymore.

The Nightmare caved in on itself, its tail whipping like a water hose on full blast. She fumbled in her attempt to get up, her hands sliding in mud. She slipped again, and this time when her arm stretched forward, pain burst from her side. She whined, pitching herself onto her back.

Red stained her ruined shirt below her ribs, hot and warm against her skin. It spread outward from a slice in her flesh. The sight of the wound stole her remaining strength as shivers invaded her limbs, the growing cold wrenching away the last of her control. She wasn't strong enough, couldn't do it on her own. She was a helpless little girl again.

"Ha-Hat . . ." She tried to call to him again, but the words died on her tongue. Her mind filled with him, the feel of him steadying her as they crossed the Veil. The smell of him, like bourbon and licorice. The sound of his voice, "I've got you, luv."

Her hand outstretched, blood smeared her fingers. The mark left by the Black Knight nearly glowed in the blue moonlight. Images of her insides blackening before rotting away tumbled over her fractured thoughts. She saw herself shifting, morphing, her body contorting into some hellish beast. She saw her mother curled in bed when she didn't come home, refusing to eat or drink until she, too, faded away.

"N-no," she gasped.

Nearby, the Nightmare finally stopped writhing, a mere boiling mess shrinking away.

So was she.

Shadows danced at the edges of her sight as the voices melded, calling to her.

"Alice."

Leave me alone . . .

"Alice." The call was more insistent this time.

Fingers latched on to her shoulder. The icy burn beneath her skin roared at the contact. She tried to scream, to fight, but the touch pinned her arms.

"Alice, open your eyes."

Her lids fluttered sluggishly.

"That's a girl." A shadowed blob hovered over her. Fingers

touched one cheek, then the other, gentle and warm. "You're burning up."

Yet her insides trembled, frozen. "H-Hat . . . tell . . . knight . . ."

"Shh, don't try to talk." The voice was soft, careful.

Mom?

Those hands repositioned and pulled, lifting her. "Look at me. Can you look at me?" A pair of eyes blazed white in the haze, sharp where all else blurred, bright where all else dimmed. "Hold on."

Something pricked her arm. The ice building in her limbs began to melt in a wave of wet warmth. A weight settled over her body and blanketed her mind. Together, the heat and the heaviness brought the darkness.

Eight
AND CURIOUSER

Alice hadn't dreamed since becoming a Dreamwalker.

"One of the prices paid to do what you do," Hatta explained once.

Dreams made people vulnerable and simultaneously strengthened the Nightmares. But now, she had to be dreaming. That's what she told herself as she stood in shadow, surrounded by nothing.

Emptiness expanded outward, endless in all directions save for a faint glow somewhere beneath her feet. It chased back the black just enough for her to see her hands. A white haze coated them, along with her arms and body.

It's me, she realized as her gaze roamed her form. *I'm the light.* Rather, she wore it.

Fluid and weightless, the brightness wreathed her body like

fabric, stark against her brown skin. The light painted her curves like a luminous corset, with hints of silver and gold streaked in vine-like detail. From there, the glow fell in thin folds forming elegant skirts concealing her legs. She gripped the fabric and lifted.

Water swirled beneath her bare feet. It tossed and turned, churning with erratic waves. The fitful roll was hypnotizing, almost concealing the fact that something waited beneath the surface, still in the midst of the maelstrom.

Alice pointed her toes and touched them against the waters. A jolt of cold shot up her leg. Immediately the surface stilled. Motionless, the waters cast her reflection at her like a mirror, except her mirrored self held a silver scepter, crowned with a stone glowing deep purple. She extended a hand, offering the staff to Alice.

Without hesitation, Alice knelt and reached into the waters. It was like reaching through pudding, thick and creamy, the surface wavering gently. A numbness traveled up her arm, prickling like it had fallen asleep. Her fingers curled around the scepter and pulled.

When the staff slipped free, the water solidified with a crackling like ice and chilled the soles of her feet. Alice gripped the scepter, examining it. The head split outward into two hands cast in silver, the purple gem cupped by their fingers. She lifted her fingers toward the glowing stone.

"No!" her reflection shouted.

Alice's finger pricked the stone's surface. The purple exploded outward. The ice beneath her feet buckled before melting, and she dropped through. Water swallowed her, filled her nose and mouth, poured down her throat. Her limbs kicked and flailed. She couldn't breathe.

Help!

Her eyes flew open. Light stabbed the back of her skull, and she snapped them closed again, pressing her palms over her lids. Her chest spasmed.

Oh, thank god. She was able to breathe, though . . . she wasn't sure why she thought she couldn't. Pressure behind her eyes swelled and deflated. The steady pounding felt like someone was holding her head underwater.

Drinking in gulps of air, she blinked her eyes open again. Unfamiliar clay-colored walls rose around her, bare and boring, with not a window between them. The white ceiling held an equally plain fan, the blades whipping the air in soft whispers. A plaque featuring a white rabbit in a waistcoat and brandishing a pocket watch hung on the wall. She knew that funky tchotchke.

I'm at the pub? She frowned, trying to remember how she wound up here. Flashes played through her mind: a white dress, her holding a stick while running through the woods. She fought a Nightmare. Then everything went dark, followed by lots of water.

It was a dream. No, she'd been attacked, she was certain.

"Ha—" Hatta's name stuck in her throat. She swallowed, and her mouth withered like grass in the hot sun. Breathing became a chore and she coughed, choking on dry air.

The attempt to roll onto her side sent shards of pain tearing through her. She yelped as much from surprise as the hurt. "W-wha?" Her voice cracked, pitching her words into a squeal.

A door she hadn't noticed swung open, and Maddi scurried through. "Don't move." She scrambled to the side of the bed.

"Not moving," Alice whimpered, frozen in an awkward position where she'd arched off the bed, partially trapped by the sheets.

"Easy," Maddi shushed. The sound of something sloshing accompanied her words, then a slippery coolness spread through Alice's side. The pain eased, and she sank against the mattress with a groan.

It was then that she noticed she was dressed in some sort of cotton tank and sleep-shorts set. She plucked at the front of the white shirt, brow furrowed. "What happened to my clothes?"

"You mean besides being muddied and bled all over?"

"Touché." She must've been pretty banged up if Serious Maddi was on the clock. Normally the sleepy girl was all riddles and nonsense talk, but funnily enough, whenever Alice was badly injured, it was like Maddi was a different person entirely, all sense and clarity.

"So you soundly boggled your scourse."

Mostly sense and clarity. "What?" Alice asked.

"You got really messed up."

"Ahh." Understatement.

"By the time we got you in here you were practically half-dead. Plus you smelled like you crawled out of Death's ass."

"Lovely." And here she was supposed to be quitting in order

to avoid this whole half-dead situation. Images of Mom crying after Alice had been killed poured over her mind. She dug the heels of her palms into her eyes. "Uuuuugh."

"I got you cleaned up and changed, no worries." Maddi patted at Alice's side with a cloth before tossing it onto a bedside table that looked more like a chemistry station, various glass containers filled with different liquids set atop it. "Sorry no one was here; we didn't expect you to be up so soon, and moving around to boot."

Questions bubbled in Alice's mind, about what happened and why she couldn't remember clearly. Only one was important enough to make the journey to her lips. "Where's Hatta?"

"Coming." Maddi turned her attention to mixing something orange in one of the glasses while Alice risked a look at her wound. Dark skin puckered around four distinct slices. Strips of tissue stretched across the gashes like fleshy string cheese, spurred on by Maddi's healing touch no doubt.

"Nasty business, that." Hatta filled the doorway, his expression drawn. His eyes fixed on her wounded side. "What happened?"

What happened? Alice frowned, the throbbing in her head kicked up. "I . . . the twins. We found something. I was coming back and—"

Images of the Black Knight darted behind her eyes. Her chest tightened, and she bolted up with a shout. Pain danced down her side, her head pounding now.

"I said easy!" Maddi called, reaching for her.

Hatta was at her side as well. He didn't say anything, just wrapped his arms around her and held her close as she shook and cried, fumbling over the words. "H-him! He happened!"

"Easy, luv," Hatta coaxed, his hands sliding over her arms, up and down her back. "Breathe."

She was trying. Deep breaths became quick hitches. She swallowed thickly, her mouth like cotton. Her vision waned in a combination of tears and the sudden decrease in oxygen to her brain as she panted.

"Drink this." Maddi offered a frosted glass filled with the orange liquid from before.

Alice downed it without a second thought, ignoring the tart lemony taste made worse by the lukewarm temperature. By the time she handed the cup to Maddi, the pain in her head was all but gone, replaced by a warm, tingly feeling, like hot sand being poured between her ears. It felt . . . funny. She was also able to actually inhale without choking on it.

"That's it," Hatta cooed. "In and out. In and out."

Her headache was gone. But she was still shaking.

"Now then. What happened?" Hatta asked.

"I was headed back when *he* jumped me," she forced between clenched teeth.

"Who?"

She shook her head, sniffing and wiping at her runny nose. "I—I don't know. He called himself the Black Knight."

Hatta stiffened. Alice could feel his muscles lock up around her. She winced, he was holding her so tight.

Something clacked to the side. Maddi quickly righted a bottle that had fallen over, spilling yellow liquid across the table. "Bobs and ends," she whispered. "Bobs and ends and round the bend." Her hands shook as she stacked glasses and jars away from the mess.

Alice couldn't see her face, but she could tell from the hitch of the Poet's shoulders something was wrong. "Maddi."

"Towel!" Maddi jumped to her feet, pink eyes wide, her brown face gone white. "I'll get a towel." She hurried from the room, slamming the door behind her.

"Um . . ." Alice stared after the Poet. "She seems awful upset."

"For good reason." Hatta loosened his hold, drawing back to ease Alice against her pillows and sit at her side. "The Black Knight was the strongest force the Black Queen commanded. He wiped out entire battalions in her name, did horrible things." Hatta's jaw tensed. His lips pursed. "No one likes talking about him or hearing about some tosser pretending to be him."

Alice frowned. "Pretending?"

"Absolutely." Hatta's multicolored eyes smoldered, his expression oddly unreadable.

Alice squirmed under his gaze, struggling to hold it. "How do you know he's pretending?"

"Because I do," Hatta snapped. Shaking his head, he forced air through his nose as he shifted his weight. "What did he look like?"

Alice snorted. "Wore armor, a mask. I couldn't see his face."

"Anything identifiable? A crest on the breastplate?"

"Not that kind of armor. More modern, *Call of Duty*–type stuff."

"Any markings at all?"

It had been dark, and they'd been moving around a lot. She hadn't seen much detail. She shook her head before blinking at Hatta.

"That's it then." He drew one leg up to tuck beneath himself. "The Black Knight—the *true* Black Knight—wore enchanted plate armor with the emblem of his queen emblazoned on the breastplate. All knights of Wonderland wear such armor. The real Black Knight is gone."

That seemed way too simple. "Then who the hell was that?"

He rolled his shoulders as he twisted one of the rings on his hand, his long fingers curling and flexing. "An imposter. Someone still loyal to the Black Queen, possibly, looking to start trouble."

"Why?"

"That is the question." He tapped his fingers against his lips. "Curiouser—"

"And curiouser, I know." Alice picked at a hole in her sheets. "He fought pretty good for just some imposter." Kicked her ass, actually. She hadn't been beaten that bad since training.

"But you defeated him."

Heat burned through Alice for a different reason now. "No, I didn't. He let me go after whoopin' my butt with his freaky sword."

Hatta straightened, eyes on her. "Sword? What sort of sword?"

An image of that weapon and the way it swallowed the moonlight danced across her memory. A shudder crawled through her, and she fought not to press back into the pillows. "He called it a Warped blade or something."

"*Vorpal* Blade?"

She nodded. "It infected everything it touched with this black stuff. The grass, the dirt, the rocks." Another shiver moved through her. She shut her eyes, trying to remember. There was something important . . . "*It* was black. He used it like some sort of reverse Figment Blade, drove it into the ground and boom, Nightmare popped up."

Hatta watched her, his head cocked to the side. The easygoing air around him had shifted, as if standing at attention. "You're certain he said Vorpal Blade?"

Alice blinked, her mouth working as words tripped over themselves, tumbling free. "It sounded—I mean—yeah, I'm sure. He said the Vorpal Blade, snicky snack, and something about cutting off someone's head."

"Impossible . . ." His gaze drifted past her to the wall and somewhere beyond. Somewhere long ago that once was, and perhaps should never be again.

Everything played across his face, through those eyes that weren't really looking at her.

Her hand fell over his. "Hatta?"

He started and refocused on her. "I should let you rest. We can talk about all of this later." He twisted his fingers to twine them with hers. "I'm sorry I wasn't there, luv."

The warmth from his hand spread to hers and up her arm. This odd, tingly feeling followed. Her gaze lifted from their fingers, and her eyes caught his. Their colors shifted. He smiled. It may have been a trick of the light, but she thought he leaned in a little.

"I'm all right," she murmured, her throat going dry. She

swallowed, sitting up. Their hands shifted, lacing their fingers together. Her palm pressed to his.

Something sparked at the contact.

Hatta yanked his hand away with a yelp and shook it out.

Alice stared at him, then her still-lifted hand, the sudden space between them like a chasm.

The hell? "I'm . . . sorry."

"No worries." He flexed his fingers, his expression faintly twisted.

"You okay?" Her tongue felt thick in her mouth, clumsy.

"What?" He rubbed his palms together, looking his hands over before glancing at her. "I'm fine. You?"

"Yeah." She shrugged, eyeing her hand. "Sorry."

"Not your fault." Another flex of his fingers.

Smirking, Hatta leaned in and brushed his lips against her forehead. Every part of her tingled lightly, heat crawling up her neck from her chest and consuming her face. "Rest, milady."

"R-rest sounds good." Alice tucked her hands between her sheet-covered thighs as Hatta moved over to the door. He tugged it open, drawing up short when he nearly ran into Maddi, who stood on the other side clutching a towel to her chest and looking like she'd been caught in the act.

"Towel," she whispered, holding it up.

Hatta chuckled and stepped back to let the mousy girl move past and over to start cleaning up the mess from earlier. The liquid had congealed into more of a greasy substance, so the towel wasn't really working.

"Good night." He waved.

Alice returned the wave, smiling faintly, all warm and fuzzy.

Then she caught sight of her palm. A pinprick of black nestled in the center. It started to grow. And grow. And she remembered. "Wait!"

Maddi jumped, jostling the table and a few jars. She reached to steady them. Hatta stood in the door, an eyebrow arched.

"He told me to give you a message." Alice held her arm out, marked palm up.

Fingers took her hand and pulled so fast she jerked up a bit. Her side stung in protest. "Ow!" She hadn't even seen Hatta move.

"Sorry, luv." He studied her palm, squeezing her fingers.

His gaze flicked up to catch hers through the veil of his dark lashes. "Does it hurt?"

She swallowed and shook her head, praying he couldn't hear how her heart thudded against her ribs. "He wants something called the Eye."

Maddi glanced back and forth between the two of them, her wide eyes shifting in color with every blink.

Alice withdrew her hand. Hatta let her.

"He says you have it and he's coming to . . . Hatta?"

Hatta traced his own palm. His lips moved the slightest bit, whispers escaping him in a rush.

"Hatta?" she tried again. When he didn't answer, she glanced at Maddi, who was watching him with a frown crinkling her normally sleepy expression.

The Poet approached Hatta and leaned in to wave her hand in front of his face. He didn't do anything, just stood there, mumbling.

Worry crawled through Alice, enough for her to draw back

the sheets, ready to go to him. Before her feet touched the ground, Maddi hauled back and slapped him. "Addison!"

Hatta jerked. So did Alice, actually.

His body snapped straight. His head lifted as he shook it. He blinked owlishly, glanced at Maddi, then at Alice, back and forth a few times before smacking his lips. "Anyone else taste chartreuse?"

"Ahh . . ." She wasn't sure how to respond to that, or to the fact that Maddi now stood with her arms folded over her chest, looking annoyed for having to slap him in the first place.

He lifted a hand to massage his cheek. "Ahem. Thank you, Madeline."

Maddi went back to cleaning, her actions stiff, her frown deepening. It was so strange to see her looking anything but exhausted.

Alice still wasn't sure what to say, if she should say anything. After a few beats, she found the words. "Are you okay?"

Hatta blinked at her as if surprised to find her there. "Ah, yes. What were you saying?"

"The message." The mark on Alice's hand seemed to stand out all the more now. "The Black Knight wants the Eye."

"Right, right." Hatta continued to rub his cheek, which had now gone an angry red. "I don't have it."

"What is it? And why is some asshole tagging my hand over it?"

The rubbing moved to his temple. "It was a magic artifact that belonged to the Black Queen. After defeating her, the Red and White Queens hid it. As I said, I don't have it."

Maddi clacked glasses against the table, spreading them

out again. The way she manhandled them, Alice almost felt pity for the dishes. She'd never seen the bartender so bothered.

"He'll have to look elsewhere." Hatta lowered his hand and moved for the door. "As for your hand, if I'm not mistaken, the mark is a conduit. It contains a Verse meant to pass from one carrier to the next. I imagine it's supposed to be a reminder."

"Mark?" Maddi glanced at Alice. "What mark?"

Alice offered her palm. Maddi stared and shook her head. "I don't see anything."

"Because you are not the bearer nor the intended recipient." Hatta kept his eyes on Alice. "It should fade soon. Maddi will finish looking after the worst of your wounds, give you something to ease the pain and speed up healing, more than your naturally enhanced regeneration. Take two swallows every few hours for four days. Or three and nine-eighths days. Just in case. If you miss a dose, take one swallow every quarter half hour."

"Every quar—that doesn't even make sense."

"And don't take the bandage off."

"What bandage?"

Maddi slapped something against Alice's side. She jumped, more from surprise than anything. The bartender slathered what looked like green finger paint against Alice's bare skin. The color gradually darkened to match her complexion, concealing the wound completely.

Alice blinked. Had Maddi used this after Ahoon? Alice didn't remember much following that fight, but this was some useful stuff. "Can I get some of this to go?"

"'Fraid not. It goes bad a few days after being mixed." Maddi turned her attention to Alice's leg. "I applied some earlier, but a second coating helps maintain the illusion."

"Literal wound dressing. Can't have you looking like you got yourself mauled." Hatta winked, then disappeared out the door and down the hall, his words trailing behind him. "Get some rest. We'll talk more later."

Alice settled against the pillows as Maddi finished applying the bandage and cleaned her hands with the towel she'd used to wipe up her earlier spill. "All light, starshine."

"Thanks."

"Yup yup. I'll let you sleep."

"Hey, you know where my bag is?"

Maddi crouched beside the bed. The springs creaked and shifted, then she popped back up, Alice's backpack in hand. "Figured you'd want it close." Which meant under the bed, apparently.

"Thanks. Again."

Maddi nodded and gathered up her supplies. "Food?"

The way Alice's stomach twisted in on itself, she didn't think she could keep anything down. "No. But some water?" Her throat was on fire.

"Mmhm." Maddi slipped out of the room, closing the door behind her.

Alice tugged her phone free, intending to call her mom and let her know she was just going to spend the night at Court's. The screen lit up. Message after message scrolled by. Missed call alert after missed call alert followed, along with several voice mails. With each notification, Alice sank in on herself, a hollow feeling widening inside her, threatening to collapse inward.

"Oh no." She kept scrolling, falling deeper and deeper. "No, no, no!"

Most of them were from her mom, the usual in her new-found practice of angry demands wondering where the hell she was. The others were from Court and Chess, wondering the same.

Above them all, 10:14 PM blazed against the screen. Beneath that, the words SATURDAY, OCTOBER 15.

Courtney's birthday party had started four hours ago.

Nine

A VERY
IMPORTANT DATE

Alice downed a couple of potions and asked Maddi for a ride home, promising her and Hatta she'd go straight to bed. Borrowing a pair of sweatpants from the Poet, which fit Alice more like sweat-capris, she sat in the front seat of Maddi's car typing and deleting text after text to Courtney. After the dozenth delete, she tried calling. Something in her chest went cold as she pressed the phone to her ear. It rang. And rang. And rang.

"Hay, it's Court-nay. You know what to do."

Voice mail. Alice didn't know if she was relieved or even more upset, but she tried again. And again. The fourth time, it went to voice mail on the second ring. Court had hit dismiss. There were few feelings worse than knowing you'd been intentionally ignored, revoked, denied.

On the next call, it went straight to voice mail. Alice sighed and waited for the beep. "I'm late, I know, I'm sorry, but I'm on my way. I got hit. Hard. I didn't wake up until like an hour ago. Maddi and Hatta can back me up, so please, call me? I'm on my way, love you, bye."

She tried Chess next. He picked up on the first ring, music blaring in the background. "Alice! Where are you, what happened, are you okay?"

"I'm okay. It's a long story. Are you with Courtney?"

"What? Hold on." He must have lowered his phone because the music hit loud enough Alice had to pull hers away from her ear. After a few seconds, it died away completely. "Sorry, what did you say?"

"I said I'm fine. Where's Courtney?"

"She's inside. Dude, what happened yesterday? Where have you been?"

Alice bit into her lower lip. "I'll explain when I get there. Can you put Courtney on the phone?"

"Um, I can try." His tone dipped toward irritated. The music kicked up again. Alice supposed she'd be in her feelings if she called someone, worried about them, and they called back to talk to someone else. Being her friend was the worst. She'd find a way to make it up to him.

For a couple of minutes Alice listened to the party music and willed Maddi to go faster. When it finally died down again, she pressed the phone to her ear, an apology on her lips.

"She doesn't want to talk to you," Chess said quietly.

The cold feeling in Alice's chest dropped into her gut.

"I'm sorry. Alice?"

She tried to respond, twice, but the words kept slamming

into the back of her teeth. She took a second to just breathe. "That's all right. Just tell her I'm on my way, okay?"

"Yeah, sure, see you when you get here."

"Mmhm." She couldn't manage anything more, the sting in her eyes spreading to the rest of her face, clogging her nose and burning her throat. She let the window down, but that didn't help. Buildings whizzed by, eventually shrinking down to houses as they reached her neighborhood. If Maddi sensed anything was wrong, she didn't try to talk about it. Alice silently thanked her.

When they pulled up in front of her house, she pushed the door open, but paused. "Maddi, I need one more favor. Can you drop me off at Courtney's?" she continued when the bartender looked at her with quizzical blue eyes.

Maddi frowned. "You're supposed to be not this."

"Huh?"

Maddi pressed her hands together and pretended to be asleep, fake snore and all.

"O-oh. I know, but it's her birthday and I'm late for her party. I'll take it easy, just drink punch and eat cake."

Maddi's eyes narrowed before she gave a single, sound nod. "Cake is important."

"Oh, thank you! I'll be right back, I need to change." Alice jumped out of the car and raced for the porch. The driveway was empty, but that didn't necessarily mean Mom wasn't home. Sometimes she put the car in the garage. A couple lights shone in the living room window.

Quiet and careful, Alice unlocked the front door and stepped inside. She held her breath, listening for signs of movement, the TV playing upstairs, anything. Silence greeted her from all directions. Light in the kitchen was dim, most likely from over the sink. The hall upstairs was completely dark. Mom was out, thank god. Alice raced upstairs and into her room. With a pang of pain here and there, she stripped down. Maddi had cleaned the blood and mud off her, but she still needed some soap-on-skin action.

After the fastest shower in human history—thankfully, the magic bandages were also waterproof—she slathered some lotion on and slipped into her costume. She'd spent weeks on this dress, trying a couple of patterns before getting it right. She was out of practice. The satin felt cool against her skin, the skirts fanning out at her feet. She pulled the shoulder puffs into place, checking to make sure they were straight. The gold collar blazed, radiant even in the dull glow of her ceiling fan light. She threw on some sneakers to wear out, then brushed her gel-slicked hair into two puffs atop her head and hastily pinned two extra-long tails of silk Yaki at the base of each. Her hands still sticky, she looped a sock donut over each puff and smoothed the hair around the material to form two buns. More pins ensured they stayed in place. She hoped. She nearly forgot her jewelry, completely skipped makeup, and raced out of the house.

Maddi made it to the highway by the time Alice worked up the nerve to call her mom. She may have evaded the threat for now, but she needed to at least put in some communication time if she didn't want Mom to go completely awf, and a text wasn't gone cut it. She steeled herself, shoulders hunched and one eye shut, and called. She felt like she was launching a nuclear missile.

Mom picked up halfway through the first ring. "What the hell is wrong with you?"

Alice flinched before launching into a story about how she

texted her a few times today, a boldface lie, but she only just now noticed that her messages weren't going through because she somehow accidentally put her phone on airplane mode. That also explained why she didn't get any of her mom's calls or messages, either. Court used that line on her mom once, and Alice decided to steal it for just this occasion, but Courtney's mom was super suburban white and Alice's mom probably had TRY ME tattooed across her knuckles in a previous life.

After Alice spun her web, she waited in silence for judgment to be passed.

"You must think I'm stupid," Mom said way too calmly.

"No, I don't. I seriously just thought you were cool with me helping Court get everything ready for the party."

"And that's where you been? Since *yes. Ter. Day?*" Mom cut the word in pieces. "'Cause that's the last time I heard from you. And even if I believe your lil story about you messin' up your phone or whatever, I called Courtney, too, and she didn't pick up. Y'all think it's a game. I could've been calling 'cause of your grandma or some other emergency, maybe to wish her happy birthday, y'all don't know. I called Maxine, but she and Robert are off somewhere neglecting their children, ain't talked to Courtney all day, neither."

Just from the way Mom chewed on her words, Alice could picture her lips twisting to the side and her head cocked, especially when she talked about Courtney's parents. Mom didn't like the way they weren't around, even when they were.

"Y'all must think I won't come over there and embarrass the both of you," Mom went on, just shy of yelling. "I'm not above scene-causing."

"I don't know what happened to Courtney's phone. She probably set it down somewhere and forgot it during all the craziness."

"Don't play me, Alison. That lil girl would lose her damn right hand before she lost that phone."

Well, Mom wasn't wrong. "I'm not. I'm on her back porch. I can go get her if you want me to." *Please don't want me to.*

A moment of silence passed. Then another. Mom sighed heavily. "As soon as that party is over, you better have your butt in a car on your way home. If I have to come get you, and I will, you're gonna regret it."

Relief swept through Alice with enough force to push the air from her lungs. "I'll come home right after, I swear."

"You better. And you better get your party on 'cause you're grounded for the next two weeks."

The relief evaporated. "What!"

"You heard me."

"But—"

"No buts, except yours in this house, you got me?"

Alice sank down in the seat, her dress bunching at her back. She bit into her lips, her grip on the phone tightening. A *crack* sounded as the screen split across the middle. Her grip eased with a faint gasp.

"Hello? I know I'm not talking to myself. You wanna add an ass whuppin' to this order?"

"N-no, ma'am. I'm here."

"Uh-huh. We're going to have a *conversation* when you get home, young lady."

"Yes, ma'am."

"Tell Courtney I said happy birthday, and she better pick up next time my name hits her screen."

"Yes, ma'am."

"I love you."

"Yes, ma—I love you, too."

"Bye." Mom hung up before Alice could respond.

Alice stared at her now-broken phone. It took everything in her not to just chuck it out the window or something.

Maddi had been shooting her looks during the whole conversation. Alice kept her eyes on the street. They rode in silence save for Alice giving directions now and again. Eventually, they pulled into a gated community. Fancy lights made to look like old-timey gas lamps lined the streets. Massive houses sat back on multiacre sites, some of them with an additional gate of their own, the driveways long enough to have separate lighting. Big and expensive, or sleek and also expensive, cars sat parked around fountains or in front of multicar garages.

Courtney's house was one of the bigger ones, a white monstrosity that looked part wedding cake, part Mediterranean castle. The lamps lining the driveway were all different colors, a string of bright bulbs threaded between them. The fountain at the center of her roundabout in the front spouted rainbow-lit water in crisscrosses. There were only a handful of cars still parked. Alice managed some eyeliner, mascara, and lipstick on the ride over. Her face wasn't beat, but it would have to do.

After a thanks to Maddi and a quick shoe swap, she hurried up the front stairs to the large double doors. She'd worry about her mom and that nonsense later; right now she had a friendship to save. She didn't know how, but she had to make this work. One thing had to work!

She rang the doorbell, waving as Maddi pulled off. When no one answered, she rang again and fidgeted with her bag. There wasn't anything but her shoes, makeup, phone, and a card for Courtney inside, but it felt like it weighed a million pounds. Alice rang a third time, her heart jumping around in her chest. Sweat slipped down her back, despite the chilled October air prickling against her bare skin. Court wasn't mad enough to leave her literally standing out in the cold, was she?

Finally, the locks clicked as they were turned on the other side, and one large door swung inward. Crystal, Court's thirteen-year-old sister, filled the small opening, blinking up at her with Court's same green eyes from behind a pair of glasses. A pointy black hat sat on top of her long, yellow hair, and a green and silver scarf curled around her neck and fell over her shoulders. Robes concealed the rest of her clothes, the Slytherin crest bright over her heart.

"Hey." Crystal adjusted her glasses, and a lightning bolt mark was visible through the fringe of her bangs.

"Hey." Alice stepped into the house, glancing around for signs of the party, but the place was pretty quiet.

"You're late." Crystal closed the door.

Alice bit down on the flare of irritation and smiled at Crystal. "You're . . . Harry Potter?"

"If he chose right." Crystal stepped around Alice and headed for the large staircase that wound up along the wall to the second floor. "They're downstairs."

"Thanks." Alice clicked down the side hall and headed for the basement. A few kids she recognized from school were on their way up, dressed as Wonder Woman, a Jedi, and something Alice didn't recognize at all. They seemed surprised to see her but greeted her all the same in passing. God, she was so late.

At the bottom of the stairs, a short hall to the right led to another pair of double doors, propped open into what was pretty much a private ballroom. The lights were up, but the decorations along the walls and high ceiling gave the impression of a dramatic Victorian manor turned rave. Balloons and sparkling confetti littered the floor. A long table full of empty trays and punch bowls sat against the far wall. On the stage, a few guys were packing up some massive speakers and what looked like DJ gear. There was no sign of Courtney or Chess until Alice stepped farther into the large room and the wall full of high windows and French doors came into view.

The amazing decorations continued out onto the terrace, where a bunch of lights had been set up to contour the space and give it the same Victorian flare. A fire flickered in the large pit at the center of the courtyard, where the furniture had been drawn back to open up the area. The large pool was also lit in various colors, the water dazzling. Courtney definitely went all out.

With a fortifying breath, Alice pushed through one of the doors. Court and Chess paused midconversation where they were seated on the large stone bench that circled the fire. Court looked stunning, and scary as hell with that glare on her face, as Maleficent. Chess was some sort of lord, maybe, in a tuxedo and cape. He didn't look angry, but he didn't look happy to see her, either.

"H-hey." Alice twisted the beaded bracelet on her wrist.

Court looked to Chess. "Did you hear something?"

He sighed. "Courtney."

"Surely, that's not my supposed best friend wandering into my birthday party four hours late after ghosting on me all damn day. Surely."

Alice swallowed. "It's not like that. I was—"

"Oh, it's not?" Court whirled on her. "You're not just now showing up after everyone's gone? You've been here the whole time, and we just kept missing each other in my freaking house?"

"There was a problem at the pub." She stressed the last few words, hoping Courtney understood what she meant. She couldn't talk about this stuff in front of Chess, though she desperately wanted to explain. "It was an emergency. I—"

"There's always a problem at the pub!" Court jumped to her feet. Her eyes glistened with anger and tears. "Or a crisis, an emergency, something important that'll just take a second, that turns into hours that turns into days. But silly me, I thought, surely, this time, my best friend wouldn't let it happen. Surely, if she didn't make it tonight, she'd at least fucking show up for my birthday!"

Tears spilled over Courtney's cheeks. She swiped at her eyes, smudging the green and black eyeshadow that had completed her look. One glance at her hand and then she rubbed it on her black robes.

"Court," Alice tried, her voice breaking. She could feel her own tears slip down her face. "I'm so sorry, I wasn't—"

Courtney lifted a hand as she stalked toward the door farthest from the one Alice stood in front of. Each angry clack of her heels sent a shard through Alice's heart. She wanted to explain, tell her friend it wasn't her fault, but her lips locked up and her throat was swollen shut. This wasn't fair. Courtney had every right to be angry, but this wasn't Alice's fault. She'd been attacked, nearly killed, recovering for over a day, but the minute she was up she got out of bed—where she was supposed to be resting—and came to this stupid party. Dammit, she was even grounded now for all this mess!

She sniffed and it threatened to break into a sob. *No.* She clamped down tight over the ones trying to follow. They bubbled up with the feeling that she might throw up. *I'm not gonna cry. I'm fine. This is fine. You're fine.*

Something soft pressed to Alice's fingers. She opened her eyes, not realizing she'd closed them, and blinked past the blur of tears at Chess. He took her other hand, holding both of them in his gloved ones, the white fabric tickling faintly. His violet gaze was dark in the party lighting, his eyebrows pinched. He tucked his head forward a little, meeting her gaze.

Alice waved a hand. "I'm fine."

"You always say that." He squeezed her hands. "What happened? You just disappeared on us."

The last thing she wanted was to have this conversation right now, tonight, and here of all places. "I already said it. There was a—"

"—problem at the pub," he finished with her, heaving a dejected sigh. "I know. But that can't be it. Can it?" His voice lifted in a plea, like he was begging for something to believe other than she'd flaked on them because of her job without so much as a text.

No, that's not it. "It's a long story."

"I've got nothing but time, if you ever feel like telling it."

"You wouldn't believe me if I did."

"At least you would've told me. I'm your friend, Alice. You're supposed to be able to talk to me." He dropped her hands and stepped over to the fire pit.

Alice watched his back, the cape billowing behind him. Her fingers curled into fists. They were her friends. Courtney was her best friend, the only person who knew what the hell was going on for real. If she wanted to act like Alice had ever just ditched her, fine. If Chess wanted to feel some type of way, fine. Everyone could be in their feelings; Alice gave no more damns. She was angry and tired and didn't feel like dealing with these two right now.

"Can you take me home?"

Chess glanced up. "Yeah. Lemme say bye to Courtney first."

Alice dug into her bag and offered him the card. "Give this to her for me, since she probably doesn't wanna see my face right now."

He hesitated, then took the card with a nod. "See you out front." He tucked a top hat under his arm, then headed inside.

◊ ◊ ◊

Neither Alice nor Chess said anything for the first several minutes of the ride. R&B music filled the silence, with him focused on the road and her focused on nothing in particular as she stared out her window. That is, until his hand closed over hers.

She glanced at him in surprise. He stole a look at her, then back to the road. "Are you okay?"

No. "I will be."

He squeezed her fingers. "Does whatever's going on have to do with Brionne?"

"No." She shook her head, but that wasn't the whole truth. "Yes? I don't . . ."

"It's okay."

"It's not!" She didn't mean to shout. But extra points to Chess for not pulling away. In fact, he squeezed her hand again and stayed silent. She snorted a laugh, though nothing was funny. "It's not. And yeah, it's fucked up, things with Brionne. She was just minding her business, wasn't looking to hurt anyone, just trying to get home from a stupid game, and now she's dead."

Chess turned the music down but didn't say anything. He pulled over and parked, but left the car running. They sat in silence. Well, the car was silent. Alice's head was a furor of anger and fear.

"It could've been me," she finally said. "It could still be me." Tears slipped down her cheeks. She stared at the dashboard and sniffed, wiping at her face with her free hand.

"It's not fair," Chess murmured.

"It's not," she whimpered around a shuddering breath. "None of it. My mom freaks out every time I don't answer my phone, 'cause I could be dead in a ditch somewhere. Talkin' about how I'm all she's got and she's afraid to lose me. I used to say she's just being extra, but now . . ." Alice shook her head. "She ain't wrong. It's as possible as anything else."

Chess stroked his thumb over the back of her hand. "I'm sorry."

Alice snorted. "You didn't do anything." She swiped at her eyes again.

"I know. I'm still sorry."

She shook her head, swallowing to try to ease the tightness in her throat. She really could end up dead somewhere. Almost did trying to tie up loose ends for Hatta. Then got grounded for trying to be a good friend. Then lost her friend anyway for trying to do her job. She sure was trying to do an awful lot of stuff for an awful lot of people and failing spectacularly at it.

"I'm doing everything right, or trying to, and it can still go all wrong." *I'm protecting the world. Who'd protect me?*

"I would."

Alice blinked. "What?"

"I'd protect you." Chess held her gaze, his violet eyes soft in the darkness of the car. His thumb kept stroking her hand.

Her face warmed. She hadn't realized she'd said that out loud. "How?" Her eyes dropped down to his lips.

"Whatever way it took." He bit his lower one.

A small shiver moved through Alice, and she forced her attention back to his eyes. He leaned toward her. She felt herself pull toward him, too.

Her phone buzzed so loud it practically screamed.

Alice's eyes widened and she drew back, scrambling to get at it.

You better be on your way.

"My mom." She sank down into the seat.

Chess cleared his throat, letting go of her hand. "Better get you home, then."

"Y-yeah." *Oh god, what just happened? Or almost happened!*

Chess pulled back onto the road and they rode the rest of the way in silence. Alice wasn't sure if she wanted to hurry up and get home or for it to take a while. Before she could make up her mind, they stopped in front of her house.

"Chess . . . Thanks. For the ride."

He grinned, though it didn't reach his eyes. "Of course."

"See you later." She climbed out of the car and headed for the porch. He waited until she reached her door, then waved before pulling off.

Alice watched until his taillights turned the corner at the end of the block.

"Oh god, what the hell was that? What the hell am I *doing*?" She rubbed her face with both hands. Her and Chess. They almost . . .

The thought sent a not-entirely-unpleasant fluttery feeling through her. "So stupid."

Her shoes dangling from her fingers, her feet cold from the concrete, Alice pushed into her house, closed the door, and sank back against it. Mom sat on the living room couch in her pajamas, head wrapped, TV off, book in hand.

"Well, now." Mom snapped the book shut. Her eyes played over Alice from head to toe. "You look nice."

Alice tossed her keys into the cat-shaped dish on a nearby table. "Hey, Ma."

"'Hey, Ma'?" Mom cocked an eyebrow. "Folk gettin' shot, I don't hear from *my* child for over twenty-four hours, and all I get is, 'hey, Ma'?" She kept her voice even, which was a good sign. But this was a trap. Alice knew it was a trap. No answer would be the right one. But not answering would be the worst.

"Well?" Mom asked.

I don't need this shit right now. "I'm sorry." It wasn't an answer, but at least it was something.

Mom released a slow sigh, then patted the couch beside her. Reluctant, Alice schlepped over and flopped down.

Setting her book aside, Mom angled herself to face Alice. "I know you're almost grown. Meaning you can *almost* not answer when I call, and *almost* not return my texts, for over twenty-four hours. But not yet."

Here we go. Alice resisted the urge to massage the ache building in from her temples.

"I'd hoped you'd still respect me enough to do all that even when you *are* grown."

"I do." Alice fixed her gaze on the carpet. "I already told you, I put my phone in airplane mode on accident."

"Don't feed me no lines, Alison. You don't put your phone on airplane mode on actual airplanes, and I'm supposed to believe it happened on accident?" She pressed her lips together, then clicked her tongue. "Sound like something Courtney would say to her momma."

"It's true, though." It wasn't, but Alice had nothing else.

"Okay, say it is. Even still, if this was the first time you didn't respond for hours, I wouldn't be sayin' nothing. It happens more and more lately." Mom sighed. "You been stayin' out late, not answering your phone, now not coming home? You know I don't play that. Especially now."

"I know—"

"A woman lost her daughter one week ago, for no reason. That baby just gone. Then mine is nowhere to be found. How am I supposed to react to that?"

"I'm sorry," Alice repeated. "I promise I am."

"Then why you tryin' me?"

"I'm not! I just . . ." She took a breath and searched the ceiling before shrugging. "It was this one time. And it was an accident. I'm sorry. I know you're shook up after what happened to Brionne and everything, but I promise I'm okay. I'm not doing nothing, gettin' in no trouble, just hanging out with my friends and stuff. Can I get a little space, maybe?" Alice hunched her shoulder and put on what she hoped was her best puppy dog face.

Mom huffed. "Space. Sure. You got space, right up there in that room for two weeks. Keep it up and you'll spend every spare minute until you're grown in there. And as far as stuff, is there some pair of legs sniffing around I need to watch out for?"

"Ma!" That's what Mom called boys. Legs. Because *that* made all the sense.

Mom lifted her hands. "I'm not saying more than what I said, and I can say that. You know the rule: Two things you cannot bring to my door are babies and police." She pushed up from the couch, took her book, and headed for the kitchen.

Alice sank into the couch cushions, shaking with the effort not to cry. *I give up.*

There was no point in fighting. Mom believed what she believed, and nothing short of the truth would make her believe otherwise. If she would even believe the truth.

Daddy would. The sudden thought of her father pressed the dam even more. If he was here, he'd at least hear her out. If he was here, she probably wouldn't be a Dreamwalker, so it wouldn't matter.

"I made brownies," Mom called from the kitchen. "If you aren't full on cake. Could've at least brought me a piece."

"I'll get some later." Alice bolted to her feet and headed for the stairs. Mentioning food meant the talk was over, for now, and she was free to go. She hurried to her room and closed the door behind her.

Letting her bag drop from her arm, she flopped face first onto the bed. She didn't even bother getting out of the costume, just wormed her way under her blanket and pulled it up over her head. The press of paws against her shoulder meant Lewis had come to check on her. She stuck a hand out from her comforter fort and was rewarded with the bump of a furry head against her fingers, letting her scratch his ears.

"At least I still have one friend." She drew back the covers, smirking faintly at the cat.

Lewis sprang up and hissed, hackles raised, before bolting under the bed.

Alice jumped. "The hell, cat? Make that *no* friends, you furry jerk."

"Oh, I wouldn't say that."

Panic bolted through Alice like lightning. She flung the blanket off and sat up, her eyes fixing on the dark figure standing just inside her window.

The Black Knight waved. "You got me, princess."

Ten

VISITING HOURS ARE OVER

Alice sat frozen on her bed as the Black Knight lowered himself to the bench in her bay window, a finger lifted to where his lips would be behind his helmet. "Let's not get Mommy involved, yes? That would be unfortunate."

That shook her out of her shock. Anger coiled in her gut, but the panic didn't wane completely. "Don't threaten my mother."

"I'm not." He plucked a stuffed tiger from the small stack of old dolls in the corner and started stroking it evil genius–like. "Just suggesting we use our indoor voices. I don't want to pick a fight. Leastwise not with you."

"Funny, I didn't get that impression last time we met." A quick glance around the room revealed nothing Alice could use as a weapon. If he came at her again, she'd be defenseless.

"It's the helmet. Freaks people out." He continued stroking the stuffed cat. "You look tense."

"I wonder why," she bit out, fingers twisting in the sheets.

"Don't be. I'm here as a friend." He sat the animal aside and patted its head. "You delivered my message. I appreciate that." He settled into the corner of the window at a lean, the hilt of his sword visible over his shoulder.

The sight of it sent a shudder through her. "What do you want?"

"The Eye. But you know that, so I'm guessing you meant to ask 'what are you doing here?'" He gestured at her with a flourish. "To visit my favorite Dreamwalker. And thank you for a job well done."

"Stop playing games," she spat between clenched teeth. "I'm not in the mood."

"Pity. Games are such fun." He pushed to his feet, and it took everything in Alice not to recoil. "Seriously, princess, job well done."

"Enough with the nicknames!"

He tilted his head to the side. "You're dressed like one."

"Get out, before I throw you out that window." Her threat probably didn't mean much considering he'd whupped her ass already.

"Ahh. You wound me." He set his hands against his chest. "Even so, you held up your end of our bargain. That deserves a reward. Brace yourself."

Before she could ask what he meant, a flare of agony tore through her stained hand, like something eating it from the inside. She dropped to her side, clutching her wrist. The mark glowed against her skin.

Hands gripped her shoulders. "Breathe through it." The Black Knight knelt beside her. She wanted to shake him off but hadn't regained the control of her body stolen by pain. She couldn't even scream.

He drew his sword, touched the edge to her palm. She felt the sensation of tiny fingers peeling back her skin, as the taint swept into the blade, blending with the black. It lasted only a few seconds, but it left her palm clean and her head spinning.

"It's almost over. I promise." He curled his gloved hand over hers.

Everything twisted in on itself as her vision danced. Her stomach threatened to roll up past her lips as something hooked beneath her knees and she was lifted. She sank into his arms.

"No," she gasped. *Please.*

He shushed her as the sky poured across her vision, white and blinding. Scorching cold creeping along her limbs. Her heart blasted away at her ribs. The rush of blood howled in her ears.

She couldn't move, could barely breathe. The warmth from his arms, his body, was the only thing keeping the cold from consuming her completely. Part of her wished it would. The other part struggled against the darkness creeping at the edges of her vision.

"That's it, kitten. Rest now." His voice washed over her, stealing what little fight she had left.

Darkness claimed her.

Ehhnn, ehhnn, ehhnn, ehhnn, ehhnn.

Her head pounding with the echoes of her alarm, Alice cracked her eyes open. Daylight streamed across her bedroom floor, gathered in her mirror, and darted across her ceiling in reflective fractures. The device in question rattled facedown on her nightstand. Fumbling with a couple of pens, she shoved them and a notebook aside to grip and silence the damn thing.

That's when last night came rushing back in a flash of darkness and pain. She bolted upright with a shout, whirling to face her empty window. Her chest heaved, her heart drowning in her attempt to take in enough air. She nearly slapped herself jerking her hand up to look at it. The mark was gone. It wasn't a dream.

The Black Knight had been here. In. Her. Room.

The panic from last night slammed into her full force, and she scrambled out of bed and raced for the bathroom, tripping over herself twice in the process. She hadn't eaten anything in almost two days, but her stomach worked to empty itself anyway. Aching, and with a mouth that tasted of snot and sick, she stumbled over to the sink. The shock of cold water against her skin dissolved the remaining haze of sleep over her brain. She rinsed her mouth out until it stung so bad she couldn't feel her tongue.

Shower. She needed a shower.

After standing under hot water for lord knows how long, throwing some moisturizer in her hair, and pulling on some clothes, she edged back into her bedroom. The space felt . . .

corrupted somehow, the air heavy and oppressive, the light—bright as it was—dimmer.

That bastard had been in her room.

Her skin felt like it wanted to crawl right off her. She grabbed her purse and her phone and raced into the hall, slamming the door behind her.

In her *room*.

A shudder rolled through her, and she started down the hall. "Mom?"

An empty house greeted her. A sliver of fear slithered down her spine.

Don't panic. This didn't mean anything. It was Sunday morning. Mom was probably at church. *Why didn't she wake me?*

Someone had to be dying or dead for Mom to let her miss service.

Don't. Panic. Alice checked her mother's room and bathroom. Empty, save for Carol lounging on the pillows like she wasn't supposed to. Lewis was curled in a small chair in the corner. No gospel music on the radio, no T.D. Jakes on the TV.

Alice raced for the stairs. "Mom?" she called, louder this time. The living room was empty, too. So was the kitchen, but a slip of paper rested on the breakfast bar.

> *Went to worship without you.*
> *You were dead sleep, guess you partied hardy.*
> *Left some breakfast in the oven.*
> *Going to see Grandma Kingston after service.*
> *Take that cubed beef out of the freezer no*
> *later than 12.*

♥ you, Baby Moon.
PS—I asked Mrs. Hughes to keep an eye on
things while I'm gone, but call me if you
need anything.

Alice sank onto the nearby stool. Mom was okay. Thank god.

After Dad died, Grandma Kingston slowly slipped away. Dementia, Alzheimer's—the doctors couldn't say what was wrong. Dad was her only child, so now Alice and Mom looked after her. Some days were good days; she was her whip-smart self and knew everything and everyone. Some days were hard days, with Grandma Kingston not so much as acknowledging their existence.

Shaking her head, Alice shoved the thoughts aside. After last night she wasn't sure she could keep any food down, but she needed to try. Surprisingly, she smashed the full plate Mom left, loaded up with bacon, eggs, hash browns, sausage, the works. Full, and slightly less nauseous, she called Hatta. No answer. She tried again. Twice. Still nothing. No answer on the pub line, either.

Pacing the kitchen, Alice argued with herself over the decision to sneak out. On the one hand, something might be wrong, with no one answering the damn phone. And she needed to tell Hatta that Black Knight bastard had been *in her room*. On the other, everything might be fine. Plus she seemed to be okay—the mark was gone—but that most definitely wouldn't be the case if Mom came back while she was out. And the Black Knight could show up anytime, anywhere, even on this side of the Veil.

The clock on the microwave read just after noon. Church would let out soon, if Pastor wasn't on a roll or the Holy Ghost didn't take over the service. Visits with Grandma Kingston usually lasted for a few hours, sometimes more. If Alice was back by three, four at the latest, she should be fine.

"I'm really gonna do this." She shook the jitters from her hands. Slayer of fear itself, and she was worried about crossing her mom. With damn good reason, but still. "Gut up, Kingston."

Before she lost her nerve she rushed out the back and over the fence, hoping to avoid the nosy eyes of her across-the-street neighbor. Mrs. Hughes used to go to church with Alice's family and babysat Alice when she was younger. Now she was Mom's watchdog, keeping an eye on things from the rocker on her porch. Thankfully, the backyard wasn't in her line of sight.

The train ride across town seemed longer than usual. Normally, she spent the time texting back and forth with Courtney and Chess, but neither of them had messaged her since last night. Instead she burned through her lives on Candy Crush, jumping every time a notification dropped onto her screen, afraid it was her mom, but it was from Court's and Chess's feeds. They were full of Snaps and Instagram pics from the party. The hollow ache in her chest returned. It looked like they had a blast without her.

It didn't take long to reach the pub. She pushed through the door and nearly tripped down the stairs when she spotted Hatta doubled over on his knees, his arms wrapped around himself. Papers lay scattered around him. Harsh coughs rattled his body as he choked on his efforts to take in air.

"Hatta!" She flung her bag aside and dropped beside him. "What's wrong?"

He pushed her off, shaking his head. "Go."

It took a moment for her to realize what he meant. "No, I'm not leaving you." She shifted on her knees to get a better grip on him.

He shuddered. The feel of it traveled up her arms. He tried to pull away. "N-no . . . get . . ."

"I'm staying here, Addison," she barked.

"Get." His head snapped up as he clutched at his chest.

Alice nearly recoiled when their eyes met. The multi-colored quality of his irises blended, melding into a burning orange like embers in a fire. The whites turned black and stuck out sharply against his sickly pale skin.

"Oh god," Alice whispered, her hand at her mouth.

"Get . . . Maddi," he gasped, gesturing shakily at the hallway.

"Maddi?" Alice repeated with a glance over her shoulder. "Maddi. M-Maddi!" she shouted, tightening her hold on Hatta as he sank toward the ground.

Alice screamed for the girl again, her fingers fisted in Hatta's shirt as he sprawled across the floor, still, lifeless. She smoothed his hair from his face as she leaned in to make sure he was breathing. It escaped him in static pants, ragged and labored.

"Okay, okay—okay." She didn't want to leave him, but she had to. She was on her feet and at the hallway in an instant. "Maddi!"

The bartender nearly slammed into her, stumbling to a stop

with a flail of limbs. "Ruckus jumps the way?" she asked, normally drowsy eyes alert.

"Help him!" Alice raced to Hatta's side. She hit the floor next to him, her knees punished even through her jeans.

Maddi's shoulders hitched. "Oh . . . oh no! Okay, one bird is not two." She raced behind the bar. "I know, I know, I know." Bottles clacked and glasses clinked as she rummaged around. Something hit the floor with a smash, and she cursed.

Alice shifted so Hatta's head rested on her lap. She brushed fingers through his hair and over his forehead. He was hot to the touch, but the whole of him shivered violently. She shushed him when he groaned. "It's okay, you're okay. You'll be fine, I've got you . . ."

He had to be. Thoughts of anything else tore a hole inside her.

Maddi scrambled over, clutching what looked like an old, black iron jewelry box. She sat it down with a scrape and reached to snatch a thin gold chain from Hatta's neck. A sliver of a key dangled at the end. Maddi shoved it into the top of the box and twisted. The lid creaked open.

Alice clutched Hatta as the other girl lifted small vials filled with various colored liquids up to the light, shaking them one by one before replacing them. When Maddi finally found whatever she was looking for, she tore the cork free with her teeth.

"Wide the door," Maddi cooed as she tipped the vial against Hatta's lips. When it was empty, Maddi leaned in and pressed her ear to Hatta's chest. Everything fell deathly still, quiet, as they waited. For what, Alice wasn't sure.

Her fingers tapped Hatta's shoulders. Her body jostled his as her knees bounced.

"Still," Maddi snapped.

Alice froze, throat working in a thick swallow.

Pleasepleaseplease . . .

"Too much of nothing." Maddi straightened and went through the selection process again, pouring another vial down his throat, then listening at his chest. "Come on, come *on*." Her hands shook as she searched a third time.

Hatta's breath sputtered and choked, like an engine on the verge of giving out.

Alice squeezed his hand. "You will live," she whispered, her fingers wound around his. "You'll be okay. A-are you listening?" Shivers wracked her body. Tears blurred her vision. She shook her head then bent forward, her brow pressed to his. "Come back to me."

Eleven

CONTAGIOUS

The clinking of vials, like the distant ringing of bells, sung a sorrowful melody. Maddi poured another potion down Hatta's throat. The fifth or sixth, Alice had lost count.

As Maddi administered the potions, she chanted Verses of various lengths, the words lost beneath her breath. Another elixir tipped from her fingers before she leaned in to listen to Hatta's chest again. "Hear me, Addison . . ."

Alice couldn't manage words, try as she might. Instead she focused on breathing, which had become increasingly difficult.

Hatta jolted with a harsh gasp, startling both Alice and Maddi, who jerked back. His eyes flew open, rolling in his head before fixing on a point overhead. The black in his eyes lightened to gray, and the fiery glow of his irises dulled.

"By the Breaking." Maddi heaved a relieved sigh and leaned back on one hand while the other pressed to her face.

A short laugh escaped Alice as she wiped her cheeks and nose with her shirtsleeve.

Maddi checked Hatta's vitals, holding his eyes open with her fingers to examine them, feeling for his pulse along his wrist. He didn't seem to notice, his gaze unfocused, cloudy. At least his breathing eased and the shivering lessened, but he was still burning up. Alice brushed damp hair from his face, pausing as she noticed a change. Green strands had lightened to blue. She toyed with them while she watched Maddi work.

"What's going on?" Alice asked.

"I'm . . . not sailing high." Maddi gathered the empty vials scattered across the floor. She placed them in the box and snapped it shut. Alice noticed only one vial had anything left in it. Maddi locked the box, then slipped the key into her pocket.

That wasn't comforting. Alice continued to toy with Hatta's hair.

"I have . . ." Maddi seemed to consider her words, pausing in action as her gaze swept the room. "I have seen a sickness. Two in one. Curse and sorrow." She held up two fingers, then tapped them together in a scissoring motion. "Two in one."

Alice didn't understand. But with Maddi, she hardly ever understood. "Curse and sorrow?"

Maddi sat back, wrapping her arms around her lifted knees. "Of brisk wings and battles." She glanced away, her face scrunched. "Her darkness. Poisonous."

Her darkness. Alice had heard that phrase before, when

the Black Knight first attacked her. She had a good idea who Maddi meant. "The Black Queen."

Maddi's head bobbed. "Verse, powerful. A cursed, poisoned body. A winged mind." Her shoulders hunched, and she sank behind her knees even more. "Bad crows, over and over. In here." She tapped the side of her head. "It's called the Madness."

Alice frowned. "It . . . what?"

"Dreams are not in Wonderland." Maddi's voice was so soft, Alice barely heard the words. "The hungry dark." Maddi swallowed. "Everything gone to near away."

With each word, the fist around Alice's heart tightened its grip, until she felt she might break. She had no idea what was going on. "I don't . . . I don't understand. What's wrong with Addison?"

Maddi pushed to her feet, disappeared behind the bar with the box, and emerged empty-handed a moment later, glass crunching under her feet. "*Maybe* is a word."

What the hell does that even mean? "Whatever it is, can you cure it?"

Maddi shrugged, her lips trapped between her teeth. "Can't say, no how. No way, knowing not a least."

Great. The last thing Alice needed right now was more nonsense talk. More than usual, anyway. She looked back to Hatta, resting peacefully. The idea that this darkness was turning him inside out sent her stomach roiling. "What now?"

"Away, away, fly to roost."

"I . . . I don't . . . what?"

Maddi made a frustrated sound before pointing at Hatta. "Rest."

"Oh." Alice carefully finagled from beneath Hatta, gently laying his head against the ground. "You take that side, I'll take this one. On three." She shifted her hold to grip Hatta under his arm. When Maddi did the same, she started the count. "One, two, three."

The girls heaved. Alice nearly toppled from the momentum, surprised at how light he was. The two girls got him up, his arms over their shoulders.

Thankfully, he stirred enough to get his feet under himself and help them propel him along the hall. Maddi called out directions, right turn, left turn. The back of the pub always seemed to grow larger and larger, expanding like some sort of mystical labyrinth.

The three of them wound up in a room Alice had never seen before. The girls maneuvered him onto the bed, where he sank against the sheets with a faint murmur, then didn't move again save for the steady rise and fall of his chest. Every now and then he'd twitch with a cough.

"Sleep now, starshine." Maddi made her way to the door.

"That's it?" Alice didn't want to leave him like this. "We leave him here to suffer?"

"Only fish flip-flop." Maddi leveled a look at her, swallowed, breathed in slow, then pushed more words out. "There . . . is . . . nothing else. Done." She disappeared through the door.

Alice hesitated, glancing at Hatta. He looked relatively at peace, his color still way off, but it enhanced the otherworldly appeal he always exuded. It made him seem that much more . . . ethereal.

You sound like a lovesick puppy. She forced her eyes away

from him and to the rest of the room. It was similar to the one she'd been treated in, though larger, the walls darker, more rust colored than plain tan. A large portrait hung directly across from the bed, the gold frame a twisting flow of gleaming metal. The picture itself poured across the canvas in a mix of color and light. A golden castle set amid a sea of green seemed to twinkle against the painted sky of pinks and blues. Flowers and trees danced in an invisible wind.

Impossible. Alice blinked, and the brushstrokes settled into stillness. It had to be a trick of the light, she told herself, and turned her gaze elsewhere. A few articles of clothing littered the floor, a haphazard trail she followed to a long, dark-stained dresser. A massive thing, the drawers scuffed and worn with use, knickknacks dotting the scratched surface. She plucked up one of several rings, stole a glance at the sleeping Hatta, and slid it onto her index finger. A simple band of silver, it fit perfectly. The metal warmed instantly.

She ran her fingers across the dresser, her eyes trailing the other items: a snow globe on a stack of old books, a Ziploc bag filled with all sorts of buttons, a half-empty bottle of cologne she barely resisted the urge to smell, a set of Figment Blade daggers still in the sheaths, scattered spools of thread of different colors—all strewn among various mugs and teacups of all shapes, sizes, and materials, stacked or alone. She went to remove the ring, planning to place it back in the pile of jewelry, but she hesitated. Glancing at the sleeping Hatta, she left it on, hoping he wouldn't mind, if he even noticed it was gone. It was some small piece of him she could keep with her and return when he recovered from . . . whatever this was. Grandma Kingston used to pray over little trinkets from friends and family; said it made it easier for the angels to know who she wanted them to look after.

Shoving her hand into her back pocket, she moved for the door but paused. She peered out into the hall, then hurried over to the bed, leaned in, and brushed a kiss to his brow. "You'll be okay."

"Mmm." He barely stirred.

Heat flushed her face and she hurried out, closing the door behind her.

In the bar, she found Maddi sweeping up the sea of shards on the floor. The pub was gonna run out of glasses at this rate.

"Tick-tock?" Maddi glanced up from her task.

Alice avoided making eye contact. "Went to the bathroom, splashed some water on my face."

"Mmhm." It didn't sound like Maddi believed her.

"What's the plan?" Alice slid onto a stool. "Or, idea."

Maddi kept sweeping. "Twinkle, twinkle. Not too far. Ideas, ideas." She paused, frowned at the floor, and then continued sweeping again. "Twinkle, twinkle, where you are." Dustpans full of glass went into the bin. "Twinkle."

Alice sat and waited while Maddi worked the broom furiously and muttered to herself. No use asking questions with the other girl wound up like this. Interrupting her while she was in the zone could make her lose whatever idea she was concocting. After putting the broom away, Maddi went back behind the bar. The way she scurried around, scooping up ice, selecting strawberries from a bowl, reminded Alice of a mouse.

"Black Queen." Maddi said the name like it tasted rotten in her mouth. "*Her* darkness. The Madness."

The whir of the blender filled the bar. Alice sat, her thoughts a jumbled mess, much like what was once fruit, ice, and juice. She doubted the outcome of her racing mind would be as tasty. The Black Knight had to have something to do with this. None of this shit started until he showed up.

Maddi clacked a glass on the bar.

"Thanks," Alice muttered as she lifted the drink to her lips.

Maddi poured a glass for herself.

The cool of the frozen strawberries did little to quell the unexpected burn of alcohol. She coughed, glanced at her glass and then at Maddi.

"Eat your veggies." Maddi shrugged as she drank her un-virgin daiquiri without flinching.

Alice swallowed and took another sip. It didn't sting as much this time. "He came to my house."

Maddi stopped fluttering about, mopping the counter, and looked at her.

"The Black Knight. He was in my room."

"It cannot cast its own shadow," she whispered, and started wiping again. "All gone."

Alice tugged at her hair, then wiped the excess cream against her thigh. "I really wish you'd . . ." She trailed off, looking at her now-clean hand. The roiling in her insides returned. "H-how did the Black Queen spread her darkness, again?"

Maddi didn't say anything for a moment, cleaning and reorganizing things behind the counter. She drew out a teal potion, then downed it. Groaning, she clutched at her throat, turning away to cough into a fist. For a second Alice was afraid she was choking, until she straightened and cleared her throat. "She used the Heart. It and the Eye were the source of her power."

Alice blinked rapidly, her head jerking back and forth. *What the—* She pointed at Maddi, staring. "So that's how you do it?"

"Do what?"

"Talk!"

The bartender made a face. "Couldn't I?"

"No, I mean—you sound not riddle-y."

Maddi lifted the empty vial. "Helps me straighten out words for human understanding. Hurts, though, so I don't use it unless it's important."

Something twisted in Alice chest. So this was how she turned into Serious Maddi. "This definitely counts. Are you okay?"

"I'm fine." Maddi flapped a hand. "As I was saying, the Black Queen's artifacts of power, born from the core of Wonderland, passed down from ruler to ruler. The Eye let her see things about people, places, things. Deep into them. Not like read their minds but, she could see *them*, and whatever ailed them.

"The Heart let her connect with her people and the land, able to draw on their essence to shape and influence both. That was before she corrupted the Heart and used it for the bad things." She went still. "She used it like a weapon. A scepter that pulled the darkness out of the ground. She sliced open her victims and poisoned them with it."

The whole time Maddi spoke, Alice couldn't move. She

couldn't talk, she couldn't think, all she could do was listen to how absolutely screwed they were. Because of her.

No. Nonono. Gripping the edge of the counter with one hand, her eyes fixed on the other, she forced the words free. "Could . . . could the Black Knight do this? Infect people with this darkness, this Madness?" He shared her other powers.

"Yes and no. Using her artifacts to command the Nox, the Black Queen forged the Vorpal Blade for her knight. He could infect others, but his power still paled in comparison to hers." Maddi turned a curious eye in Alice's direction. "Why?"

The trembling had intensified to full-blown shakes now. Hatta had said she was a conduit for a powerful Verse, meant to pass it on to an intended target. "I did it," she whispered. "It's my fault. H-he cut my hand! He put it in me! I gave it to Addison!" She shouted now, clutching her hand against her chest as it threatened to cave in on itself with each rattling breath. "I poisoned him!"

Twelve

THE PUZZLE

Alice gazed at Hatta, stretched across the bed. **His chest** rose and fell with erratic breaths, and his eyes rolled beneath his lids. His lips trembled as he spoke in his sleep, too quick and too quiet for her to make anything out. He jolted and twisted, as if caught in a nightmare.

He was.

Trapped in his mind, as Maddi had explained it, living horrors known only to him.

And it's my fault.

She reached for his hand, but hesitated. Her touch did this. So stupid, how had she not seen it? The Black Knight played her, and now Hatta was . . .

The ache in her chest cut off the thought. No, this wasn't going to happen. The knight wasn't going to win. Alice would find him and *beat* answers out of him if she had to. He was going to find this kitten had claws.

"Got it." Maddi entered the room, Hatta's phone lifted like a baton. Alice recognized the case covered in teacups. "Spoke with the Duchess. There's a way to help him." Maddi paused, her attention on Hatta.

Swiping her eyes, Alice cleared her throat to untie the knot lodged in it. "What did she say?"

"The Heart."

"The . . . what now?"

Maddi moved to lay a hand to his forehead, then pressed two fingers to his neck. "The Black Queen used the Heart to infect her victims, but it can cure them, too. The Red and White Queens hid the Heart. Only they know where to find it, and only a member of the royal family can then use it." She wrung the phone in her hands. "You have to fetch that piece of the puzzle."

Alice snorted a laugh that didn't have any real joy behind it. "And how am I supposed to 'fetch' a member of the royal family?"

"By asking very, very nicely. Follow me." Maddi led the way out of the room.

Alice hesitated, reluctant to leave Hatta's side, but followed Maddi out into the pub.

As Alice slid onto a stool, she stole a glance at the cat clock on the wall. He wagged his tail and cut his eyes back and forth, marking the seconds. Mom wouldn't be home for another few hours, giving Alice time to concentrate on helping Hatta.

Maddi slipped behind the bar, chewing her nails. "The Red Queen is missing, so that leaves us with one person who can help." She rapped her knuckles three times against the mirrored wall behind the bar. "Open my eyes."

The surface rippled like troubled waters. The bottles lining the shelves in front of the mirror vanished, along with the reflected image of the bar itself. When the waves settled, the mirror appeared more like a window.

Wonderland, with its pink-tinged sky and wildly colored plants, stretched out before her. The scene sped through the Glow as if it were on fast-forward, a bird's-eye view that crossed the Bubbles and ventured into distant territories. Eventually, everything slowed as the image came upon a castle.

"Where?" Alice whispered. Sparkling spires reached toward the sky. Archways and columns circled the levels lined with parapets cast in silver, polished marble, and crystal. The castle glistened like a jewel. Something about it pulled at her mind, a ghostly touch of familiarity.

"Legracia, the White Palace. Go and tell the White Queen what happened—we need their help." Maddi tapped the mirror again and the image faded, returning it to its original state, the bottles reappearing. "The Tweedles will meet you partway. Together, you'll go to Legracia, ask the Queen to reveal the location of the Heart; you go get it and bring them both back so she can use the Heart to cure Hatta."

Alice gazed at her reflection as she absorbed the information. Go to Legracia, get the White Queen, bring her and the Heart back. Alice's mind bubbled like a pot left to boil too long.

Blinking rapidly, she lifted her hands, waving them in the air. "Waitwaitwait. You want me to go to the White Queen and convince her to come help someone she tossed out of Wonderland on his ass. I don't know what happened between them; I don't know anything other than the Black Queen went bananas and started killing people, her daughters had to stop her, and people were exiled; it—I need something to work with here. Give me the whole story."

For a moment Maddi didn't say anything, just stared at Alice with this look on her face like she was debating whether or not to let her in on some secret. After the cat clock above the bar wagged two minutes' worth of tail flips, she set her hand to the mirror again.

The surface wavered and shifted, revealing the image of another castle. The spires reached just as high as Legracia's and shone just as bright, but the structure was wider, struck with more earthy colors, the stone appearing gold in the daylight. Larger, and more and more stunning the longer Alice gazed at it, this castle put Legracia to shame.

"This is Castle Emes, home to Her Royal Highness Portentia of Harts, High Queen of all Wonderland." Maddi's voice was soft, wistful almost. "Before she became the Black Queen." She waved her hand, and the image shifted, taking them into the castle. A world of gold glass reflected light every which way, painting the palace with cold flames. A throne sat at the center of the room, and on it perched a woman, her hair pulled back from her elfin face. Her flawless skin was rich copper and shine, almost as if a sheen of metal had been cast against her flesh.

"The Queen of Harts ruled with the love of her people and her daughters." The image revealed two girls who didn't look much older than Alice standing on either side of the throne, and a third little girl sitting in Portentia's lap. The child looked sweet, with a round, brown face and eyes the color of earth. Her hair was cotton candy pink and pulled into poofy pigtails atop her head. She couldn't be more than seven or eight. Well, the Wonderland equivalent of seven or eight.

One of her older sisters had red hair pleated away from her face and left to fall against her back in long braids, her skin like bronzed mahogany. There was something strikingly familiar about her slate gray eyes: sharp, focused, though sparkling with a hint of knowing mischief. The slight twist of her lips silently spoke of the same. The image shifted to the other daughter. Her skin was whipped-cream white, and her hair the color of snow. It fell over her shoulders, long enough to reach the floor. A warm smile stretched her slightly rounded face, and her dark eyes held such kindness.

"Mm. Almost forgot what they looked like." Maddi gazed at the image, sadness deepening lines in her face Alice had never noticed before. She sniffed before touching the mirror again. The scene warped into a forest Alice didn't recognize. A massive tree, several of its roots arching out of the ground, stood nestled amid bushes covered in violet leaves and sprouting roses.

Between the roots, small fingers dug at the grass, pulling, working, until a little white girl emerged from a hovel, hidden at the base of the tree. The girl, who looked as young as the small princess, pushed her hairband up from her plump face and glanced around. Her eyes widened and her mouth dropped open.

Alice smiled faintly. She'd reacted similarly her first time in Wonderland. The little girl quickly repositioned the headband, brushed dirt from the previously white apron tied over her blue dress, and hurried into the forest. She was adorable, from her curly blond hair to her shiny little Mary Janes.

"She comes and goes, the first human in Wonderland. First to walk the dreams. To fly and—" Maddi lifted a finger before rooting around behind the bar. Emerging with another teal potion, she downed it and nearly hacked up a lung again. "I *hate* using these."

She turned back to the image of the little girl. "This child was the first human being to set foot in Wonderland. The first Dreamwalker, although unintentional. To this day, no one's entirely sure how she managed to cross over, only that she did, and her presence set off a chain reaction within Wonderland's very makeup. That child crossing the Veil did something to it, weakened it, changed it, we're not sure. The result was the Nightmares became aware and started to try to cross it, to get to this world. At least, more frequently than they had in the past, to horrible effect."

"Right." Nightmares were attracted to humans. Ironic, humans being the only things that could kill them.

Maddi tapped the mirror again, and an image of the Glow faded into view. The human girl ran in circles, laughing as she chased the young princess with pink pigtails. "Princess Odette befriended the child. The two were inseparable for years, the human visiting Wonderland frequently. No one knew what was happening with the Nightmares at first. There were more sightings and attacks, but those had been increasing steadily over time anyway, due to the increase in the human population. Then, one day, both girls vanished in the Glow. A search party went after them. Days passed before the princess's body was discovered." The heaviness in her voice was so foreign. Alice wouldn't have believed it was Maddi if she wasn't sitting in the same room, watching the words fall from her lips.

The sorrowful tone tugged at her heart, but not as much as the image of the Queen and her two remaining daughters mourning near a small casket of crystal, the young princess resting inside. When the Queen threw herself atop the coffin, Alice had to look away, thankful the images didn't come with sound.

"The human girl was never found," Maddi continued, her voice thick. "Grief-stricken, Portentia sought the growing darkness left in the human child's wake, hoping to restore Odette's life."

Mercifully, the image shifted to the Queen alone, locked in some gloomy room. Reading by firelight, she frantically flipped pages, her attention rapt, her face gaunt and dark rings hugging her eyes.

"But nothing worked. She blamed the human world for her pain, saying if the child had never entered Wonderland, the princess would still be alive. Eventually, the darkness warped her mind. She became the Black Queen, and her kingdom transformed into the Harrows, dark heart of the Nox. Her ambitions turned from reviving her lost child to taking her revenge on mankind. But without humanity, Wonderland would not be. Destroying them would be destroying us, too, so some of us fought against her. The Black Queen ripped apart anyone who stood in her way."

The image shifted to the view of the palace, but the golden glow of Castle Emes was gone, now dark and shadowed. The entire palace was misshapen, formed from broken crystal with hard lines and jagged edges fused together like bone that hadn't healed correctly. Dark clouds swirled to fill the skies. Red lightning struck the ground.

Within the palace the Black Queen sat on her throne. Gone was Portentia's gentle bronze skin, replaced with harshness the color of stone. Her eyes were snow white, cold, and her features still beautiful—but pointed and sharp. Darkness and living shadow filled hidden corners of the room, enveloped her body, dancing and coiling, occasionally exposing naked skin. Beside her stood the original Black Knight. Alice shuddered. This one was taller, his armor more medieval, ragged and sharp, formed from the monstrous dark. The Vorpal Blade hung at his hip.

"Portentia's eldest daughters knew she had to be stopped, but couldn't bring themselves to kill her. So, with the help of Hatta, the Duchess, and a few others who once fought for the Black Queen but now saw what was in store for us all, the princesses mounted their forces for a final assault. It was a hard battle; so many died, but they won. They sealed her away deep in the Nox and scattered her items of power to prevent her resurrection. Then they split the kingdom, became the Queens Red and White."

Maddi wasn't looking at the mirror. In fact, she had her back to it. When she pulled her hand away, the surface distorted, shattered, then re-formed to its original state, bottles and all.

"Hatta and those like him were exiled, but given a duty to guard weak points in the Veil that had been discovered. They were then charged with finding Dreamwalkers, humans sensitive to the Veil, to help protect it. It's funny. A human started all this, and now humans are the only ones strong enough to keep it from escalating. Sure, we can fight the Nightmares, but not like you. You hold the greatest power over your fears."

That made Alice feel like shit. Sure, none of *that* was her fault, but still. She slid from her seat, then made her way around the bar to wrap her arms around Maddi. The Poet stiffened, blinking up at her.

"Thanks. I know going through all of that had to be hard."

Maddi relaxed enough to return the hug. After a squeeze, they parted. Maddi started mopping the countertop, and Alice went for her discarded backpack, tossed to the other side of the room when she first ran to Hatta.

"Is that why he wants the Eye?" she asked. "To resurrect the Black Queen or whatever?"

Maddi stilled, her shoulders hunching slightly. "That is one possibility. The Eye can do many things, *if* you can use it. But our focus is on the Heart now."

"How long will it take to get to Legracia?"

"Once you cross over, four, maybe five days."

Shit. That was going to take much longer than a couple hours. Maybe. She could go in, travel for a week, but return to find she'd only been gone an hour. Or an actual week. Freaking Wonderland.

"Okay, but if I go, someone needs to keep an eye on my mom. The Black Knight was in my freaking house, and he's going after people I care about. I can't leave her without protection."

"One sec." Maddi hurried down the back hall, her footsteps clapping against the tile. She returned several seconds later, Alice's Figment Blades and belt in hand. "Take these with you."

Alice shoved the daggers into her backpack. She already felt a bit better. "Thanks. What about while I'm gone?"

"The Duchess and I will take care of everything. We'll make sure she's well-guarded. I swear."

That was somewhat comforting. Alice had never seen Maddi fight, or heard anyone say she could, but it was better than nothing. Maybe she could convince Mom to spend some time with Grandma Kingston or something.

"Okay, okay, so I'm gonna need to grab a few things from home before crossing." And change her clothes. There was no way she was wearing a pair of good jeans and booties on a four-day trek through the wilderness.

"I'll get you some supplies, rations and stuff. You'll be back soon?" Maddi asked, a slightly desperate tinge to her voice.

"I can't leave until late. I'm kinda grounded, so I'm gonna have to sneak out."

Maddi arched an eyebrow. "You have a plan for that?"

"The start of one. I'll figure it out. Hopefully, I can manage this before shit hits the fan." She shrugged into her pack. "Call me if anything changes with Hatta?"

Maddi gave her a thumbs-up, and Alice headed out. On the train home, worry ate at Alice like an infection. She tried calling Courtney to let her know what was going on at least. Straight to voice mail.

"Fine, if she wants to be like that." She sent a text with a breakdown of what was happening and noting that she had to go into Wonderland. She didn't know how long, but it would be longer than anytime before and she might need a cover, especially since she was supposed to be grounded, if Court was done being mad at her for being late to her party because she nearly freaking died.

Uuuuggggh! After a few calming breaths—irritating as hell—she called Chess.

He picked up on the first ring, like always. "Hey."

"Hey. Look, I gotta cancel, no, ask for a rain check on our undate tonight."

"Uh-huh. Problem at work?"

She scoffed. "Way to sound broken up about it. And no, a friend is really sick and I gotta help 'em out." Then there was the whole being-grounded thing.

"Oh . . ."

That's right, oh. Jerk. But she couldn't be mad. Not for real. He didn't know what was really going on. Courtney did. On top of that, Alice and Chess almost . . . she wasn't sure, but the memory sent this fluttery feeling through her and, ugh, this was not the time.

"Who?" he asked, sounding all interested now.

"Friend of the family. If you talk to Court, tell her I sent her a message and it's important. She doesn't have to talk to me, just read it."

"Okay. Look, Alice, I didn't mean—"

"I know. It's cool, talk to you later." She hung up, anger and a billion other emotions simmering through her as she shifted against the uncomfortable plastic seat. The city whipped by outside her window as they rode over the platform just outside Little China, the angled buildings modeled after old Hong Kong architecture, pale and rustic in the daylight.

Her phone buzzed in her hand. Chess. She didn't answer. She didn't know what to say to him, and she couldn't get wrapped up in that right now. She had to focus. She'd deal with it all when she got back and after Hatta was cured. Her phone buzzed again. Her annoyance spiked, until she saw a message from her mom.

On my way home. Did you take the beef out of the freezer?

She hadn't. "Shit. Shit shit shit *shit*."

"Hey!" An old Chinese lady a few seats in front of her turned around, frowning. "Language, young lady."

"Yes, ma'am," Alice responded automatically. "Sorry."

Shaking her head, the lady faced forward, muttering something about kids.

Alice sank in her seat. How the hell was she gonna do this?

Thirteen

HURRY

By the time Alice climbed the fence and dropped into her backyard, she had formed what she hoped was a solid plan. She'd sneak out tonight and leave a note saying she went to school early. She hadn't since she stopped playing softball, but it was believable. As far as skipping class, it was risky as hell, but an email from her mom should cover her. Unless they did something like call to confirm, but hopefully it wouldn't go that far. If it did, detention, suspension, or whatever they threw at her was more than worth saving Hatta's life.

Alice couldn't see the driveway from here, but she didn't think Mom was home yet. At least she hadn't gotten any furious texts or calls. She slipped into the kitchen, one Figment Blade in hand. A careful search of the house, closets included, left her confident that she was alone, at least for now. She slipped the dagger back into her pack and set it on the kitchen counter before going for the freezer and yanking out the beef. It was forbidden, but she tossed it on a plate and shoved it in the microwave, hitting defrost. Fifteen minutes. She'd check on it in five.

There was no telling how much time she had to get things together for tonight, so she better get started. Upstairs, she packed a bag, throwing in an extra set of clothes, just in case. Once she was sure she had everything she needed, she headed downstairs to check the garage for anything that might look useful.

The smoky smell of exhaust and oil hung in the air and only seemed to grow stronger as she reached the cluttered shelves and storage cabinets on the other side. Cartons of Christmas decorations, yard tools, and old clothes and toys likely didn't hold any potential treasures. Alice maneuvered her way to the workbench.

Pristine, organized, and untouched since her dad died, the whole area was off-limits thanks to an unspoken understanding between her and Mom. It had taken months for Mom to donate a lot of Dad's things, and she kept more than she let on, but this? This was a frozen shrine to his memory.

Her lungs tight with a sudden difficulty breathing, Alice inched toward the tool chest. She ran her fingers over the silver surface, the metal cool to the touch. A misting of dust covered the tools spread over the breadth of the bench. Soft light caught in the steel, causing it to shine.

Alice could see her father clearly in her mind, taking each tool from its place and disappearing around to the front of the car, the hood lifted, and the radio blasting "Word Up!" by Cameo. The whir of the air compressor, the studded roar of the ratchet, six-year-old her sitting in the front seat eating a sandwich while her legs swung as she asked a million questions. He always had an answer, patiently responding while simultaneously maneuvering through the complexities of the engine. Eventually, her questions turned into complaints as she grew older: she was hot, she was tired, she didn't understand why she had to be out in this stank garage learning how to check fluids and change out crap.

"'Cause there's not an app for that." He had stared at her phone and then at her until she put it away. "What's a man's most useful resource?"

Alice rolled her eyes so hard she saw the back of her skull. "His head," she regurgitated. She'd only heard this a million times.

"Right." He wiped his hands on a rag that probably added oil instead of removing it. "To know a thing, or be able to learn a thing, makes good men great. That goes double for Black men, triple for Black women. Knowledge is power, and this world is set against you knowing anything, so when someone's trying to teach you something, pay attention. Take it all in, you hear?"

"It's just changing the oil." She gestured at the car, annoyed with yet another speech on how she had to do better, think better, fly faster, blah blah blah.

"It's never *just* anything." He held out the wrench, the silver gleaming in his dark, sludge-covered fingers. "I showed you. You do it."

The memory faded, leaving Alice in the shadow of his presence, the quiet of the garage amplifying the sound of her choked sobs as she tried to stifle them. Her eyes burned. Her throat closed off. Her face ached like it was too small for her skull, stretched open to fit. Grief burrowed its way into her chest and dove for her stomach, pulling her insides with it. She'd give anything to have him back, lectures and all. She'd listen to a thousand of his lessons if it meant hearing his voice again. She'd tell him about Hatta, about the Black Knight, about all of this, and he'd know what to do. He always knew what to do. He always . . .

Fighting the scream building inside, Alice backed away from the workbench. Her feet caught in a hose coiled on the floor and she went down. The sting in her hands and legs faded under the hurt washing through her. Gathering her knees to her chest, she folded her arms around them, buried her face in the sleeves of her shirt, and let go.

She had no idea how long she sat there, sobbing into her arms, until pressure at her shoulders alerted her to another's presence.

"Alice?" Mom whispered.

She didn't want to look up, not yet, but the touch slid up and down her arms, then over the top of her head. She sniffed, wiping snot away, then on her jeans. Finally, she glanced up. "H-hey."

Mom, her expression pinched with concern, clicked her tongue. "Oh, baby, what's wrong?"

That set off another wave of tears.

"Okay, okay." Mom settled next to Alice, wrapped her arms around her, and held just tight enough that she felt like she wouldn't come apart entirely. "It's okay."

Alice cried for a few minutes more, soaking the sleeve of

Mom's blazer, which smelled of her jasmine perfume. The whole time, Mom spoke in soft sounds, hums, and whispers. The words sounded like nonsense strung together, muddled by her crying, but she didn't care. All that mattered was the voice was there, with her.

When Alice felt like she could manage more than two words without breaking down, she lifted her head from her mom's shoulder, sniffing all over again.

"There you go." Mom brushed Alice's hair back, swiped glistening trails from her own face, and released a huff. "What are you doing out here?" There was no scolding in her tone.

"I—I, um." Alice wiped her face to give her a few seconds to think. "I—I needed a screwdriver."

"There's one in the kitchen drawer." Mom fussed over Alice's clothes.

"Oh." Alice shrugged, and stretched her legs out. "I came to borrow one and . . ." She held her hands out, offering her current state as explanation.

"Well." Mom wiped at Alice's face again. "I bet some jambalaya will set you right."

"Nana Suebell's recipe?" Her great-grandmother made the *best* jambalaya this side of the Mississippi.

"And a fresh jug of sweet tea." Mom smiled. "Just help me bring the groceries in."

Alice nodded and got to her feet. Mom had already brought in a handful of bags, resting on the counter. She sent Alice for the others. There weren't that many, and Alice managed to bring them all in, just as the microwave beeped.

Uh-oh.

"What the—I know you didn't put my meat in this micro-wave. Alice!"

◊ ◊ ◊

After a thorough lesson on why the defrost function on the microwave is as useful as a paper spoon, Mom set to making dinner with Alice assisting, meaning she chopped, peeled, and sliced whatever was needed. A haze of steam, smoke, and stir-fry thickened the air. As she went along, Mom flipped on every light in the kitchen, flooding the room with pale brightness. She liked to see while she cooked, whatever that meant. Just the overhead light would've gotten the job done.

Mom bopped in front of the stove as she stirred a couple of skillets, singing along to Whitney Houston's "I'm Your Baby Tonight." "Sang it, Whitney!"

Chuckling, Alice finished unrolling some biscuits onto a pan. She tried to relax, or at least look like she was relaxed. But every time something thumped or thudded in the house, she froze, her hand twitching toward her pack. Likely, it was one of the cats, but still. She was *not* about to be caught off guard again.

"How was service?" she asked, attempting conversation even as she stared at the ceiling.

"Don't know." Mom tossed a towel over her shoulder as she checked the Crock-Pot. "After praise and worship I went to the funeral service for that little girl." Her pleasant expression deflated a little bit. She ran a hand over her hair, puffed out in big curls, and came over to kiss Alice's forehead. "The family is

shook up, but by the grace of God, they'll get through this."
She went to fetch something out of the fridge, muttering about
senselessness and it shouldn't be like this.

Alice fidgeted with a spoon. "I meant to go with you." With
everything happening, Alice had forgotten about the service.
They'd planned to attend together, but bastard entities of evil
had a way of derailing things.

"I know, but you wouldn't move this morning." Mom
smirked over her shoulder, an eyebrow arched. "Partied harder
than you intended, huh?"

"Something like that." *If you mean facing off with the resurrected knight of darkness from a secret world of dreams, sure.*

"Glad you had a good time. Now, go get washed up—oh,
this is my part!" Mom reached to turn up the volume and
belted out, "I wanna run to youuuuu!"

Wincing, Alice made a hasty retreat, but not before stealing a bite of red pepper from the plate on the counter.

During dinner they talked about Brionne, the funeral service, how Alice missing praise and worship this morning meant
she was definitely going next week, Sunday school included.
She kept stealing what she hoped were discreet glances at the
clock.

After the leftovers were put away, Alice spent the rest of the
evening up in her room pretending to read a book about a Black
girl and some dragons. Normally, she'd be all about that Khaleesi
life, but a combination of worry for Hatta and just plain old
boredom—she'd been trying to get into this same book for a
week now—kept her from making it past the first chapter.

Finally, ten o'clock hit. Mom's bedtime and morning

routines were damn near sacred, so she'd be knocked here in about ten minutes. Alice checked over her things one more time, then peeked out the door and down the hall just as Mom's light cut off under her door. Talk about perfect timing.

Heart racing—she'd never done anything like this before— she swung her bag onto her back and slipped out, quiet as a cat. With every second she spent feeling her way down the stairs, her heart beat faster and faster. She swore it was gonna give her away, but she made it to the door with no problems. She eased the locks free, cracked it open, and slipped out, careful not to let the screen door bang behind her. Thankfully, Mom got one of those fancy dead bolts installed, the kind that locks itself when you twist it.

Chest heaving, Alice said a quick prayer to protect her mother, then raced down her porch stairs and toward the end of the block. If she was lucky, Mom would sleep through the night. If she wasn't . . . well, at least she wouldn't be around for it.

◊ ◊ ◊

Maddi was waiting behind the bar when Alice reached the pub. Judging by the pile of pouches and packs on the counter, Maddi had been busy. "There you are."

"Sorry it took so long." She wasn't exactly a pro at this sneaking-out thing.

Alice joined Maddi and laid out what she had brought. Between the two of them, they managed to fit the essentials into Alice's pack, leaving the extra set of clothes for her return.

She'd braided her hair on the train. It wasn't pretty, but it would keep her hair under control and safe from the Wonderland elements.

Maddi went over the plan while Alice changed into something more hike appropriate.

"You've got food, a sleeping bag, a couple purge potions, precautionary. I threw in something for pain, in case your injuries start aching."

"They're mostly healed now." They'd been a little achy this entire time, but Alice had been so distracted by everything going on that it had barely registered.

"I talked to the Duchess. The Tweedles are going to meet up with you along the way to Legracia. She's going to come here and help keep an eye on Hatta and protect your mother."

"Thank you for that. Really." At least she would be able to focus on the task and not worry about the Black Knight hurting her family. Not worry as much, anyway. Alice laced her last boot and moved to grab her daggers from the bar. She fastened them in place, then pulled out her phone. "Speaking of my mom, I need you to do something for me. While I'm gone, if my mom texts me, I need you to answer." Alice held out the phone.

Maddi eyed it like it was going to bite her. "What do I say?"

"Anything you think I might. Mostly stuff like 'Okay' or 'Yes, ma'am. I love you.'"

"Ahh." Maddi gingerly took the device. "Doesn't Courtney usually do this?"

"Yeah. But she's not being super cooperative." Alice

pulled an envelope from her bag, pushing down her rising irritation. *Deal with it when you get back.* "This is the log-in information for my mom's email and a letter. I need you to send the letter to my school. I've written it, so you only have to type it, word for word, and send to the address in here. Then delete it from the sent folder. The school might send some sort of confirmation. Delete that, too."

Maddi blinked wide blue, then green, then purple eyes at her. "You've given this a lot of thought." She took the envelope.

"Well, I'd like to live past saving Hatta, so it's necessary. My phone has an alarm set for 7:30 a.m. You have to send the letter then." Mom would be up at seven, cup of coffee and breakfast, kiss Alice good-bye—only she wouldn't be there—then into the shower to finish getting ready for work. That shower was the only time for certain she wouldn't be checking her email.

"Mission accepted." Maddi set the phone and the envelope on the bar. "Ready?"

"Let's go." They hurried down the hallway, with Alice pausing briefly to look in on Hatta. He was still sound asleep, fretting only a little. Her heart twisted with each small sound of distress. Maddi had given him another potion while she was gone.

"Move as quickly as you can, but pace yourself. You have a long journey ahead of you." Maddi closed the broom-closet door behind them, plunging them into darkness. The drop through the Veil was nauseating and harrowing as ever, and left Alice doubled over. Without Hatta there holding her, his scent and the feel of his arms to distract her, the motion sickness hit hard.

Maddi stood in the Gateway, her lips twisted as Alice dry heaved into a silver bush. "You really do get sick."

"What, you thought it was a myth?" She spit, curled her tongue with a *ycch*, and straightened.

"That he exaggerated the amount." Maddi tilted her head to the side, her nose crinkling. "And the noise. Sounds like you dislodged something."

"Thanks for your overwhelming concern." If she weren't so queasy, she'd have the energy to be embarrassed.

She breathed deep, hoping to quell the dizzying buzz between her ears. "There wouldn't happen to be a Follyshroom or two in here, would there?" She hooked a thumb over her shoulder at the pack.

"'Fraid not." Maddi fidgeted with the collar of her shirt, leaning out to glance around without actually setting foot through the Gateway. "They turn hours after being picked. Nothing keeps 'em fresh. Trust me, I've tried. You got your mirror?"

Alice shook her head. It was still at school.

"Here." Maddi produced a small, mini-me version of the one Hatta kept in his desk. "Use mine."

Alice fingered the silver surface before shoving it into a pouch on her belt. "Anything else?"

"Yeah." Maddi took a few steps back as the Gateway started to curl shut. "Hurry."

Fourteen

THE DUCHESS

With the use of the mirrors, and Maddi's instructions, Alice was able to navigate her way toward the rendezvous point with the Tweedles. She kept her head on the swivel the entire time. Just because the last place the Black Knight showed up was the human world didn't mean he couldn't pop up here.

The mist of the freshly risen morning clung to the grass and plants in pearls of dew. Wonderland's pink sky bloomed bright and streaked white, but black clouds curled on the distant horizon. Her path took her past the Bubbles, where she was able to grab some Follies to ease her stomach, and across a stretch of literal rolling hills. Seriously, the hills slowly rose from the ground, traveled a handful of miles over the course of the day, then sank back into the earth. She'd ridden one with the twins before, just taking a break for a bit and soaking up some Wonderland . . . well, there was no sun. The hills weren't fast, but you could definitely tell you were moving.

Working with the somewhat rudimentary map Maddi had drawn—seriously, it was like something out of a coloring book— Alice used the landscape and a few landmarks to find her way. Like the rainbow river that changed colors as it cut through the grassland. In the river, large and small glass fish twinkled in the light. There were no towns or villages on Alice's trail; she was crossing wilderness in a direct line, the fastest way through. She did pass what used to be an old lookout tower, white stone rising into the sky, but it was long abandoned.

After a few hours, she spotted the crossroads where she was supposed to meet the twins. A woman stood with them, dressed similarly in dark pants, boots, and a formfitting black shirt. Alice couldn't be certain from a distance, but she appeared armed with what looked to be sheathed long knives strapped to both thighs. A rope of red hair swung past her hips as she moved.

The Tweedles waved. So did Alice, hurrying up to meet them. "Hey," she panted, eyes on the woman. She looked the same age as Hatta, but that didn't mean anything. She was almost as tall as him, too, her frame lithe but round in the important places. "Didn't keep you waiting long, did I?"

Dem shook his head. "Nyet. Maybe half an hour?" He looked to his brother for confirmation.

The woman cleared her throat, and both boys straightened a bit. Her green-eyed gaze bounced between them before landing on Alice. Dramatic makeup highlighted her cheeks, made her eyes gleam, and painted her lips the color of blood. "I apologize for their rudeness," the woman said in a less thick Russian accent. It surprised Alice, though she guessed it shouldn't. Hatta spent most of his time in Atlanta and sounded like he was from London. At least this lady's accent made sense. "I am Anastasia Petrova, but you most likely know me as—"

"The Duchess." Alice took the woman's offered hand. Meticulously manicured nails the same red as her lipstick flashed.

"Da."

Alice had guessed right. "I'm sorry if *this* is rude, but weren't you exiled like Hatta?"

The Duchess arched a sculpted eyebrow.

Alice swallowed. "It's just, being this far in would cause him pain—are you okay?"

The Duchess smiled, showing off pearly whites. "I am, but the terms of my banishment were not as severe as Addison's. Neither were my charges."

"What charges?" Alice asked.

The twins shared one of their creepy glances.

"It is not my place to say. Perhaps a conversation to be had once we are finished." The Duchess folded her arms over her chest.

Feeling somewhat scolded, Alice cleared her throat. "Are you going with us?" That wasn't the plan Maddi laid out, but something told Alice the Duchess was a woman who did things her way.

"No. I'm going to help Madeline. I have more experience dealing with what ails Addison. If she's going to slow the progression of the Madness, she'll need my assistance."

Oh, well, that made sense.

The Duchess faced the twins, who both snapped to attention. She barked what Alice assumed was an order in Russian. The twins responded in unison. Patting their shoulders, the Duchess looked to Alice. "Make sure they don't get into too much trouble." She winked, then stepped past, heading in the direction Alice had come from at a brisk pace. "See you soon," she called as she set into a steady jog.

The three of them watched her for a moment before turning to continue toward Legracia.

"So much for retirement, eh?" Dem said.

Alice tried not to grimace. "Something came up. That was the Duchess. She's . . . tall."

The twins snickered, Alice smiled, and, like that, the odd tension the Duchess had left behind dissolved.

"So, Legracia." Dem came up on her left. "Have you ever been to the White Palace?"

Alice shook her head. "Have you?"

"Once." Dee came up on her right. "Before you became a Dreamwalker."

That was a while ago. "What's it like?"

"It's beautiful. Right out of a fairy tale." Dee smirked.

"Sounds nice." Alice hoped this fairy tale had a happy ending.

Most of the conversation as they traveled centered on why they were going. The Duchess had explained that Hatta was ill to the twins, and the White Queen was the only one who could help, but none of the other details like the Black Knight and his wanting the Eye. Naturally, the twins asked about a million questions Alice didn't have the answers to: Who was the Black

Knight? Wasn't he dead? Why did he want the Eye? On and on. Alice realized how little they knew of the Black Knight and his plans. So far, everything they did was in reaction to him. Made it pretty easy to fall for his tricks, like using her to poison Hatta. She'd left that little detail out.

"Maybe he wants the Eye to try to resurrect the Black Queen, I don't know." Alice took in their surroundings. Orange grass spread out around them, cresting stationary hills and dotted with silver flowers. In the far distance, numerous curls of smoke drifted toward the sky. A village maybe. The air smelled like roasted garlic, fresh bread, and lemons.

"So she could finish what she started?" Dem toyed with a switchblade.

"Maybe." Alice gripped the straps of her pack, for something to do with her hands. "If that's the case, we definitely need to help Hatta. They couldn't beat her without him before; we wouldn't stand a chance now."

"You thinking that's why the Black Knight did this to him?" Dee said, watching her as they walked along.

"It makes sense." She'd been turning this over in her head since leaving the bar. Only one person can keep you from doing the thing? Handle 'em. A play right out of the how-to bad-guy handbook. But she wasn't going to let that happen. Hell to the naw.

Hours passed with little fanfare, but Alice couldn't relax. If the Black Knight wanted Hatta dead, and somehow found out she and the twins were here to get the one thing that could cure him, he'd come after them, right? But so far, nothing. A suspicious amount of nothing, to be honest.

She tugged the mirror out and tapped against it. "Open my eyes."

It took a few seconds before the swirling calmed to reveal Maddi's face.

"Everything okay?" the bartender asked.

"Yeah, everything's good. Too good, s'why I'm calling. How're things on your end?"

"All quiet. Hatta is resting, and the Duchess is looking after your mother. Discreetly."

Some of the tightness in Alice's chest eased a bit. "No sign of the Black Knight?"

"Nothing. I assume the same for you."

"Mmhm." Alice heaved a sigh and rolled her shoulders to ease the strain in her muscles. "Okay, well, keep me posted."

"Likewise." Maddi's face swirled out of sight before Alice's reflection replaced it. She put the mirror away and updated the twins on everything being quiet back home. Maybe things were actually starting to work out. She pushed the thought aside, not wanting to jinx it, and focused on chatting with the twins about this area of Wonderland. It was closest to their Gateway in the north.

Wonderland didn't really have seasons. There were areas where it snowed, areas where it rained, deserts, mountains, all of that. Sometimes the weather would change in these places, but never drastically enough or predictably enough to be called winter, spring, and so on.

The Northern Gateway, the twins' gateway, was settled on a ridge at the start of the Tashinewa Mountains. The area was usually all snow and wind but ended with a sweltering jungle.

No reason for it; just two feet to the left there would be a blizzard with sometimes purple snow, and two feet to the right was a jungle of bright colors with trees both tall and tiny, all manner of flowers, and metallic vines that crisscrossed the canopy. She'd never been there, but listening to the twins, it sounded beautiful. It was nice to think of something so simple but positive, even for a little while.

They stopped briefly to rest and eat at midday, observing the Mending as they filled their canteens in a stream of what *looked* like water. The twins said it was safe to drink. They'd been this far into Wonderland before, so she trusted them.

Every time something moved nearby or made a noise, Alice went on alert. The Black Knight had sneaked up on her twice now, and like hell there was gonna be a third. She even drew a dagger on what appeared to be a fox. Dog? Canid creature. The twins told her to relax, just a little. Mind her surroundings, of course, but they had her back. She was going to exhaust herself at this rate, and they were right. Besides, they needed to save their energy for the night watch.

The journey was easy enough, their path curving over hills and dipping through valleys and once around a marsh so foul she couldn't hold her nose tight enough and thought she was going to be sick more than once.

Eventually, day began to bleed into night. Dee called for them to make camp before darkness fully descended, thankfully, far, far away from the marsh. He dug a ditch while Alice and Dem gathered wood for a fire. At least, it was the closest thing to wood they could find. The trees in this area, tall and pole-thin, were more like wire than anything else and bent instead of broke when she yanked on the gray branches. They had to cut some free.

She settled near the silver flames, admiring their pale light. She rubbed her palms together and flexed her fingers, her hands sore from fighting with the firewood. Heat wafted over her body, smelling of metal and cotton, soaking into her bones. She inhaled the soothing scent as her eyes fell shut.

"It's the wood," Dem said.

"Mmm?" Alice tilted back on her palms and basked in the warmth.

"From these trees," he continued. "You burn it, and the smell relaxes you. Like aromatherapy. And the light from the fire helps ward off unpleasant company."

Alice stretched out on her side, grateful for the sleeping bag. "How much longer till we get there?" She dug into the leftover jambalaya she'd brought along. Nana Suebell's recipe never disappointed.

"Another three days. Maybe four." Dem munched on some sort of sandwich.

Not soon enough. Three more days until they reached the White Palace. That meant it would take four days to get back to the Gateway. Hopefully, the time difference between the worlds would work in their favor.

"Think we can pick up the pace tomorrow?" she asked.

"Doable." Dem nodded. "You are okay for this? Your injuries."

"I'll be fine. Almost one hundred percent."

They ate quickly, then checked their weapons. Nighttime in Wonderland always carried the danger of running across a

Nightmare or two. They weren't near any Gateways, but still. There was also the chance of the Black Knight showing up, unless he was causing trouble back home. Maddi would let her know if there were problems, right? Alice's hand went to her pouch, where it hung against her thigh.

She'd call. Stay focused. Sheathing her daggers, Alice stretched over her sleeping bag and gazed at the starless sky. The moon's blue face blazed, peeking between purple clouds. In a few hours it would all shatter with the Breaking.

"How did you guys become Dreamwalkers?" she asked. They had been working together for just under a year, and she never asked how they got into all of this. She figured it was probably similar to how she and Hatta met, but that was just a guess.

The twins never asked her, either. This was the longest she'd ever spent with them in one go, with more time ahead. These were her friends, her literal brothers-in-arms. She should know more about them.

They glanced at her, at each other, then back to her. The white glow of the fire washed their skin in ghostly light, making their movements in tandem creepier than normal. "Like usual, I guess," Dee said.

"Define *usual*." Not being jumped in a back alley by some monster, she hoped.

Dem shrugged and took a bite of what looked like a blue apple while he looked over his things. "The Duchess found us when we were young. She and the other Gatekeepers go around searching for Dreamwalker candidates from time to time, so they have prospects when the position needs to be . . . filled." Which was a nice way of saying *when the current ones died off. Or quit.* "She came to us in a dream. Said it was to test our connection to this place." He gestured around them.

"If a Gatekeeper can make contact from this side of the Veil, they've found a candidate." Dee settled atop his bag, already finished with his weapons. He wasn't slowed by snacking, like his brother.

Alice snorted. "So, what, the Duchess showed up in your dream one night and asked if you wanted to fight monsters in your spare time?"

They grinned.

"Not entirely," Dee continued. "She told us who she is, what she does. We didn't believe it at first, but she told us where to find her if we were interested."

"That's not creepy at all," Alice muttered.

"We went through the Gateway for the first time that day." Dee pushed to his feet. "Passing through the Veil makes you stronger, faster. We could feel the change."

"*Then* we agreed to fight monsters in our spare time." Dem's grin widened.

That was completely the opposite from her "call to arms." Hatta found her in real life, not a dream. He trained her three months, *then* took her through. Maybe the twins needed convincing, whereas she'd already seen a Nightmare.

She frowned, lips pursed. "How old were you?"

"Thirteen," they responded together.

Alice nodded slowly. So, they'd been at this for a good while before she came along.

"What about you?" Dem asked.

Alice curled on her side, her eyes fixed on the fire as it faded to embers that looked more like charred diamonds. "A Nightmare attacked me the night my dad died. Hatta said it was drawn to my grief. He saved me, decided to train me. Here we are."

Silence settled over them, interrupted now and then by the dying snap and crackle of the embers. She took a stick and stoked the flames to a low burn. Wonderland nights rarely grew cold, but a chill washed through her that had nothing to do with the temperature.

"We are sorry," Dee murmured.

"For your loss," Dem added.

"Thanks. It was a long time ago." The words tasted bitter, but she didn't want to dwell on this. Not tonight, not when she had a job to do. "I'm okay."

The twins nodded.

"I'll take the first watch." Dee strapped his weapons in place.

"I'm second." Dem stifled a yawn. "Wake me when it's my turn."

"Then me." She shut her eyes and focused on trying to rest. It wasn't easy, especially when Dem started snoring behind her.

Eventually, sleep took her.

Fifteen

LEGRACIA

Alice woke to Dem shaking her shoulder gently, letting her know it was her turn to watch. She spent the entire time doing all she could not to think about Hatta or the disease eating away at him. It only worked for an hour or so. Thankfully, morning came without incident, and the twins were early risers.

Alice checked in with Maddi and the Duchess. The two of them reported her mom was safe and sound and there was no change in Hatta's condition. This could be a good or bad thing; only time would tell. Time, something they didn't have much of.

Time stretched into the blooming day, torching the sky bright pink. The three of them set off at a brisk pace, even jogging when the landscape allowed for it. They filled the passing hours with trivial talk about family and school, hobbies and movies, pretty much anything and everything that wasn't their mission. Then came a night of restless exhaustion where Alice's mind refused to calm while her body begged for sleep. The result was visions of the Madness spreading through Hatta's body, blackening his veins, moving like fire through his blood. When it wasn't that, she dreamed of the Black Knight slicing her hand open, black blood spilling over her fingers, filling the room, then her throat. She couldn't breathe. She couldn't move.

She woke with a start every hour or so, sweat soaking her face and shock icing her limbs. This wasn't possible; she shouldn't be able to dream anymore. But either of those images waited for her every time she closed her eyes.

The twins offered to take the full watch since she was having such a hard time sleeping, but she refused. They needed rest as well, and she needed yet another distraction. Thankfully, they had no trouble from Nightmares or any other nighttime critters. One blessing amid a pile of crap going wrong.

By the time they set out that fourth morning, she didn't have the energy to join their conversations and instead moved with them in silence.

The urge to check on Hatta again grew with each step, but she didn't want to keep pulling Maddi from her work. Potion mixing was equal parts art and science, and the mousy bartender was flighty enough without the added distraction of answering Alice's every call. That, and she figured Maddi or the Duchess would let them know if anything was wrong.

Alice's fingers curled around the mirror. She gazed at her reflection as she walked, the twins marching ahead of her.

Closing her eyes, she pressed the mirror to her chest. *Please hold on . . .*

"We're here."

Dee's words snatched her from her mental wanderings, and she glanced up.

The trio stood atop a large hill overlooking the massive and majestic castle. Translucent stone formed the outer walls and curved spires reaching for the heavens, the entire structure tall and glittering. High silver gates surrounded the palace grounds and swung open to bid them enter.

Wide lawns shifted between blue and purple as the grass waved in the wind. A few statues and fountains carved from the same dazzling stone as the palace dotted the lawn. Even the road had transformed from cobblestone to something resembling stained glass.

The road ended at a set of stairs, which arched up and widened as they reached the landing. Two huge silver doors stood watch. Alice and the Tweedles stopped at the foot of the stairs and waited.

And waited.

"Is anyone home?" Alice asked.

"Should we knock?" Dem asked. "I can knock."

"Just wait," Dee murmured. "You know the drill."

A soft chime played over the wind, faint at first, then louder. Metal clanked against metal. It wasn't a harsh bang, but more like someone shaking a bag of change. She knew that sound.

As Alice racked her brain, trying to figure out where she'd heard it before, a figure emerged along the walkway lining the front of the castle. A woman who moved briskly, her steps quick and confident. She wore white plates, though the pieces weren't chunky like the stuff from the Middle Ages. No, this armor was streamlined, elegant. Spaulders, breastplate, greaves, boots—and between them Alice glimpsed leather and chain mail that looked more like gems than steel. It rattled with each footfall.

A cape of deep blue cloth fell from the woman's shoulders to the ground, gathering at her feet when she stopped at the top of the stairs. She didn't appear much older than the twins, but in Wonderland, who knew.

"Lady Xelon," Dee said, nodding.

Dem did the same.

Xelon returned the gesture. "We did not expect you. Is something wrong?" She looked at Alice.

Even at this distance, Alice could feel the power behind Xelon's gaze. She blinked bright, upswept eyes that held an odd light. Her brows lifted and nearly vanished into her hairline as she angled her head to the side. Platinum strands fell around her pale face and over her shoulders. She looked like she'd stepped right out of a manga. Alice felt a little flurry in her stomach. And there was something familiar about her voice.

"This is Alice." Dee set a hand on Alice's shoulder.

"I know who she is." Xelon looked her up and down in a way that left her feeling flattered or insulted, she wasn't sure which. "I am merely surprised she is here."

"I take it you know *of* me." Alice finally found her voice and was glad she sounded more annoyed than gooey. "'Cause we've never met." She'd definitely remember running into an armored hottie.

Xelon descended the stairs. "You weren't very coherent at the time. You'd just been attacked by a Nightmare."

The steady rhythm of steps distracted Alice as Xelon came to stand in front of them. Alice knew that sound. Realization bolted through her.

"You rescued me!"

Xelon smiled, the expression lighting her face. Up close, Alice could see why her eyes had seemed so strange. They were light gray, so pale they appeared white at a distance.

"Saved her?" Dem asked.

"After Ahoon. When the Black Knight jumped me. I passed out, but I remember someone carried me. Talked to me."

"That was indeed me. I was returning from the southern reaches and heard the battle. Unfortunately, I was too late to stop the initial attack. I am glad to see you've recovered." One corner of Xelon's lips lifted higher than the other, and a dimple appeared on the left side of her face under a high cheekbone. "I admire your strength."

"Oh . . ." Once again, Alice thanked the heavens her dark skin concealed her blushes. "Thanks."

"Milady." Xelon bent forward slightly. "What brings the Dreamwalkers to our door?" She addressed the three of them.

"We came looking for help." Alice took a steadying breath as Xelon fixed her gaze on her. "Addison Hatta's been injured by someone calling himself the Black Knight. He poisoned Hatta with a curse called the Madness; now he's fading."

Xelon's eyes narrowed, and her sharp jaw tensed. "Fading?"

Alice described what had happened to Hatta, how he'd changed before Maddi gave him the potions. How he was still fighting it when Alice left. "Only a member of the royal family can save him, with the Heart," Alice continued. "Maddi said the White Queen knows where to find it."

Xelon frowned, her gaze dropping to search the ground. The twins exchanged a glance, but Alice kept her eyes on Xelon.

"That is going to prove difficult." Xelon finally looked at them again. "Come with me."

The three of them followed her up the stairs and along the walkway. Alice glanced at the imposing doors that remained shut. It was probably a lot of trouble to unlock and open them. Xelon led the way through a smaller set of doors that resembled the main ones at the front.

Inside, the palace was equally stunning. It held the same shimmering walls adorned with crystal sconces and chandeliers. Light poured in from the glass ceiling, catching every glossy surface before being reflected out again. It filled the place with energy and life.

"This way." Xelon headed down one of the carpeted halls. Her cape billowed behind her with each step. People roaming through the halls moved out of the way and bowed to Xelon as they went. More than a handful of curious stares trailed after Alice and the twins, accompanied by hushed whispers.

The guards stationed at intersections of hallways and in front of a door here or there wore armor similar to Xelon's, just no cape. Paintings of oddly dressed persons seemed to watch the group as they passed by. Every bit of furniture looked delicate enough to crumble at the slightest touch, so Alice kept to the center of the corridor.

Xelon stopped outside a pale blue door, nodding to a pair

of guards who stood on either side, a man and a woman with deep, earthy brown skin and flame red hair. A small silver stone sat at the center of the woman's forehead.

The woman gripped the door's sloping silver handle and spoke to Xelon in a language Alice didn't understand, the sound centered at the back of her mouth. Xelon responded in kind, the two going back and forth a bit before the woman released the handle, looking less than thrilled about it.

Xelon cleared her throat, looking from the woman to Alice and the twins. "This is Malal and her brother Kapi. Like me, they are part of Her Majesty's personal guard."

"Her Majesty is not expecting an audience." Malal eyed the three of them, her brown-eyed gaze hard. "She will not be pleased." She aimed this statement at Xelon.

"No, she will not." Xelon took hold of the handle this time. "I apologize in advance," she said to Alice and the twins, then swung the door open and stepped through.

"Majesty, you have guests." She waved them in.

The twins entered first, flanking the doorway and Alice, consequently, as she stepped through, into some sort of sitting area given the lush-looking couches, chairs, and chaise longues.

At the center of the room, draped in silver and white fabrics that fell over her body like water, sat a girl. She glanced up from a book, blinked large blue eyes, brushed snow-white strands from her face, and scowled. Despite the ugly expression, she was storybook pretty, with round features and rich, amber skin. Like Malal, a small silver jewel rested in the center of her forehead. Her eyes pinged on Alice with a hardness that didn't match the rest of her.

That's the Queen? Prom queen, maybe. She looked Alice's age. Then again, she could be Methuselah.

The door shut behind them, and Xelon made her way between the trio and the girl, gesturing to her. "May I present Her Royal Highness, Princess Odabeth of Legracia, daughter of the White Queen and heiress to the throne."

"Princess?" Alice cut a look to Xelon, who nodded.

Odabeth's nostrils flared slightly. "What is this?"

Xelon bowed at the waist, deeper than she had before to Alice. "Dreamwalkers. They've come with an urgent matter for Your Highness to hear."

"Urgent, you say." Odabeth snapped her book shut and set it to the side. Brown markings decorated her hands in what looked to be an intricate, flowing design. The princess's fingers fell to her chest, then shifted and revealed a jewel star hung on a thin, white chain around her neck. She toyed with the gem, twirling it so it caught the light in soft glints.

"We know the Tweedlanovs, but you'd bring a stranger before us?" Odabeth waved and Xelon crossed to stand beside her.

"This is Alice, Addison Hatta's charge." Xelon gestured to Alice, who felt the need to step forward.

Alice cleared her throat. "A pleasure, Your—"

"Is she?" Odabeth interrupted, sounding disapproving as she smoothed out imaginary wrinkles along the front of her skirts before toying with her necklace again. "I'm surprised to find someone trained by none other than Addison Hatta has such poor manners."

Alice blinked. "Excuse me?"

"So rude, talking out of turn. Hatta must not be instilling proper etiquette in his charges anymore." Odabeth drummed her fingers against her thigh. "Very well. We shall hear them. You may speak, Alice."

She'd never heard her name spoken like it was a cuss word before. Swallowing her retort—this was for Hatta—she bent at the waist the same way everyone else had. "Thank you, Your Highness. We're actually here to talk to the White Queen. Iiiis that possible?"

Odabeth eyed Alice up and down. "Our mother is currently indisposed. We will relay your concerns."

"That's not—"

Xelon cleared her throat.

Alice's teeth ground together. "Thank you. Addison Hatta's been hurt, bad. Someone calling himself the Black Knight att—"

"The Black Knight?" Odabeth sniffed. "Impossible."

"You are the third person to say that, but it's what he calls himself." Alice waited a moment before continuing. "He poisoned Hatta with the Madness. We need the White Queen to tell us where the Heart is so we can find it and she can use it to help him." She hated herself for letting her voice break. She didn't want to appear weak in front of the princess.

Odabeth's arrogant expression softened. Her fingers tapped her thigh all the faster. "Our sympathies. Hatta has been good to this family. Good to us."

"So can your mother help?" Alice asked, her breath catching.

Odabeth peered down her nose. "The Heart is gone."

"Right." Alice pushed down on a twinge of irritation. "But

your mother and her sister are the ones who hid it. We can go get it, we just need to know where it is."

"You don't understand—it's *gone*," Odabeth pressed. "My mother and aunt hid my grandmother's artifacts, but they didn't do it together. Each sister took *one* artifact, so neither would ever know where both lie. My mother hid the Eye, and my aunt took the Heart. It disappeared with her."

Alice stared at the princess, her mind tripping over what was said. The Red Queen had the Heart. The same Red Queen who went missing decades ago. This wasn't happening. They'd come all this way! "S-so the Heart is . . . gone?"

"That is what we said. At least, the one person who knows its location is gone." Odabeth folded her hands against her stomach. "We regret to say we cannot offer more than this."

Ice poured through Alice. With the Heart gone, there was no way to save Hatta. Tears burned her eyes. *No.*

A hand fell on her shoulder. One of the twins, but she didn't know which. "Alice—"

"No!" She shook her head, swallowed the tightness in her throat, and drew in a slow breath. The pain in her chest left her lungs rattling. "No, there has to be a way."

Someone pulled at her elbow, trying to get her to head for the door. Xelon bent near the princess, saying something under her breath. Odabeth looked less than pleased. Everything slowed as Alice's heart and mind raced. *There has to be a way!*

"The Eye let her see things about people, places, things." Maddi's voice practically rang in Alice's ears.

Her head snapped up. "The Eye." She planted her feet and

shook loose of whichever twin had hold of her. "It sees things, or whatever. Right? We can use it to find the Heart. *Right?*"

Odabeth blinked in surprise, though whether it was at what Alice said or because she was still present was unclear. The princess shared a look with Xelon before both of them focused on Alice. Odabeth refolded her hands. "This is plausible. But as we explained, The Eye has been hidden—"

"Then *un*-hide it!"

Both Odabeth and Xelon tensed at Alice's shout. The princess's lips tightened and the knight shook her head, but Alice was past caring. Hatta was dying and they were just going to let it happen.

"You said Hatta has been good to your family." Alice's hands fisted at her sides. Anger bubbled at the base of her skull.

Xelon shook her head again, more adamant this time.

Alice ignored her. "You called him friend, but this. Is. Not. What you do to *friends.* You people wouldn't know that, though. After everything Hatta did during the war, you banished him from his home, and now you're going to abandon him to die?" Fury pounded through her, red-hot. She should stop, part of her rationed. With each word, another section of Odabeth's amber face burned red. She'd never help now. But that didn't matter. It wasn't Odabeth they needed anyway. "I don't have time for this—where's the Queen? I came to talk to her, not some bougie-ass princess."

Silence descended on the room. Odabeth sat rigid, as if her body had turned to stone. Her nostrils flared with quick breaths.

Xelon stood to the side, eyes on the princess, looking like a woman waiting for lightning to strike. The twins were silent and unmoving somewhere behind Alice, who held Odabeth's thunderous gaze.

The princess's heaving chest slowed. The color in her face slowly evened out. She toyed with her necklace, playing it between her fingers again and again. Over the next several seconds she gradually calmed, but the storm smoldering behind the princess's bright blue eyes intensified.

Finally, Odabeth brushed her hands against her legs and rose to her feet, all while holding Alice's gaze. Xelon dropped to a knee beside her.

"The power of my mother's crown has passed to me. As Lady Regent and acting ruler of Legracia, I hereby dismiss you." Odabeth flung her finger at the door. "Get out of my sight."

Sixteen

WHAT MOTHER WANTS

The silence was thick enough to push the oxygen out of the room. Alice's eyes remained locked on the princess, but this time shock kept her in place.

Oh shit.

"Milady." Xelon shifted to place herself between Alice and Odabeth, facing the princess. Odabeth's furious gaze fell to the knight, who bowed deeply. "Milady, I'm certain Alice speaks from her concern for Hatta and means no disrespect to Your Highness." She straightened, but not fully, and gestured for the princess to take a seat. "If milady will permit me."

Odabeth cast a glare over Xelon's shoulder. It took everything in Alice not to recoil, but the princess lifted her chin and lowered herself to the chaise longue. Xelon thanked her, before murmuring something Alice couldn't hear over her heart, beating like a bass drum. "I know this looks bad," Dem whispered while the princess and her knight conversed, which consisted of a lot of placating and flailing gestures. "But for what it's worth, you're my hero."

Alice would've been amused if she wasn't terrified.

"Mine, too." Dee kept his eyes on the show. "I've never seen her this pissed."

"Is she always like this?" Alice asked softly, her stomach squirming.

"Yes," they both replied.

Xelon stepped aside to reveal Odabeth. Her face had gone a deep coral color, her fingers curled in the fabric along her thighs.

"The princess, in her great wisdom and endless compassion, has conceded her previous position." Xelon retook her place at Odabeth's side. "You may remain, so long as you are *respectful.*" Xelon looked straight at Alice.

Alice sighed in relief. "Thank you, Princess." She bowed again, this time sincere. "I'm sorry, I . . . Hatta is important. To you, to me, to a lot of people. I can't let him die."

Odabeth scowled, though not as deeply as she had before. "You say this Black Knight has poisoned him?"

"Y-yes." Alice rubbed her unmarked palm against her thigh.

"What are his symptoms?"

Alice blinked. That was a weird question, but she answered anyway, laying out the details of Hatta's episode.

Xelon stepped forward slightly. "Your Majesty, it's the same as—"

Odabeth cut the air with her hand. Her expression twisted briefly, pain fluttering over her face, before she schooled it back into place. "In theory, the Eye could locate the Heart. The two had never been separated before my—our mother and aunt hid them away. Unfortunately, our mother is unable to tell us where she put the Eye."

"Why not?" The question leaped from Alice's lips before she could stop herself. When Odabeth tensed, Alice bowed her head. "Apologies, Your Majesty. If you would explain?"

The princess eyed Alice, the tension in her shoulders drawing them up. At least, until Xelon placed her hand on one. Odabeth relaxed with a sigh.

"What we are about to say must never be repeated without our explicit permission. Swear it. On your honor and duty as Dreamwalkers." Odabeth looked from Alice to the Tweedles. "All of you."

"I swear," Alice offered immediately.

"I swear," the twins repeated together.

Odabeth nodded but didn't say anything just yet. Xelon rubbed the shoulder she still had hold of and the princess reached up to lay her hand over the knight's.

"My mother was attacked." Odabeth's quiet words rose between them. "A fortnight ago, while we were out riding."

Xelon's free hand went to her sword. Her jaw tightened.

"A figure cloaked in shadow," Odabeth continued. "I think he may have been this Black Knight of yours."

Alice bristled. *Not mine, but okay.*

"He demanded my mother give him the Eye. He threatened to take my head if she refused." Odabeth's hand went to her neck. "My mother tried to reason with him. She said that she was no longer the Eye's protector. That it was gone, and she couldn't give it to him even if she wished to because she had no idea where it was. He didn't believe her. Then he went for me, and she threw herself in front—" The princess's voice cracked and her voice trembled. Tears sprung to her eyes.

Xelon looked away but continued to stroke Odabeth's shoulder as she breathed through a faint sob, wiped at her face, and straightened her shoulders.

"My mother took the blow. It wasn't deep, she even managed to fight him off. We came home and the next day, just after the Mending, she showed the same symptoms as those you described plaguing Addison Hatta."

Alice's pried her tongue from the roof of her mouth. "H-how is she?"

"This morning, the Poets tending her said she would not see the next Breaking."

"Oh my god." Alice's hand went to her mouth, her eyes wide.

"So they put her in stasis to preserve what little health she has left while they search for a cure."

"The night I rescued you," Xelon began, "I was riding south to seek aid from a Poet known to produce extremely strong potions. We believed it was a simple poison, but now we know what truly ails her."

"And only the Heart can cure her," Odabeth said.

A flicker of hope sparked in Alice. "So, you'll help us find it?"

The princess sniffed softly and nodded.

The twins whooped. Alice was torn between the want to holy ghost stomp and hug Odabeth, so instead she shouted,

"Yes! Thank you, thank you, thank you! And I'm sorry about your mom." She knew the pain of losing a parent, and it wasn't something she'd ever wish on anyone, even a pompous princess.

"Mmm." Odabeth squeezed Xelon's hand and the knight withdrew to stand at her side. "There is still the complication of my mother being unable to give us the location of the Eye. If she even knows."

And like that, Alice's joy deflated. Even with Odabeth's offer, they had no Eye, and without that, there was no Heart. And without *that*, Hatta would . . .

Alice groaned, rubbing her hands over her face. What were they supposed to do now? All-powerful heirlooms didn't just disappear. In every book she'd ever read, every video game she'd ever played, every movie, TV show, and anime, magical shit went missing but turned up eventually. The One Ring, the Deathly Hallows, the Triforce—this stuff didn't just drop off the edge of the world.

Unless it did . . .

Alice's head snapped up.

If you wanted to hide something forever, sending it off the edge of the world is exactly what you would do, or rather, to a completely different world. Alice's eyes slowly widened. It couldn't be that easy, could it? Of course it could; only she would miss something so obvious staring her right in the face. "Uuuugh, I'm a moron!" And Hatta was a lying liar who lies! As soon as she saved his lying ass, she was gonna kill him. "But I'm a moron who thinks she knows where your mom hid the Eye."

By the time Alice got Maddi and the Duchess on the mirror and finished explaining her theory, everyone looked half confused but also half convinced she was right. It'd be funny, if she wasn't so irritated.

"The Queen even said it herself; she's no longer the Eye's protector. With Hatta being exiled for treason, he's the last person anyone would expect to have it, making him the perfect person to give it to."

"Many were exiled," Xenon said. "Why would it go to him?"

"Because his sentence is the most severe." At least, the way he and the Duchess spoke, it was.

"That does make a ridiculous sort of sense," the Duchess said from where she and Maddi had managed to squeeze half of their faces into the mirror. "No one would believe he could be trusted with anything like that."

"I would." Alice grunted. "And obviously the Black Knight."

"It sounds like something Her Majesty would do." Xelon set her hand against the hilt of her sword. From anyone else, the action would have come across as threatening. "This way, not even she could use the Eye if tempted."

"So what now?" Dem asked around a mouthful of a purple pear. Odabeth had ordered food be brought in when his stomach interrupted Alice for the third time. A trolley sat nearby, covered in various dishes of funky fruit, weird bread, and sweet-smelling pastries, cheeses, and tarts.

Alice realized she hadn't eaten anything since breakfast when her gut gave an embarrassingly eager churn.

"We'll look for the Eye," Maddi said. "You bunch hurry back, quick as you can."

"Got it," Alice nodded. "How's everything?"

Maddi puffed her cheeks. "Hatta's doing okay. Anastasia was going to check on your mother right before you contacted us."

"On my way now." The Duchess waved before stepping away.

Maddi's full face filled the mirror. "Remember what I said about hurrying."

"Yup. See you soon."

The image faded to a regular ole mirror again.

"Let us begin preparations to depart immediately." Odabeth rose to her feet.

"Hold on," Xelon cut in. "If the White Queen hid the Eye with Addison Hatta, clearly she did not wish it found. No matter the circumstances."

"We're certain our mother, even with her vast wisdom and insight, could not have foreseen these events," Odabeth countered.

"I don't think Her Majesty would want this."

"What my mother would or wouldn't want is irrelevant," Odabeth barked. "On *my* order, we leave for the Western Gateway as soon as possible."

Xelon bent at the waist. "At once, milady."

In a flourish of satin and gossamer, Odabeth crossed to the

door. Xelon beat her to it, drawing it open for her to pass through. On the other side, Malal and Kapi stood at attention, then fell into step behind her. Xelon heaved a sigh before facing Alice and the Tweedles.

"I'll return shortly. Help yourselves to all you wish." With that, the White Knight slipped out the door.

Alice dropped onto the chaise longue Odabeth had vacated, draping herself over it spread-eagle. The twins stood over the trolley and talked to each other in soft, somber Russian between bites. The tone made it easy to guess what they might be discussing. Alice snagged a small sandwich from one of the lower trays. Nomming eagerly, she let her gaze wander the room. Several large paintings hung on the walls, including one of a woman and little girl near the door.

Alice recognized the White Queen, though she appeared a bit older than the image Maddi had shown her in the bar mirror. The little girl, clearly Odabeth, looked thrilled to be getting her picture painted, beaming, blue eyes full of life.

Still chewing, Alice approached the portrait. Beneath the massive frame, a small plaque read HER ROYAL HIGHNESS QUEEN EMALIA AND THE CROWN PRINCESS ODABETH.

Alice examined the Queen's smile, those eyes. There was a light in them Alice recognized, one she saw in her mom, and missed in her dad. The Queen was probably a loving mother, the right amount doting and attentive mixed with strength and firmness.

Overcome with a sudden want to burrow into her parents' bed and snuggle between them like when she younger, Alice lowered her gaze to the floor and wrapped her arms around herself.

A light touch at her elbow drew her out of the memory. Xelon stood beside her.

"I came to let you know we will be ready to depart within the hour. The princess and I are the only ones making the journey with you."

"Sounds like a plan." Alice looked at the twins, whose quiet conversation had turned to bickering. Again. "I'll let them know."

"Very good." Xelon turned, her cape sweeping out behind her.

"Wait." Alice reached out to catch Xelon's arm. The armor warmed beneath her fingers.

The knight faced her, brows lifted in the same curious manner as when they had met on the stairs.

"Thank you. For the other night." Alice dropped her hand to her side, fingers tingling where she rubbed them against her palm. "Saving me."

Xelon's lips ticked upward before she dipped her head in a faint bow. "An honor, milady. By your leave." Xelon swept from the room, calling something in Russian to the Tweedles over her shoulder. They howled with laughter.

A faint smirk tugged at Alice's lips. It was nice to hear laughter, with everything going on. Her attention shifted back to the portrait. She didn't know why, but she'd always thought the beings of Wonderland were immortal. Now, it was more than obvious they weren't.

Seventeen
D IS FOR . . .

Alice gazed at Maddi's face, centered in the mirror. "We'll be leaving shortly. Hopefully, we'll reach the Gateway a lot faster than it took us to reach Legracia." They were bound to make good time, with the princess packing a whole carriage for the trip.

"Keep us informed," Maddi said.

"Talk to you when we reach the midway point." Putting the mirror away, Alice joined the Tweedles at the base of the stairs by the castle entry. Xelon approached, guiding a pair of lily-white horses by the harness, where they pulled along a coach fit for royalty indeed. All ornate silver, white, and pearl trappings, it looked more like a massive accessory than a mode of transportation.

Dem whistled as he pushed away from where he'd been sitting on the stairs. "Looks like we'll be riding in style."

"Style and speed," Alice said, encouraged.

"Indeed." Xelon patted one of the horse's necks. Dapples of blue and purple shifted in and out of sight along the hair beneath her fingers. "These are Moondance horses. They'll ride through the night, meaning we'll reach our destination that much faster."

"Can they outrun Nightmares?" Dee asked, eyeing the shimmering animals.

"If not, we've got three Dreamwalkers with us." Xelon stroked one of the horse's silvery manes. "There's enough room for one of you to join me in the box. The other two will ride inside with Her Majesty."

"Dibs!" Dem darted forward and hauled himself up onto the driver's seat. Or the passenger's seat—Alice wasn't familiar with the specs on magic carriages.

"Guess that means we're in first class." Dee approached the side of the carriage and tugged open the door.

"Oh joy." Alice climbed inside, taking in the posh interior of royal blue velvet seats and the coach's single occupant.

Odabeth sat in the center of the rear bench, taking up the entire thing. Not a problem. Alice settled across from the princess and moved over to give Dee room to join her.

"Highness." He nodded in Odabeth's direction as he settled in, his weapons in his lap.

"Mmm." She sat with her back straight and her hands folded atop her thighs, her eyes fixed on something through one of the small windows on either side of the coach. She had changed into a lavender dress with golden embroidery dancing along the pleats. Shimmering fabric gathered at her left shoulder, fell down her back, pooling on the bench.

Xelon stood outside the door, holding it wide, her eyes on the princess. "If you are ready, Highness, we'll be on our way."

Odabeth waved a gloved hand without looking away from whatever had her rapt attention.

Xelon bowed and shut the door. The carriage rocked slightly as she climbed into place. Then, with a slight lurch, they started forward.

The creak of wheels made a steady rhythm as the carriage carried them across the wilds. Xelon and Dem spoke to each other, their words muffled through the walls of the coach. Odabeth shoved her nose in a book, apparently unable to be bothered. Dee was similarly occupied with the same little tome from the other night.

Alice busied herself with watching Wonderland race by. A couple of weeks ago, she would have been beside herself at riding in a carriage, with an actual princess, pulled by magic Moondance horses. Seriously, she'd be no more good. Now, she was too occupied with thoughts of Hatta, the White Queen, and the Black Knight to fangirl properly. She scanned the trees and brush, her wet palms resting on the pommels of her daggers.

As they rode on, the landscape around them shifted. The trees thickened and grew taller. The ground softened, the canter of hooves muted against a carpet of moss that spewed an orange mist in their passing. Alice frowned, taking in the forest.

Odd plants with red stalks as tall as men and bulbous, white pods sprouting in every direction grew in twos and threes. They swayed in the wind, the pods swiveling back and forth, at least until the coach drew near. Then the stalks went rigid and the pods whipped around, revealing black orbs at the base of each one. It was a ripple effect, and within seconds what looked like hundreds of massive eyes fixed on the carriage, following it as it rode by. Maybe it was the shadows dancing beneath the canopy, but she could've sworn the "eyes" blinked.

Alice withdrew from the window. She and the twins hadn't passed anything like this on the way to Legracia.

"Where are we?" she asked.

Both Dee and Odabeth lowered their books to peer out the window.

The princess's face scrunched. "We're on course." She lifted her book, a shield against further questions.

Gee, so helpful.

"The Blind Thief's Forest." Dee settled back in his seat. "We'll reach the main road soon."

"We didn't come this way." Alice rubbed her arms, trying to banish the crawling-beneath-her-skin feeling of being stared at, watched, the fabric of her shirt suddenly scraping like sandpaper.

"Too long on foot. By carriage, faster."

Made sense. Her knuckles cracked as she fisted her fingers. Swallowing a groan, she shoved her hands under her thighs and fought the urge to rock. "Blind Thief, hmm? That's not creepy."

Dee smirked. "There's an old myth the Duchess told us when we first came to this place, about a witch who lived out here: a woman of great power and greater beauty. She wore this gold mask rumored to be the source of her magic. That or she was cursed by jealous gods so no one could ever see her face. Either way, she never took the damn thing off.

"Along comes this thief one night, breaks into her cottage.

He creeps in and removes the mask while she's asleep." Dee snapped his fingers and Alice jumped, glowering as he grinned. "Just like that, the gods' holy fire burned his eyes out of his skull. The witch took pity on him and restored his sight, but she couldn't completely undo a divine curse. So, every night the thief's eyes would fall out of his head, and every morning the witch would give him new ones. Over the years, the thief placed his discarded eyes on branches in the forest surrounding the house, to warn others to stay away."

Alice stared as Dee finished his story. "Well, that's gruesome."

He chuckled and went back to his book. "Is just a story."

"Still pretty gross."

Being watched by the forest was not something she wanted to remember, and she didn't want to spend the rest of the trip staring at the back of Odabeth's book, so she settled against the cushion of the bench and closed her eyes.

When she opened them again, night had fallen, and two shafts of azure light poured through the windows on either side of the coach, splitting the darkness. Odabeth, her book closed on her lap, tilted against Xelon with her head on her shoulder and her eyes closed. Xelon slept as well, her arms folded across her breastplate. The two of them shifted slightly with the sway of the carriage, two glimmering statues undisturbed in their rest.

"Hello there, sleeping beauty." Dem had taken Dee's place beside her. He grinned, his teeth white in the gloom. "Have a good nap?"

"Why'd you guys let me sleep so long?" She sat up and rubbed at her face, shaking herself to full wakefulness.

"You needed it. You barely got any sleep last night, and since we're making good time, we figured it wouldn't hurt. Travel during the day is pretty safe. It's now when we need to be alert, so you have perfect timing."

Alice grunted, not sure if she was more grateful or annoyed. She shifted in her seat to peer out the window. They were gliding through another forest Alice had never seen, but this one was decidedly less creepy. A couple of times Alice thought she saw movement in the distant trees, alerting Dem, who searched the darkness with her, both of them drawing their weapons and Dem opening the window to the driver's bench to let his brother know what was going on. Nothing came at them, but that didn't mean something wasn't out there. Something was *always* out there.

Night bloomed into morning, and daylight crept through the windows, gradually filling the coach. Xelon woke first, blinking her eyes open. She bade Alice and Dem good morning and asked a few more questions about the Black Knight, but did not so much as move until the princess woke as well. Odabeth yawned and stretched, then seemed to remember Alice and the twins were there and went right back to her book.

The hours ticked by, steady and silent, until, *grrrrrrrrrbbbblbllbllll*. The familiar sound of an empty stomach filled the quiet, and all eyes went to the princess. She kept her book firmly in place, but the blush creeping up her neck was a dead giveaway.

Odabeth cleared her throat. "Could we, perhaps, pause for a rest?" She peeked over the top of the book, her eyes fastening on Alice. "Not long, merely enough time to give the horses a chance to catch their second wind. And I'm certain everyone could benefit from something to eat."

Alice started to refuse, but realized the princess had asked, not commanded. And she seemed willing to wait for an answer. Alice fingered the pouch, where the mirror rested. There had been no word from Maddi on any change in Hatta's condition.

"Fine." Alice sighed. "We'll rest, but not too long."

Relief washed over Odabeth's expression like she'd avoided an execution. "Thank the heavens."

"Breakfast sounds like a good idea to me." Dem turned to rap on the window behind his and Alice's heads. "Though it's probably lunchtime by now." Three knocks and the carriage slowed to a stop.

Xelon pushed open the door, spilling bright light into the cab. Alice blinked back tears as her eyes adjusted. Xelon exited first and extended her reach to Odabeth. With her aid, the princess descended to the ground. Dem and Alice followed, though she paused when Xelon offered her a hand as well.

"Uh, thank you."

A faint smile stretched Xelon's face as she nodded. "Of course." The metal of her gauntlet was cool to the touch, sending a faint shiver through Alice even in the warm Wonderland afternoon.

Outside, she drew in deep breaths, the faint smell of pine and something fruity filling her nose. Behind her, Xelon unhooked the horses to allow them a bit of a rest while the twins sat two buckets of water into place in front of them. The steeds nudged the Tweedles gratefully, earning pats to their noses as they drank.

"We'll need more water," Xelon said as she pulled a parcel free from the back of the coach.

"We passed a stream not far back," Alice said. "Two, maybe three hundred yards."

Dee held up a large canteen.

Alice snagged it with thanks and started in the direction of the stream. "Don't let Dem eat everything while I'm gone."

"Then hurry back," Dem said around the half of something already shoved in his mouth.

"Really?" Dee asked. "You couldn't wait for everything to be prepared?"

"What's to prepare?" Dem shot back at him.

As Alice followed the trail the wheels and hooves had left, the sound of Dee and Dem arguing in Russian faded. Clusters of trees eventually blocked the others from her sight. As she walked she breathed carefully, evenly. In and out.

Like Dem said, everything would be okay. Addison would be okay. She repeated this in her mind over and over until the sound of rushing water filled her ears. She followed it to the stream cutting its way through the forest floor.

Unscrewing the canteen cap, she knelt at the creek bed. The cool dampness of the earth seeped into her jeans. The metallic scent of the minerals in the mud mixed with the perfumed smell of the lilies growing nearby. She dipped the canteen into the icy water, a chill dancing up her arm.

While the canteen grew heavy in her grip, her thoughts wandered again. She hoped Hatta hadn't worsened.

Hold on, I'm coming . . .

"Aww, you're worried about him."

Alice's head snapped up. The Black Knight hovered in the air on the other side of the creek, his legs crossed at the ankles and his hands hooked behind his head.

She surged to her feet, daggers in hand.

"Easy, I'm not here to fight." He rolled his shoulders. "But talking might be nice. Get to know each other since we're spending so much time together now." He worked one foot back and forth at the ankle. "Open and honest communication is essential, don't you agree?"

Stance set, she watched him. If she shouted, would the others hear her?

"Such a Chatty Cathy." Sarcasm coated the lazy way he drew out the words. "Look, I'm a big fan, Alice, I really am. I mean, brains, beauty, magic daggers, and the know-how to use them."

Alice scowled. "Bet you say that to all the girls with lethal weapons."

"Naw, most of them aren't as . . . skilled. It's a shame your partner doesn't share my high opinion of you." His tone sounded troubled, and far more genuine than she believed him to be capable of. "He thinks you're losing your edge, if he ever believed you had it."

"Right." Alice eyed him. "And you're an expert on what he thinks about me?"

"No, I'm an expert on stealth and observation. What, you think this getup is just for the aesthetic effect?" He gestured to himself. "What I've observed is a capable fighter—that's you—getting trounced repeatedly and constantly playing catch-up because her partner, or whatever he is, didn't trust her with vital information. If he told you about the Eye to begin with, maybe you would've been more prepared for our first little dance. And I *know* you wouldn't be scrambling now. Congratulations on putting the pieces together on that one. I knew you could do it."

Anger flashed through Alice, red-hot. "There's no one to blame for all of this but you. I won't let you win."

"Mmm, you're not good enough to stop me. Not yet. And with him keeping things from you like this, weakening you, you'll never be." The knight lifted his hands. "I can't make you hear the truth. But when he *shows* his lack of faith, remember I told you so," he said, singsong.

"What do you want?" she growled through clenched teeth, so over this guy and his bullshit. Her voice stayed steady as the rest of her shook.

"Always the same questions with you." The Black Knight lowered his legs so his feet hit the ground. She could tell the instant gravity took hold of him again by the way his armor shifted downward slightly. "I'm starting to think you don't pay attention when we talk."

She wanted to punch him dead in his mouth even though his helmet covered it. Her nerves buzzed with the effort to hold back. "Why. Are. You. Here?"

"To distract you." He twisted his wrist as if looking at a watch. "Cue music."

A shriek bored into Alice's bones. Icy dread followed.

Odabeth . . .

Eighteen
FIENDISH

Alice raced for the campsite. Wind smacked her ears in a whistling rush. Blood galloped through her veins.

Stupid. She dodged trees and vaulted stones and dips in the ground. *Fell for it, again.* This was her fault. If anyone was hurt, she was to blame. But she couldn't focus on that now.

Lungs on fire, muscles screaming, heart beating a panicked rhythm in her ears, she pushed herself to move faster. Another scream cut the air, following by the shriek of metal.

The carriage gradually came into sight, and with it signs of battle. The twins fought, back-to-back, against creatures with massive bodies like wolves but heads like cats, with fangs and claws that lashed out in attack. Inky fur glistened in the daylight.

Xelon fended off two with her sword. Behind her, Odabeth

cowered near the trunk of a tree, frozen, her mouth working in silent terror.

"Nyet!" Dee shouted as the creature he'd been battling tore away and raced toward the princess.

"Kill the girl!" it howled.

Alice hit Odabeth at full speed, diving into her from the side, her arms around her torso. Odabeth squawked, pain, shock, and fear rolled into the same sound. There was a loud WHAM as the monster slammed into the tree.

The girls flew a short distance. Alice did her best to angle them so she took the brunt of the fall. They hit the ground in a tangle of limbs and lace. Pain spasmed along Alice's body, filled her head, lit stars in her eyes.

Get up.

The smell of dirt and vanilla perfume coated her throat. Her lungs kicked at her ribs in their struggle to take in more air.

Get up.

Odabeth groaned. The sound bounced between Alice's ears, along with her racing pulse. The harsh throbbing took a dizzying twist.

The beast snarled somewhere nearby. "Take her! Take them *all*!"

Get UP!

Alice twisted and flung Odabeth to the side as she kicked to her feet. Her hands flew to the daggers at her hips. Muscle memory brought her into a defensive stance, weapons lifted.

The beast struggled to free its claws, embedded in the tree.

It yanked loose and turned on her, snarling, black lips curling from glowing fangs.

"You think you can protect her. You can barely protect yourself."

Alice's mind went back to that alley, the monster that called to her from the darkness. None of the Nightmares she faced spoke, from then until now. A shudder moved through her. She shook away the vision. Withdrawing as the monster paced forward, she searched for weak spots—eyes, nose, ears. It had none, just a mouth full of teeth.

Hackles raised, it pounced.

She leaped to the side, twisting to rip at the creature as it sailed by. It yelped and dropped. The instant it hit the ground she was on top of it. The fear from before, the hesitation, was gone. She moved like a girl possessed, her body working outside of her thought processes. Her hands tingled; her palms ached with her tight grip on the daggers. The Figment Blades found giving flesh, again and again, their glass-like surface catching the light in ways that made them shine.

She countered one swipe of claws, but another caught the meat of her thigh.

"Hng!" Her groan sounded loud in her ears. Blood ran warm against her skin. The tears in her flesh stretched as she ducked another swipe.

Knees bent, she exploded forward and hit the beast broadside, daggers first. Both blades plunged into its exposed ribs. Something slick and putrid erupted over her hands. Nausea reeled in her gut. Bile kicked the back of her throat, but she swallowed and twisted.

"Ahhhh!" Canine-like legs kicked and pumped. Claws caught her arms and legs, tore at her clothes and skin. She let go and scrambled backward.

"Thank you," the creature hissed, then twisted and flopped, its death throes pitching it over. With one final buck it fell still. The skin went fluid and slurped to the ground, spreading outward until it solidified with a crackle. The body should've caved in on itself, but instead it fissured, fizzled, and dissolved slowly. Particles rose into the air like a fine dust, carried up and away on the wind. Alice drove her dagger into the ground. Light exploded from the blade with a sound like warped thunder. She threw her hands up to shield her eyes, blinking as the roar and brightness faded. The ground where the monster had fallen was now white.

Alice sat there, eyes wide, chest heaving. "What . . . the hell . . . was that?" Her fingers hovered over the pale grass the color of ash. Movement to the side drew her attention. The Tweedles clutched their swords, the blades buried in another beast as it flailed. One creature hobbled away, tossed its head in a howl, then darted off into the woods.

Xelon threw herself down at Odabeth's side. "Your Highness?" She gathered the princess into her arms, hands carefully surfing her body in search of injury.

Alice shut her eyes as everything wavered in and out of sharp focus: the stink on her fingers, the burn from her injuries, the ache in her muscles. That damned thing talked. It *thanked* her for . . .

"Alice." One of the twins took her face in his hands. "Open your eyes."

She obeyed, peeling her lids open. Dee's ice-blue orbs locked with hers.

"She all right?" Dem demanded, standing behind his brother, his left leg working in an anxious bounce.

She would have smiled, but guilt settled into every muscle, including the ones in her face. This was her fault. She'd let the Black Knight distract her. If she'd just walked away, or attacked— anything but flipping *talk* to him.

Dee shifted his attention to the slices in her clothes and skin. She winced when he pulled at cotton and denim to get a good look.

"Nothing too deep, no sign of venom," Dee reported clinically.

Dem released a hard sigh and ran a hand through his short hair as he spun in pointless circles. "Bozhe moi."

"How is the princess?" Dee called without taking his eyes away from his work checking Alice's wounds.

"None too worse for wear." Xelon smoothed her hands over Odabeth's arms, examining her similarly. The knight murmured something. Odabeth sniffled and nodded, then wiped her face.

Alice met Odabeth's bleary red gaze. Swallowing, the princess glanced away, hands gripping the grass-stained folds of her dingy skirts.

"Look at me." Dee gently guided Alice around to face him. "You didn't hit your head, did you?"

She started to shake it, but then thought better of it. "No," she rasped, despite the thunder between her ears. "But . . . did you hear them talk?"

Dem turned from where he was surveying the area. "Talk?"

"Those Nightmares." Alice lifted her hands helplessly. "They *talked*!"

"I heard." Dee finally sat back, breath escaping him in a rush through his nose. "That was wild. And also not normal." He frowned, looking around as well. "I've never seen Nightmares like—"

"That was incredible." Dem dropped to the ground beside his brother, eyes on Alice. "You took that thing apart—you were a beast!"

Alice looked over her injuries herself. Serious or not, they still hurt like hell. "Just doing my job." The words tasted like a lie. If she'd been doing her job, she'd have been here to help.

"I've never seen you fight like that. Have you seen her fight like that?" Dem asked.

"No. You sure you're okay?" Dee asked.

She nodded, tucking her hands into her lap. "Fine."

The twins stood, Dem helping Alice up before he held out her daggers. She took them with thanks, swiped them against her jeans, and caught sight of cracks in the blades.

"Great," she grumbled, sliding them into the sheaths. Busted already. Her Muchness must be real low.

"Here." Dem offered one of his dual swords, harness and all. Alice started to wave it off, but he pressed the weapon into her hands. "Not smart to go unarmed now." He was right. Her daggers could shatter in another fight, leaving her helpless. She thanked him and worked to fasten the sword to her back.

"So I'm straight—are you guys okay?" She rocked with the adrenaline still surfing her system.

"Good." Dee traced a trio of thin slices in his cheek.

"All limbs accounted for." Dem wiggled his fingers. "And I'm gonna have a new scar." He winced as he lifted his shirt to reveal a shallow slice along his side. It still bled, but looked clean. There were other scrapes, probably a few bruises blossoming unseen over both of them. "Chicks dig scars."

"So sexy." She rolled her eyes and looked to Odabeth and Xelon. Both were on their feet now as well, Xelon fussing over her princess gently.

"Sooooo," Dem dragged out. "Those things didn't look like any Nightmare I've ever fought."

"We already covered that. Keep up." Dee glanced at the white-washed grass. "Didn't purge like one, either."

"They're called Fiends." Xelon finally turned from the princess, though Odabeth shifted closer to her side.

"Fee-what?" Dem asked.

"Fiends." Xelon retrieved her sword with a slight jerk, or was that a wince? Alice couldn't see if the knight had been injured, her cape falling down around her and blocking any view as she sheathed her weapon at her hip. "Using the power of the Nox, the Black Queen was able to corrupt those who didn't swear loyalty to her, morphing them until they were monsters that had no choice but to follow her. They're faster and stronger than natural Nightmares. More lethal all around."

Alice shuddered. "W-wait. Some Nightmares were people once?"

Xelon shook her head, pushing platinum strands out of her face. "Not humans, but my people. I lost many good friends that way."

"Those were hard times." Odabeth set a hand on Xelon's shoulder. "My mother and aunt were able to reverse my grandmother's work, but only for her more recent victims. The others h-had to be . . ."

Xelon covered the princess's fingers with her gauntleted ones.

"Podozhdite." Dee waved his hands. "Who's running around turning people into Fiends?"

The sinking feeling from before returned full force. Alice sighed, her gaze falling to the ground.

"It's got to be the Black Knight," she murmured. For an imposter, this dude was pulling off some super real shit.

Surprise flickered over each pale face.

"The Black Knight?" Xelon asked. "What makes you think—"

"I saw him. While I was getting water from the creek." Alice smoothed a hand over her braids. "He showed up and started . . . *talking*. A-about nothing. I was ready for him to attack, not strike up a conversation. So I stood there and listened like an idiot. It was a distraction."

All eyes focused on her; Alice fought like hell not to squirm. Instead, she smoothed her hands over her arms, mindful of her scrapes. "I'm sorry, I—I should have realized sooner."

After several painful seconds of silence, Xelon stepped forward to meet Alice's gaze, her motions somewhat disjointed. "You're not to blame for his deception."

Part of Alice wanted to believe her. The other part knew better, but said nothing.

"We need to move," Xelon said. "We've still got an hour's ride before we reach the Western Gateway."

"If we leave now, we can make it before sunset." Alice eyed the sky, where bursts of orange mixed in with pink. "Even then, we'll be cutting it close." That's when she noticed their party was two travelers short. "Where are the horses?"

"They took off the minute the fun started." Dee jerked a thumb over his shoulder.

"They'll find their way back to the palace, where they'll be safe." Xelon scanned the area.

"Good for them." Alice scrubbed her face. "Meanwhile, the rest of us will be stuck out here in the dark with Fiends running around all . . . Fiendish."

"What about the supplies?" Odabeth asked as Dee gauged the direction of the Glow and started walking. "The coach?"

"Leave it." Dem fell into step at his brother's side. "No time."

The princess gave a noise of protest, but Xelon said something Alice couldn't make out and she fell silent.

As they trekked along, everyone seemed jumpy and turned to look whenever something moved in the brush nearby. Twice they'd increased their pace, but there was no way they could make it before nightfall.

After a while, Alice's legs started to ache, and a hitch in her shoulder made itself known, but there was nothing for it. They had to keep moving.

Xelon caught Odabeth when she tripped over something for the millionth time. Normally, Alice would have questioned the ridiculous decision to wear those silly, strappy shoes, but three things stopped her: One, she was almost positive Odabeth only owned those kinds of shoes. Two, even if Odabeth did indeed own other shoes, Alice was sure hiking boots were not included. Three, the princess hadn't complained once since they started off again, about having to walk or no longer having her things. She was holding her own, in the best way she could.

"Not much farther," Alice offered.

Not that it mattered. They were going to run out of daylight a couple of miles shy of the Gateway. The darkness itself wouldn't be a problem—the Glow provided more than enough light to see by—but another Fiend attack was definitely on everyone's minds.

When the last swells of daylight faded, a heavy tension fell with the darkness. The soft whisper of leather and cloth sounded as everyone who was armed drew weapons. The only other sound permeating the night air was the thump of their footfalls, the crunch of grass and leaves, the occasional snap of a twig. No birds, no insects, no nighttime creatures.

Then Alice heard it, faint and distant. "Wait," she whispered as she threw up her hand. Everyone froze. "You hear that?"

They glanced around, their heads tilting. It sounded like the whistle of the wind at first. Then it grew louder, into a howl. And there was more than one.

"Move." Dee took off at a run.

Odabeth and Xelon followed. Alice and Dem brought up the rear. The princess gripped her skirts, wheezing around harsh pants. She slowed their pace, stumbling over her own feet. The howls grew louder, closer. The baying rose to a sound like hyenas cackling.

"Strewth!" Odabeth gasped, throwing glances over her shoulder, her eyes bright in the blue light of the moon.

"Almost there," Dee called over the collective symphony of their efforts.

The group burst from the edge of the forest and plowed into the tall grass of the meadow. Ahead, the Glow burned, intense in the night.

Another howl.

"If we can reach the Glow, the light will hold them off," Xelon hollered.

"I don't recall them being picky about that sort of thing." Dem panted around the words.

"It's sacred ground," Xelon said. "They'll come apart if they set foot there."

The howls became snarls.

Claws pounded against the ground.

Odabeth whimpered.

"Don't look back!" Xelon shouted.

Everyone ran as fast as they could. Alice kept sight of the princess ahead of her.

Behind her, teeth gnashed. Alice imagined fangs sinking into the exposed flesh of her neck.

The Glow loomed close. Thirty yards to go.

Another snarl. One of the Tweedles shouted a curse in Russian.

Twenty yards.

Alice's legs burned. Her calf cramped.

Ten . . .

Nineteen

JAWS THAT BITE

We're not gonna make it! Alice chanced a glance over her shoulder. Fiends were closing in.

Xelon looked back as well, just as the closest beast leaped. In one motion she spun, drew her sword, and slammed into the monster. Both of them went tumbling.

"Xelon!" Odabeth screamed, her voice cracking. The twins turned, spitting curses.

"Get her out of here!" The knight was on her feet, fending off a swipe of claws. "Go!"

Everything in Alice wanted to stay and fight, but the princess was the priority. "Guys!" Alice called to the twins as she took hold of Odabeth, who fought against her, screaming for Alice to let go. Dee grabbed her other arm and together they hauled her toward the Glow.

Alice hit the wall of crystal foliage at full speed. Leaves

smacked her face; branches scratched exposed skin and yanked at her clothes. When she emerged in a small clearing on the other side of the tree line, she stumbled to a stop. Odabeth dropped to her knees, whimpering around sobs of Xelon's name. Alice's chest heaved. Her face and hands throbbed. She fought to stay on her feet. Dee stood over the princess, eyes alert.

Dem exploded from the bush, wearing half of it. He lumbered to a stop, his and Dee's eyes asking each other if they were all right. Alice kept her eyes on the shimmering leaves, her chest tightening with every second that ticked by.

The typhoon of emotion loosed inside her made her dizzy. "You two get Odabeth to the Gateway." She darted back into the brush.

"Alice!" one of the twins shouted, but she didn't stop.

She stormed through, running, praying. The brightness of the leaves blinded her, their edges like razors against her skin. She ignored the stinging, pushed through the aches coating her body. She broke through. Darkness hung thick on the other side, the haze of the Glow fighting for dominance. She blinked as her vision clouded to adjust, like trying to see the world through murky water. Her head whipped around, searching.

Howling and cries of effort drew her attention. Xelon stood maybe fifty yards off, braced against a silver tree, one arm wrapped around her torso, the other gripping her sword as she swung. Two Fiends circled her, snapping shy of where her blade cut an arc in the air.

"We'll peel you out of your armor," one Fiend snarled.

"It will be quick and painless, dear one, we promise."

Xelon could turn, try to run to safety, but they'd get her

before she made it, drag her into the black, and tear her apart. Alice darted toward them as one beast dove to the side and lunged, digging teeth into Xelon's leg. She shouted.

"No!" Alice screamed. Her hands went to Dem's sword at her back.

The Fiends' heads snapped up. Their lips parted with fanged snarls. Xelon screamed at Alice to go back.

She drew the sword free and gripped it in both hands so tight her knuckles popped. Heat suffused her arms, her hands, her fingers. Her pulse pounded like war drums in her limbs.

Barking, the Fiends came at her, monsters charging in the night.

She lifted the blade. The thrumming in her arms shot to her palms. Her hands burned, the sensation familiar from the ache when she killed the Fiend before. This time the pain was excruciating, and she nearly lost her grip on the sword. Shock locked her fingers around the hilt as her body leaped into action without her permission.

"Be gone!" Her voice rang like a stranger's in her ears as she twisted into a swing.

Light erupted from her sword and sliced a clean arc into the air. Like some sort of lethal crescent moon, it slammed into an approaching Fiend, sending it flying with a yowl. The other Fiend peeled off, stamping the ground as it circled her instead of attacking.

Alice swung again, and again, hurling blades of light at the monsters. They dodged and ducked, the arcs shooting off and vanishing into the night when they missed. Those that hit hammered their targets, flinging them to the ground.

The beasts withdrew, their howls fading as they ran. She gazed after them, her lungs drinking in gulps of air that raked her throat like shards of glass. Every muscle ached. Her body swayed like a sail in a battering breeze. Her fingers finally loosed their death grip on the sword. It thudded to the ground, and pain radiated from her palms. She eyed the reddened skin where it rose in clustered welts.

Someone called her name. She wanted to answer, but her lips remained closed, the words trapped in her cotton mouth. Her knees knocked. Fatigue flooded her system, soaking her like a sponge. It pulled at her, hauling her toward the ground, and she hit the grass knees first, sinking to sit. Dem dropped beside her, grabbing her hands to examine them, asking all sorts of questions that were a hum in her mind.

What . . . what just happened? The sword. That light. Her head snapped up, and her eyes homed in on Xelon, who remained tilted against the tree. The surprise on her face equaled Alice's own, and something more, something questioning.

Xelon shifted, flinching as she gripped at red-stained armor.

"We have to help her." Alice made to get up, but Dem's hold kept her still.

"Are you all right?" he demanded, sounding concerned and a little annoyed.

"I—I'm fine. Get Xelon."

"Can you move?" Dem asked.

"Yes, *go*." She waved him in that direction, and he jogged over, his voice quiet as he asked Xelon the same line of questions, no doubt.

246

Alice took a few deep breaths before forcing herself to stand. The instant she was certain her legs would hold her weight, even though they felt like overcooked spaghetti, she joined the other two as quickly as she dared.

As she approached, the severity of Xelon's injuries became clear. Blood and dirt coated her armor. Deep grooves from claws and teeth scored the white plates. Pieces were missing, exposing rips in leather and broken links. Pale as she was before, all color had fled her face, slicked with sweat and blood, her expression pained as Dem examined her.

"How is she?" Alice asked, her eyes following a trickle of red as it slid along Xelon's thigh.

"Not good." Dem straightened from where he'd been looking over the bite in Xelon's leg.

"Can you walk?" Alice asked. Worry pitched her voice high.

"With that leg, she'll be lucky if she can stand." Dem shook his head. "Here, get her on." He spun around and knelt, arms out expectantly.

Xelon shifted forward, and Alice helped her into position against Dem's back wincing at the stinging in her hands. The younger Tweedle locked his arms under Xelon's legs and stood with a grunt of effort.

"You good?" Alice asked them both.

Xelon, one arm draped over Dem's shoulder, the other clutching his torso, nodded.

"Da." Dem shifted Xelon's weight before heading into the glowing brush.

Alice moved to follow, though she paused long enough to grab Xelon's sword. She hesitated before lifting the one she'd borrowed from the Tweedles. It looked like a regular Figment Blade again, no glowing or shooting light. She grit her teeth against the pain—god, her hands hurt—and sheathed it on her back and hurried to catch up.

As they stomped through the tangle of glass-like branches and vines, she ignored the looks Xelon threw her. She'd seen it, the light in Alice's sword. Dem must not have, otherwise his mouth would be going a mile a minute. Thank goodness, because she didn't have an explanation to offer.

When they emerged, Odabeth and Dee stood waiting for them. The princess took one look at her knight and burst into tears, hurrying to Xelon.

"I'm all right, milady." Xelon smiled with a wince. "Alive and well."

"Define *well*," Dem grumbled.

"You were supposed to take her to the Gateway," Alice said.

Dee shook his head. "She refused."

"We need to hurry, get her through so she can get looked at," Alice urged.

"Need a hand?" Dee asked his brother.

Dem shook his head and adjusted Xelon, who flinched. "Sorry. And no, at least not yet. But she's not exactly dainty, so . . ." He nodded toward the Gateway, and Dee led the way, deeper into the Glow.

As they hobbled along, the mist swirling between the trees parted for them. The bell-like laughter that usually filled the trees faded to whispers. No Flits or Sparks danced through the air, no flowers sang. The Glow itself seemed to recoil at their passing, the branches shifting ever so slightly, as if to move out of the way. Even the light itself was different, harsh and painful. Alice squinted and had to shield her eyes on occasion.

Odabeth, still in tears, fawned over Xelon, going on about how she was sorry and she was going to make sure she got the best care possible. The knight took it in stride, reassuring her.

As they moved, Alice gingerly pulled her mirror free and knocked against it.

"Open my eyes."

The surface shifted and warped until the Duchess's face filled the frame. She looked Alice up and down. "You look like hell."

"We're almost to the Gateway. Xelon's hurt pretty bad; she'll need to be looked at."

Maddi's face appeared over the Duchess's shoulder. "How bad? What happened?"

Alice swiped at her forehead with her sleeve as words caught in her throat. "W-we were attacked. Fiends, they ambushed—"

"Fiends?"

"Uh-huh."

"Did they bite anyone?" Maddi demanded, yellow eyes wide, a panicked note in her tone.

Alice looked over the five of them trudging through the Glow. From what she had seen, the only one to sustain any bite injuries was the knight. "Xelon. She was bitten."

Maddi grumbled something Alice couldn't make out. Maddi's head disappeared.

"We're preparing a room," the Duchess said. "Is everyone

else all right? The boys?" Worry was etched into her face, her tone pitched higher.

"We're fine."

"Be sure and keep it that way. See you shortly."

The image winked out, the surface of the mirror swirling to its original state. As Alice placed it in her pouch, she picked up the pace. Not since the battle at Ahoon had she so desperately wanted to leave Wonderland. And with those Fiends now running around, she wasn't too keen on return trips anytime soon.

Twenty

THE BLACK KNIGHT

As happy as Alice was to be back in the pub, her insides reeled from the journey between realms. She pulled in careful breaths, in through her nose and out through her mouth, as she clutched a small wastebasket to her chest, her face inches shy of pressing into it.

"Uuuuuugh, I hate feeling like this," she moaned.

"That . . . is super gross." Dem made a face where he stood over her. The two of them remained in the broom closet, the last ones through from Wonderland. She'd been eager to go after Xelon—who'd been taken away to be seen to—and check on Hatta, but first needed to be able to walk without throwing up.

"I don't know what's wrong." She squeezed her eyes shut and rocked a little, settled on her knees. "It hasn't been this bad in a long time."

"Bad enough to shove your face in a trash can," Dem muttered.

"And bad enough without your commentary—shut up." When she felt she could lift her head with no problem, she pushed the trash can away and hugged herself with mostly healed but still slightly sore hands. It was weird she hadn't recovered yet. Hell, her other cuts and bruises were still fresh.

Dem continued to pat her, unbothered by the hot mess she'd become. She released a low grown and murmured her thanks.

"Knock, knock." Maddi rapped her knuckles against the doorjamb. "Here ya go. Thought this might help." She handed over a glass filled with a brownish liquid.

"God, yes." Alice reached for the potion.

Dem took it and transferred it to her. She knocked it back like a woman dying of thirst.

"Smells like dog shit," he complained.

Alice shut her eyes and focused on the feeling of the liquid slipping past her throat, fizzy and bubbling. It tasted like a Coke infused with Tang and was like magic for her nausea, dog-shit smell or not. It coated her insides and tamped down the churning.

"Thanks." Alice sighed, the empty glass warming her fingers.

"Again. Gross." Dem stood and helped her up.

"This way." Maddi headed down the hall.

Now that Alice's stomach troubles were over, worry for her friends took the place of the nausea, and she was still pissed at Hatta for lying about the Eye. Ass. "How are they?"

"Xelon's injuries themselves aren't fatal," Maddi explained. "Still looking her over."

"And Hatta?" Alice clutched the glass a little tighter.

"He's . . ." Maddi paused in front of a closed door, her hand on the knob. "Stable." She didn't glance at Alice before pushing her way in.

Alice didn't like the way Maddi said that. "What do you mean *stable*?" she asked, trailing after her.

"The traditional definition, I'm sure," Hatta said, sitting on the edge of the bed. He gazed at her with ringed eyes, the color all but drained from them. The rest of his face pasty and clammy, he managed a smile that was more a grimace.

Her earlier anger at being lied to faded under relief, and Alice rushed to throw her arms around him, mindful of his weakened state. He felt thin, but at least he was awake and talking. She took a deep breath, reveling in his candied bourbon scent.

"Glad to see you, too." He curled an arm around her waist and gave her a weak squeeze.

"How are you feeling?" she asked without letting go.

"I've had better days." He patted her back, and she finally withdrew, but didn't go far.

She planted herself on the edge of the bed beside him, eyes moving over every inch she could see. "We brought Princess Odabeth. We're going to find the Eye, use it to find the Heart, and make you better."

"Hn." Hatta leveled a dark look at Maddi, who busily packed up her mixing tools while meeting his glare. "I'm touched you went through all this trouble, but you shouldn't have."

That was not expected. Alice glanced between the two of them.

"What's wrong?" Alice asked.

"Madeline and Anastasia have brought me up to speed on this rescue mission you all planned. Hunting for the Eye? Planning to go after the Heart—you're doing this imposter's work for him."

"I think he may be more than an imposter," Maddi murmured. "They were attacked by Fiends."

"What?" Hatta's gaze flew to Alice, then back to Maddi.

"I've never seen anything like them." Alice chewed at her lower lip. That wasn't exactly true. "Except the night we met. Outside the hospital. That one talked to me. These did as well. And Xelon said they were Fiends. She'd know, right?"

"Damn it," Hatta snapped. "How many were there?"

"Three." Alice held up that many fingers, as if that would help. "I killed one. I didn't know . . ."

"It's okay. You did what you had to do." Hatta reached to squeeze her fingers. She didn't even flinch this time.

"Addison," Maddi started. "The signs are all there."

Hatta shook his head. "Impossible."

"What?" Alice asked.

Hatta remained quiet.

Maddi cleared her throat. "All remaining Fiends were either killed or cured after the war. Or so we thought." She looked to Alice. "When you were attacked that night outside the hospital, we figured we missed one. Or something. But three?" Maddi glanced at Hatta, then back to Alice. "What if someone is turning people?" she asked quietly. "He has a Vorpal Blade—"

"No. No, it has to be something else," Hatta said.

"There is nothing else." Maddi stepped forward, almost pleading.

"No!" Hatta snapped. "It's not possible."

A hard pounding set in between Alice's ears. Why was Hatta being so stubborn about this? "This guy can summon Nightmares, poison people with this Madness mess, and maybe even create Fiends, but you're still convinced he's some random wannabe."

"He's *not* the Black Knight." Hatta pressed his hands to the sides of his bowed head. "He can't be."

"What makes you so—" Alice's words dried up on her tongue when Hatta jerked and lifted his head.

His eyes flew wide, the colors dark again. The black in them set off the burning amber.

Alice shifted backward despite herself.

Dem jolted where he still stood in the doorway, his hand on his sword, his body tense. Alice had forgotten he was there. His gaze bounced between her and Hatta as if asking her what to do.

Hatta shut his eyes and took a slow, shaky breath, a hand lifted. "Sorry, sorry, I can't—I'm trying to fight it, but it's hard." He released a low groan, strained.

Maddi moved forward, setting her hand to his forehead, then his chest, murmuring words too low to make out. She gave him a glass of something red that he swallowed without question.

"I'm not convinced he's an imposter—I know it for a fact." Hatta spat the words from behind clenched teeth. "Because *I'm* the Black Knight."

Twenty-One
BEST-LAID PLANS

Alice didn't believe one word that came outta Hatta's mouth. What he said made a painful amount of sense, but wouldn't compute. Her brain refused to accept the information, so she sat there, staring, waiting for him to say something else.

"*You're* the Black Knight?" Dem sounded as surprised and disbelieving as she felt.

Impossible, she wanted to say, but the word stuck in her throat. Hatta was sweet and funny and got worried when you were hurt and made sure you got home safely at night. He laughed at bad jokes and preferred stories with happily ever afters. He put more effort into looking after lost strangers that wandered into the pub—like Sprigs—than some people put into looking after loved ones. He *defended* people, protected them, pushed them when they needed to keep going or held them when they needed to break down. He was gentle, patient, and self-sacrificing, everything the Black Knight wasn't.

So why was he nodding?

"Rather, I *was*. The original." Hatta smoothed his hands along his thighs. "Back when I was simply the knight, I served my Queen and her daughters. My duty composed all of me, and I excelled at it. Until I failed miserably."

Ice poured through Alice's veins, numbing her from head to toe. But that didn't stop the pain twisting in her chest. "Odette," she whispered.

Hatta nodded without looking up. Maddi withdrew her touch, backing away as he sank even farther into himself, back rounded, arms draped over his thighs. "I was supposed to protect them, protect her. I—I . . ."

"That wasn't your fault." Alice clenched her fists. She surprised herself with the forcefulness of her words, but she believed them, and she needed Hatta to believe, too. "You can't blame yourself fo—"

"I was supposed to *protect* them!"

Alice had never seen Hatta like this before. He was all writhing fury one second, then deflated anger the next. Sorrow twisted his expression. She moved forward, her arms encircling him, squeezing.

He pressed his face to her shoulder.

"It's okay." She choked on the whisper, clutching him. "It's okay."

He shook faintly, and she let him take his time, concentrating on her own breath, on the thickness in her throat. The area between her shoulder blades ached as she fought to keep still, solid, rocklike, for him.

She refused to cry. Hatta didn't need her pity. He didn't need her sympathy. He needed her to wait until he pulled himself together.

They stayed like that. For how long, she wasn't sure, but when he withdrew, she dropped her arms to her sides. There were no tears on his face—she wasn't sure he *could* cry—but she knew the value of having someone there while you disappeared into yourself for a little while.

Hatta cleared his throat, his gaze playing over the room before drifting to her. "You're better at that than you let on."

Alice smiled faintly. "All I did was sit here."

Maddi offered Hatta a tumbler with a touch of amber liquid inside. He took it with murmured thanks and downed it in one go.

"Could I get one of those?" Dem asked.

Hatta chuckled, and the tension dissolved in shared, slightly awkward but genuine, laughter.

"So, if he's *not* the Black Knight, how is he tied to the Black Queen? How does he share her powers?"

"I'm . . . I don't know," Hatta said. "All the more reason you should *not* have gone after the princess."

"She's the only one who can help you," Alice stressed.

"Exactly." Hatta shot a look at Maddi before wincing, shifting on the bed. "The Heart and the Eye are useless without a member of the royal bloodline. Even if the imposter managed to find either of them, he couldn't use them on his own. Attacking Queen Emalia, then me." Hatta shook his head. "I should've seen it. He did this to ensure you'd bring him the last part of the equation."

"Odabeth," Alice murmured. Swallowing thickly, she pushed down the small voice inside her head that said she'd screwed things up, again. The Black Knight continuously played her, and somehow she kept falling for it. She was supposed to be smarter than this, better. "So what, we just let you die?"

Hatta met Alice's gaze, his softening. He lifted a hand to the side of her face, his touch gentle but brief. "I'm not worth the risk."

"You are to me," she whispered, her voice cracking.

He smiled, though it didn't reach his eyes. "And Queen Emalia is worth it to Odabeth. Between the two of you, we were bound to end up here."

"Hate to admit it," Dem started, "but this Black Knight bastard is brilliant."

"Maybe," Alice said. "But maybe he overplayed his hand. Now we know his plan, we know what he wants, and he has to come to us to get it. We find the Eye, find the Heart, but keep them separate. That way, we cure you, cure the White Queen, then she can scatter everything again. We'll just stay ahead of him this time. He can't beat *all* of us."

"Heart, Eye, starting to sound like we're building Frankenstein," Dem murmured.

"This is all real interesting." Dee stepped into view beside his brother. "But I was sent to fetch you lot."

Alice hadn't even heard him approach. She wondered how long he'd been standing there.

"What's wrong?" she asked.

"Nothing, just finished with Xelon."

Alice had nearly forgotten about the injured knight. She'd been rushed off to be treated with anti-venom.

Everyone but Maddi—she said she had a bit more work to do with so many busted-up people—moved to follow Dee. They filed down the hall and then an adjacent corridor. Dee ducked through yet another mystery door, which opened to what looked like a hotel room of some sort. The generic green-and-black-plaid comforter stretched across the king-sized bed, and a little chair and desk sat off to the side. There was even a kitchenette complete with a minibar.

Xelon rested in the bed, wrapped in bandages. Concern tugged Alice forward, but she stopped at the foot of the frame.

"Will she be all right?" she asked.

"Yes." Odabeth stood near the window, still wearing her tattered dress, staring at a view of the downtown area that was obviously not real. For one, it was at least a tenth-story view. "She'll be fine." The princess twisted her necklace. The jeweled star at the end danced like a puppet on marionette strings.

Dee joined his brother, who rummaged through the fridge. The two spoke in whispered Russian that came out garbled every time Dem took a bite of a sandwich.

Hatta sat on the edge of the mattress and reached to lay a hand over Xelon's arm but stopped short, his fingers hovering over pale skin. "She does good work."

"A compliment, coming from you." The Duchess emerged from the washroom, the sound of running water fading behind her. Dee and Dem leaped to their feet and stood at attention when she entered. She waved them off as she wiped her hands on a towel, then tossed it aside. It landed in the mesh basket near the door. "How are *you* feeling, Addison?" She perched beside Hatta and angled herself forward to place her palm on his thigh.

His hand fell atop hers. "I've been worse, Anastasia. You know that."

"But you've also been better. I know that as well." The Duchess smirked and withdrew her touch.

It happened so quickly there was nothing to be bothered about. The concern in the Duchess's tone meant nothing. And there was certainly nothing to be worried about in Hatta's returning her friendly gesture, or the way he smiled at her. And definitely nothing troubling in the way they used each other's names like that.

Nope.

Nothing to be upset about.

Alice stood there, watched the exchange, and when it was over, she lifted her chin and cleared her throat a little.

"It's good to see you again, Alice." The Duchess nodded at her.

"Good to be seen." *Her eyes are like emeralds. Who actually has eyes like emeralds?*

It was silly, complaining about the color of someone's eyes. Green, like envy.

"How's she doing?" Hatta asked, drawing the Duchess's attention to the bed and Xelon.

"She's stable. This news of the White Queen's condition troubles me, though. It's a shame we weren't alerted sooner."

The Duchess tossed a glance at Odabeth's back. The princess's shoulders stiffened, but she remained silent. The Duchess looked back at Hatta. "If she's been poisoned for as long as I believe, we're running out of time."

Odabeth turned to face them, tears in her eyes. She clutched at the chain around her neck. "How long does my mother have?"

"Days. Maybe." The Duchess looked at Hatta again. "Tell us where you hid the Eye."

"And risk plunging both worlds into darkness if this all goes tits up?" Hatta countered.

"Hatta." Alice looked at him. "We've been through this. We have a plan."

"*You* have a plan. So far your plans are how we wound up in this mess."

Alice jerked as if slapped. "What?"

He lifted a hand, as if to ward off what she was thinking. "I know, it was also Madeline's plan. And this one's." He eyed the Duchess.

It was a nice save, but Alice didn't buy a word of it. "You think this is my fault." The Black Knight had been right. After everything they'd been through, Hatta didn't believe in her. She didn't believe in herself half the time, but she'd always thought he had. That's what kept her going. Now, looking back on everything, it was clear she was fooling herself. He lied to her about the Eye because he didn't think she could handle it.

"Alice, listen." Hatta approached her, stopping just shy of reaching out to her. His fingers flexed and his arms shifted as if he wanted to, but they remained at his sides. "However you're taking it, that's not how I meant it," he murmured, searching her face with those oddly colored eyes.

Alice nodded, blinking rapidly to fight tears. "Whatever. You're dying. The White Queen is dying. *Your* plan is to just let that happen."

"What?" Odabeth squawked, her wide eyes dancing between the three of them. "No. No! This is the only way to save my mother, it *will* be done."

Hatta sighed, his entire body sagging with it. "Your mother and her sister gave explicit orders. Under no circumstances are we to risk bringing the Heart and the Eye out into the open, Your Majes—"

"Don't you 'Your Majesty' me, Addison Hatta." Odabeth chewed on his name. "You may be in exile, but you are still duty bound to my mother's crown. With her ill, it is now mine and you are hereby ordered to do everything in your power to save her, and thus yourself. I won't hear a word otherwise."

"Ummm . . ." Maddi stood in the doorway, blinking wide brown, then black, then green eyes.

"Yes, Madeline?" Hatta sighed, pinching the bridge of his nose.

"Right. Your friends are here," Maddi said, looking at Alice.

Alice shook her head, blinking. "What?" She hurried out of the room, nearly bowling Maddi over in the process, and down the hall. Her chest tightened with each step. There were only two people the bartender could be talking about.

Out in the pub, Alice slammed to a stop, her shoes squeaking against the floor. Courtney stood at the bottom of the steps to the door, her arms folded, her eyes fixed on Alice, who couldn't read the blank expression on her face. Joy warred with irritation and a little bit of fear. Was she still mad?

None of that mattered when Chess stood from where he'd been seated on the stairs behind her and the twisting in Alice's chest went into full-on *oh shit* mode.

"So." He let his violet gaze dance around the room, then back to her. "About this job of yours."

Twenty-Two

FIVE DOWN

Alice stared at her friends, and her brain promptly dumped all information on how to speak. Or move. Or do anything useful except blink like some fool.

Chess glanced back and forth between her and Courtney before sighing and rolling his eyes, then nudging Court's arm.

Courtney yanked away from him as if burned. "All right!" Chess lifted his hands as Court cleared her throat, blinked at Alice, released a faint breath, and said, "Hey."

Hey. Hey? That was it? "Hey." Alice, apparently, didn't have better. Her tongue felt too big for her mouth, her stomach twisting. "What're you guys doing here?"

Court shrugged, looking everywhere but at Alice now. "I maybe told Maddi to call me when you got back."

The twisting eased a little. "You got my message?"

"Mmhm." Court fidgeted with something shiny hanging off an expensive-looking purse.

"That's new," Alice said, indicating the bag.

"What?" Court looked at the purse as surprised to find it draped on her arm. "Oh yeah. It was a birthday present."

The twisting tightened right back up again. "You got a matching wallet? 'Cause I still owe you one. A present, not—not a wallet."

Chess groaned, flinging his arms into the air. "Oh, come on! Not five minutes ago you were ducking in and out of traffic like you were in *The Fast and the Furious* to get here. Could've gotten several tickets, definitely almost got us both killed, all 'cause you were worried sick about her!" He pointed at Alice. "Now, you wanna act like you're not happy to see her alive and well and not, quote, 'torn to shreds'?"

Court stared at Chess like he'd started spitting fire from his eyes. He just held a hand out, indicating Alice, who'd started shaking, her lower lip trapped between her teeth. Courtney had been worried about her. Enough to speed over here the second she got a call.

Alice sniffed as her throat closed off. The tears started before she could even try to hold them back.

Court looked at her again, red crawling up her neck and over her stupid flawless face.

Alice lifted her arms, and Courtney all but flung her bag aside as she crossed the room and threw her arms around her.

"I'm sorry," Court sobbed, gripping Alice tight enough it was hard to breathe.

It didn't matter; Alice was having trouble with the snot and tears anyway. "Me too!"

"It was just a party. I was so stupid." Court hiccuped.

"I-it was important—I didn't mean to miss it."

"You were nearly killed!"

Alice held on to her friend as they cried and apologized, cried some more, promised to never fight again, cried some more. They finally let go, and the twisting in Alice's stomach faded completely, replaced by this warmth that spread through the rest of her, healing a part of her she didn't realize was broken. She wiped her eyes, sniffling, and smiled like an idiot.

Court smiled, smearing her makeup as she wiped and sniffed as well.

"Your face looks horrible," Alice giggle-whined.

"Yeah, well." Court sniffed and wiped at her nose. "You literally smell like shit."

"I know!" They both laughed, the sound like so much music to Alice's ears. "Gawd, we're a mess."

"You have no idea." Chess offered them both tissues from lord knew where.

Alice ignored it, instead stepping between his arms and wrapping hers around him.

He made an adorable little noise of surprise but folded her into a hug.

"Thank you," she murmured into his shoulder.

"Anytime." He squeezed her gently.

She returned the gesture, then stepped back, taking the tissue and blowing her nose. Court was dabbing at her makeup, compact already in her hand from where she'd fetched her purse.

"Now, then," Chess heaved a dramatic sigh, glancing between them with his attention settling on Alice. "You were nearly killed?"

Oh right. Alice heaved a sigh, looking to Courtney. "You told him?"

"No. I didn't. Nosy Nancy here went snooping through my phone." Court glared at him in the process of touching up her mascara.

"I didn't go—look, the phone buzzed, it was sitting on the couch next to me, I went to hand it to you, and the message was on the damn screen. There was zero snoopage involved."

"Uh-huh. Anyway." Court paused to reapply her lipstick, which was probably all somewhere on the side of Alice's face. "I told him you had an important position that sometimes led to dangerous things and, well . . ."

Chess looked to Alice. "I tried calling you, but no answer. I texted you, and you said you were with Courtney, which you weren't."

"Ahh, yeah." Well, at least Maddi was on top of the text thing. At least, Alice hoped she was.

"I spent *for-ev-er* trying to ditch him after school, but he was determined to come—"

"Wait." Alice lifted a hand. "What time is it?" With a wormy feeling in her stomach, she hurried around Courtney and ducked behind the bar, searching for her stuff. Her phone sat on one of the shelves, plugged in. The screen read 6:38 PM on Monday night. Her heart up around her ears, she checked her messages. There was no indication of trouble from school, so far. Mom had checked in right after class let out, telling her to come straight home. Maddi responded masterfully with a "yes, ma'am." Everything was cool until Mom got home from work about an hour and a half ago. Three missed calls and a bunch of messages demanding to know where the hell she was.

Shit shit shit. Alice unplugged the phone while calling her mom, who answered not two rings in. "She lives. For now."

"Hey, Mommy. I'm sorry, I—"

"Don't mommy me. Where are you, Alison?"

Alice's phone jumped out of her hand. She reached after it, only to blink as Courtney held it to her ear.

"Hey, Mrs. K! It's Courtney. Y-yes. Yes, ma'am. Yes, ma'am. She told me. Yes, ma'am. It's my fault she's late. My car got a flat, and we had to wait for my dad, but he was stuck in traffic. Yes, ma'am. No, ma'am, we were coming straight from school. Yes, ma'am. He's already done. We're on our way. Yes, ma'am. Here she is."

Court handed the phone over.

Alice took it and pressed it to her ear like it might just bite it off. "Hello?"

"You better have your ass in this house by eight thirty. Don't walk in at eight thirty-one, or that's the last thing you do."

"Yes, ma'am. I love you." It was worth a shot.

"Eight. Thirty. I love you, too, now bye."

Alice heaved a sigh, folding her arms over the counter and pressing her face to them. Her nose wrinkled at the sharp stink of Nightmare, rather, Fiend guts. Court was right, she did smell like shit. And she hugged Chess like this. *Uggggh.* Straightening, she looked to her friends. Court had finished her touch-ups, looking like she hadn't shed one tear. Chess just looked vaguely confused, but intrigued, as he took in the pub decor.

"So," he said as Alice came around the bar, her pack of clothes in hand.

"So," Alice repeated. "We need to leave, or my mom might actually kill me."

"She sounded on the edge," Court murmured.

"Let me tell the others what's happening." She was already partway down the hall. Voices greeted her, rushed, clipped, and angry. Hatta and the Duchess still debating about the risk of revealing the Eye. Maddi looked over a still-sleeping Xelon. The twins had slipped off to who knows where.

Alice didn't try to make out who was saying what, just knocked on the door to gain their attention.

"I have to go," Alice said when curious eyes turned her way. "Not for long. It's my mother . . . she's . . . worried." The last thing she needed to explain was how a freaking curfew was throwing a monkey wrench into her plans.

The Duchess sighed. "It's not like we're racing the clock or anything."

"Anastasia," Hatta snapped.

"I know," Alice cut in before he could continue with whatever he was going to say. "I know we don't have a lot of time, but I'm all she's got, and I've been hiking through the wilderness and fighting off fucking monsters and shadow-wielding assholes, and I've only got more of that to look forward to, so I'd like to take a couple of hours to hug my mother!"

Three pairs of wide Wonderlandian eyes blinked at her. One pair kept changing color.

"Then, take them." Hatta broke the silence. He struggled to his feet with a wince, moving over to her. "Like you said, you've been pushing through for what had to be days on the other side. A few hours isn't going to hurt us." He pitched a look over his shoulder at the Duchess, who just wrinkled her nose a little but remained silent, then ran his hands up Alice's arms to her shoulders, squeezing. "Hug your mom. Get some rest."

Alice nodded, hoping he didn't feel the shiver that moved through her. "This doesn't mean I'm giving up on this. Or you."

He smirked. "Never. Go on now."

"I'll be back." Alice looked to Maddi. "Call me if you need me, okay?"

The Poet gave a thumbs-up, and Alice turned to make her way back out to the bar. She scrubbed her hands over her face and swallowed the groan welling against the back of her throat. Could this night get any worse?

"Of course it can, so just shut up," she hissed at herself as she rounded the corner and nearly ran into Odabeth, who stood in the entry to the bar. She'd changed into a pair of sweatpants and a Hello Kitty shirt that were too small, clearly borrowed given the way the sweatpants hugged the princess's frame and didn't reach past her ankles. She still managed to look regal as hell as she toyed with the jewel around her neck.

The twins had come out as well, pausing their quiet conversation in Russian as Alice entered the room. She looked from the twins to Chess and Court—the latter eyeing the boys like they were a double scoop of ice cream—then to Odabeth. "Your Highness."

The princess lifted a hand. "After today, that won't be necessary. I owe you my life, Alice. I'd hoped that this is where we might be able to call each other friend."

Well, that was a surprise. Alice blinked before smiling. "I'd like that."

"Then please, call me Odabeth. You two as well," she said, looking at the twins.

"O-okay." Alice hadn't expected that. Neither had the twins, given the looks on their faces.

"Good, good. Now then . . ." Odabeth nodded as her jaw tightened. "How do we proceed with the plan to help my mother? And Hatta," she added, hurriedly.

"You mean where we gather all the magical body parts so this Black Knight can resurrect an evil queen and let her lay waste to our world and yours," Dem muttered, arms folded over his chest. "That plan?"

Alice cut a glare at Dem. "Yes, that plan. Only we'll stay ahead of the Black Knight so the laying waste doesn't happen."

Odabeth nodded. "Tell me what you have in mind. What do you need from me?"

"We find the Eye, use it to locate the Heart, then keep them under close guard until you're able to use the Heart to cure Hatta and your mother. Then one, or the both of you, scatters it all to the winds again." Now that she said it out loud, it didn't sound like a plan so much as what she hoped would happen.

"You're really going through with this?" Dee asked, his gaze bouncing between Alice and Odabeth. "Even though the Black Knight might be tricking us into doing it?"

The princess peered down the length of her nose at the twins. "Am I wrong to believe you Tweedles are up to such a task?"

"Not wrong at all," Dem snorted. "But there's a difference between being able to handle trouble and walking face-first into it."

"Get that out of a fortune cookie, did you?" Dee eyed his brother.

"Zatkn'ees." Dem shoved his twin, and the bickering picked up instantly.

Court "mmphed" under her breath. "I can maybe appreciate why guys like watching catfights . . ."

Odabeth ignored the twins, looking back to Alice. "I saw you face those monsters. I know how capable you are. You saved me. Twice. You saved X-Xelon." She looked away then, her breath catching. "I did not get a chance to express my gratitude." She faced Alice again with a regal lift of her shoulders. "You have our thanks."

Alice hesitated, rubbing at the back of her neck. "Uh, you're welcome. Just doing my duty or whatever."

"Exactly. You are a great warrior who sees her duty done. Ignore what Hatta said before. You and I, *we* can do this. They can help." She gestured to the twins, who were in a full-blown spitting match. Court ogled them, biting her lower lip, like she was watching a striptease instead of a battle.

Alice turned the words over in her mind. She understood the reasons for Hatta's refusal. Doing all of this would almost be like flipping the switch on a nuclear power plant. So much could go so wrong so very fast. But with fail-safes in place, and people who knew what they were doing—like Alice, the Tweedles, the Duchess, and Xelon when she was healed—they could definitely handle the Black Knight.

"All right," Alice answered. "We got this."

"Excellent!" Odabeth clapped her hands together, and the twins stopped bickering to glance over.

"We're with you," Dee said.

"Okay, well, what's our next move?" Court asked.

Alice faced her friend, arching an eyebrow. "*Our* next move?"

"Oh, I'm part of this. You want me to keep covering your ass, you let me in on the juicy bits." Court lowered her gaze before mumbling, "The Russian-speaking juicy bits."

Alice rolled her eyes but smiled. *You are impossible.* The look Court gave her in return made it believable she'd heard.

"I'm in, too," Chess said. "I literally have no idea what's going on, but it sounds like you're going to need all hands on deck. Even clueless ones."

"So." Court clapped then rubbed her palms together. "Next move."

"Next move, we find the Eye," Alice said. "Wherever Hatta's hidden it. And he's not in a sharing mood."

"I may be able to help with that." Odabeth fingered the jeweled star hanging around her neck. "There's a Verse my grandmother would use to invoke the power of the Eye. Since her downfall it's been forbidden to cast. I tried it once, when I was younger, when I was missing her. Nothing happened, but the Eye was in another realm at the time. Now that I'm here as well, maybe it will work."

The twins looked skeptical.

Alice shrugged. It wasn't much, but she said, "What've we got to lose."

Odabeth nodded, though she hesitated. "Perhaps it is best if we try this in a less restricted space." She glanced around the bar. "The results in the past could be . . . intense."

Alice pointed at the door. "Everybody outside."

They all shuffled through the exit, out onto the sidewalk, and into the nighttime chill. Streetlights filled the air with an orange glow, hazy against the sparkling backdrop of downtown. Alice checked her phone. 7:56 PM. Still time. Hopefully.

When they'd all gathered in the cracked parking lot beside the building, Odabeth studied the clear sky. Cradling the gem in her hands, she released a soft breath, then held it up.

"Twinkle, twinkle, all-seeing star. Show us wonders near and far." As Odabeth spoke, her voice took on a faint, echoing quality that hung in the air, building instead of fading. The words grew louder, meshing together to become a hymn-like resonance.

"I've never heard this version," Court whispered. Alice shushed her, eyes on the princess.

"In the midnight sky you keep," Odabeth continued, "watch over the dark and deep. I beseech the masters old, search my heart for worth bestowed. Menders of the breaking skies, clear my mind, open my eyes."

As the sound of her voice rose, the pendant in her hand began to shine, softly at first. Then the glow grew, brightening until everyone squinted or lifted their hands to shield their eyes. The light burned, blinding, then flickered and went out completely.

"Did it work?" Chess asked after several seconds of silence.

Alice squinted, trying to get her eyes to adjust to the sudden darkness. Court rubbed her eyes. The twins shook their heads as if trying to clear them.

Odabeth stared at the ground.

Chess did as well, eyes wide. "That was a magic spell. Like actual magic. Holy shit."

Alice looked down, blinking to clear her vision. With each fall of her lids, a soft trail of gold revealed itself. It started at Odabeth's feet and fissured outward, split into six lines. Two of them led out of the parking lot and made a sharp right turn along the sidewalk. A third darted out into the street and kept going. The remaining three lines trailed to each of the twins and Alice. They pulsed gently, winking in and out as they climbed their legs.

"Kakogo cherta?" Dem smoothed his hands over one thin streak of light where it ended at his thigh.

"No clue." Dee traced the trail up his leg with his fingers, then rubbed them together.

Alice smoothed her hand against her own leg, marveling at the phenomenon.

"Um, Alice?" Court tapped Alice's hip where a faint glow the same color as the trail pulsed in tandem with it.

"What the hell?" Alice shoved her hand into her pouch, fingers wrapping around something hard and warm. She pulled the object free and held it up.

The mirror Maddi had given her before she went into

Wonderland, identical to ones the twins now plucked from their pockets. All three shone with the same light, thrumming like a faint heartbeat.

"What's going on?" both boys asked.

"It's in pieces," Alice murmured. "The Eye. That's how Hatta hid it."

Dee flipped his mirror over in his hands and played his fingers against the reflective surface. "Six lines, six pieces."

"And we already have three," Dem said. "Convenient."

"Maybe." Alice followed the two lights that made a right at the sidewalk. "Or maybe something more. These should lead us to the remaining sections of the mirror." The trail turned again, right into the pub.

"One's gotta be the Duchess," Dee said.

"Then the other is Hatta," Alice said.

"What about this one?" Odabeth stood at the lone trail a few feet off to the side. It continued up over the hill, vanishing from sight.

"I don't know." Alice glanced in that direction, wondering where the trail might end.

"Since we already know where these two lead," Dem said, pointing, "I say we find the mystery piece."

"Okay." Alice paced back and forth a few times, her fingers tapping at her lower lip. They needed to be smart about this, stay ahead of the Black Knight. "Dee, Dem. You two stay here, with the princess and your mirrors. Take this one." She handed Maddi's mirror over to Odabeth. "More shards here, more muscle to guard them. Let the Duchess know what's going on, and you all can work together to get Hatta's mirror. That's five down."

The twins nodded.

"And you?" Dee asked.

"I'll track down the last piece with Court and Chess."

"Sounds like a plan." Dem headed for the pub, beckoning Odabeth to follow.

"What about your mom?" Court asked. "She expects you home soon and is already fit to be tied. If you're late . . ."

Alice flung her hands into the air. "I know! She'll probably ground me forever, or kick my ass—but this is literally life or death. I'll take the beatdown, just . . . let's go."

Alice, Court, and Chess piled into the Camaro. The instant the engine turned over, Court peeled out of the lot and onto the street. During the ride, Alice managed an awkward-as-hell explanation of Dreamwalkers, Nightmares, Wonderland, and everyone back at the pub while trying to focus on the road and the thin trail of light that disappeared now and then under the direct glow of streetlights. They lost it a couple of times, having to backtrack here and there. Chess took all of it in stride—seeing Odabeth perform the Verse probably helped. His knee was bouncing awful hard in the back seat, though. He nodded. And nodded. And nodded, repeating the phrase "Well, all right" whenever a new bit of information was offered.

"Why didn't you tell me any of this before?"

Alice shrugged, fighting the urge to sink down in her seat. "I didn't know you. At first. Then I didn't know what you'd think of all this, of me. If you even believed me."

"Yeeeaaaaah, it . . . it's pretty damn unbelievable." He reached to set a hand on her shoulder. "But I did just watch a princess from another world perform a spell to find a magic talisman to save your boss and possibly the world from an ancient evil. Which is equal parts unbelievable and awesome. So you're still the coolest person I know."

Alice twisted in her seat to find him smiling at her. She couldn't help but return it, feeling some of the tightness in her chest loosen a bit. It felt good, telling him all of this, telling somebody all of this. Courtney knew, but she knew from the beginning. It had been over a year of keeping this secret. Now it weighed a little less.

"Um, this has got to be a joke." Court guided her car into a wide lot.

The three of them stared through the windshield, Chess leaning in from the back, as they pulled up in front of their school.

"We sure they got the right place?" Court asked.

"Uh-huh. There's the path." Chess pointed to the trail of starlight that led up to the building, climbed the wall, and vanished into a third-floor window.

Alice suddenly knew, without a doubt, where it would lead. "It's in my locker."

Twenty-Three

ONE TO GO

Alice gawked at the school through the Camaro's windshield. Everything looked different in the dark. The brick of the building had taken on a purple quality, shadowed under the cloudy night. The windows were dark, the blinds pulled, closing the entire place off. The empty parking lot stretched on like a concrete desert.

"Didn't know this place could look so creepy." Court cut the engine.

Alice kicked the underside of the dashboard.

"Easy!" Courtney held an arm out in front of the dash protectively.

"I can't believe I didn't realize it sooner." Alice knocked her head back against the headrest. "Or that I have a piece of a powerful relic just chillin' in my locker." If Hatta had *told* her what it was, she would've taken better care of it, gotten an extra lock, locked it in a box inside the locker *with* the extra lock, something! *But no, can't tell Alice anything important, apparently.*

"Soooooo," Alice drew the word out as she straightened in her seat. "Any idea on how to get inside?"

"And somehow get to your locker, get the mirror, and get out without breaking any windows, picking any locks, setting off the alarms, and possibly winding up in jail?" Court glanced over her shoulder. "Not one. 'Cause Hatta's hot and all, but I don't do time for a pretty face."

Alice eyed the metal double doors at the front of the building, her mind working out just how the hell they were going to do this.

"You're seriously considering breaking into the school?" Court asked.

"I could get us in," Chess offered from the back seat.

Both girls turned to stare at him.

He lifted his hands. "If it's important, I wanna help."

"You could get us in there?" Court asked, eyes narrowed in suspicion.

He pressed his lips together, glancing to the side, and shifting a little before meeting their gazes again, though he didn't hold them. Finally, he sighed and said, "I may or may not have been kicked out of my last school for . . . similar activities."

Court's face went from suspicious to shocked, then sly all in a blink, a smirk curling her lips.

"It's not what you think." Chess waved his hands. "I didn't steal anything. It was a stupid dare-slash-bet. I wasn't caught, but the jackass who dared me ratted me out instead of owning up."

Court snickered.

Alice couldn't help grinning, too. "Looks like I wasn't the only one keeping secrets."

"Touché." Chess sighed before looking back to the school. "We can't do it right now, though. It's too early, and I need to get a few things."

"Chester." Court purred his name. He flinched. "I didn't know you had this darker side. Think I'll start calling you Clyde."

He scowled, though there was no real malice behind it. "Only if I can call you Bonnie."

"Right, so." Alice took a breath. "We take you home, you get your cat-burglar kit together, and you meet us back here when?"

"Late, like three," Chess said. "And not here, a few blocks over. Don't want our cars on the security cams."

"Huh." Court eyed Chess, her mouth turned down as she gave an impressed nod. "I like this Clyde-Chess."

"Just Chess is fine," he muttered as Court started the car and pulled out of the lot.

After they dropped Chess off at home, Alice called the bar and let Maddi know what the plan was and was pleased to find the Duchess had handed her mirror right over. They found Hatta's in his office. The good news was he didn't put up a fight about it. The bad news was he didn't put up a fight because he'd had another episode. After five minutes of assurance from Maddi that he would be okay, it wasn't half as bad as before, Alice hung up and flung her phone into the back seat.

"What's wrong?" Court asked quietly.

"He's getting worse. Can you believe that fool is ready to die?" Anger warred with the burn of tears. "On top of that, his headass is ready to make me watch it happen."

"It's okay, Alice." Court glanced back and forth between her and the road. "Seriously, everything's gonna be fine. We'll get your mirror, then get the Eye thingy and all that other stuff. He'll live. You two still have to hook up; he can't go out before that."

Alice barked a laugh, shaking her head. "You back on that, huh."

"Always. You two are my OTP."

"Whatever."

"Though Chess might be looking to give Hatta a run for his money," Court singsonged.

"Okay, now I know you buggin'."

"I'm just sayin', I see the way he looks at you when you're not lookin'."

"And what way is that?"

Court heaved a dramatic sigh. "Seriously, where did I go *wrong* with you?"

Alice shook her head, though she couldn't ignore that bit of warmth that filled her face at Court's talk about Chess. "Let's worry about this heist and keeping my Black ass out of prison, *then* you can worry about my love life."

"And what about my white ass?" Court asked, feigning indignation.

"It's white, so it'll be just fine. Hell, they might give you a medal for bringing me in."

Court humphed. "I could hang it on my wall."

"Girl, shut up!" Alice laughed. Court did, too. It felt good. *Okay, one to go. Let's do this.*

◊ ◊ ◊

Alice checked her phone for the third time as they climbed the stairs to her door. 9:16 PM. And no calls. No messages. To anyone else, this might be a good sign. To Alice, it meant one thing: DEFCON 1.

Court squeezed one of Alice's hands as she lifted the keys in the other. She barely touched the lock when the door flew open and her mom filled the frame, all silent rage, nightgown, and curlers.

"Get your ass in this house." She pushed the quiet words from behind her teeth, then stepped back so the girls could enter.

"It's still my fault, Mrs. K," Courtney started. "I took Chess home first because he was closest and—"

Mom clamped her fingers together in the air, and Court shut up. She wasn't her child, but she knew that wouldn't save her. Mom glanced between the two of them, and Alice did her best not to look away. The silence was way worse than any yelling. The quiet before the mother of all storms. The muscle at the back of Mom's jaw kept working as she ground her teeth.

"I said eight thirty."

Alice didn't say a word. Neither did Courtney.

"I meant eight thirty. Since you can't manage to tell time between the both of you, I will be dropping you off at school in the morning and Mrs. Hughes will be picking you up."

Alice's stomach dropped to her feet. "But we—"

"I'm not finished." Mom's expression didn't budge even when she shouted. She cleared her throat. "When you get home, you will call me from the house phone to let me know you are here. You will do whatever homework you have, then start dinner. After, you'll do those dishes and clean whatever else around here I can think of. Then you will go up to that room and sit. No TV, no computer, just you thanking God for how he blessed you—against all odds and my patience—to see another day. Am I clear?"

"Yes, ma'am."

"Good. Now, gimme your phone." Mom held out her hand, and Alice placed it on her palm. It disappeared into one of the pockets on her robe. She turned to Courtney, who jumped slightly. She'd been watching with eyes the size of dinner plates. "Your tire okay?"

"Y-yes, ma'am."

"Your daddy get you a spare?"

"Yes, ma'am."

"He teach you how to change it?"

"No, ma'am."

Mom snorted. "Tell him I said he should. Can't have my girl getting stranded out there, maybe by herself next time."

"Yes, ma'am."

"Say your good-byes." Mom gestured between them.

Court mumbled a "see you tomorrow" that Alice returned before Court headed out the door.

"Drive safe." Mom held open the screen, watching Court head for her car. "Text Alice's phone when you get in."

"Yes, ma'am," Court called. The driver-side door thumped shut, and the Camaro started up.

Mom closed the door as Court drove off, the sound of the engine fading.

Alice stood in the middle of the den, not quite sure what to do with herself. She felt two feet tall.

Mom tied her robe and folded her arms over her chest. "You know better than this. And now I have to go in late 'cause you act like you don't. You got homework?"

"A paper. English."

"Due when?"

"Next week."

"Lights out at midnight. Shove that laptop under my door. I'll give it back in the morning." Mom brushed past her and headed for the stairs.

◊ ◊ ◊

By the third set of search results for "How to Break into a Building," Alice was convinced that any second now the FBI, CIA, and any number of acronym-armed men in black suits would burst through her front door.

"It's all videos of guys doing stupid crap." Court's voice carried over Alice's headphones.

"Did you really think they'd put legit instructions for this online?" Alice knelt in the space between her bed and dresser, going over the supplies she'd stealthily gathered from the garage: some rope, cargo hooks, hammer, wrench, two cans of spray paint for the cameras—it worked in the movies—duct and electric tape, all just in case Chess was missing something from his burglar kit. That still tripped her out. Chess, sweet-smile-and-soft-eyes Chess, breaking into buildings. Man. She kept throwing glances at the door, nervous Mom might pop in for a random search or something.

"They have instructions for how to make a bomb. Figured this isn't as bad," Court said from Alice's laptop, where it sat on the floor nearby.

"You keep thinking that." She stole a glance at the clock. 2:13 AM. "You almost here?"

"Five minutes. Meet me at the end of the block?"

It was craziness, sneaking out after all this mess, but she didn't have a choice. Hopefully—God please—they'd be back before her mom woke up. Court could take the mirror to the pub, and Alice would figure out a way to get over there tomorrow.

"End of the block. See you in five." Alice shut the laptop and hopped to her feet, wriggling into her pack.

A quick glance down the hall showed Mom's door shut and the light off. Alice crept as quietly as she could toward the door, slipped the laptop under it, then headed for the garage for one last thing.

The same gassy, oily smell lingered in the air. She clicked on the light and made her way over to the workbench. The same tightness from before wrapped itself around her lungs. She took a steadying breath and set her hand on the chilled metal surface.

"I need your help, Daddy. To save someone else important to me." Carefully pulling open the top drawer, she plucked free the crowbar before eyeing the empty space where it sat.

"Know your resources, Baby Moon," she could hear him say. "Right tool for the right job in the right hands? Anything is possible."

The sting of tears resurged with a vengeance. "No," Alice whispered, taking slow, deep breath after slow, deep breath. She couldn't do this right now, couldn't go into the dark. "Please," she begged the emptiness. Leave her be. Just for now. Just long enough to get this done.

She couldn't lose anyone else. Not again.

Sniffling, she closed the drawer and turned off the light. The garage door was only a few feet from the front one, but it may as well have been a mile. Stealing glances at the top of the stairs, expecting her mother to appear at any second, Alice didn't breathe until she was outside and racing toward the end of the street, the lights of Court's car beckoning.

Alice threw herself into the front seat and gestured for Court to go. She didn't relax or stop glancing out the back window until they left the neighborhood completely.

◊ ◊ ◊

Court parked on a side street a few blocks from the school, like Chess said to. He told them to meet him on the north side of the school and to leave their phones in the car. Alice was salty all over again for having hers confiscated. Neither of them said a word, anxious energy ping-ponging between them, rising with each step. The chill did little to calm Alice's buzzing nerves. Every muscle tensed to the point of shaking. She felt like she might come apart at any second.

Court's pale face stuck out in the moonlight, faintly flushed from running and the cold, floating between her black wool cap and thief getup. She looked like something out of a sitcom, though her wide eyes darted around every few seconds.

The girls slowed as they approached the school, ducking behind a wall of shrubbery surrounding a house next door.

"Can't believe we're really gonna do this." Court rubbed her gloved hands together.

Alice shot her a look. "You sound way more excited than someone about to commit a felony should."

"Oh, this wouldn't count as a felony. Just burglary. Not even theft, 'cause we're taking something that already belongs to you."

Blinking at her friend in the dark, Alice shook her head. "How do you *know* this?"

"Google," Court chirped. "Didn't learn how to break into a school, but there was a lot more interesting stuff."

Keeping low, the girls circled around to where they were pretty sure Chess said to meet them.

"Pssst," a nearby bush whispered. A hand extended and beckoned them.

They hurried over, joining Chess, who'd also dressed for the occasion. "You two ready for this?"

They nodded.

"Good. What's in the bag?"

Alice unzipped it. "Few things I figured wouldn't hurt. Just in case."

Chess rifled through before pulling out the crowbar. "Very nice."

"Careful with that, it's my dad's."

"I'll take care of it. Okay, we're gonna go in low and fast. Stay on me, move when I move, okay?"

The girls nodded again.

"Let's go."

It wasn't too far from the bushes to the nearest wing, and the three of them crossed the yard at a run, Chess in the lead. Frost-slick grass squeaked under their shoes, their steps thudding faintly in the dark. They reached the outer wall and pressed against it, chests heaving, pants escaping in bursts of mist. The chill of the brick at her side crawled through Alice's clothes, licking at her skin.

Chess peered around the far corner, then over his shoulder at them. "We're gonna run, on three." He counted up with his fingers, and the three of them took off, Alice and Court on Chess's ass.

They made it to the other side of the building, ducking into an alcove where the air conditioners and furnaces were tucked away. The machines growled and rattled, pumping heat into the building. All this noise was sure to mask any noise they made, from the outside at least.

"Give me a boost." Chess pointed to a window about four feet above their heads.

Court lifted her hands. "You're the superhero."

Alice glared at her before crouching down and lacing her fingers together for Chess to place his foot. "On three. One, two, three," she grunted, heaving as Chess pushed off.

"W-whoa!" He went up pretty fast, but Alice was able to get underneath him, guiding his feet to her shoulders.

The two of them wavered for a second, then held.

"Wow," Chess whispered.

"Be impressed later," Alice grunted. "Get to work." Chess's shoes dug into her shoulders till she felt his weight in her bones.

There was a bit of clanging, a shrill grind, then a hard *snap*. "I'm in! Push me up."

Chess's weight eased a bit—he'd probably grabbed hold of something—and Alice got her hands under his feet to give him a shove. She turned just in time to see him disappear through the window. His face reappeared long enough for him to hiss, "wait here," then he was gone again.

"You are such a badass," Court whispered, shaking her head.

Alice grinned. "Thanks."

Both girls watched the dark window as seconds ticked by. The seconds stretched into one minute. Then two. It felt like ten, and Alice would've believed it was if she wasn't counting the seconds off in her head.

At three minutes, Court cursed under her breath. "What the hell is he doing?"

Another fifteen seconds slugged by.

Alice was just considering going and searching for him when a clank from above made both girls leap away from the wall and whirl around. The window overhead slid up, and Chess poked his head out.

"Up and at 'em, ladies." He extended the crowbar.

"You first," Alice said to Courtney. With Chess pulling and Alice lifting, Court climbed through the window with ease. Once she was inside, Alice backed up a few feet, took a short running leap, caught the edge of the sill, and hauled herself up. She spilled into the room, landing beside Court in a crouch.

"Wow," Chess murmured, his eyes were on Alice, his hand out to help her up.

She cleared her throat, rising with a thanks, grateful her gloves concealed her sweaty palms. "Security system?"

"Took care of it." Chess headed for the door. "We've got about twenty minutes."

"And how do you know how to do *that*?" Court asked.

"Now, now," Alice said. "Play nice now; interrogate later."

"Oh, there will be a later," Court murmured.

Out in the hall, the echoes of their steps filled the building as they raced to the third floor, the dull shine of security lights guiding their way.

Alice reached her locker first, the other two sliding in behind her as she spun the lock. The mirror glinted when the door clanged open. *Oh, thank you.* She didn't expect it to not be there, but seeing it safe and sound settled a rising unrest inside her.

She plucked the mirror free, wrapped it in a dish towel, and tucked it into the pack before slinging it over her shoulders. "Okay."

"Perfect." Chess grinned. "Plenty of time to make our getaw—"

Court screamed, the sound raking against Alice's ears, sending shards through her body. She caught a glimpse of the horror etched on her friend's face, eyes fixed at the end of the hall, as she spun, and froze.

Dread dropped cold and hard in her stomach. The world

went out of focus. Everything dissolved in shades of fractured gray, falling away as a low snarl slithered across the floor.

A Fiend paced forward, its limbs hunched, hackles raised, leathery skin pulled back from fangs. "There you are." Its inky hide reflected the pale flare of hazy light.

Alice's skull buzzed, her thoughts scattered, as she struggled to comprehend the fact that a Fiend was here. At her school.

"Oh my god." Court whimpered as she edged backward. "Oh my god, what is that thing?"

"I—I don't know." Chess raised an arm in front of the girls, eyes fixed on the monster at the end of the hall. "I don't—that's not . . ."

"Run," Alice breathed, the shaking in her limbs coating her voice.

A second Fiend emerged at the top of the stairs.

"Run!"

Twenty-Four

A DEAL

"**In** here!" Alice led the stampede into an open classroom. The three of them barreled through the door, Chess bringing up the rear. She all but shoved him out of the way so she could close and lock it behind them. He caught himself against the edge of a table, the legs scraping the linoleum floor just as something slammed into the door from the other side.

Everyone jumped and scrambled back. Shadows danced beneath the door. Claws scratched at the wood, knocked at the handle. Fingers clutched at Alice's arm, and she nearly shook them off before she realized it was Courtney.

"Are those . . ." Court stared at the door, barely able to form words for her trembling. "Are those?" she repeated.

"Yes," Alice panted, shifting to move around a desk, putting more distance between them and the door. "Chess!"

He snapped around from where he'd been staring, too. She

waved him over, her heart leaping when the door shook with another bang. The Fiends snapped and growled, wood splintering under their claws.

"They're gonna get in," Court whispered, her voice cracking on the words.

Alice knew the Fiends were here for her, for the Eye, but that wouldn't keep them from ripping Court and Chess apart.

No. No, she wouldn't let that happen.

"Stay here." She shook off Court and gestured for them to keep back while she searched for something to block the door. A bookshelf stretched from the floor to the ceiling and across most of the wall. She gripped the open end and pulled.

Wood creaked and screamed as the bottom of the shelf scraped across the floor. She hauled it out, then pushed it forward against the door. Winded by the effort, she rejoined Court and Chess.

BAM. The door shook so hard it knocked a few books loose, and they clapped against the floor. Teeth and claws flashed along holes worn into the wood. The makeshift barricade wouldn't hold for long.

Alice raced to the windows, fumbling with the lock before shoving one open. Cold air blasted her face as she pushed the pane up and out of the way. It stuck a couple of times, but she managed to wedge it high enough to wiggle through and out onto the ledge.

"We need to jump," she said.

"What?" Both Chess and Court recoiled.

"It's that or *that*." Alice pointed at the door as a Fiend hit it with another bang.

Her friends joined her at the window, peering out into the chilled night. Chess made some faint, reluctant sound, but pulled a chair over from the nearby table and propped it into place beneath the window. "Ladies first."

"Go," Alice said to Court, whose gaze flickered uncertainly over the window, but with another thud against the door, she bent to work her way onto the ledge.

"Be careful," Alice called, though Court was already half-way out. Once she was through, her hand dropped into view, her fingers beckoning. Alice passed the pack out, then followed.

The ledge was about three feet wide, just enough space for her to plant her knees and catch her balance to stand. The cold seeped into her arms and legs, stiffening them on contact.

Court handed over the pack, sliding over to make room for Chess, already on his way out. Alice shouldered the bag as her mind worked on possible ways down. Climbing wasn't an option. Neither was jumping. The fall wouldn't hurt her too much, but Chess or Court would definitely break several somethings.

At the end of the building, a walkway connected the main structure to the cafeteria. They could drop to it and then the ground, cutting the distance almost in half. Much better odds.

"That way." Alice pointed. Court, the whole of her shaking, edged along the ledge.

Alice turned to check on Chess, who slid in behind her, his eyes fixed on the ground, his body stiff. All color had drained from his face. Alice took his hand. He latched on, his grip crushing.

"We're okay. Come on." It took a couple of tugs, but he finally followed.

Heel-to-heel, the three of them scurried along the ledge as fast as they dared. From the outside, there was no way to tell when one classroom ended and the next began, no way to tell if they'd made it far enough so the Fiends couldn't drag them, screaming, back inside. Alice pushed the thought aside, instead focusing on getting out of here.

They'd only made it about twenty feet when Court stopped, cut off by a stone pillar sticking out from the building.

"We gotta go around," Alice said.

Court looked ready to protest, when something hit the floor with a crash in the classroom behind them. Books tumbled, their pages flapping. Wood and metal clanged and banged against the desks and the floor. A howl tore through the night. Court edged up to the pillar and, with a yelp, swung herself around it. She teetered, hollering, and Alice reached to steady her as a window shattered.

"Holy—!" Chess pushed Alice farther along the ledge.

She stumbled, one foot slipping free. She'd have fallen if he hadn't pressed against her, wedging her face-first into the pillar.

Pain blossomed where her arm was pinned behind her, and where Chess's elbow caught her in her side. Motion fluttered in her peripheral vision, and Court dropped out of sight. Alice's stomach plummeted.

"Courtney!"

"I'm okay," Court hollered from around the other side of the pillar. "I made it!"

Behind, jaws snapped and snarled. Claws raked against concrete. Chess hissed a curse as he shifted, pushing harder against her.

"You're smashing me." She wriggled to glance over her shoulder as best she could, catching sight of a Fiend hanging halfway out a window, twisting to try to catch hold of Chess's leg. Talons scraped the ledge inches shy of his foot. Something, presumably the classroom wall, kept the monster at bay.

Until it climbs out here and kills us. Alice worked one arm free, careful not to jostle Chess too much, then swung it around the pillar.

Court seized her wrist. "I've got you."

Alice shimmied around the pillar and managed to pull herself loose without shoving Chess into eager jaws. With Court's help, she braced one foot on the ledge long enough to swing around completely, joining her friend on the other side.

Court started for the walkway, and Alice braced herself to reach for Chess. "Come on!"

He shuffled on the other side, his shoes scuffing against the ledge. For a handful of seconds, the only sound was the crack of glass and the Fiend's snarl as it worked its way out the window. When Chess's hand appeared, she grabbed it, waiting until he positioned himself. Then he swung and she pulled.

He almost bounced off the building, but Alice yanked him in against herself. His arms caught hold of her, tight enough to squeeze the air from her lungs. He tensed; she felt it through layers of cloth. His breath caught while hers came in shaky, deep gasps, drinking in the crisp smell of the cold air and heady aroma of citrus mixed with whatever he'd used in the shower that morning.

"It's okay. You're okay," she coaxed, detangling herself from his hold. He seemed reluctant to let go at first, but loosened his grip while stealing glances at the ground.

"I have this . . . thing with heights," he explained, his expression tight but pleading.

Alice nodded and took his hand. "I've got you."

Court had already made it to the walkway below. Alice gestured for Chess to go first, letting him scoot around her. He steadied himself before climbing down, dangling from the edge for a second before letting go. Once he landed and backed away, she jumped after him, knees bending on impact as she tucked into a roll. She came out of it just as the distant echo of howls filled the air.

"Oh god," Court whispered. "Can those things get up here?"

On the other side of the walk, the outdoor eating area stretched toward the far parking lot. Metal tables dotted the courtyard.

"Those bushes." Alice pointed to the shrubbery lining the adjacent wall. "We jump."

Chess looked a little green, backing away from the edge. Court didn't look too pleased, either, but at another howl—this one closer—she took a running leap.

Alice held her breath as her best friend dropped into the shrubbery with a pained shout. The initial thud, the sound of branches snapping under Court's weight, turned Alice's stomach.

She thought she was going to be sick until Court rolled free and pushed to her feet. She clutched her arm against herself, but she looked okay, sticks and leaves stuck to her clothes.

Relief threatening to weaken her knees, Alice turned to Chess. "Your turn."

Lips pursed, he took a deep, shaky breath. His fingers clenched and unclenched at his side before he pressed the heels of his palms into his eye sockets. "Jump off a roof. I'm going to jump off a roof."

"Only if you want to live." Alice took his hand again and tugged him forward. "Come on."

"N-no." He yanked free and lifted his hands. "I can't, I—I. I need a second." His voice shook. "Just a second. You go. I'll follow."

For that second Alice debated throwing him over.

"I swear," he added.

"No. I'm not leaving you up here." She slipped her pack off, clutched it to her chest, then held out her hand. "We'll go together."

He swallowed, peering down at the ground where Courtney beckoned. "I-it's not wide enough. What if you miss?"

Another howl sounded, closer. They didn't have time for this.

"Chess, Chester! Look at me!"

He jerked around, his expression twisted with fear.

She grabbed his hand and squeezed. "I've got you, okay? I'm the superhero, remember? I've got you."

Chess stared at Alice, looked down at the bushes, looked over his shoulder the way they'd come, then back to Alice. His head bobbed in quick nods. His chest heaved. She could feel his shaking in his hand, his grip iron-tight.

"One. Two. Three!"

They kicked off the edge of the roof.

Chess barked a shout.

Alice's body hung weightless in the air briefly before gravity latched on and yanked her down with an almost personal vehemence. Chess's hand slipped out of hers. The rush of wind, the sting of the cold, was short-lived before she was stabbed, pricked, and poked in every inch of her back, arms, and legs.

Twigs snapped and cracked like fireworks in her ears. Leaves rustled, and the pain strewn through half her body burned, but she was alive, unbroken. She shifted in a roll to the side, fighting her way free of the shrubbery cage. She tasted blood, hot and sour, against her tongue. The smell of it filled her nose. She finally tore away and hit the ground.

"Chess! You good?" She pushed to her feet, shuffling the pack around onto her back.

Court stood nearby, gaping up at the roof.

Alice spun, ready to face off with a Fiend, unarmed if she had to, only to freeze.

Chess hung in the air, like he'd gotten stuck by his shirt on the way down. His arms and legs hung limp, his head dropped forward, his eyes closed.

"Chess?" Alice called, fear sluicing cold through her body.

Court croaked a confused "How?" beside her.

He jerked up and over the roof, out of sight. Alice started forward, prepared to climb up after him, when footsteps sounded along the stone. They stopped at the edge of the roof, and *he* leaned forward, hands on his hips, his armor swallowing the moonlight.

Court gasped somewhere behind Alice as the Black Knight angled his head to the side.

"Fancy meeting you here." He crouched at the edge of the roof, arms draped over his knees. He said something else, but the pounding of Alice's heart had risen from her chest to fill her ears. Her stomach headed the opposite direction. The rest of her body went numb.

"You don't look so good." His words finally penetrated the buzz of her frantic thoughts. "Maybe you should sit down a second." He lifted a hand to wave. "You brought a friend. Hello there."

"Kiss my ass," Court snarled, then flipped him the bird.

"Ooooh, fiery."

"What . . . what did you do to him?" Alice demanded. Her voice cracked with the force of her fear, her fury. Both filled her, dueling one another in a frenzy that left her shaking.

"Calm down, he's fine." The Black Knight glanced over his shoulder. "Well, maybe not *fine*. I mean, he'll probably have a helluva headache when he comes to." He waved a hand and Chess floated into view beside the Black Knight, hovering unconscious in the air.

She wanted to hurt the bastard, to punch his stupid face in, but there was no way she could reach him to do it. The urge to find something to throw swept through her.

The Black Knight leaped from the roof and descended to the ground gradually, landing a few feet in front of them. Alice shifted to place herself between him and Court. Her eyes found his, or where they would be under his mask, and she hoped he felt the anger burning in her glare pierce through to the back of his skull.

"The Eye. I know you have it."

"I *don't.*"

"But you can get it. Don't say you can't—lying doesn't become you—so let's make a deal." He hooked a thumb over his shoulder. "Bring it to me, and the boy lives. Don't?" He reached to draw his sword free. The black blade hung against the night, the dark surface like a slice in the very air.

The Black Knight vanished, appearing above Chess. With a flick of his wrist he drove the blade down through his chest.

Courtney screamed.

Chess didn't move.

Alice's body went rigid and cold. Her heart jackhammered at her ribs, screaming when she couldn't. She jerked forward, but the Black Knight lifted a hand. "Ah, ah, ah, let's not be hasty. And don't worry." He pulled the blade free. Chess's body jolted. "He's not dead. Buuuuuut he'll turn into another of my little friends. You met them, back in Wonderland, then on the third floor just a moment ago. They're kinda shy."

Alice stood frozen, her fingers curled into fists at her side. Courtney cried quietly behind her, sniffling around *oh gods* and *oh nos.*

"I know this isn't easy." The Black Knight's voice washed across the space between them. "And I don't . . . *want* to hurt you."

"Bullshit," she hissed from behind clenched teeth. Anger stampeded through her, so hot she couldn't see straight.

He gazed at her in silence for a moment. "Whether you believe me or not makes it no less true. This was never about you. It should've never gotten this far. But the powers that be are . . . stubborn." He grunted, then floated back down to hover in front of them. "I tried to spare you, truly. I'm sorry it's come to this. But it's an easy fix. Just bring me the Eye, and I'll reverse the transformation."

Her pack suddenly felt like a ten-ton weight against her back, the shard tucked inside it, threatening to pull her to her knees. Without the Eye, they couldn't find the Heart. Without the Heart, Hatta died. So did Odabeth's mother. But if she didn't give it up, then Chess wound up on the chopping block. This is exactly what Hatta had warned them about.

"How long does he have?" Alice whispered.

"The change usually takes a day, but I wouldn't wait too long. Never did this to a human before. There are bound to be side effects."

Every horrible outcome immediately swam through Alice's mind. Chess could wind up one of the monsters, or worse! Her vision blurred. She wavered on her feet. The Black Knight's hand shot out to steady her.

"No!" Court grabbed hold of her other arm.

The Black Knight yanked away as if burned. "I'll give you a little time to think about it." He cleared his throat. "After all, such decisions shouldn't be made under stress. It's not healthy." The slyness slithered back into his tone. "Sunrise tomorrow, bring me the Eye. Or don't. Your call."

He backed away, his feet leaving the ground, his body floating toward the walkway and Chess's unconscious form.

"Wait." She stepped after him. Court tightened her hold on her arm.

The Black Knight paused, hovering midair, like some dark specter.

"Where . . . w-where do I meet you?"

"Don't worry, princess. I'll find you." Rising higher, he and Chess faded from sight.

Twenty-Five

REFLECTIONS

Alice barely remembered the drive to the pub. She remembered needing to look for Chess. She remembered Court holding her back, shouting how the twenty minutes he bought them with whatever he did to the security system was almost up. How there was no helping him if they got in trouble. They had to leave.

The pub was completely dark. The tables and chairs appeared afloat in the black, shafts of light cutting through the shadows from small windows near the ceiling. A little light spilled from the hallway, too.

With the front door locked, and her phone still at home, Alice borrowed Court's to call Maddi. The bartender sounded sleepy, but glad for the good news about the final piece of the Eye. Alice didn't mention the Black Knight, or his ultimatum. Yet.

After a couple of minutes, a figure emerged from the back, gliding toward them. Alice couldn't tell who it was, until they flipped on a light.

Dem, disheveled and half-awake, rubbed at his face with one hand while he unlocked the door. "You got it?"

Alice held up the mirror just as someone screamed, "Help!"

Dem bolted across the bar and down the hall. Alice followed, Courtney behind her. They rounded the corner, following the shouts to one of the back rooms—Hatta's, Alice realized with sudden dread. Dee and the Duchess were already there. They pushed through the door just as Alice slammed into the doorjamb, her breath catching at the sight of Maddi tussling with Hatta, who had hold of her, half hanging from the bed.

His eyes had gone midnight fiery, wide and wild. Maddi struggled to pull away from him, shoving and slapping, but he held on, stammering some sort of gibberish.

"Addison, release her!" The Duchess was across the room in an instant, latching onto Hatta and pulling. Alice jerked from her shock and moved to help Maddi wriggle free. Together, Alice and the Duchess managed to separate the two of them.

Maddi stumbled into Alice, who caught her while the Duchess practically mounted Hatta. One of the twins asked Maddi if she was all right, but Alice didn't hear the mumbled reply, focused on how the Duchess pressed her brow to Addison's, her eyes shut as she murmured in the same odd language he'd been stuttering. She carded her fingers through his hair and stroked the side of his face.

There was no change at first. He thrashed and writhed, but

as the Duchess spoke, he calmed, and sank against the mattress. The Duchess shifted forward with his descent, until she lay on top of him. She continued speaking softly until he appeared to slip into a fitful sleep, twitching and whispering. She rested against Hatta for a moment, then straightened, her clothing and hair disheveled. She swept red strands from where they had fallen free of her braid into her face and looked at Alice, whose entire body had gone cold.

The Duchess climbed off him, smoothing her hands over her clothing. "Until he is treated, these . . . episodes will not be uncommon." She grabbed a vial from a nearby table, slid her free arm beneath Hatta's head, and lifted it to coax him to drink. She set the vial aside when it was empty and snapped her fingers. Maddi hurried forward, looking through the other vials before offering another.

Alice stood frozen, a deluge of emotions short-circuiting her ability to move. The mirror dug into her palm, the sting barely registering.

"Come on." Court had hold of her shoulders and, with some coaxing, guided her out of the room. The boys led them to another room, the one from before that resembled a hotel.

Xelon was awake, and sitting up this time. Odabeth sat beside her. Both of them looked up as the group entered.

"What happened?" Xelon asked, frown in place.

"Another episode," Dee explained. "He had hold of Maddi. She is fine, they are fine. The Duchess is taking care of it."

Something twisted and clenched in Alice's chest, tightened around her heart.

Xelon settled against the pillows, her white hair loose and

falling over her bare shoulders. She exchanged a look with Odabeth, squeezing the princess's hand where it rested on her leg. "The Queen had similar . . . reactions."

"Did you get it?" Odabeth interrupted, pushing to her feet.

Alice presented the wrapped bit of mirror. Odabeth came around the bed, and Alice handed the shard over.

"All six," Odabeth said as she made her way to the dresser.

She pulled open the top drawer and lifted the other five mirrors free, laying them out along the top. Then she unwrapped the final one and set it with the others.

"What now?" Alice asked, trying not to think of how Hatta had looked, lying against the bed, practically the same color as the pale sheets. Or of how Chess could be morphing into a literal monster right now. She couldn't imagine the pain. The fear.

"I'm not entirely sure." Odabeth gripped the edge of the dresser. "Let me try the Verse again." She took hold of her necklace. "Twinkle, twinkle, all-seeing star. Show us wonders near and far. In the midnight sky you keep watch over the dark and deep. I beseech the masters old, search my heart for worth bestowed. Menders of the breaking skies, clear my mind, open my eyes."

Nothing.

No bright light, no soft bells, not a thing.

Alice glanced back and forth between Odabeth and the shards. "Is that it?"

"I-I-I don't know," the princess stammered.

Alice did not like the sound of that. "What do you *mean* you don't know?"

"I don't know!" Odabeth slammed the drawer shut, her face red. "The last time I saw my grandmother use the Eye, it wasn't shattered into several pieces. The Verse I know is for a whole Eye, not this." She flung a hand out, indicating the fragments.

Fire burned through Alice, anger ready to fling itself at the princess. After everything—traveling to Legracia, being attacked by Fiends, Xelon being bitten, Chess being taken—this is where it ended? But none of this was Odabeth's fault; it was hers. It was always hers.

"The important part is we have the pieces," the Duchess said from the doorway, surprising everyone. She made her way over to the dresser and lifted one of the shards to examine it. "In the morning, we can journey to Legracia to ask the Queen."

"No, we can't." Alice wanted to sink into the floor when Odabeth and the Duchess turned twin expressions of confusion her way. Not looking at either of them, she launched into the story of what happened at the school, how the Black Knight ambushed them, took Chess. "He stabbed him in the heart with the Vorpal Blade. He won't reverse it unless I deliver the Eye by sunrise."

Xelon, the Duchess, and the princess all stared at her, their expressions ranging from shock to disgust. Alice knew it was aimed at the situation, but the guilt roiling in her stomach said she deserved it, too.

"This is unfortunate." The Duchess stroked her chin as she paced the small space.

"That's an understatement," Alice bit out.

The Duchess paused, blinking at her. "Of course, but we must keep cool heads about this."

"Cool heads? That asshole has my friend!"

"I understand how you feel, Alice, believe me I do. I had comrades captured during the war that I would've given anything to save, but making rash decisions won't help anyone." She set a hand on Alice's shoulder, squeezing. "We need to think this through. Besides, we don't have a fully assembled Eye to give to the Black Knight or be used to seek the Heart, so there's not much we can do either way."

The Duchess was right. About the Eye, not about there being nothing they could do. They could go find that Black Knight bastard and beat the shit out of him, but that was one of those rash decisions the Duchess was talking about. Chess would likely get caught in the middle.

Alice curled her arms around herself, shuddering at the thought.

The Duchess went back to pacing.

"Are you cold?" Odabeth tugged at the boa-like scarf around her neck. "Madeline was gracious enough to give this to us. It helps. You can have it."

Alice started to protest, when she spotted something bright against Odabeth's chest.

"Your necklace." She pointed at where the scarf fell away from the princess's neck. Something glowed beneath her collar.

Odabeth blinked, tucking her chin to peer at her chest, then reeled the jewel up from beneath the fabric. The star pulsed as it had last night, growing brighter until it blazed. The mirrors caught the light and burned with it, a white-hot glow spreading out from the reflective surfaces. They lifted from the dresser, hovered a moment, then shot through the air like bright bullets. Everyone dropped to the ground as the shards circled the room, then darted out the door.

Odabeth squawked when the necklace tried to follow, dragging her with it. She flailed in an odd stumble that was more her trying to dig in her heels than walking.

Xelon pushed from the bed to go to her aid, but the Duchess intercepted her. "Let it lead you, Your Highness."

"What?" Odabeth shrieked, dubious.

Alice took her by the elbow. "Follow it. I'm with you."

The princess looked reluctant, but stopped fighting and started walking. Now her stagger was more from being hauled forward. Alice moved with her. The Duchess and Xelon trailed behind, with the sharp clap of boots and the slap of bare feet.

They rounded a corner, and a perplexed-looking Maddi, with an armful of vials, shifted aside for their little parade.

"Do I wanna ask?" Maddi blinked her sleepy eyes, her head cocked to the side.

"The Eye," Alice said as she escorted Odabeth into the main bar area, then called over her shoulder, "I think."

Out in the bar, Dem and Court stood near the bar. They wore similar looks of confused shock, their attention fixed on the six shards—still glowing—that hovered midair, circling one another slowly.

"Alice!" Court hurried forward. "What the hell is going on?"

"I don't know, but—"

The mirrored wall behind the bar shifted. The shelves and bottles disappeared, but there was no picture or scene this time, only swelling, swirling, glinting waves, like a silvery sea. One by one the shards dove into the mirror, vanishing from sight. Then the star dragged a screaming Odabeth toward the bar.

"I got you!" Alice took hold of the chain and yanked. The links snapped. Free, the princess dropped to her knees, and the gem shot straight into the mirror.

Odabeth rubbed her neck, a red line visible on her brown skin. Xelon moved to her side, and together the knight and Alice got the princess to her feet.

Everyone crowded in around them.

Alice eyed the fluctuating surface of the massive mirror, struck by the oddest sense of déjà vu. She'd seen this somewhere before, the silver tossing, roiling. An image flashed through her mind of her hovering, water rippling beneath her feet. The longer she watched the water, the more she could make out an image waiting on the other side.

On the other side . . . Alice stepped forward, her hand extended.

"Don't," Court protested somewhere behind her, followed by Maddi's voice urging everyone to stop, wait.

Alice gazed at what should have been her reflection but instead was a distorted vision of something else, something . . . more. She faltered for just a second, then pressed her palm to the mirror.

The stirring waves stilled, flattened, and solidified into a crystal-clear image. The room was reflected back at her, including everyone's shocked faces. The mirror was back to normal, except Alice's reflection.

Her reflected self held something in her hands. It was a crystal, braided with twists of gold and silver curling around the elliptical face. The setting held the same shape and pinkish color as the jewel, only larger, the entire thing dazzling. Reflection-Alice held it out in offering and whispered, *"Take it."*

Alice's fingers shifted, and the surface of the mirror wavered beneath her hand with a gelatinous feel she knew would give if she pressed hard enough. She took a deep breath and pushed.

Her hand plunged through the mirror. The sudden shock of cold against her skin made her gasp, and her entire body jerked. It burned, so much so that she nearly snatched her arm free. The silver swallowed her arm clear up to her elbow, and the pain traveled even farther. She fisted her other hand, her knuckles popping with the strain, and bit down on the inside of her jaw to keep from crying out.

Her fingers brushed something solid and the pain vanished, all at once. Chest heaving, she curled her fingers around whatever it was and pulled. Inch by inch her arm withdrew.

Reflection-Alice wavered, washing out completely as more of actual Alice's arm emerged. The watery surface faded, solidifying into a regular mirror along the wall. The bottles and shelves gradually reappeared. A faint tingling peppered Alice's skin as she gave a tug.

Her hand finally came free.

Twenty-Six

THE EYE

The jewel Reflection-Alice had been holding rested in Alice's palm. The crystal sparkled. The gold and silver shone. She turned it over in her hands, careful, gentle, mindful of squeezing too hard or doing something to break it.

It's beautiful, Alice mused, until a groan grabbed her attention. She turned to find the Duchess straightening from where she'd sunk against a wall, a hand pressed to the side of her head. Maddi, Odabeth, and Xelon looked to be equally shaken.

"What happened?" Alice moved to help the bartender to her feet, Court and the twins helping the others. "Are you guys all right?"

"The Eye," the Duchess said. "The power it possesses, the link to our world, I could sense its awakening."

"We all did." Maddi thanked Alice and shook her head,

crossing her eyes briefly. "You don't fire up a hoodoo that powerful and not feel it. Like the shock wave of some mystic bomb."

"Do you think the Black Knight felt it?" Alice asked.

"Perhaps, though I imagine proximity is a factor. He could be completely unaware." The Duchess straightened her shirt, brushing herself off before fixing her eyes on the jewel. "I never thought I'd lay eyes on this again."

"It's been so long." Maddi's gaze shifted to the Eye as well. Something like awe mixed with fear played across both of their expressions.

"This really is it, then?" Alice asked.

The Duchess nodded.

Finally, something had gone right. Alice dared to hope, to believe everything would be okay, or at least better than it had been. She nodded. "How do we use it?"

"Only a carrier of royal blood," the Duchess said. "The princess must be the one. Madeline, let us check on Addison. I'm certain he felt the effects of the Eye's assembly as well." The Duchess headed for the hall.

"I'll let you know how he's doing," Maddi said to Alice before following.

"Let's do this." Alice carefully handed the jewel over to Odabeth, who held it out slightly, like it might bite her.

Clutching it to her chest, the princess took a slow, shaky breath. "Be with me, Mother."

"I don't like this," Xelon murmured, her fingers curled into fists at her sides. She would have looked more imposing in something other than a large Chococat sleep shirt. The two must have borrowed clothes from Maddi.

The princess trailed her fingers across the jewel's surface, then pressed the back of it against her bowed forehead, over the smaller gem already centered above her brow.

The same light from before flared anew, and Odabeth jerked with a gasp. The Eye remained fixed to her forehead as her hands dropped away, growing brighter and brighter. Light burst forth from her eyes. It filled her mouth when her lips dropped open in a scream, the sound mixed with a crack of thunder.

"No!" Xelon reached for her, but Alice caught her around the waist.

"Don't." She held on, despite the knight's struggles.

Odabeth's body jolted as if struck by some outside force, but she stayed upright, nailed to that spot on the floor. Gradually, the light filled all of her. Her arms and legs went white. Her body lifted from the floor, hovering in the air, her hair floating around her. The glow intensified, like in the parking lot. Alice had to turn away.

When it died down, Alice blinked to clear her eyes. Everyone else did the same, and one by one they came to stare at Odabeth with various expressions of shock. Everyone except Xelon, who sagged in Alice's hold, her face drawn up in a mix of concern and amazement.

"Your Majesty," the knight whispered.

Odabeth stood on the ground again. Her skin had gone white, a webwork of gold veins glowing from within. Pools of white light took the place of her eyes. Her hair caught on the very air, white strands flowing and waving as if she was underwater. She blinked, lids falling over those shining orbs. "What?" When her lips parted, the same light poured from behind them. She lifted her hands, gasping as she caught sight of her flesh, running her fingers over her arms. "Oh." Her head lifted as she jumped, glancing around at each of them. "Oh heavens."

"What is it, Your Highness?" Xelon pulled toward Odabeth.

Alice let her go, but the knight stopped shy of touching the princess, hands lifted.

"I can see," Odabeth whispered.

"See what?" Alice asked.

"Everything."

◊ ◊ ◊

Hatta sat on a barstool, leaning heavily against the counter, his expression a storm on his face. Maddi stood just behind him, peering over his shoulder with wide, surprised eyes. The Duchess stood directly in front of Odabeth, who still glowed like some sort of Wonderland fairy godmother. Alice had gone to Anastasia after Odabeth's change. Hatta, more himself, insisted on joining them.

"Incredible," the Duchess murmured. "And you feel all right?"

"I feel amazing." Odabeth laughed the words, her voice taking on a faint echo. "And I can see the Heart." Her white face scrunched. "I think."

"Show us."

"This is still a horrible idea," Hatta muttered as Odabeth moved behind the bar. She pressed her hand to the mirrored wall. Like before, the surface rippled before fading to black, like a dead screen. Odabeth grunted in effort, and an image of the Glow flickered to life. The woods blazed radiant in the dead of night, but their light soon faded as the scene transitioned to the main road that led to Ahoon. It followed the road away from the village, passed the turnoff to Legracia at the edge of the Blind Thief's Forest, and continued on. The landscape changed along the way, rolling into rocky crevices and cliffs dotting sweeping gold plains. Eventually, the path met a stone bridge collapsed over a rushing river, the purple waters blazing in the moonlight.

Across the bridge another forest waited, this one a tangle of vines and thorns. The image lifted into the air then, gliding over a span of meadow, all of it nothing Alice had ever laid eyes on before. The meadow gave way to marshes, glistening and crystalline, lilies sprouting along the waters. A single road stretched across the vastness, gated at one end, lined with stone columns topped with arches. Another castle waited beyond, this one not quite as tall as Legracia, but it stretched wider, solid and firm and just as breathtaking with its crimson overlay that burned in the twilight.

"Castle Findest," the Duchess whispered.

"Castle where?" Alice asked.

"The Red Palace," Xelon murmured, her eyes moving between Odabeth and the mirror, her brow furrowed. "Home to the Red Queen before she vanished. Now it's known as the Royal-less Palace."

"The Heart is here," Odabeth said.

"That's impossible." The Duchess shook her head. "We've searched Findest many times over the decades. Turned over every stone in that blasted place."

"You mean Romi and Theo searched," Hatta corrected. Alice recognized those names. Romi, the eastern Gatekeeper in Tokyo, and Theo, the southern Gatekeeper in South Africa. She'd never met either of them, but Maddi and Hatta had spoken of them on occasion. "They could have missed something," Hatta continued.

The Duchess grumbled in Russian as the mirror zoomed in on the castle. Everything was gray stone lined with gold and red trappings, solid and thick, far less delicate than Legracia. The mirror finally settled on a lengthy throne room, empty and somewhat dark, where curtains had been drawn. A golden throne sat desolate.

"Somewhere in this room." Odabeth withdrew her hand, and the mirror returned to normal, bottles and all. She reached to set both hands on either side of the Eye, where it glowed at the center of her forehead. "Sleep now," she whispered.

The light in the Eye faded, and with it whatever had illuminated the princess from within. Eventually, the jewel was little more than that, catching the glow of the lights overhead. When Odabeth lowered her hands, the Eye came away from her forehead, leaving the much smaller gem behind.

"A-ah." The princess faltered, falling to her knees. Xelon was across the room in an instant, her arms around Odabeth, holding her up.

"Princess?" Xelon pressed her fingertips to the side of Odabeth's face.

The princess blinked up at her knight, blue eyes slightly hazed with fatigue. "I'm all right." She set her hand over Xelon's. "Just tired." Her other hand kept hold of the Eye, fingers curled around it.

"Well done, Princess." The Duchess knelt beside them and took up Odabeth's hand, pressing it and the Eye to her chest. "Your mother would be proud."

Odabeth smiled, bright but with a tired edge.

The Duchess stood and snapped her fingers. "Mal'chiki, help the princess to her room."

"No." Xelon slipped her arms beneath Odabeth and with a brief wince playing across her face, lifted the princess as she stood. "I'll look after her."

Odabeth gazed up at Xelon before resting her head on the knight's shoulder as she carried her down the back hallway.

"That is the most romantic damn thing I've seen in a long time," Court said from where she was seated with the twins at one of the tables across from the bar.

"Yeah." Alice smiled, her stomach all fluttery. It jumped when a hand came down on her shoulder.

Hatta stood at her side, looking less pissed but not pleased. His expression softened as their eyes met, his dulled but not black. The Madness was clearly taking a toll.

"We need to talk."

Twenty-Seven

FAMOUS LAST WORDS

Alice stood in Hatta's room, tilted against the closed door, rubbing her palms together.

"How was your mother?" Hatta asked, back in bed at Maddi's insistence. She'd have a few potions to help him get back on his feet for a short while, but they weren't finished just yet.

She snorted, shaking her head. "Fine." Livid, and probably going to kill her when she woke up to find Alice gone, but she couldn't worry about that now. She could be dead later, after making sure Chess wasn't.

"Good, good. So. The Eye has been restored and the Heart located." Hatta patted the bed beside himself.

Reluctant, Alice moved to sit. "Somewhat." They'd been shown a room, after all, not the Heart.

He rubbed slow circles into his temples. "Not surprising. It takes a disciplined and practiced mind to master the Eye fully."

He looked at her, his eyes still dim. "Seems we're moving along with this plan of yours."

She laughed. She didn't mean to, it just came out. "Right. My dumbass idea. That you said I would screw up. And you were right."

"Alice."

"I mean, of course you were. I've done nothing but screw up. The Black Knight has kicked my ass twice, yeah?" Anger roiled through her, hot and unceasing. It pushed words out of her mouth, completely bypassing any filters or care for any damage they might do. "He tricked me, got me to poison you, fooled me into bringing Odabeth here. I'm just messing everything up."

"Alice . . ."

"It's fine. It's fine! It's *fine*." Her voice broke a little, but she swallowed the sadness peeking through, burying it under the anger. Her hands screamed where she'd curled them into fists again. She opened her fingers, eyeing the small cuts in her palm.

"When did this happen?" He took one of her hands.

She snatched it away and tucked them between her thighs. "I'm fine. It's just scratches."

"You should have Maddi take care of these. Or the Duchess."

"I said I'm fine."

Silence hung between them, swallowing everything they didn't say. Alice's heart beat so loud she swore they both could hear it in the thick emptiness.

"I'm sorry." Hatta shifted against the headboard and stared

at the ceiling. "What I said before. I didn't mean it that way, but it doesn't matter. I hurt you. Which is the last thing I ever wanted." He heaved a slow sigh. His eyes fell shut. "The night you were attacked, I was waiting for you, in the Glow. I heard you scream; I . . . haven't been so afraid in such a long time. He could've killed you, nearly did, and I wasn't there to stop it." He pursed his lips, shaking his head. "If Xelon hadn't—I almost lost you."

Alice's breath caught in her throat. Her heart fluttered somewhere between her ears. Hatta had never talked like this before. She didn't know what to say, didn't think she could form the words if she tried. So she just stared at him, her heart in her throat now, trying to work its way back into her chest.

"When Maddi told me you'd gone back, where you'd gone, and knowing I couldn't follow, I panicked." He lifted his shoulders. "How could you be so stupid, I thought. But that was my fear talking. We were wrong."

That fluttering feeling in Alice's stomach returned full force. "I did it for you."

"I'm *not* worth it, Alice." He shook his head, adamant. "The things I've done to my own people. The evils I've unleashed."

It wasn't lost on Alice that Hatta had something to do with the Fiends from the war, since he was the Black Knight. Emphasis on *was*. "That's not who you are."

"You have no idea who I am!" The ember glow filled his eyes. He pressed a hand over them, taking a slow breath as he turned away from her. "No idea who I was. What I was." He chuckled. "Or maybe you do."

"You could have told me." She twisted to face him. "About

the Eye, the Heart, the truth about the Black Knight, all of it. You didn't have to keep it secret. I wouldn't—"

"Is there nothing in your past you want to forget? Nothing you'd give almost anything to erase? To make it so it never happened?"

The sharpness in his raised voice wavered at the end. He blinked rapidly, his eyes blazing, but beneath that Alice recognized the pain. A pain she knew all too well, of wanting to change what's happened. Of trying to get past it and being unable to.

Her shoulders lowered from where she'd hunched them. She gazed at him, lips pursed, brow pinched. She understood, more than he knew.

Slowly, the fury faded from his face, melting away under a sudden wave of sadness that took her by surprise. He pressed a hand over his eyes, whispered something incoherent as he sunk against the pillows.

Alice scooted in close, their thighs brushing. She wanted to help, wanted to let him know everything would be okay. With no idea what tormented him, she had no clue how she'd do it, but she had to try.

His face buried in both hands, he didn't see her reach out. He stopped muttering when she gripped one of his wrists, tensed when she pulled that hand away from his face. He looked up at her, a question clear in his eyes, so normal and still gorgeous.

What are you doing? she could imagine him thinking. She didn't know. She just wanted . . .

He straightened slowly, angled his body to face her as she drew his hands around to hold in her own. She gazed at him, teeth pressed to her lower lip. He watched her, eyes flickering over her face, which flamed under his gaze. When it settled on her lips, that heat traveled through the rest of her.

She leaned forward. Somewhere in the back of her mind, a frightened part of her said this was stupid. If he was interested, he'd make a move. But she'd done it, and he probably thought she was some fast little—

He caught her lips with his in the same instant he did this tiny scoot across the bed. The contact sent a shiver through her, and she flung his hands aside to lift her arms and curl them around his neck. He tasted like she expected he would, sweet and tangy. Had she thought about how he tasted? She couldn't remember, couldn't think about anything outside of holding on to him, of having him hold her.

His hands smoothed against her sides, his touch warm and firm. She wanted to feel more of him and pressed closer, nearly sliding into his lap. He finished the job for her, pulling her against himself, their bodies held tight together. Her focus went to his lips with the sudden urge to nip at them. She drank him in with every breath lost between them, the rushed pants and faint sighs. And his hands were everywhere, drawing on feelings she hadn't known were there, eliciting soft shivers, and when she couldn't swallow the faint groan that rose in her throat—

"No." The word was muffled, her mouth over his, but she made it out as he pushed her away. It was like pulling the plug on an energy source she needed to keep running. Her arms fell useless to her sides, and for a few seconds neither her mind nor her mouth worked.

Her fears from before came rushing in, taking advantage of her paralyzed state. *Oh god . . . this was a mistake . . . I went too far, he hates me now.*

He must've seen it in her face before he looked away, chest heaving, his face flushed, his fingers gripping her shoulders hard enough to hurt where he held her at arm's length. He shook his head, his throat working in a thick swallow. "No, I—I can't . . . this isn't . . ." His quiet words lacked surety, as if he was trying to convince himself and not her. "We can't . . . I'm not . . ."

Alice sat there while Hatta fumbled over whatever he was trying to say. In the end he only managed a frustrated sound that pulled at something inside her when she realized the negativity flowing off him wasn't aimed at her, but at himself.

"No," she whispered, a mirror of his previous declaration, but with vastly different meaning.

He met her gaze finally, his self-loathing crystal clear in his eyes, along with confusion, and fear. She took his face in her hands and leaned in, her brow touching his, like when she'd comforted him while Maddi gave him potions during that first episode. He shut his eyes with a shudder and sank forward so his head fell to her chest. She wrapped her arms around him and held him tight.

"No," she repeated, more forceful this time.

Again he drew back, and Alice was afraid he'd pull away altogether. Instead he held her gaze, his eyes clearer now, the fear gone, replaced by a flicker of desire that called to her own. He closed off the distance between them, renewing the kiss with fervor. She matched it, pulling at him as he moved in over her. Her fingers raked through his hair. She tugged soft strands in her enthusiasm, swallowing the faint hiss he gave in response.

It was happening. She couldn't believe it, and at the same time wanted more, but the jiggle of the doorknob sent a jolt of panic through her so powerful it flung them apart. She yanked away the same time he let her go. They sat there, separated by feet that felt like miles, chests heaving.

The door opened.

Alice silently cursed whoever chose *this* moment to come check on Hatta, as the Duchess appeared. She arched an eyebrow, her gaze bouncing back and forth between Alice and Hatta, finally resting on him.

"Everything all right?" the Duchess asked.

"Fine." Hatta licked his lips.

Alice cleared her throat, trying to concentrate on anything but the need to kiss him again. "Was just checking on him."

"Well, let's have a look, then." The Duchess crossed the room and set one hand to Hatta's forehead, the other to his chest. "How're you feeling?"

"I've been better." He grinned. "But I'll live."

"Of course you will." The Duchess removed her hand, but not before stroking the side of his face.

Alice's entire body went rigid.

"I've been working with Madeline on an elixir that should slow the progression of the Madness. Hopefully. If it works for you, we'll take some to the White Queen, try to buy more time to figure out this Heart situation."

"I thought your days of looking out for me were over. Something about my ignorance not being worth the trouble."

"You'd be dead without me, we both know that." The Duchess leaned in and pressed a kiss to his forehead. "Besides, you're just the guinea pig."

It's nothing, Alice told herself when she shut her eyes to avoid seeing red. *Just one friend caring for another. It's nothing.*

"Have you told him about your friend?" the Duchess asked. "The one the Black Knight took hostage?"

Alice's eyes flew open at the mention of Chess. Worry for him swelled all over again, along with a sliver of guilt she tried her best to ignore. He was being held captive by that bastard while she was here . . . doing . . . things.

Hatta frowned, glancing between the two of them. "What?"

It was Alice's turn to massage her temples, pushing at the pounding that was starting to pick up. "Things have gotten complicated."

◊ ◊ ◊

Out in the bar, everyone gathered to come up with a plan to address the latest development in the debacle that was Alice's life, namely the recent kidnapping of one of her friends by a dark minion that wanted to resurrect the entity of evil he served. Alice explained what happened at the school and the Black Knight's ultimatum. She fidgeted with the hem of her shirt, fighting the burn that closed off her throat and muddled her vision. She was not going to cry. She was Not. Going. To. Cry.

She was going to fix this.

Wiping discreetly at her eyes, she kept glancing at the clock on the wall. Only an hour until sunrise.

"I didn't know humans could be affected in such ways." The Duchess paced near the bar. The rhythmic thumping of her boots was like sandpaper against Alice's nerves.

"It's never happened before," Hatta said. "And we can't let it happen now. A human Fiend? A creature of both worlds; it could tear the Veil to shreds, just to start."

"But we can't just hand over the Eye," the Duchess countered. "And even if we did, how do we know this Black Knight can reverse what he's done? Could you?" She looked to Hatta.

So did Alice, every inch of her praying, hoping the answer was yes.

"I don't know." He shook his head. "As the Black Knight, I was only able to unleash darkness. The power to undo it lay with the Queen."

"And the Heart," Alice murmured. Which they didn't have. Yet. "How long before the transformation becomes permanent?"

Hatta and the Duchess exchanged a glance.

"A few days." Hatta gestured. "A week. Depends on how strong-willed the victim is."

A few days. That wasn't a lot of time. What if Chess turned before then? What if they couldn't find the Heart? Dammit, this was all her fault. Every step, every action she took to try to stop the Black Knight only furthered his plans and put people she cared about in danger.

So what you gone do, Baby Moon? Dad's voice washed over her, through her.

Alice shut her eyes and took a slow breath. Then another. And another.

That's my girl.

"A few days." She nodded. "W-we can work with that."

"What did you have in mind, luv?"

Suddenly aware of all the eyes on her, Alice tugged at the hem of her shirt. "We don't have to give the Black Knight a damn thing—just let him think we are long enough to get close and grab Chess. Everything else stays the same: use the Eye, find the Heart, get the cure." She looked to Hatta. "I know you think that's a bad idea, but we have to now. For Chess. And not just because he's my friend. You said it yourself: He could rip the Veil apart."

Hatta watched her with something she couldn't really identify in his gaze. "That I did."

The warmth that spread through Alice threatened to consume her. "Okay then. No bargains. No deals. We take this asshole down."

The Duchess smacked the bar top. "Agreed. We'd best get to it." She gestured for the twins to follow her. "Mal'chiki."

"Get ready." Hatta wrapped his arms around her and squeezed. "We've got a helluva fight in front of us."

◊ ◊ ◊

Alice paced near the bar, along the same path the Duchess had earlier. Her gaze flickering to the cat clock every few seconds. Forty-five minutes to sunrise, give or take. She slid her hands over the sword at her back. Dee had insisted she keep it, what with her daggers still in disrepair. Her thoughts traveled to the last time she'd used it, the strange way the blade had glowed, and the arcs of light she'd fired from it. She hadn't told anyone about that and was certain Xelon hadn't, either. If she had, there would have been questions for sure. Besides, it wasn't important, not in the grand scheme of things. She could figure out what it was all about later.

"Okay, this is it." Hatta emerged from the hallway. He'd changed to something more battle appropriate that mirrored the twins' leathers. This was the first time Alice had ever seen Hatta armored up. Not like Xelon, but definitely ready to throw hands. It was weird but . . . sorta sexy.

The Duchess, now dressed similarly, reached to stop him with a hand planted firmly on his chest.

He grunted. "What?"

She pointed at the hilt of the sword visible over his back. "What is that?" Irritation sharpened her accent.

Hatta heaved a sigh. "Better get this over with." He drew the weapon and held it out. The black blade swallowed the pale light in the room, almost dimming the bulbs.

Dee loosed a low whistle.

The Duchess gave a sort of strangled gasp. "You *kept* it?"

"I had permission." Hatta turned the sword over in his hand. "Needed to be able to protect the Eye."

"What is it?" Dem asked.

Alice had only seen that blade twice since he used it to slay a Fiend the night they met, but she had a pretty good idea.

"The Vorpal Blade," the Duchess said, glaring at Hatta and confirming Alice's suspicions.

"The original one, anyway." Hatta slipped the blade back into the sheath. The room brightened again. "I'm not sure what the imposter wields, but it is not this."

Alice couldn't remember if the Black Knight's sword had such an effect, but it had been night when she'd seen it so she wouldn't have been able to tell either way.

"You two ready?" Hatta looked between Alice and the White Knight.

"Hell yes," Alice said. The three of them would face the Black Knight while the Duchess and the Tweedles stayed behind to guard Odabeth. Maddi was busy mixing potions and preparing healing salves. No one expected this to be an easy fight.

Odabeth twisted the collar of her sweater where the necklace once rested. Xelon stood beside her in her full suit of armor. It had been cleaned and repaired a little, but the damage was still clear.

Court stepped forward and squeezed Alice, who returned the hug.

"I'll be okay," Alice murmured.

"Damn right you will. And so will Chess. That Black Knight asshole has no idea who he's messing with." Court swiped at her cheeks. "I'll be here helping Maddi mix some celebratory drinks for when you all get back. Definitely gonna use the hard stuff. Turn up!"

Alice rolled her eyes but chuckled, shaking her head. "Love you, girl."

"Love you, too."

"Worry not, milady." Xelon bowed to Odabeth, whose tight expression looked as uneasy about all of this as Alice felt. "You will be well protected in my absence."

"I worry for you." The princess clutched at the empty space near the center of her chest, likely missing the necklace she used to fidget with. "I order you to return to me."

Xelon deepened her bow. "As you wi—mmph!" As she came out of the bow, Odabeth latched onto her and pressed their lips together.

A few whoops from Courtney and the twins filled the air.

Xelon stood arms frozen where they were lifted on either side of her, eyes wide as windows. When Odabeth pulled away, the knight blinked rapidly as red crept up her neck. "I—I . . . of course, Your Majesty. Always."

"This way, Your Highness." The Duchess, a knowing smile in place, led the princess around the corner and down the hall, no doubt to one of the many rooms hidden in the back of the pub.

Xelon cleared her throat and refused to look at either Alice or the grinning Hatta as the three of them made their way out into the chilly Atlanta night. Court was a gem and let them borrow her car. Alice drove, with Hatta poured into the passenger seat and Xelon in the back, looking more than a little on edge.

"Pre-battle jitters, Xelon?" Alice asked, trying to ignore her own shaking as the break of day encroached on the edge of the horizon. Light steadily filled the darkness. "I mean, that's a thing, right?"

"I'm not concerned with the battle ahead, more for what I

leave behind." Xelon gazed out the window, watching the human world float by. "I already failed my Queen. It cannot be the same with the princess."

"You know Anastasia as well as I do," Hatta said. "Anyone foolish enough to go to that pub looking for trouble will most definitely find it. You've got nothing to worry about."

Alice tightened her grip on the wheel. *Famous last words.*

Twenty-Eight

EYES OF FLAME

A nearby football field was the only readily available place they could go that was open enough to face the Black Knight. It would be empty and out of the way. But Alice's stomach still tied itself in knots as they circled the block to park. Not because of what was going to happen, but because it was where Brionne had been shot. Small gatherings of flowers, stuffed animals, and crosses dotted the parking lot, positioned around a larger vigil where she had probably died.

Taking a deep breath, Alice fastened the decoy Eye around her neck and dropped it down into her shirt.

"You ready, milady?" Hatta downed his second stamina potion, the sky pinkening outside the window behind him.

"As I'll ever be."

The three of them made their way along the grassy stretch

lining the outside of the field. The sun's light poured across the sky, a streaked mix of pale blues and peaches.

Right on time . . . I hope.

Alice led the way into the tunnel from the backfield onto the main yardage. Their steps echoed in the shadows. When they emerged, the stadium rose around them. She'd never been on the football field before, always relegated to sit in the stands with the rest of the cheerers. From down here, the place was enormous, stretching out like a great behemoth of brick, ready to swallow them whole. The space was both freeing and oddly claustrophobic, with no way out except the tunnel at their back, or a similar one directly across from them.

A quiet tension settled over the trio as they came to a stop at the fifty-yard line. Minutes ticked into eternity as they waited, fingers flexing around various hilts, heads on the swivel.

Xelon cleared her throat. "Are we in the right place?"

"There is no right place," Alice explained. "Not really. He just said have the Eye ready at sunrise, and he'd find me." A cliché bad-guy line if she'd ever heard one.

"So I did." The voice came from the south, and everyone spun to find the Black Knight hovering in the air, arms folded across his chest. "And so I have." His head tilted to the side. "Didn't expect you to bring friends, kitten."

"*Don't* call me kitten. We brought the Eye." She pressed a hand over the chain where it rested cool and concealed against her skin. "Where's Chess?"

"We'll get to that in a minute. First things first." He waved her off, his head angling around in a manner that indicated his attention had shifted to Hatta. "I suppose I should've expected you, but I'll admit I didn't. Still, I'm glad you're here. I need your help." He swung around to face away from them, his arms out to the sides. "What do you think?" He faced forward again. "Not as pointy or cape-y as your original getup, but still a good look."

"Who are you?" Hatta growled, his expression calm, almost serene, but the menace in his tone was downright lethal.

The Black Knight snorted and set his hands on his hips. "She didn't tell you?" He looked to Alice. "I luv ya, hun, but you suck at this."

"I know who you *claim* to be, but that's not what I asked." Hatta's fingers flexed at his sides.

"Is it childish to say that's for me to know and you to find out?" The Black Knight tapped the chin of his helmet.

"Enough." Alice stepped forward, clutching the chain. "We had a deal. I brought it. Let go of Chess. Now."

The Black Knight shook his head. "Y'know, if take-charge girls didn't drive me wild, I'd be kind of offended right now. Relax, kitten, the stiff's fine." He snapped his fingers.

With a whooshing rush of sound the immediate area behind the Black Knight shimmered like the street on a hot day. Two Fiends emerged on either side of him, one of them dragging an unconscious Chess by the back of his collar.

Alice's chest tightened at the sight of him. Blood crusted the side of his face. He hung limp, bound and gagged, his clothes stained black and torn in places. He was pale, near white, except for a stretch of blackened skin visible from his chest to his neck. His left arm was twisted behind his back, though she could see through tears in his shirt that it was black as well. He was changing.

"Chess." She started forward, but Xelon gripped her arm, shaking her head.

Fear and panic warred for dominance within Alice, but rising anger won out. She glared at the Black Knight, her hands going to her sword.

The Black Knight extended his hand. "All right, I showed you mine."

Every muscle in Alice's body tightened. This was it. She started forward, slowly lifting her hand to slip into the collar of her shirt and around the chain. She yanked. The chain snapped against the back of her neck. When the Black Knight curled his fingers expectantly, she pressed the decoy into his palm, hers still covering it.

"You'll pay for this," she hissed between clenched teeth, eyes fixed on his helmet, hoping he could feel the burn in her glare through it.

The Black Knight tugged his hand away. "Promises, promises." He opened his fingers to inspect his palm. His head jerked back slightly as a Time Turner came into view. "What is—"

Alice's foot slammed into that bastard's chest with a scream that rose from the soles of her feet. She'd reared back and poured into it every ounce of anger, of pain, of frustration for what he'd turned her life into, for how he'd tortured those close to her. It all burned through her in an instant, and she loosed it against him.

With a sound like a wounded animal, the Black Knight flew backward. He tumbled, rolling out of his fall into a crouch, but Hatta was already on top of him. He barreled into the Black Knight with a sound like metallic thunder, driving him back with a spray of dirt and AstroTurf.

The Fiends were distracted by their master's peril, and Alice yanked her sword free and raked it across the muzzle clamped onto Chess's shirt. The monster yowled and pulled away, dropping its captive. Alice knelt at his side, fingers going to his neck, her heart frantic as she searched for his pulse.

"Is he?" Xelon asked as she stood over them, her sword drawn.

Alice couldn't answer, she wasn't sure, and that uncertainty washed cold through her. "I—I . . ." Then she felt it, the weak jump beneath her searching fingers. Again, and again, present but fluttery. "He's alive!" she shouted, relief flooding her. "He's alive."

Xelon shifted her stance to keep herself between Alice and Chess and the Fiends pacing nearby. The beasts seemed less than keen on attacking for some reason, their lips curled, fangs bared in snarls.

Nearby, Hatta and the Black Knight dueled. Alice had never seen Hatta fight like this, twisting with the flow of his sword, executing strikes and parries with speed and agility. The Black Knight met his attack with equal fervor, the two exchanging bone-jarring blows. The clash of their blades erupted in shrieks of metal and white and black sparks. Wherever they fell, the ground burned black, scorched. Hatta was a force to be reckoned with, but he couldn't keep this up forever.

"We have to get Chess out of here," Alice said. Then Hatta could pull back.

"That's going to be easier said than done." Xelon's head whipped back and forth as the Fiends split to circle the three of them.

Alice stood and placed herself between the unconscious Chess and the beasts. Breathing deep, she reached for the energy that filled her the last time, that enabled her to drive them off.

Nothing.

Of course nothing. Why would some special ability surface when she needed it most? The Fiends drew closer. Chess groaned behind her, the sound garbled. Alice's heart filled her throat.

One Fiend darted forward. Xelon struck it from the side, earning a pained yowl. Alice focused on the monster pacing toward her, the wound on the side of its face oozing black blood. Chess shifted behind her. She wanted to check on him— it sounded like he was in pain—but the Fiend came first. Squaring her feet, she dove.

The creature pulled wide, but she was ready to follow, twisting and swiping, narrowly missing catching it along the flanks. It bounded around, lashing out with wicked claws that caught her forearm.

Pain lanced clear up to her shoulder, and she cried out. She tucked her arm behind her, backing away a few steps and chancing a glance at the wound. The leather arm guards beneath her sleeves had absorbed most of the damage, but her torn skin bled freely. It could have been so much worse. She'd have to thank the Tweedles for the loan.

The Fiend came at her again, though a plated foot slammed into its head and sent it tumbling. Xelon spun to parry another glancing blow from claws. "Your friend!" she shouted.

Alice's eyes shot to Chess, who'd regained consciousness and rolled onto his side, trying to get up.

"I'll hold them." Xelon dodged another lunge. "Get him out!"

She didn't want to leave the knight to fight alone, but she raced to Chess's side, dropping next to him. "I'm sorry." She sliced the binds at his ankles, then his wrists, and yanked the gag free, tossing it aside. "Come on, I'm getting you out of here."

Behind her, Xelon roared as she drove the monsters back. They howled in pain as her sword found flesh.

"Alice," Chess wheezed. Red stained his lips and ran from the corners of his mouth. It soaked the gag and spread over most of his shirt, near invisible in the black material.

"Shh, don't speak. I've got you." Her entire face was on fire, her eyes burning, her vision blurry. Alice tried to ignore the coppery scent, the feel of wet warmth slick on her hands. Chess clutched at her, his fingers fumbling for purchase. His entire body shook. "Here we go." She shifted closer, caught him under his arm and hauled him up into a seated position. He screamed. The sound shot straight to her gut. "Oh my god!" The words faltered around a sob as he fell back into her arms, his hand at his side.

His teeth clenched around a groan. "Side, on fire!"

"O-okay, okay, let me see." She pulled his shirt back to reveal the tears in his side, split and bleeding out. Red smeared the ground beneath him. She was almost sick with disbelief that she hadn't noticed this before. *Oh no. Oh please, no.* "I-it'll be okay." The words fell out of her mouth. Lies. "I'll get you help, you'll be okay." She fumbled through the pouches on her belt. Between the blood and her shaking hands, she could barely hold on to the few vials she had.

Chess writhed against the ground, his eyelids fluttering. His chest heaved with wet, choppy sounds rising at the back of his throat.

"Damn it!" Alice reached for a dropped potion, and his hand fell over hers, slick and sticky.

With deep, shaky breaths, he forced a word free. "L-love." His grip went slack. His fingers slipped through hers. He sank against the ground, his red-smeared face no longer contorted with pain or effort.

No. "Chess?" She shook him. "Chess!"

His eyes stared past her, unfocused, lost.

He wasn't . . .

He couldn't . . .

Alice clapped a hand over her mouth. Her insides frothed up. She screamed. Her entire body rocked with it, quaking till she felt like she'd come apart.

He did this, something inside her hissed. Red-hot fury exploded in her chest. She straightened from where she'd curled over her friend, her face slick with tears and blood. *He did this!*

She whirled, eyes moving over the field. Xelon battled the Fiends, more ducking and dodging than anything else as they attacked while retreating. Hatta and the Black Knight twisted around each other, the tarnished ground writhing beneath their feet.

The Black Knight deflected a blow, flinging Hatta over his shoulder and away. The knight moved as if to go after him, but jerked to a stop and twisted around to face Alice. With his helmet on, there was no way she could see it, but she knew the instant their eyes met.

Her teeth ground together. *You* . . . She surged to her feet.

Hatta had regained his, moving in to attack the Black Knight's open back, but it was too late.

In one fluid motion, the Black Knight gripped his Vorpal Blade in both hands and plunged it into the bubbling ground. The earth split with a shriek that burrowed into Alice's bones. The ground quaked as liquid black rocketed into the air like a geyser. Some of it rained down, but most of it spread overhead, arching out until darkness domed the entire area, leaving everything gray, as if a filter had passed over the world. Alice squinted, her head whipping back and forth as she searched the field for any sign of the Black Knight. Nothing.

He was gone.

The geyser screamed, Alice's ears ringing with it. The black was everywhere, coating everything. It oozed across the field, giving the impression the ground was alive. Mounds of it seeped together, writhing, thrashing, congealing into at least a dozen half-formed Nightmares. Instead of attacking, the blobs of appendages, tentacles, and torsos crawled, hobbled, limped, or lobbed their way across the field. Toward her.

"Alice!" Xelon raced up, her face red with effort, her sword and some of her armor covered in ichor. "The Fiends have retreated. I don't know to where or for how long, but we can't . . ." She trailed off as her gaze played over Chess.

Alice didn't move. Didn't speak.

Xelon's mouth snapped shut, and she took Alice's arm. "We have to get out of here."

"I'm not leaving him."

The ground shuddered beneath Alice's feet. It pitched and rolled, tossing her over. Xelon dropped beside her, shouting something in what sounded like Korean.

Across the field, Hatta yelled for them to run.

The half-formed Nightmares were nearly on top of them.

"Come on!" Xelon sheathed her sword and got her arms around Alice, hauling her up and away from Chess.

Alice twisted and pulled, kicking to break free. "No! No, we can't! They'll get him!"

"He's gone, Alice. I'm sor—"

Alice drove her elbow up into Xelon's face. Xelon shouted, releasing her hold, her hands going to her mouth. Alice was free, and she threw herself toward Chess just as the Nightmare blobs flung themselves on top of him.

"Chess!"

The quaking beneath her feet intensified. The blobs kept coming, piling on top of one another, their growing mass rocking back and forth. The whole of it twisted with a low rumble.

Not a rumble, a roar.

The mass swelled before one side erupted outward. A hand the size of a compact car slammed into the ground, just shy of squashing Hatta flat. Huge fingers dug grooves into the earth. Hatta scrambled to his feet as the sludge continued to take shape, the torso of a man, legs of a goat. Black, leathery wings spread from its shoulders, tendrils of ooze clinging to spindly joints or glopping to the ground. It swung its snakelike tail and threw back what became its head, pointed like a dragon, rows of jagged teeth bared. Two horns twisted upward from its head. It gave another bellowing roar, its forked tongue lashing.

The feeling of lightning shot through her left arm, searing the nerves. The flames of the Nightmare's eyes struck with life, red fire burning. That same fire erupted from its mouth with a crackle of embers and the rotten stench of sulfur and decay. She'd smelled it only once before.

At Ahoon.

Twenty-Nine
CLAWS THAT CATCH

Alice crouched, frozen as tremors twisted through her. This couldn't be happening. She was dreaming, she had to be, even though her body ached, her head and chest pounded, and her nerves screamed as her muscles tightened.

The Nightmare stomped its hoofed feet and lifted its arms, getting a feel for its newly formed body, bigger than the one she'd faced in the village.

Crossing the Veil makes them more powerful. The thought struck her like a slap. So stupid, coming here, where Brionne had . . .

So much fear, so much sadness.

My fault.

Pitch oozed off it like embryonic fluid. Its wings shuddered as it snorted a cloud of ash before fixing flaming eyes on Alice. All feeling left her body.

She screamed.

With a rumbling chuckle it stomped toward her, shaking the ground with each step. She scrambled backward in a frantic crab-walk before pitching herself over and clambering to her feet. She ran, with everything she had, she ran.

The ground cracked under its hooves. The air snapped with heat when it roared, just like last time. Flashes of the encounter tore through her mind. The pain of talons tearing at her skin, of breath hot and foul in her face. The pressure of a hoof against her chest, pushing until she felt her whole body might cave in. If the Tweedles hadn't been there . . .

But this time she was alone.

Until a familiar voice reminded her she wasn't.

"Here!" Hatta shouted. There was a sound like cloth ripping, and the Nightmare howled in rage and pain.

Alice stumbled to a stop and glanced back. Hatta, sword in hand, evaded the monster's claws as he cut into its calves.

Xelon dove around and between its legs, slicing at the beast while dodging claws.

It roared, swiping faster and faster, gaining more control of its huge limbs. It stomped, trying to catch them under its hooves. They were quick enough to avoid it so far, but they were battle worn, growing weary. Claws glanced off Xelon's armored shoulder, but she still cried out in pain.

Hatta drove his sword into its side. The massive Nightmare snarled and backhanded him away. Hatta flew through the air, then hit the ground hard enough to send dirt and grass spewing. He tumbled to a stop and was still. Alice screamed his name and started for him.

The creature turned toward her, and she froze. Her entire body locked up, trembling.

Pools of fire where its eyes should be fixed on her from across the field. It took one rumbling step toward her, then stopped. The flames in its gaze dimmed. The snarl on its lips died away as it stared at her. The orange burn cooled to white, then vanished altogether. It watched her with huge, violet eyes.

"Al . . . ice . . ." The monster choked on her name, more a growl than a word, but she'd heard it. Her heart pounded against the inside of her chest.

"Chess," she whispered.

With a cry, Xelon flung herself at the beast's back, driving her sword home. It roared, the flames in its eyes bursting back to life. It clawed at its shoulders, flapping those massive wings, trying to get at Xelon.

It was all beast and fury now, but Alice had seen it. Chess was in there. Somehow.

Xelon shouted. The monster had her by the leg, dangling her upside down. She yanked a dagger from her boot and plunged it into the Nightmare's hand. It released her with a roar. She hit the ground in an armored heap, rolling onto her side.

The beast howled with rage, spewing fire into the air from its nose and mouth. It gripped at something stuck in its side and yanked it free, flinging it aside. It landed several yards away. The Vorpal Blade. *A blade so black.*

Alice's eyes went back to the battle. Addison was still down. Xelon had regained her feet, but didn't look like she would be on them for long. The Nightmare was busy trying to dislodge Xelon's sword from its back.

Alice's chest tightened. Tears streamed hot against her face. She'd let this happen. She let the Black Knight play her at every step, and now Chess was trapped in a Nightmare, with no way out. Except one.

The Vorpal Blade went snicker-snack.

The words played over in Alice's mind.

She shook her head even as the thought bounced around inside. A sob forced its way from behind her clenched teeth. She was too late to save him, but that didn't mean she had to leave him like this. She could free him.

Do it. Alice took off running. *Do it now, before you can't.* Her body ached, her lungs burned, but she didn't stop. She dropped to slide, snatched up the Vorpal Blade, and kept going.

The beast tugged Xelon's sword loose, flapping its great wings as it faced the unarmed knight. It laughed, a low, rolling boom as it tromped toward her.

"Hey!" Alice shouted as she came to a stop, gripping the Vorpal Blade with both hands. The monster paused, spinning to face her.

"Alice!" Xelon shouted. "No! Run!"

Alice's heart clenched, fear trying to work its way inside, but she refused to be taken by it. Not this time. Instead, she embraced it. She was afraid, terrified, but not of the monster, not anymore. Even as it bore down on her.

What scared her was her friends being in danger.

What terrified her was the thought of losing anyone else.

That fear rooted itself in her center, along with the anger and determination from before.

You can't have them.

The Nightmare swiped at her. She darted to the side, slicing into its thigh. It stumbled as it tried to come after her. She took the chance to stab into its calf. Another roar. She thought she heard someone call her name before the back of a huge hand collided with her. She flew, pain rocketing through her. The ground rushed upward. She braced for impact.

Light exploded across her vision. It swept around her, cocooning her in its radiance. She hovered midair, stunned as the glow wrapped around her, flowing outward from the sword.

"How . . ."

As the light lowered her to stand, a roar from the creature pulled her attention back to the battle.

The monster stood maybe fifty feet away but didn't approach. Staring down the beast, Alice held the glowing blade in front of her and started forward. The Nightmare bellowed threateningly but drew back. It lifted its arm to shield itself before suddenly planting its feet and rearing up. Red welled between its lips. Its wings unfurled, and with a howl it released a wall of flame that ate up the ground between them, galloping toward her.

Alice dropped to the ground, hands over her head. A rush of light enveloped her, red warring with white, a radiant firestorm. She curled on her side, tucked into herself as the sword's power wavered visibly around her. Another roar, more fire. Then it all stopped with a yowl.

She lifted her head. Hatta gripped the hilt of Xelon's sword where it disappeared into the monster's side. The beast flailed, trying to get at him as he yanked the sword free. Yellow poured from the wound, slopping onto the ground. The

Nightmare released a shriek and twisted, grabbing Hatta around his neck, its claws tearing into his back. He cried out.

"Addison!" Alice scrambled to her feet.

Warmth burst outward from her center, hot with her resolve. It shot along her arms and legs, clear to the soles of her feet and the palms of her hands, tingling. She gripped the sword, yelping at the burn. Her fingers tightened when she felt she might drop it. Her body acted before her mind could catch up, and she swung. Light arced from the blade and shot through the air. It slammed full force into the Nightmare and sent it reeling.

"You give him back!" She swung again, and again, sending light hurtling into the beast until it dropped Hatta in order to defend itself. "Do you hear me? You give him back!"

She left it dead . . . More words whispered against her mind. Another voice joined hers, the same but different.

The warmth surged. She didn't try to pull it up, or force it out; it was just there. The energy spread through her fingers. It flared brighter than when she fought the Fiends. Her body sang with the power pumping through it and into the sword, which brightened until she could barely make out the blade itself.

The monster roared.

And with its head . . .

"You can't have anyone else." Alice stepped into a spin that brought the sword all the way around, then pushed everything rushing through her into the blade and hurled it outward. "I won't let you!"

She went galumphing back.

A massive arc exploded from the sword with so much force it knocked her over as it shot straight for the beast. This light hammered home, and the monster's entire body ruptured. It shrieked in pain as some invisible force tore it open from the inside. The combination sent it into wicked throes, wings spasming, arms thrashing, until it exploded.

No! She hadn't meant—Chess was still in there!

Liquid black filled the area in a rush, a massive wave sweeping outward. Alice, her strength waning, sank to the ground as the dark waters overtook her. She tumbled end over end, unable to see or hear. She bounced against the ground, then angled herself around to push off it. Her head broke the surface. She gasped for air, arms flailing, legs kicking as she spun, out of control. A short ways off, Chess bobbed into view. He floated along the inky surface for a second before disappearing beneath the black.

Alice kicked off toward him, pushing with everything she had, but the current was too strong. It pulled at her, yanked her toward some unseen vortex at the center of the liquid darkness.

She tried to fight, tried to swim, but the fatigue settling through her limbs and over her mind made it hard.

"You won't get in my way again," a voice snarled. Pressure clamped on Alice's ankles, dragging her down. She choked and coughed, her chest aching, stretching. She was going to burst.

"Begone!" a different voice shouted, and light filled the void, driving back the darkness. Alice's body went limp, and with it the pain that threatened to tear her open. All that remained was a soothing tingle cascading through her limbs.

Reflection-Alice suddenly appeared in the murky waters, her dress flowing around her as it had before. *"Rest now."* She pulled Alice into her arms, and together they tumbled through the deep.

I did it.

"You did." Reflection-Alice smiled, but she still looked sad.

I did it . . .

It was over. She could stop fighting.

That thought settled warm inside her as she and Reflection-Alice sank into the dark.

Thirty

NOT OVER

Alice stood on the ridge of a chasm and gazed out into the abyss. Black sand shifted beneath her feet, the skies darkened by rolling clouds of pitch. Every now and then purple lightning scorched the air. The land around her was void and desolate, all rock and stone, barren.

She felt she should be afraid, but she wasn't. This wasn't real; it couldn't be.

But a part of her knew it was, or . . . it would be? She didn't understand.

"Alice."

The sound of her name swept up in echoes from below, rising out of the chasm. She peered into it. Shadows waited at the bottom, concealing whatever rested on the floor.

"Alice." Again.

She thought she recognized the voice but couldn't put a name to it.

"Alice!" More insistent this time. "—back, please! Come back . . ."

Come back? But she hadn't gone anywhere.

She lifted her bare foot. The hem of her skirt wafted in the breeze, stark white against her dark skin. Arms out, she stepped over the edge.

The darkness swallowed her, and spit her out with a jolt. Her eyes flew open wide, and a sudden heaviness slammed into her. She twisted onto her side, coughing.

"Oh, thank god." Arms curled around her, shaking as Courtney sobbed, her face pressed against Alice's cheek. "Y-you're okay! You're okay."

Alice twisted against Courtney, her head pounding. "Where—" She tried to speak, but her throat seized around the words with the feeling of swallowing sand. She coughed to clear it, breath catching. "W-where am I?"

Court finally drew back, swiping at her nose with a sniff, then wiping her puffy eyes. "The pub. You're at the pub—oh my god, you're okay." She started crying again, weeping into her hands, smeared with makeup. "I thought . . . I—I thought . . ."

Alice wanted to reach for her, but her limbs felt like they'd been filled with hot metal. Her muscles burned; every inch of her throbbed. Her mind danced with flashes of faces and light as the pounding intensified.

The door behind Courtney opened, and Maddi hurried in with a tray of vials and glasses full of various swirling and glowing fluids. "You're awake. Good." She set it down on the bedside table and took up one of the vials, popping the cork and handing it over.

Alice had some trouble gripping the vial, but with Court's help, drank it down without question. It slid along her throat, coating it in a layer of cold, easing the hurt.

"Better?" Maddi searched her face.

She nodded. "Better." Though it didn't help the migraine, the churning in her stomach, or the images dancing against the back of her eyes. "Augh." Faces flickered in and out of her vision. Some she recognized, some she didn't. There were voices as well, screaming. It all tried to come together but vanished like so much smoke through her fingers. "My head."

"What's wrong?" Maddi asked.

"It *hurts*. I keep seeing flashes. Faces." She blinked rapidly, but that didn't help. "Feels like my brains are gonna leak out of my ears."

"An effect of taking in so much of that sludge." Hatta stood in the doorway, watching her. He sported a few cuts and bruises, some bandages here and there, but looked to be in one piece.

"It's rude to lurk in doorways," Alice murmured.

Hatta smirked, but there was no joy behind it. As he approached, Maddi drew back, leaving him to take her space. He settled on the edge of the bed and, his touch gentle, reached to gather Alice into his arms.

She went, eagerly, sinking into him with a soft sound. Her eyes drifted shut as his arms wound around her, warm and safe. She tried to return the embrace, but her arms refused to obey.

Instead she buried her face in his chest, breathing him in. His hand went to the back of her head.

"I'm so, so sorry, Alice."

What? That didn't make sense. Neither did his tone. He sounded like somebody die—

The images flashed against Alice's vision again. This time they held, solid, familiar.

Chess.

Chess laughing with her. Chess asking her out, or making a face when someone used his full name. Chess with his bright violet eyes and wide grin.

Chess lying on the grass as blood poured out of him. Chess struggling to take in air. Chess . . .

Someone screamed. It wasn't until the images faded that Alice realized it was her. She clutched at Hatta and wailed into his chest as something inside her cracked apart and hung open. Ice coated her insides, the cold twisting within her like a living thing. Hatta held tight to her, muttering something she couldn't hear over her sobs.

Warmth pressed against her back. Courtney's voice joined Hatta's, shaky and just as broken as Alice's. They held her, together, as she fell apart.

◊ ◊ ◊

Alice curled on her side in the dark, staring at the bare wall across from her. She didn't know how much time had passed, and she didn't care. Maddi had come and gone a couple of times, offering her food she couldn't eat. After holding her through the worst of her crying, Hatta had slipped out and hadn't been back. Alice asked where he'd gone.

"To take care of your friend," Maddi explained quietly. They'd brought Chess back. Alice wasn't sure if she was grateful they didn't just leave him lying out there or angry for . . . she wasn't sure. Just angry.

Her fault. All of it was her fault.

Courtney had lain with her, cried with her more. Then she left, saying she would take care of Alice's mom who, on waking to find an empty house, had called Court immediately. She had no idea how that went or what was said. She couldn't bring herself to care.

Her mom was angry, but at least her daughter was alive.

When Alice couldn't take being alone with her thoughts anymore, she picked herself up and made her way out into the bar. The main area was empty, the sign on the door still flipped to CLOSED. Maddi stood behind the bar, speaking softly with the Duchess. Both of them glanced up when Alice walked in. The cat clock above their heads read 6:37, but the tail had stopped wagging, so that couldn't be right.

Her lips pursed, the Duchess came out from behind the bar, grabbing a glass of water from the counter in passing. "How are you feeling?" She offered the glass.

Alice didn't take it. "I don't know."

The Duchess sighed softly. "I am sorry, Alice."

Sorry. People were always sorry, weren't they? Her father was sorry when he said she'd have to find a way to make it without him. The doctors were sorry they didn't know what happened and couldn't stop it. Her mother was sorry after she checked out after he was gone, leaving her all alone. Everyone at school and church was sorry for her loss. She'd gotten so damn sick of the sorries. Now they would start again.

"Where is everyone?" Alice asked, glancing around again as if they'd all pop out of hiding.

"Your friend went to get something from her vehicle." The Duchess moved to place the glass on the counter, then stepped behind it to start mixing potions again. "The princess is with Xelon, who's resting. The twins are making sure the Nightmare essence from your battle is subdued until you can get to it. Hatta is in the back but asked not to be disturbed."

The bell over the door rang, and Courtney tapped down the stairs. "There's my girl." She hurried over and pulled Alice into a hug she only half returned. Drawing back, Court flashed a smile that was all teeth but little joy. That's when Alice realized she wasn't wearing any makeup. Not even lip gloss.

"Hey," Alice murmured.

"Your mom is livid." Court's voice broke a bit, and she forced another smile, sniffing. "I told her you were with me and you were okay. There was a lot of cussing, but I got the gist of what she was trying to say, which is, I think we're forbidden to hang out now."

Alice half-hiccuped, half-laughed. It wasn't funny, but she couldn't help it.

"I'll take you home, if you want. Or to my place. Wherever. Your stuff is already in the car, so just meet me in the parking lot when you're ready, okay?"

"Okay."

Court squeezed Alice's hands, hugged her again, and then went for the door, wiping at her eyes.

"Heading out?" Hatta came up behind Alice, hands in his pockets, his expression unreadable.

She nodded, releasing a slow breath. She looked to the hall, then back to Hatta. "What'd you do with him?"

"We're taking good care of him, milady, I promise."

Alice wanted to know more, but at the same time didn't. She couldn't go back there, couldn't see him. Not right now. "What do we say h-happened?" Her voice broke and her eyes burned, but the tears wouldn't come.

"One of a few things, but you don't worry about that right now." He drew his hands free and placed them on the sides of her face. "Go with Courtney. Get some sleep." Hatta took her hand and led her through the bar and out to the sidewalk. Court's Camaro waited at the curb. Hatta opened the door so Alice could climb in.

"What now? We just give up?"

He gave her a look before sighing. "Now, we regroup, which is not the same as giving up. This isn't over. Not by a long shot." Hatta leaned into the window and pressed a kiss to the top of Alice's head. "Rest well, milady."

She watched Hatta in the side mirror, who was watching them as they rode away.

Court put on a jazz station to fill the silence. Alice didn't ask where they were going.

As they drove, the croon of a saxophone filled the car along with the hum of the engine. It should've been a relaxing mix, but Alice's thoughts were far from calm. They kept tumbling over everything, from the night the Black Knight attacked her to Chess lying on the ground, his eyes . . .

He did this.

The anger from the field returned. It swallowed the hurt peeling away her insides. It burned, hot and heavy in her blood. She shook with it, gripping the bottom of the window so tight it buckled under her fingers. She let the anger swallow her and pushed back the image of Chess in her mind, replacing it with the Black Knight.

I'm coming for you.

And she hoped he knew it, like he knew on the field. She hoped he could sense her fury from wherever he'd crawled off to and realized it was for him. Hoped he understood just how little time he had before she found him and made him suffer the way he'd made her friends suffer. Hoped he searched the darkness for signs of her, glancing over his shoulder at every unknown sound or slightest movement. Hoped he was afraid, like she had been afraid, but wasn't anymore. Because Hatta was right.

This wasn't over.

Epilogue
IT'S ONLY
A DREAM

He couldn't run. He couldn't scream. All he could do was be.

Pain and anger. They didn't stop, they didn't start, they just were. He didn't know if he even had a body to hurt, but there it was. Agony. Rage. There *he* was. Alone.

Darkness went on in every direction.

Quiet.

Still.

Everything and nothing all at once.

He floated in the void, fear slithering cold through him. He couldn't move. He couldn't speak. He could only lie there as the black consumed him.

Flashes of a face interrupted the fear every now and then. Whisperings against his mind, of bright laughter and brown eyes, kept him from giving in entirely. He clung to them, with his nothing arms and his trembling essence. This was all he knew. He couldn't let her go.

"You poor dear." A voice. The shadows shifted but did not fade. Someone stood beside him. Over him.

He couldn't see.

"Look at what they've done to you. What *she* did to you."

She? The flashes again. More this time—a smile, a voice, but not this one.

"Yes, her. She did this to you. Don't you remember?"

More flashes. A sword, burning bright. It hurt. The light burned. The fire filled him, ate him from the inside. Every inch of him screamed, every nerve like lightning. He wanted it to stop, tried to beg, but he couldn't speak. Could barely breathe.

Without warning, the pain vanished. The cold rushed in to fill him, the relief hit hard enough to hurt.

"There you are. All better?"

He wanted to nod. The pain was gone, but so were the flashes. The eyes. The laughter. He was alone, again.

"Oh, my lovely, you're not alone. I'm here."

Warmth blossomed in his chest. It spread through him, filling him from top to bottom. It chased away the remaining jitters of pain. Calm. Peace.

"You see? I have not forgotten you. I am always here. You can come with me, if you like. Leave this place."

Yes! That's what he wanted. To escape, to get away from the nothing. To not be alone.

"Come to me. Be with me. Be mine."

The darkness drew into itself and let him go. He floated

higher now, up and away, leaving everything he knew and was behind.

"That's it. Come to me."

A pinprick of light flickered to life above him.

"Come to me."

He reached for it.

"Come to me."

It filled his vision, filled his body, filled everything. There was nothing but him and the light.

He opened his eyes. A brown ceiling stretched overhead. A fan rotated slowly at its center. Walls the same color, bare and cracked here and there, surrounded him. He shifted his body, wriggling his fingers and toes. He had fingers and toes. Maybe he always did, but now he could control them. He lay on a bed, the softness against his skin intriguing. He inhaled, slow, careful, his chest burning as it took in air, like his lungs had forgotten how. The smell and taste of dirt and copper filled his nose and mouth. His face scrunched.

Something clicked to his right. A door opened, and a small, dark-haired brown girl slipped through, closing it behind her. She held an armful of vials and bottles that she promptly dropped to the floor when she looked at him.

"Strewth." She all but threw herself against the door, back pressed to it, shoulders hunched. "Ch-Chess?"

He tilted his head to the side, observing her.

"This . . . no way, no how, the crow flies." Her wide pink eyes held his. She blinked. Her eyes were now purple. Then green.

He studied the way her mouth quivered and the rest of her trembled. She stank of fear. It rolled off her in waves.

"Alice. A tale to tell. Must tell." Her fingers fumbled at the knob.

"*Take her*," the voice echoed between his ears.

He bolted up from the bed and across the room.

She screamed.

His fingers closed around her throat.

ACKNOWLEDGMENTS

I cannot begin in any form or fashion without first thanking my heavenly Father the Lord God and His son Jesus Christ, my personal Lord and Savior. Thine is the honor and the glory, and I would not be here without Your guidance, Your grace, Your mercy, and Your blessings. Thank You for guiding my steps, for putting those who would lift my dreams in my path, and for being with me from the first word of the first story I ever wrote.

Thank you to Melissa Nasson, who fell in love with Alice enough to stand by me and her through the years we searched for the right home for this story. You kept my spirits lifted and my hopes high. You made what would've been a difficult time surprisingly easy. Not once did your belief in me or this story and these characters falter. Thank you to Rubin Pfeffer, for backing Melissa as she backed me.

Thank you to Rhoda Belleza, who took a chance on me and convinced her team to take a chance as well. I could tell from our first phone call, when you said you were willing to go as far as I wanted with Alice's story, steeped in Black Girl Magic, that I had nothing to worry about placing this book in your hands. You pushed me to be a better writer, a more capable storyteller, and a stronger artist.

To Erin Stein and all of the Imprint team who've made me feel welcome at every turn with this project. You guided me through this entire process, included me whenever and wherever you could, and shared your insight into the industry.

I want to thank my family, my mother, Yolanda, and my father, Carl Jr., who saw my passion for words and writing and let me do my thing. You supported me, encouraged me, and prayed for me through this nearly decade-long struggle. I always wanted to make you proud, from when I was a wee thing to the woman I am now. Seeing your joy at every success leading to this one has filled me up and pushed me in ways I honestly cannot describe. Seriously, when I try, it just ends in incoherence and tears. I love you, Mom and Dad.

To my sisters, LaQuisha, Carlanda, and Richetta, the first audience for my first stories, which I ~~made~~ asked y'all to act out with Barbies and action figures. Thank you for all those years of indulgence and the (mostly) constructive criticism. Seriously though, you guys are my heart, along with Carl III (RIP) and Carl IV, my baby brothers.

To my Granny, I miss you every day, may you rest in peace, and to my Papa, who gave me my first typewriter—yes, the old-timey kind—and laptop respectively, thank you for making sure I had the tools and resources to pursue my dreams. I wasn't even all that serious about it back then, but you two were serious about me being able to be serious if I ever chose to. Guess I did. I love you both so very much, and words can never express the impact you've had on my life and my creativity. I certainly wouldn't be here without you.

To my Grandma Richie, who kept me lifted in prayer and gave me a quiet space to gather myself. Sometimes I had to escape and you were someone I could go to for that, and so much more. You provided peace, clarity, and a covering I'm eternally grateful for.

My BETAs and two of my besties, Craishae Johnson-Sarol and Angie Meyers—the geekery and fandom are endless with us, but so is the love. You two have supported me since I said I wanted to do this thing, for real for real. You held me accountable, demanded updates, then read this and other stories over and over, providing feedback that helped mold me as an author and develop this story. All while going on about how excited you were for the future fanfiction. I love you.

So many people touched Alice's story as critique partners, and it's so much stronger for it. Winter Jones, Margaret Owen, Megan Bannen, your constant cheerleading kept me going, and your excitement and support at each new accomplishment filled my well.

My Novel Clique ladies, my writers group, my fellow story-tellers, and fighters. Natasha Hanova, Dawn Allen, Nicole McLaughlin, and Marsha Lytle, for seven years you taught me, pushed me, consoled me, guided me, instructed me, and held me down whenever I felt like giving up. You were the first ones to lay eyes on this, the first ones to offer feedback, the first ones who showed me what my words were capable of. You were there during the rejections, the rewrites, the revisions, the resubmissions, and everything else. You're my friends, my sisters from another mister. I love you guys.

My Wakanda ladies: WAKANDA FOREVER! Angie Thomas, Adrianne Russell, and Camryn Garret, you three are warriors. From the moment I read your words, I knew you three were going to rattle the stars and leave *everyone* shook. I'm glad to say I told you so while doubling down on wait and see. Your fire burns bright and I cannot wait to set it all ablaze with you.

To Dhonielle Clayton, Heidi Heilig, Justina Ireland, Zoraida Cordova, Cam Montgomery, and Tehlor Kay Mejia, your industry, insight, knowledge, support, and all-around bad-assery are an inspiration. Knowing you're in my corner emboldens me to take on the industry and the world.

And to those black kids searching countless shelves and between endless pages, hoping to catch a glimpse of themselves in galaxies far away, fantasies long ago, and stories here and now: This one's for you. Shine on, and drive back the dark.

In this thrilling sequel to
A BLADE SO BLACK,
Alice goes deeper into a
dark version of Wonderland.

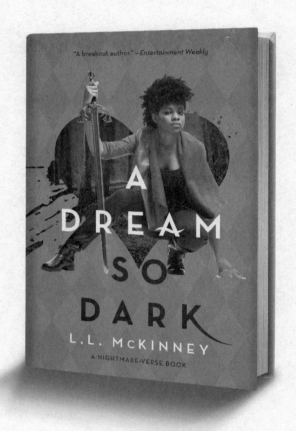

Keep reading for an excerpt from
A DREAM SO DARK!

One
GONE

Alice couldn't run. She couldn't hide. All she could do was sit there as her mother *went. In.*

"Must be out your got. Dayum. Mind. Just doing whatever you please." Mom paced in front of the coffee table, her steps barely muted by the carpet. She'd kicked off her heels, abandoned one near the door while the other was over by the fireplace. This alone was a sign Alice was well and truly screwed. "Like you run things 'round here. Like you pay bills, do you pay bills?" Mom whirled on Alice, who had pressed so far back against the couch she felt she might slip between the cushions and be lost.

"No, ma'am." Alice's voice sounded as small as she felt in the path of her mom's fury.

A little muscle in Mom's jaw jumped as she ground her teeth together. "I can't hear you."

"No, ma'am," Alice managed, louder this time, the words thick with the emotion coursing through her. Fire licked at the center of her face, and a feeling like fingers around her neck closed off her throat. She just wanted to go to bed. Couldn't she go to bed?

"Got the school calling me 'cause you decided you just wasn't gone show up, I guess. Now I'm missing work, and for what? For *what*, Alison? Knowing I didn't raise you like this, *knowing* this wasn't gone fly. Then walk in here covered in lord knows—what is that mess?" Mom flapped a hand at Alice, indicating the black splattered against her clothes and skin. "And *what* is that smell?"

Alice eyed the stains. Yeah, that inky shit stank to high heaven, but that wasn't why her eyes started to water. It wasn't why her chest went all tight, like the space was suddenly too small for her lungs. She smoothed her fingers over the rusty red splotch on her shirt. A handprint hidden under all the other yuck. *His* handprint.

The heat behind Alice's eyes filled the rest of her face.

"I know you not ignoring me." Mom's tone went razor sharp.

Alice wanted to answer, but the words tripped over her tongue and hit the back of her teeth. What escaped instead was some sort of whine.

Mom's eyes widened slightly. Her arms unfolded from where she'd crossed them under her chest, and she shifted as if to reach out to Alice, but lifted a finger in warning instead. "No, ain't no crocodile tears gonna fix this."

The tears came anyway. They welled up and spilled over

Alice's cheeks as she stared at the floor while fighting to keep from all-out sobbing. The carpet's shaggy white tufts went brown and green, the memory of the shredded football field dancing in and out of her vision. The rumbling snarl of Fiends and the shriek of clashing weapons filled her ears. Her heart knocked against the inside of her chest, its *thump-thump* rising to join the crash.

Voices surfed the waves of chaos.

Side, on fire!

I-it'll be okay. You'll be okay.

Lies.

You lied to him.

She flinched. She hadn't meant to lie. She gave everything she had to try and save him! The Black Knight, he was the one that didn't keep his end of the bargain. He was the one that let those monsters tear her friend apart! Chess was gone because of *him*.

Maybe, but Chess would be at home right now if you hadn't pulled him into this.

"Alice," Mom barked.

If it wasn't for you, he'd still be alive.

A buzzing prickled beneath Alice's skin, spreading over every inch of her. It pressed at her temples and filled the space behind her eyes.

You did this. You killed him.

Her vision darkened at the edges. Her jaws throbbed, the muscles so tight her teeth ached. She couldn't cry. She couldn't—if she did, she wouldn't stop.

Just like Dad.

The sobs tore free. Hard, unforgiving things that clawed their way from the depths of her. They stole her breath, shook her frame, and bent her in half until something deep inside cracked open and bled familiar shades of shame, anger, and regret.

Fingers played against Alice's shoulders before the cushion beside her dipped with sudden weight. The smell of floral perfume reached her before Mom's arms tucked around her.

Let me go! Alice wanted to scream, but she could only cry and gasp and cough and cry some more.

"Come 'ere." Mom drew Alice up, then guided her deeper into her embrace. "I don't know what's going on. You don't tell me nothing, you just out running these streets. Is it something happening at school?" She rubbed at Alice's back, her fingers pressing steady circles between her shoulders. "Talk to me, baby."

Talking. That wasn't possible. The very idea of words shriveled in Alice's mind. Whatever managed to make it to her tongue just dissolved entirely. A groan slipped free, muffled against Mom's shoulder, but that was it.

"Okay, baby, okay." Soft shushes and faint humming filled the silence between hiccupped sobs. Every now and then a whispered *Jesus* accompanied them.

Jesus had nothing to do with it, Alice wanted to say.

Eventually, the sobs died away enough for Alice to cobble together a couple words. "H-he's gone." She coughed like she was six years old again. Snot slipped over her lips, between them. She rubbed at her mouth. Her throat burned.

"Who's gone?" Mom smoothed hands over Alice's braids, then wiped at her cheeks. "Is this about your daddy?"

Alice shook her head. The action made her dizzy and left wet, slick patches on what felt like one of Mom's really nice shirts.

"Look, whatever's going on, you don't have to deal by yourself." The arms around Alice tightened in a squeeze. "We'll get through it. Together, okay?"

A sudden edge of anger scissored through her thoughts. *Together. What, like with Dad?* There wasn't much "togetherness" in dealing with her father's death.

"But you gotta tell me, baby. I can't help you if you don't talk to me."

That anger sharpened. Alice tried to approach her mom after Dad died, but the woman either retreated so far into herself it was like she was looking for Narnia, or she threw herself in the opposite direction and got lost in her work. Meanwhile, Alice ended up crossing into another world and killing shit as a hobby.

And say they *did* have a sit-down or whatever, how in the hell was she supposed to explain any of this? Hatta, the pub, Wonderland? Chess . . .

Would her mother even believe her? And if she did, what then? She'd probably forbid Alice from going to Wonderland or seeing her friends. She might go off on some mess about how she believed Alice believed what she was saying, then make her "talk to someone" about it. Maybe she'd yell at her for making shit up and never trust her again.

Or maybe, just maybe, Mom would understand for once, or at least try to. A small, hopeful part of Alice latched onto that barest sliver of a silver lining. Maybe all this could be one less thing she had to carry, to hide. Maybe it *would* be okay. Mom wasn't a liar, like her.

But Alice had no idea where to start.

Begin at the beginning, something whispered against her mind. A gentle touch. A calming press.

The night Dad died. The night she met Hatta. The night everything changed.

Her racing thoughts settled on the memory. It was so crisp and clear in her mind she shivered at recalling the cold press of stone against her back. The stink of the fetid puddles and heat-soaked dumpsters nearby stung her nose. She could practically taste the salt of her tears. Then a beast slithered out of the throbbing dark, followed by a monster slayer, an invisible boy bright and shining.

Begin at the beginning.

Alice took a slow, deep breath. She sniffed and swallowed and swiped at her nose "I—I . . ."

"Yeah, baby?" Mom encouraged.

Alice licked her lips and tried again. "It . . . a-after Daddy . . ."

"Take your time."

Her throat closed up, *again*.

The rest of the words refused to come. They gathered at the back of her tongue, piling on top of each other like rocks after a landslide, heavy and broken. It was as if part of her still wanted, needed to keep the secret.

Something shifted in Mom's expression. The corners of her mouth turned downward, and Alice felt the tightness in the arms still wrapped around her.

Get it together, Kingston. She had to say something.

Janet Jackson and company belted *We are a part of the Rhythm Nation* from Mom's pocket. She huffed in annoyance before pulling her phone free. "It's Courtney."

Alice blinked, surprised. Court just left not twenty minutes ago, after getting her own cussing-out. Something was wrong. The flutter between Alice's lungs agreed.

Mom slid her thumb across the screen. "I can tell her to call back, so we can finish talking."

"She probably left something." Alice hoped she didn't sound too eager as she wiped at her still-aching face. "Or I left something in her car."

Mom squeezed Alice, rubbing at her arm, and lifted the phone. "Yeah, honey?"

Court started screaming.

Mom jerked the phone away from her ear, her expression twisting, before telling Court to calm down and try again. Alice couldn't make out what she was saying, but whatever it was, it didn't sound good. The fluttering in Alice's chest turned to full-on flailing.

A frown wrinkled Mom's forehead. "Chester is where?"

Alice's insides went cold. Chess's body was still at the pub. Had something happened to it?

"A what? Oh lord, hang on, baby. Here." Mom held out the phone. "I can't understand her."

Alice reached for it, her fingers shaking. She didn't want

to take it. Whatever was going on had to be bad, and she was so done with bad, but Mom was already pressing it into her hand. Chewing at her lower lip, she lifted it to her ear. "Yeah, Court?"

"Alice! Ohmigod, I'm coming to get you."

"Wait, what? Why?"

"Something happened with Chess, we need to go to the pub."

"Som—" Alice blinked rapidly, her brain misfiring for a second. Did she hear that right? "With *who*?"

"Chess! Hatta called and said we had to come back, right now." The rising panic in Courtney's voice mirrored Alice's. "Then someone started hollering and he hung up."

Alice shook her head. "No . . . he's not . . ." Her chest tightened all over again. She couldn't catch her breath, and it left her with a feeling like water sloshing around her thoughts.

Mom leaned forward to catch Alice's attention. "What's going on?"

"I tried calling back," Courtney said. "But no one's picking up!"

For a few seconds, Alice couldn't remember how to speak. Her mind was working so fast trying to keep up with what Courtney was saying, what Mom was saying, with her own thoughts, and it kept misfiring.

Something happened with Chess.

Hatta said to come back.

But Chess was dead.

They had to hurry.

Chess . . .

"O-okay." Alice finally managed, one hand pressed to her mouth. She shut her eyes and tried to focus on breathing as the burn of tears made a comeback.

"I told your mom Chess was in an accident and we're going to see him. I—I didn't know what else to say!"

"Okay," Alice repeated, her voice thin.

"Shit, this is so fucked up." The sound of sniffles and whimpers carried over the phone.

"C-Court?" Alice croaked. She swallowed to ease the ache in her throat.

"I'm okay! I'm okay." Court sniffed again and whispered something Alice couldn't make out. "I'm okay. ETA two minutes."

"O—" Court cut the call. "Kay." Alice lowered the phone. Her heart buzzed in her ears as her mind continued to tumble over everything. Something was wrong with Chess. But Chess was dead. Hatta said to come. Something was wrong. Hatta said . . . Was something wrong with the body? Something was wrong with the body. Why else would Hatta send for her so soon?

Bad. All bad.

"Alison!" Mom snapped her fingers in Alice's face. The sound sent shards of pain dancing behind her eyes. "What's happening?"

"U-um, Chess." The words got stuck again. She pressed her hands over her face and groaned. Her fingers came away wet with fresh tears. "S-something—oh my god. He was in an accident? Court's coming. We're gonna go see him. Please, Mommy." Her voice cracked on the plea. "Please. I—I—I know,

I'm grounded, but I have to see him. It's bad. It's real bad, *please*. Please."

Mom pinched her lips together and held Alice's gaze, her brown eyes questioning. For a perilous stretch of seconds, the only sound was Alice's harsh sniffles and choked breaths. Mom licked her lips and glanced to the side before sighing through her nose.

She's gonna say no. Raw, unrelenting panic jolted through Alice and knocked an equally unforgivable idea loose. "O-or! You can take me. He's at Grady."

The small sound Mom made at the mention of the hospital sent Alice's stomach plummeting. It was a low blow, and god, she felt a whole ass for doing it, but she *had* to get out of here.

Swallowing the sour taste at the back of her throat, she pressed on. "You can drop me off on your way back to work, and I'll call when I'm ready."

Another handful of seconds passed.

Mom pursed her lips and leveled a look at Alice. She opened her mouth, and the blast of Courtney's horn made them both jump. Mom shut her eyes, pushed to her feet, and started pacing in front of the coffee table again.

Alice glanced at the clock. Both hands stood nearly straight up, putting the time at just noon. "Or you can, um . . . pick me up when you get off. Please," she pressed. She had to sell this. Sniffing she wiped at her nose. "Court can bring me home, whatever works, I just need to—"

Mom lifted a hand, gesturing for quiet. She paced a bit more. Her shoulders hitched when Court blew again, but

Mom remained focused on Alice. "I don't know what's going on with you. And I hate thinking I can't trust you."

Alice couldn't deny she had that coming, but it still hurt to hear it. She fought to hold her mother's gaze.

"But you're not leaving me much of a choice here, Baby Moon," Mom continued.

"I know." The words leaped free before Alice even realized they'd hit her lips, her mouth suddenly dry. "I know. I—I'm sorry. I just . . . there's a lot—"

Another blast from Court's horn. Mom grunted before stalking over to the door, yanking it open, and stepping partway onto the porch. "I will rip that horn out and choke you with it, lil girl!" Then she turned back to Alice, letting the screen bang closed behind her. She eyed her a bit longer before jerking her head toward the door. "Come on."

With her heart in her throat, Alice hopped up, grabbed her bag, and hurried after her mother, who padded down the front steps. Her feet had to be freezing—pantyhose didn't do much protecting from the cold. Alice followed close behind as they headed down the driveway, toward Court's Camaro.

Court's wide green eyes, red and puffy from crying, watched them approach through the passenger side window, which she rolled down after Mom twirled her finger.

"Here's the deal." Mom bent forward so she could meet Court's gaze, then glanced back and forth between both girls as she spoke. "The *instant* you get to that hospital and find out how Chester is doing, call and let me know, and not from Courtney's phone. Use the phone in his room, or the nurse station, or information booth, or security, or something, I don't care. Then you can sit and visit for a little while. Just a little while." Mom looked to Alice. "Your ass is in this house by three o'clock. Not three-oh-one."

"Yes ma—" Alice started, but fell silent when Mom lifted her hand again.

"I'm not playing with either of you. This is it. Last damn chance. If you mess this up, you two won't see each other outside of school until college." She swung a manicured finger back and forth between the girls like the sword of Damocles. "I mean it. I love you, Courtney baby, but you will *not* be allowed in this house for the rest of the damn year." The finger stopped at Alice. "And I'm putting bars on your window. Don't. Test. Me."

"Yes, ma'am," both girls chimed together. Alice's voice shook almost as much as she did.

Mom tucked her hand into the crook of her elbow, arms folded again. "What time I say?"

"Three o'clock," Alice answered.

Mom peered into the car. "What time I say?"

"Three o'clock," Court answered as she swiped at her flushed cheeks. Her whole face was bright red.

Mom stepped back and gestured for Alice to get in the car, which she scurried to do. She was fastening her seat belt as Mom practically leaned in through the window to stick them both with a healthy dose of side-eye. "*What* time did I say?"

"Three o'clock," the girls said together.

With a nod, Mom threw an arm over Alice to give her one of those awkward half hugs that she did her best to return. "Drive safe."

Court waited until Alice's mother had backed up a few feet before pulling off. Neither girl seemed to breathe until they turned the corner, but Alice could feel her mother's glare following them, like heat from a comb on the back of her neck. Court kept her eyes on the road, her grip on the wheel so tight the color had drained from her knuckles.

"What all did Hatta say?" Alice asked, anxiety crawling through her. She fought to keep her breathing even, but it felt like her whole body had turned against her, still trembling as she sunk farther into the seat.

"S-something happened with Chess a-and, um . . ." Court took quick, deep breaths and blinked rapidly. "And we needed to get back there right now."

"What kind of something happens with a . . . a—a dead . . . He's dead . . ."

"I know!" Court slammed her fist on the wheel. "That Duchess woman started screaming in Russian and Hatta hung up! I don't—" She pursed her lips and stared ahead.

Shit. Alice glanced around. "Where's your phone?"

Court pointed to the cubby under the center dash. Alice snatched the phone up, punched in the lock code, and hit the pub's number.

It went straight to voice mail and Alice's body went tight. A wave of . . . of rage washed over her. How the hell you say some shit about someone's dead friend, hang up, then don't answer when they call back? Alice had to force herself to relax or she might crush Court's phone like hers. She waited a bit, then hit redial. It rang this time. And kept ringing.

Voice mail.

She tried again, her knee bouncing.

Voice mail.

"Damn it!"

On the fourth try, someone finally picked up.

"Looking Glass."

Alice's heart jumped at the sound of Hatta's voice. There was an edge to it, an unease that plucked at the already frayed whispers of remaining strength barely holding her up. "Hey, it's me. What's going on?"

For a moment the line went so quiet she thought the call had dropped. She even pulled the phone away to double-check. Then Hatta said the absolute last thing she could've expected.

"Chess is gone. And he took Maddi with him."